Memories: his sisters' hair combed out be-tween their fingers to catch the godsvoice.

Still earlier memories: plain people in plain clothes. They had found him—so small a child to be crying and alone—and fed him on plain foods and love. They filled his emptiness and helped him grow, until one day...

Darkchild gasped, trying to force his way out of the trap of memory. But there was no escaping.

Two peoples had cared for him. Two peoples had taken him in and fed him, fostered his growth, formed him in the ways of love.

And both times had come the droning in the sky. Both times had come the screaming ship....

Berkley books by Sydney J. Van Scyoc

DARKCHILD
SUNWAIFS

DARKCHILD

SYDNEY J. VAN SCYOC

BERKLEY BOOKS, NEW YORK

DARKCHILD

A Berkley Book / published by arrangement with
the author

PRINTING HISTORY
Berkley trade paperback edition / September 1982

ISBN: 0-425-05644-9

A BERKLEY BOOK® TM 757,375
The name "BERKLEY" and the stylized "B" with design are
trademarks belonging to Berkley Publishing Corporation.

PRINTED IN THE UNITED STATES OF AMERICA

For my parents, John W. and Geneva

1/*The Boy*

The day was overcast, the sky a lowering grey. In the forest, it was a morning of fevered breezes and distant thunder. The boy's slender limbs glistened with perspiration as he slipped through the dense underbrush toward the voices. His slight body was tense, his eyes vigilant. They had accepted him now, these bristling people with their hooded eyes and their blunt husking-teeth. They treated him as they treated their own children: with offhanded brutality. So long as he jumped to his tasks when commanded and didn't get in the way of the adults, he went unmolested. But let him pause a moment in his work, let him hesitate, particularly let him question, and a heavy-handed blow caught him. Usually the blow was accompanied by the staccato grunts the boy had come to recognize as laughter.

He had never learned to share these people's laughter, any more than he had learned to enjoy the tasks they set him and the other children. He paused beneath a sour-leaf bush and gazed down at his hands, frowning. They were rough from the rock harvest. With the others he had scrabbled through tons of river pebbles yesterday, sorting out trade rocks while the riverbed was briefly dry. The tribes to the south favored the tiny nodules of crystalline grey stone while the more primitive tribes to the east and north were eager to trade for glassy blue and green stones. All were buried in deep banks of less desirable pebbles and stones. The other children's hands were covered with protective bristles. They could grub anywhere without harm. The boy's hands were not so equipped and one of his fingernails was torn back deep into the quick.

He touched it experimentally and winced. In addition to the damage he had done his hands, his arms and shoulders were stiff and his back ached. He peered up through the trees at the grumbling sky. Surely it would rain again today and flood the pebble beds.

But earlier this morning there had been unaccustomed sounds from deep in the forest: a grinding, whining drone followed by the tearing sounds of some jarring impact. After a moment's startled silence, the adults had abandoned the harvest and disappeared into the forest, not even bothering to call back threats. Later one of the men had come back to the pebble bank flashing some metal-bright device and laughing hoarsely. He had refused to let the harvesters examine his booty and finally the youths and children had given up their work and disappeared into the brush too, harking to calls from the distance.

The boy had followed, but cautiously. As he drew nearer the source of the calls, what he heard chilled him. There was a ship in the dell, fallen from the sky, a ship like those that came sometimes to trade. Nervously the boy bit at his torn nail and tried to deny the images that rushed into his mind: the flash of a metal hull, dark markings upon it; an opening port; a capsule unwinding toward him, grappling; a suited figure. He had never seen the trade vessels—none had come since he had been here—and from what the people told at night around their cookfires, no one had ever been abducted by one. Yet his mind held these stark memories and his heart pounded with them.

He gasped at a moment's sharp pain and saw he had torn his nail completely away. His finger bled. Frowning, he popped the injured finger into his mouth and sucked it.

The chilling images continued to unfold. He was in the belly of the ship, captive. It was a place of harsh lights and metallic odors, a place of smooth hard surfaces and smooth hard faces. Cold-eyed people dressed in black seized him by both arms, pinioning him to a padded table. They hardly seemed to notice his angry struggles. As he fought, one of them seized his arm and stung it with a needle. The boy's vision blurred then and a peculiar paralysis overcame him. Although his anger and fear remained as violent as before, his arms quit thrashing and his feet quit kicking. As he lost consciousness, someone lowered a metal helmet over his head. And after that came emptiness. Whatever life he had known before the ship had seized him, the metal helmet had stolen memory of it. The helmet had left him virtually nothing, not even—at first—the knowledge that he had been robbed.

Not again. It had taken him too long, a full year, to emerge from the vacuum, to begin to find himself again. For deep down in some secret place, he had managed to hide a bare scrap of identity from the helmet. He had even contrived to keep knowledge of that precious, flimsy scrap from the guide, the implacable voice that directed him now night and day, driving him to observe and classify, to question and learn—no matter what the price he paid in blows.

He knew, for instance, that he had not always lived among brutal people. He did not yet remember where he had lived before the glinting ship had taken him, but flashes of clear golden skies came to him sometimes now and other times he remembered faces that must belong to that previous life. Certainly they were nothing like the bristled faces he saw here.

He sighed, touching the memory: fair faces but with eyes so somberly violet they were like night. And hair that fell in midnight reams.

But the guide did not like it when he remembered those faces. Sharply the guide demanded that he stop and classify an unfamiliar seedling growing in the underbrush. The boy managed to retain a ghost-vision of golden skies while he crushed the seedling's tiny leaves. Their scent was tart. Quickly, hardly thinking, he made a lateral slit in the plant's tiny stem and studied it in cross-section. It was clearly related to the yellow-blooming creeper that grew on the verges of the creekbed when it rained. Deftly he stirred the soil where the tiny plant had sprouted, analyzing its organic content. A single insect clung to the underside of one leaf and he studied it minutely. No detail was too small for the guide. He insisted upon knowing everything, from the form of speech an adult male used to address his most remote female kin to the pattern of cross-hatching on the underside of a clay water pot. The guide was voracious.

He was generous too, sometimes. Since the boy had come here, the guide had given him refuge from care any number of times. The boy stood, sighing. Certainly he was tired and anxious now. If the guide would let him rest, let him crouch in the humid shadows, drop his forehead to his knees and join his brothers for just a few moments . . .

But the guide denied him. Except under the most gruelling circumstances, trancing with his brothers was a reward to be saved for night, when there was nothing left to do or see. For now, there was much to be done. The boy sighed heavily and continued through the brush. The soil was springy underfoot, the distant thunder indistinct, little more than a promise of rain.

Reaching the edge of the dell, the boy slipped forward cautiously. If the ship had the remembered markings on it, he wanted to be away quickly, before he could be taken again. He did not like this place and these people, but they were better than the emptiness the metal helmet had made of his mind.

Then he saw the ship and there were no dark markings on it. It carried a bright crest on one metal pod, a similar identification on its tubular body, and it was crumpled awkwardly between the trees. It would not fly again. And if there were crew members, they had died in the crash or had been dispatched by the people. No one appeared to defend the ship from looting.

Grunting with laughter, the people dragged crates and cartons from the fallen ship. The containers were of many sizes and shapes, but each had its own identifying markings. The boy crouched in the brush, studying the markings, memory stirring. These people did not so much as draw in the mud with sticks. But hadn't he clutched a marking instrument in his hand once, somewhere? Hadn't he made marks that had meaning upon some smooth surface? It almost seemed he could feel the instrument between his fingers now, could feel it move purposefully over the marking surface.

He frowned, absently wiping perspiration from his chin with the back of his hand. Did he know how to record meaning with quickly inscribed symbols? If not, why did he understand the concept? Why did he understand that the markings on the crates and cartons identified their contents? Quickly the boy snapped a brown pod from a nearby bush and began pulling it apart, examining it minutely, feeding sensory data to the guide. He had learned months ago that intense sensory activity served as an adequate screen for his private thoughts.

He sniffed the pulpy interior of the pod, then extracted one round black seed and crushed it on his tongue. As he relayed its sharp taste to the guide, distracting him, with his left hand he seized a small stick.

He did not attempt to guide the stick consciously, but let his hand move of its own volition. It moved rapidly, leaving a series of marks in the soft soil. He flicked a second seed into his mouth and let instinct move his hand again. Then he glanced down.

His hand had not made random marks. He recognized with a quick surge of triumph that the lines and circles on the ground had meaning. Studying them with narrowed eyes, he even found certain similarities to the symbols on the broken crates. Eventually, if he could find time, he might even be able to interpret them. Somewhere in his mind he must hold the key. Otherwise, why had his hands made the marks so readily?

It was another step. If he could take enough of these steps, surely they would eventually lead him back to knowledge of the violet-eyed people whose faces he remembered. He settled back on his heels, summoning up faintly curving lips and deep eyes. There was one face in particular, the face of a woman, someone who had given him food and care—

An unexpected sound interrupted his reverie. In the dell, the people had broken into a tall carton. They pulled out brilliant skeins of silken fabric: azure, crimson, chartreuse, emerald, lilac—an entire silken rainbow. There was a single white silk too, shot with flecks of color. Chuckling, the people unrolled the skeins of fabric and slapped the luxuriant stuff against the damp morning breeze. And uncannily, as the fabric rippled, it made more than the rustling sound of fluttering cloth. It both spoke and sang in a multiplicity of alien voices.

The boy stood, drawn. It was as if the morning rainbow sang, its tones clear and yearning. The boy raised his hands to his ears, hearing color, sweet and pure and hypnotic.

The people shouted in rough delight, their hooded eyes glittering. They seized the silken lengths of fabric and slapped them against the air, making them whimper and moan and sigh. Then one man, more inventive than the others, seized a crimson length and tied it to the limb of a small tree. The silk's free end fluttered languidly in the breeze and its silken voice fell into a seductive melody. Fluttering, floating, moving like a thing alive, it sang its siren song to an increasingly enthralled people.

Quickly then the people tied the other bright swaths to the trees and drew back, superstitious awe on their heavy faces. They grunted to each other as the silks filled the dell with a symphony of voices. The breeze was damp, heavy. Yet the silks were not oppressed. Each gleaming length of fabric seemed to speak its own vivid hue, light become music. The boy moved forward, aware of the people's panting breath and the distant mutter of thunder. The guide was not much interested in the silks, but the boy was drawn as if magnetized.

Then one of the silks, the white one, began to speak. Not in a trembling moan, not in a seductive sigh, but in a hard-edged masculine voice. The voice crackled through the dell, crisp, urgent, somehow demanding, like the restless fingers of lightning that sometimes probed the treetops. The boy halted, his jaw dropping. A shock of recognition stiffened his limbs. *The voice—*

The white silk continued its statement and somehow the other silks seemed to resent its presence. One by one their voices fell to a dissatisfied murmur. Reacting, one of the other people reached up and yanked at the white silk, muttering angrily. Another applied her nails to it, tearing at it.

The boy was stunned. *He knew the white silk's voice.* He didn't know where he had heard it or when, but it struck a chord of recognition. If he could listen to it alone, listen without the increasingly angry jibbering of the people and the sullen whine of the other silks—

Sometimes the boy found himself moving to the guide's directive without conscious decision, as if he were a creature of the guide's will, nothing more. This time it was not the guide's will but his own that launched the boy from the undergrowth. He darted across the dell and flung himself up the trunk of the tree where the white silk flapped. His fingers, damp with perspiration, tore at the knot that held the silk. Then he slipped back down the tree, gathering the silk around him, running.

The people were outraged. They surged raggedly toward him, grunting. One of the adult males, Ramar, caught him with a slicing blow to the jaw, hooded eyes staring with rage. The boy staggered, almost falling against a second indignant male. But he caught himself and managed to slip between the two, leaving them glaring at each other. Before any of the others could catch him, he had thrown himself into the brush, the white silk clinging to him, silent now.

He ran through the dense brush, across the dry riverbed, and into the trees beyond. His feet caught on runners. Low-hanging branches scratched at his face and tried to seize the white silk from him. When he paused, listening, his thin torso was slick with perspiration and he gasped raggedly for breath. But he heard no sound of pursuit. He heard only the thunder, nearer now, less indistinct.

Still panting, he secured the white silk to the trunk of a young tree. His fingers trembled as he first smoothed the slippery fabric, then released it and let it speak.

The breeze was reluctant at first. Then it caught the length of silk and lifted it and the fabric resumed its plea.

The boy recognized it for just that now. Although the voice was incisive, commanding, it pleaded with him. The boy pressed a knotted fist to either temple, trying to heighten his concentration. Had he heard the silk's language before? Were the words, the intonation familiar? Quickly he stooped and uprooted a plant specimen. He crushed its leaves and pressed them to his nose, screening his thoughts from the guide. The guide was not pleased that he had run from the dell with the silk. Almost absently the boy touched the bleeding cut Ramar had inflicted upon him when he fled. His jaw would be scarred.

That didn't matter. *Where had he heard the voice?* He was certain it had not spoken then the language it spoke now. The language it spoke now triggered no memory at all.

If only he could remember the language of the violet-eyed people. He would someday, he was sure. But now, today—

He had no time to pursue his line of thought. The indistinct mutter of thunder had become something more ominous. The sound grew, harsh, rising, until it was a wrenching scream directly overhead, as if some mammoth metal throat cried fury at him. The boy's head snapped back, and at that moment he felt himself caught in an invisible beam, his arms pinned to his sides, his eyes wide, helpless. The paralyzing ray held him for moments.

Then it passed, his eyes cleared, and he saw the ship overhead: a metal hull with familiar dark markings; a port that slowly opened; a metal capsule that descended slowly, grappling. For him. The ship had come to rob him again with its metal helmet.

His heart beat wildly and he tried to shrink back into the brush. But his knees stiffened and instead of carrying him away, his legs carried him toward where the ship lowered. The guide wanted him to go to the ship, wanted him to walk to the dry riverbed and hold up his arms, signalling to the suited man in the capsule.

He would not. He struggled against the guide's imperative. With fierce effort, he seized control of his legs. Jerkily, as if his muscles fought each other, he backed away into the trees, then turned, running, his heart pounding furiously with anger and fear. As he ran, his leg muscles writhed and cramped, trying to hold him back.

He had to remember the voice and its words. He had to save them from the helmet. Otherwise he would never know why the voice pleaded with him, why it was trapped in a length of silken fabric.

He ran through the trees knowing it was useless. Three kinds of thunder sounded in the morning forest: the helpless pounding of the boy's heart, the distant grumble of the heavens, the sharp throb of the ship's engine. The grappler caught him as he plunged down a shallow bluff near the compound where the people lived. It hooked his sparse clothing and then the suited figure jumped from the capsule and plunged toward him, something glinting in his hand. Too exhausted to struggle, the boy felt the sting of a needle. For a moment he swayed dizzily, his mouth suddenly dry, his vision blurred. As he fell, a burst of fury exploded in his mind, blinding him. It surged through his body, a last useless resistance.

The voice. The words.

The boy was unconscious. The suited man lifted him into the capsule. As the ship lifted again, rain began to fall, the drops fat and blood-warm.

2/Khira

Khira woke to the cheerful whirring of the dried rattleweed she had hung over her bed. Morning sunlight reached through her window and touched the rugged stone wall of her sleeping chamber, picking out the detail of centuries: pits, gouges, discolorations. The breeze that swept through her unshuttered window was fragrant. Beyond the palace precincts, beyond the leveed growing fields, hundreds of fruit trees were unfolding leaves and blossoms to trap sunlight and turn it to sugar. Khira's wall hangings rippled heavily, stirred by the quick breeze, and faded tapestry figures danced in the sun. It would be easy, so easy, to stretch out on her covers and let the sun warm her before she dressed and went down.

But today—

She stifled the troubling thought at the stamp of feet beneath her window. She threw off her covers and ran to the window in time to see the redmane guardian pass with her plow teams. Yvala was the guardian's name and sometimes she nodded austerely to Khira, although she ignored the other children. This morning the redmanes tossed their heads and danced with pondersome playfulness, pleased to be going to the fields. They were a Brakrathi breed, sturdy animals who stood barely waist-high to their guardian. Their stocky bodies were densely grown with shaggy grey hair and their auburn manes and tails swept the ground. With quick excitement, Khira saw that the mare with the dark forelock did not accompany the teams this morning.

Khira turned from the window, tempted to dress and run directly to the pens. Sometime since the teams had returned from the fields the evening before, the mare would have pulled out her shaggy outer coat and trampled it into a springy nest. There she must lie now, dressed only in her soft silver undercoat, coddling a newborn foal, a velvety creature with vestigal mane and questioning eyes.

Was it her own guardian ancestry, so remote, that urged her to visit the new foal? Khira sighed, putting the impulse aside. Yvala would be displeased if the mare were disturbed, even by the palace daughter. And there was a more compelling reason not to go. Khira's heart clenched and the sunny morning turned cold. Today Alzaja went to the mountain.

Today.

Khira shivered. Alzaja had charted the seasons and marked this day months ago, shortly after Darkmorning. Khira had clear memory of her sister stretched out on cushions on the throneroom floor that afternoon, the shadows of winter gathered around her, in one hand her life-scroll, wound into a tight cylinder. The throne on its dais stood over her like a dark predator and on Alzaja's shadowed face was an expression of finality, of decision.

"I've chosen my day," Alzaja said when Khira paced hesitantly across the polished floor. "The sixth day of Nindra's first spring crescent, because Nindra is my hostess and I'm the sixth daughter of the palace. I'll have perhaps five hands of days to train after spring warming. More if I go to train before the melting." The firmness of the words contrasted with the remote quality of her voice. It seemed to float in the chill air, something separate from either of them, an impersonal instrument of declaration.

Even then, with Alzaja's chosen day more than a season away, Khira felt her muscles tighten with apprehension—and a craven sense that Alzaja was abandoning her.

Alzaja was slightly built, hardly bigger at twenty-and-three than Khira at eleven, but she had been Khira's guide and caretaker through most of her years. Tiahna, their mother, was a remote figure. Sometimes she called Khira to the throne for an accounting of her time. Sometimes she advised her. But they were never alone together, because Tiahna caressed the pairing stone at her throat and spoke silently with her stone mate, Rahela, even as she talked with Khira.

Most often Tiahna was distracted by the functions of the throne. And with the coming of the cold, when the people of the stonehalls returned to wintersleep, Tiahna made the trek to the peaks to gather weak winter sunlight for spring, leaving Alzaja and Khira alone in the palace again.

Alone—yet together. Alzaja had taught Khira her first words and helped her take her first steps; had taught her running and jumping games when she was small, singing and counting games when she was older. Sometimes Alzaja took Khira to the stonehalls to play with the ruddy, white-haired children who lived there. Each time Khira returned to the palace with relief. She was a child of the palace, accustomed to its tall, stalk-grown chambers and its sparsely populated corridors. The bustle of the stonehalls was not for her. Nor was the companionship of so many children who were so much like each other, yet so different from her.

So long as she had Alzaja, she was never lonely. They were much like each other, both delicately made with auburn hair that hung straight down their shoulders and autumn-gold eyes. Sometimes Khira watched Alzaja covertly, studying the delicate bones of her wrists, the fine grain of the flesh of her forearms, and imagined that behind this primary image she saw the images of the others, the sisters she had never met: Mara, Denabar, Hedia, Kristyan, Sukiin.

Seven sisters—five of them gone now, dead on the mountain.

Today Alzaja went.

Khira laced her clothes with trembling fingers. *Today*. She wanted to dress quickly and run anywhere but to the dining hall. To the fields perhaps, to watch the redmanes draw the plows. To the canning shed, where the produce monitors would be counting containers, trying to estimate how many would be needed this year. Or to the pottery, where the wheels would be turning already, the slippery clay spattering the potters' aprons.

Today.

Khira dressed and went nowhere but the dining hall. Alzaja already sat at the table, her hair veiling her cheek. She glanced up when Khira entered and smiled when the cook's assistant appeared immediately with Khira's platter.

Today everything upon it was flesh of Alzaja's hostess. The bread was ground from grain harvested when Nindra was at her autumn fullness. The butter was churned from milk drawn at the same phase. The boiled eggs had been placed in cold storage the autumn before. And all the condiments had been gathered during Nindra's same fullness.

Today, in honor of Alzaja's challenge, every person in the valley would eat the food of Nindra's autumn fullness, even the seed monitors and the breeders, who discounted the very concept of hostess' flesh, who insisted that grains of wheat held equal nourishment whenever harvested, if ripe.

Let them choke on Nindra's bread, Khira decided, knowing she would choke on anything she ate today. With effort, she chewed a small pinch of bread and swallowed it dry. It caught in her throat and she coughed violently.

She glanced up to find Alzaja studying her. "You're pale this morning, Khira." Alzaja's voice was serene, as passionless as a dying breeze.

"I sat up the night ciphering," Khira said, although they both knew she had spent the night tossing in her bed.

"Then tonight you must sleep," Alzaja said with a smile that didn't reach her lips. Undisturbed, she turned back to her platter.

Khira studied her narrowly as she disposed of her meal. Alzaja had trained on the mountain for six hands of days, but the sun hardly seemed to have touched her. Her skin was fair, almost transparent. Through the thin flesh of her temples, Khira could see the beat of blue veins. Training had not hardened her hands, although she had honed her nails before coming down this morning. Khira frowned. Slashing-sharp nails and a bare trace of sun-darkening did not make Alzaja any more imposing than she had been before training.

"Alzaja—" But she couldn't say the rest: *Don't go! Don't leave me alone!* Perhaps if she could have said it calmly, reasonably—but just the act of biting back her plea made her head beat with emotion: fear for Alzaja; anger; dread. Even if Alzaja returned, Khira would be alone. Because if Alzaja returned, she would be changed. That was why she went to the mountain: to make her challenge and gain her barohnhood.

Alzaja read her unuttered plea and smiled palely. Pushing back her platter, she stood. "It's time for me to go now. Will you come to the orchards with me?"

Did she think Khira would relinquish her sooner? "Yes—I'll carry your pack. And your pike. Alzaja—"

"I'll carry them myself, Khira," Alzaja said with a floating smile, as if her spirit lingered somewhere outside her body, lost to its concerns. Her fingers didn't even tremble as she strapped on her pack with its single day's rations—flesh of the hostess, everything, down to the smallest bit of dried fruit—and picked up her pike. She didn't wear a hunter's leathers. Instead she wore the same bleached woolen shift she had worn to Darkmorning Evefest last autumn. Her arms were bare, as were her legs, except for her laced boots.

"You'll be cold," Khira said. "Alzaja, tonight—you'll—"

"We won't talk about it," Alzaja responded, but a bare frown marred her serenity and for a moment her fingers whitened on her pike.

Their footsteps echoed through the corridors. Spring was a quiet time in the palace, a busy time outside. They met only a pair of trimmers, who were snipping down overgrown stems of stalklamp and sweeping the glowing runners into a pile. And they met a cook's assistant, who responded to their appearance with a startled jerk and hurried away.

Once they heard a group of Arnimi nearby, discussing some project. Khira's lips tightened with distaste. She did not care to deal with the Arnimi and their cold-eyed questions today. Neither apparently did Alzaja. She quickened her pace.

They found Tiahna upon the throne, the mirrors that banked the throneroom walls focused upon her. She sat in a flush of light and the throne glowed warmly beneath her. Her skin was still blackened from the spring thawing and her eyes glowed impassively in her dark face. When Alzaja and Khira crossed the polished stone floor, she unconsciously touched the pairing stone which hung at her throat. That was her only betrayal of emotion.

"I see you have your pike, daughter," she said. "And your pack." Her voice was low, from deep in her throat.

"Yes, I'm going to the mountain now," Alzaja said, as if the entire valley didn't know. Her voice was light, clear, unaffected. "Either I will come back as tall as you or not at all."

"Come back tall then," Tiahna said huskily, the pairing stone glowing blue under her fingers. "There are valleys with empty thrones, cold places where no one lives. Let this valley be warm with the sun that touches your face." The words were ritual. Barohnas had spoken them to departing daughters for centuries. Their meaning hardly seemed to touch Tiahna.

Yet somewhere there was emotion. There had to be, unless all

Tiahna's caring was directed to Rahela. Surely she felt something for Alzaja, some fear, some regret—some anger that Alzaja had to go as Tiahna once had gone.

Khira gazed at Alzaja. No one even knew what beast Tiahna had killed for her throne. She had never made a tale of it. Would Alzaja come back as much a stranger as Tiahna? As tall, as strong, as remote? And when some traveling gem master fastened a newly cut pairing stone at her neck and it took fire—but Khira did not want to think now of the loss of intimacy that would come when Alzaja found her stone mate.

"I'll bring light to the throne when I come," Alzaja responded ritually. With a nod, she turned and led way from the throneroom. Khira glanced back once. Tiahna peered impassively after them, her sun-darkened face betraying nothing. But Khira noticed that she clutched her pairing stone with tightening fingers.

It was tradition that no one of the stonehalls take leave of the palace daughter on her chosen day. And so as Alzaja and Khira left the palace and crossed the plaza to the stone avenues, the people who passed them, the runners, the stonemasons, the launderers, averted their eyes or nodded covertly. And the occasional child too young for the fields skipped past them with flushing face, lips bitten to silence.

The palace was built upon a rise at the center of the valley. Stonehalls, work buildings, and stock pens had grown up in concentric rings about it. Stone avenues stretched from it, narrowing as they neared the fields. The precious soil of the fields was carefully contained within a series of broad, interlocking stone levees. In the first days after the spring melting, thaw-water stood to the tops of the levees, making a series of drowning pools of the fields. Gradually the water seeped down until the soil could be worked.

Shading her eyes, Khira saw Yvala leading one of her teams down broad levee steps. A crew of workers followed with the plow the team would pull. In the distance, the other team was already at work in a separate leveed field. A group of Arnimi observed them from the levee, their silver suits glinting in the sun.

The tops of the levees were broad, and foot traffic from the fields passed across them to the avenues. Khira followed Alzaja across the levees, keenly aware of her sister's composure. Alzaja hardly looked where she placed her feet. Instead she peered serenely toward Terlath, as if she could already see her beast somewhere on those frozen slopes— as if she could already see him dead.

Or as if . ... But Khira dismissed the thought unconfronted. The morning was clear, the breeze warm. No one could die on a day like this one.

But on Terlath's slopes, there was snow and ice. It would be several hands of days before the first spring grass greened the mountain's stone shoulders and the herders took their sheep to pasture.

"At least the winter beasts will be weak," Khira said aloud. Perhaps the most fearsome of them would still be in wintersleep.

"No one goes to the mountain to challenge an animal who is weak."

Khira looked at Alzaja sharply. Was she really so unaffected? But Alzaja was right. The inexplicable glandular rush that brought barohnhood could not be conferred by confrontation with a beast whom winter had left weak. Quickly images of breeterlik, of rock-leopards, of snowminx flashed into Khira's mind. The snowminx were rare, elusive white shadows that prowled the winter snows. She had seen rock-leopards more often, patrolling the rocky ridges of the mountain, and she had several times seen breeterlik. They were lumbering, shaggy beasts with hot eyes and writhing belly sphincters that oozed acid. Once she had even seen a crag-charger bumping and tumbling down the slopes in its hard carapace. When it reached a level area, it took to its feet—its stubby feet set on short, retractable legs—and pounded away without seeing her. If it had sighted her, if it had charged—

But it had not. Khira shivered. The hunters took the mountain beasts with bladed pikes and with bows. Alzaja had only a simple wooden pike and her sharpened nails. But where the successful hunter brought home meat and hide and little more, Alzaja could return with the power to capture the sun's energy and store it in the sunthrone.

If . . .

They crossed the last levee and descended into the orchard lands that ringed the growing fields. Here, so near the mountain, the air was chill. The trees bloomed anyway, their petals fluttering seductively in the breeze, promising summer fruit.

"Have you ever guessed, Khira, who I named you for?" Alzaja said as they entered the trees.

Khira abandoned her thoughts with a start. "You said you would tell me," she realized. "And there was something else you said you would tell me today." For once concern had outstripped curiosity. She had completely forgotten Alzaja's promise.

Alzaja bowed her head. Sunlight passing through bright petals dyed her pale cheeks. "I've been careful to leave you with only those two promises. All the other things I've ever promised, I've fulfilled." She paused, glancing up into the trees. "It was different when Mara went."

Khira glanced sharply at her sister. Her voice was so light, so unconcerned. They might have been on their way to gather string-grass for the cook. She tried to match Alzaja's unaffected tone. "You told me—there were things Mara never did. Things she said she would."

"Yes, so many things she promised me. Talks we would have. Scrolls she would letter for me, stories she wanted me to remember, sketches she would make. But all she left me was promises."

"She thought she would come back," Khira said uneasily.

Alzaja nodded gravely. She began to walk again, deliberately, never looking where she put her foot. "She never even considered that she might not. She was so certain, she trained for just a few days. And after she went to the peaks, the lens tenders found her pack on a rock beside the trail. She hadn't even eaten her bread. I suppose she thought she would eat it later, when she came down from the peaks."

Khira frowned. Mara had thrown her life away thoughtlessly, carelessly. Yet Alzaja was not angry, had never been. She spoke remotely, as if Mara's recklessness had not affected her at all. "Alzaja—"

"I named you from one of the early scrolls, Khira. For Khirsa. Do you remember?"

"I—" Distracted, Khira groped for memory. "She was a herder," she said uncertainly.

"Yes. In those times, there were more predators in these mountains. And the people were much more dependent upon their sheep than we are now. Each spring the young herders took their sheep to pasture and if predators came, the herders had to go against them. There was no other way. Each year herders died protecting their flocks.

"But the people had a belief then." Alzaja halted again, peering toward the flashing mirrors that beamed sunlight down the mountain. "They believed that if they saw a silverwing above the mountain, it was because one of the herders had died killing a mountain beast."

"They thought the herders actually became silverwings," Khira said, remembering the story. Frowning, she tried to concentrate her attention in the moment. There would be time later to wonder why Alzaja had not been angry at Mara, why she was not frightened now. "They—they thought the mountains had power and when the herders drew on the power to kill a predator, they were transformed."

"Yes, and transformed they lived one year in the form of a silverwing. Then they joined the web of mountain power and lived there forever. They didn't know that the sun is the source of power, not the mountains.

"But when Khirsa called on the mountain power to kill the breeterlik that had taken her ewes, she didn't change. She killed him and yet she didn't become a silverwing. And then when she started back down the mountain, she found a nest of fledgling silverwings behind a boulder— and broken shells. She learned that when you see a silverwing in the sky, it means only one thing. Somewhere there is a broken shell and a mother bird watching her fledgling fly."

Khira caught her lip in her teeth. In the story, Khirsa had been angry—angry that the people who sent her to guard the sheep had lied. Didn't Alzaja remember that?

But when had Alzaja ever been angry? Khira tried to remember a time and remembered only patience and laughter and much of the same serenity she saw in Alzaja today. Khira had always been the storming one.

"I named you for Khirsa because I wanted you to look for the truth behind whatever legend you might hear. I wanted you to know that our mother was once a palace daughter and now she is a barohna because she was strong and self-willed and went to the peaks well-trained. I wanted you to know that when you come across a killed beast, it is because someone or something has made herself stronger than the beast and has willed her life over the beast's. I wanted you to know that when people rely on powers outside themselves, or power within themselves that they haven't taken the trouble to develop—"

"Like Mara—"

"Like Mara. I wanted you to know that if you fail to prepare, your beast will have you." Her glance flickered sideways, momentarily evasive. "But Khira, there is something else. There is—"

Khira could not listen to more. "Alzaja, don't go," she pleaded, an eruption of emotion. "There will be other years. No one will say anything if you come back with me. They'll be glad. And next time, you can set your day later. You can train harder. You don't have to go today!"

"No, Khira. I have to go now," Alzaja said simply, faintly troubled. "But before I do—"

"No!" How many reasons could she name—all of them coming down to just one agonized plea? "I'll be alone."

Khira's plea seemed to stir the breeze through the trees. Leaves rattled and spring fragrance drifted heavily through the air. The twisted limbs of the orchard were thick with blossoms. Soon there would be laughing children under the trees, and this summer there would be every kind of fruit. But today there was only Khira, crying, and Alzaja, embracing her. "I have to go, Khira. Another year and I will be too old for the peaks. This is my year."

"You won't be too old!" Khira insisted. "You can set your day later next year. You can train longer and be stronger. And we'll spar during the winter. The pads Hassel made for us so we could work with the pikes—we hardly used them." Khira had laced into hers twice. They were cumbersome and scratchy. But if she had insisted Alzaja spar with her through the winter, Alzaja would already have been hardened by spring thawing.

Gently Alzaja drew Khira down to sit under the trees. "I'm not thinking of piking strength, Khira. I'm thinking of the courage it takes to leave you. Every year I have less of it. I know you will be alone and I'm sorry for it. But you're older now and you're strong. Old enough, strong enough. And I've told you everything now—except the one thing. I haven't told you about the ice and the stone."

The one secret, barely hinted at in the scrolls. How often had Khira teased Alzaja for it? How often had Alzaja evaded her? Without meaning to, Khira seized Alzaja's arm, her fingers closing tight in fresh anger. "You saved that until now just to keep me from arguing with you. You saved it—" To distract her, as she might distract a toddler from a cut finger with a piece of dried fruit. "You—"

"I saved it because this is the time when I must tell you. Now, just before I go. This is when Mara told me. I walked this far with her and we sat under the trees and after she had told me about the ice and the stone, she went up the mountain and I went back to the palace. And it was the same with the others. Sukiin told Kristyan here, Kristyan told Hedia, Hedia told Denabar—"

"Well, even if I let you tell me, I won't leave you here," Khira retorted fiercely. "I don't care what the others did. I'm going to walk to the lower pasture with you. I'm going to—"

"You will leave me here," Alzaja declared. "And there is no question of refusing to hear me. The ice and the stone come from the earliest time of the barohnas, from the days when the first barohnas learned to use the sunstone—from the time Niabi turned the fire loose and saw

Lensar fall in ashes. It is always passed from elder sister to younger. When finally a sister bronzes, it passes from her to her first daughter."

"Then it's no use telling me. I have no younger sister."

"There was no younger sister when I was eleven either, Khira."

"I was expected," Khira insisted. To all her other angers she added anger that she could not break through the barrier of Alzaja's composure. "And I don't think there will be another. I'll have no one to raise. I'll be alone and I'll be the last." Miserably she recognized the tone of a spoiled child, petulant, whining. And she did not want her last hour with Alzaja to be an hour that would sour in memory. She bit her lip, her voice tearful. "Alzaja—"

"You have to know," Alzaja said. "You have to know how a barohna dies."

Khira sucked a quivering breath, caught by a numbing chill. Was that the secret of the ice and the stone? She had asked often enough when she was younger what became of the barohnas. The scrolls were full of the dying of other people—silently in wintersleep, valiantly during the warmseasons defending their stock, grimly during the brief times of trouble. But when a barohna retired to the plains, she simply strode off the story-scrolls into mystery, without ceremony, without explanation.

"I know how redmane guardians die," she said reluctantly. She and Alzaja had gone to the plain where the redmanes lived two years before at bonding time. They had visited their grandmother, Kadura, retired there with her stone mate Upala. She shuddered, the scene still vivid. First was the silence of the gathered herds, thousands of animals standing motionless under the dusken sky, dark-robed guardians watching them from every prominence. Then the moons came across the mountains and the redmanes began to pound their padded feet. They pounded until the entire plain seemed to reverberate to the beat of a single heart; pounded ever more insistently, ever more rapidly, until Khira's own heart took up the rhythm and surged with it. The blood pulsed through her body more and more quickly. Consciousness became a whining drone in her ears and she had no thoughts, only consuming awareness of the herd and of the heartbeat of the plain. She had fallen finally, when her heart beat too frenetically, had lain helpless on the shuddering ground until the bonding was done and the redmanes padded silently away, leaving their own dead behind.

Guardians had been left dead too, those too old or feeble to stand the frenzied pounding of their hearts. On their faces Khira had seen surprise and rapture. Alzaja had led Khira away by one numb arm.

The first barohnas had come from guardian stock, but barohnas were not guardians. Barohnas did not die in the bonding. Did they?

Alzaja's arm tightened around Khira. "Sister, look at the blossoms," she urged softly. "See them, so bright, so happy. I've told you what the first timers thought—that the trees made blossoms to attract insects. That the insects trapped pollen on their legs and carried it from flower to flower, pollinating them."

Despite herself, Khira laughed.

"Well, that's what they thought," Alzaja said, laughing too. "Maybe it was so where they came from, before the stranding. Maybe insects flew like birds. But we know the blossoms are to please the children who come with the brushes. And before that, they are to send out perfume so the orchard monitors will know it's time to send the children. Then when the children have come with their brushes and pollinated the flowers and the fruit is started, the blossoms fall off. Because they have served their purpose.

"I've served my purpose in your life now. I'm ready to fall away. And as I do, I hope that your harvest will be sweet, Khira. But your harvest can't come until I fall away from you."

Was she to think of Alzaja as a blossom then, with glowing blue petals and velvet stamen? A blossom warming in the sun, then silently drifting to the ground, to be lost in the multitude of fallen petals that fell under the trees each year? "You aren't done, Alzaja!"

"But I will be as soon as I tell you about the ice and the stone," Alzaja said with gentle insistence. "Won't you listen peacefully, little sister?"

Khira did not miss the rebuke. "Alzaja, you know I wasn't born to a peaceful star." Not for Khira the serene Nindra or the peaceful Zan, coming and going in white silence. Adar was Khira's host, a fiery red star that came in the west, a host of beating drums, of clattering reeds, a host of militant chants from times of trouble.

But Alzaja had always known how to temper Khira's defiance, how to leash her impatience, how to turn threatened turbulence to compliance. And that was the fullest measure of Khira's loss. Whether or not Alzaja bronzed on the mountain, their days of closeness were ending now. Khira would have to monitor her own moods, mediate her own behavior. And if she ruined these last moments, there would be no others to remember. These were the only last moments they would have before Alzaja's bronzing.

Khira closed her eyes, gathering at reserves of composure Alzaja had long tried to foster in her. "I'm ready to listen."

"Then I'm ready to talk. But what I have to tell you isn't just how a barohna finally dies. First you have to know how a barohna lives, how she becomes a living barohna."

Despite her resolve, impatience sprang to Khira's tongue. "Everyone knows that. She makes her challenge."

"She makes her challenge, yes. But there's more. If she had only to kill the hungriest beast she could find, her bronzing would lie with the beast, not with her. No, the real secret of bronzing lies in the stone."

"The sunstone?" But how could that be? No one was permitted even to touch the sunstone of the valley throne but one who was already a living barohna.

Alzaja smiled wistfully. "The stone in her heart, Khira." She touched her chest lightly with her fingertips. "That's what really happens when a palace daughter goes up the mountain and challenges her beast. She takes stone into her heart, fully and finally. She becomes hard there where she lives, hard enough to challenge the fiercest breeterlik and live, hard enough to chase a rock-leopard to its den and break its neck with her bare hands, hard enough to put herself in a crag-charger's path and find the only chink in its armor with her pike. And that's when the bronzing changes come to her.

"If she goes to the mountain with a heart that can never take stone, she may place herself in the path of the crag-charger but her pike will never find its target. It doesn't matter how hard she has trained her body if her heart stays flesh."

Confused, Khira tried to understand, tried to relate what Alzaja said to the sisters who had already gone to the mountain. "But Mara—"

"Perhaps Mara could have taken the stone. I don't know. I do know that she didn't train because she was so blindly certain that she was to be like our mother. She worshipped our mother, Khira. You've heard stories of people who took gods, people who went out of the valleys carrying stone images and never came back. Our mother was Mara's god, and Mara thought worshipping her was enough. She didn't look deeply enough. She didn't see the stone in our mother's heart, even though Denabar told her it was there. And she didn't look to her own heart. She thought she had only to walk up the mountain with her shoulders drawn back the way our mother walks, with our mother's frown on her face, and any beast would fall before her."

"And then she would go back for her pack and eat the bread she brought," Khira whispered, beginning to understand.

"Yes." Alzaja smiled again, in memory. "I wish you had known her. You would understand about her better."

"But you understand. You know about making—making your heart stone." For the first time since Alzaja had announced her day, Khira felt a lessening of dread. Alzaja's fate did not depend entirely upon physical prowess. There was another factor, and although Khira did not fully grasp the concept of stone, surely Alzaja did. And surely Alzaja would come down the mountain again a barohna.

A barohna. For a moment Khira frowned. But if she had to have Alzaja a barohna, so be it. Alzaja remote and impassive would still contain the germ of Alzaja as she was today, her hair floating on the breeze, her cheeks blue-stained by the sunlight that glowed through the petals of the trees. "You know," Khira said.

Alzaja sighed deeply, peering down at her crossed ankles. "Yes, I know. I know a number of things about Mara and you and our mother— and myself." For a moment she was silent, staring at her fingers, long and slender, the nails honed. "But beyond the stone lies the ice, Khira. And that's easier, I think. The stone—the stone has to be bred into you. Unless there is some small grain of it there when you are born, I don't think it will ever come, no matter how hard you train. But even that small particle won't be enough unless you strengthen it by learning and training. Even the stone can't save you if you throw your life to the beast.

"But once the stone is there, once you've lived with it there, and when it finally leaves you—when you have served your throne and your heart turns back to flesh—" She glanced down at Khira, pain shadowing her eyes for the first time. "I hate to think of you that way, hard where I'm so tender, but I feel it in you. I know the stone is in you, Khira, and I know you will serve a throne if you train properly. And I know someday your heart will turn to flesh again.

"Then you must discover how to take the ice into your heart instead. Not immediately, I'm sure. Perhaps you will want to spend some time in the plain with the redmane guardians and your stone mate as Kadura does. Perhaps you will want to follow the herds and watch autumn sunsets. Perhaps you will bond yourself with the herds for many seasons.

"But one day it will be enough. Too many of your guardian companions will fall in the bonding and leave you standing. Then you must take the ice into your heart and end it." Seeing Khira's uncomprehending expression, she reached for her hand. "You don't understand what I'm saying, of course. You're too young. But all you have to do is remember. When the time comes and you are tired, take the ice into your heart as you once took the stone. You'll find the way.

"That's the whole secret. Stone and ice." She smiled, her gaze lingering back across the valley. "Although I will tell you this. We come from a race that has been changing for many, many centuries. When the first timers were stranded here, they were hardly fit to survive on Brakrath. But over the centuries, they changed—dozens of small changes that made them an entirely different people.

"I think the changing will continue. I think one day there will be palace daughters who can bronze at will, without going to the mountain to make a challenge. And perhaps there will be enough of them that none must live long with the stone in their hearts. Instead they can let the stone go while they are still young and live years and years with hearts of flesh before they finally take the ice."

Stone, flesh, ice. Khira's head churned with half-apprehended thoughts. They formed and dissolved so rapidly she could hardly catch their flavor. Alzaja thought she had stone in her heart. But if her heart was hard, why did she feel as if it were being squeezed to the bursting point? If she were meant to be like their mother, stern and strong, why were tears slipping down her cheeks?

And there was something else Alzaja had said, something she did not want to confront. "Please—" she begged.

Alzaja held her tight then and rocked her, stroking her hair. "You'll understand one day. I promise you will. The way will be hard, you'll be lonely, but one day you'll understand, Khira. You'll be a link in the chain of mothers and daughters."

But she was already beginning to understand something she did not want to understand. Its dimensions were becoming clearly delineated in her mind. It reached out for her awareness, reached to wound her, so deeply, so painfully—

"I have to go," Alzaja said.

No! It was coming clear, this new thought, and it was unbearable. She could not live with it, not alone. "Alzaja—"

"I have to go," Alzaja repeated, releasing her. "Sit here. This is the same place where Mara left me, where Denabar left her. Stay here until I wave to you from Borton's Cropping. Then get up and walk back to the palace, slowly, and I'll walk slowly toward the peaks. We will both walk today, Khira, at the same time.

"Think about that, Khira, only that. Think about walking. Every time you place a foot to the ground, I will too. We'll walk together." Slowly she stood. "We'll always walk together, Khira. I'll never leave you."

Yet she did. Despite the tears that burned down Khira's cheeks, despite the color that finally touched her own face, Alzaja left. She turned, took her pack and her pike, and walked away beneath the blue-blooming trees, petals brushing her hair and spiraling to the ground behind her. And Khira remained under the trees—not because she didn't want to shatter Alzaja's parting serenity, not because she didn't want to intrude her own suddenly renewed dread into their last moments, not because she had stone in her heart.

But because she knew with sudden and utter certainty that Alzaja would never come down the mountain again. And that certainty paralyzed her.

That was the terrible thing that had taken shape in her awareness: certainty. "I hate to think of you that way," Alzaja had said, "hard where I am so tender." And it was true. Despite the pain, there was a hardness in Khira that Alzaja did not have, had never had. Alzaja had other things: serenity, subtlety, grace—but there was no stone in her.

Paralyzed, Khira watched her walk up the first slopes of the mountain, her white shift bare protection against the cold. She had no inner protection either, no gritty substance, no granular core. And she recognized the lack. She had trained, but half-heartedly, hardly raising a callus on her slender hands. She had trained because it was expected, but she had known that no strength of muscle could substitute for what she lacked.

Finally, as if stunned, Khira took her feet. Alzaja turned from Borton's Cropping. She was a gash of white against that dark stone formation. Snow lay above; Tiahna's spring thawing had reached only to the Cropping. It seemed to Khira that Alzaja raised her hand and waved almost gaily before she turned again. It seemed to Khira that she climbed more quickly, with nimble abandon, when she had looked back for the last time.

Khira walked heavily from beneath the trees, her feet like the stone Alzaja saw in her heart. Every particle of her body was weighted down by gravity. Her spirit was borne down as if it had petrified. She could not even find her anger again, and that might have comforted her.

It was mid-afternoon when she reached the palace. The sky was darkening into an early spring dusk. Khira walked down stone avenues without seeing any of those who turned to look after her. She felt old, as if she had left childhood beneath the trees, scattered there like dead petals, something to be remembered but never held again.

Tiahna sat upon the sunthrone at the focus of the dying light, her face stiller than Khira had ever seen it. When Khira entered the throne-room, Tiahna's sun-darkened hand unconsciously touched the stone pendant at her throat. But she said nothing. There were no ritual words for the moment and no one to hear them if there had been. The runners and monitors were gone. The room held only Tiahna and Khira.

"She's not coming back," Khira said finally.

Tiahna sighed heavily. "No, she will not," she said huskily. "You see that too."

"She's not coming back," Khira said again, employing every bit of her control to keep the words from ending shrilly, in tears. "I don't understand why she went when she knows she won't come back." She couldn't bear to think of Alzaja simply falling away from her life like drying petals. She could not bear to think of herself as some budding fruit that had pushed Alzaja away.

"It was time she went," Tiahna said, shifting her eyes from Khira's pleading gaze. The pairing stone glowed softly under her fingers. "She was not one to stay here as a permanent daughter. Her spirit became a woman's years ago. How long could she live in a girl's body? Yet if she had stayed much longer, she might have lost the strength to go up the mountain."

"But—but she's going to die there! She's going to let some beast kill her!" That was what she had gone for, to shed a life that had no further meaning to her. Or a life that held so much meaning that she knew she must shed it while she still had the strength.

"Or perhaps she will simply lie down in the snow and sleep there," Tiahna said softly.

Khira shuddered. She could not bear the hollow compassion in Tiahna's voice. She had never heard it there before, or anything like it. "She'll die there and you don't care!" she cried. "You don't care about her—or me—or anyone except Rahela! You're stone where everyone else lives!"

Sobbing, she ran from the throneroom, ran down empty corridors to her own bedchamber. There she threw herself on her bed and let her confusion, her inadequacy, her anger vent in strangling sobs. If that was what it meant to have stone in her heart, if it meant sitting uncaring while a daughter died, then let her have a heart as tender as Alzaja's. Let her die on Terlath as the others had and leave Tiahna alone with her glowing throne and the blue pairing stone that linked her to Rahela.

But I do care. The thought entered her mind almost impersonally. *I care.* Was it hers? And if it was her thought, why was the voice Tiahna's? And why did it go on and on, repeating the same two phrases, as she sobbed herself to sleep, tangled in her covers?

It was dark when she wakened. She jumped from her bed with a wild cry and ran to her window. Clouds hid moons and stars. Nowhere on the mountain was there sign of a white shift toiling its way upward. Nowhere was there sign of Alzaja. Emptily, Khira stumbled back to bed.

Early the next morning. Khira dragged herself from bed again. Her face was puffy, her body leaden. In the night someone—a servant?—had left a white mourning sash at the foot of her bed. She refused to touch it. Instead she sat at her window peering to the mountain until the sun stood high. She was oblivious to the breeze, to the fragrance of the orchards, to the bustle on the avenues and in the fields beyond the palace. She didn't even frown when one of the Arnimi ground cars purred beneath her window and down the stone avenue to the levees.

It was mid-morning when she picked out the glint of silver wings above the western peak of the mountain. The wings hung there, spread to the sun, then swept sharply down behind the thrusting rock of the mountain and did not appear again.

She didn't have to see the flashing wings again. She knew their message. She knew it with a hollow heart, a heart that had already hurt as much as it could and now was numb. She turned from the window and dressed, lacing her clothes with trembling fingers. Somewhere, she told herself, tears gliding down her face unnoticed—somewhere on the mountain was a broken shell.

Silently Khira tied the mourning sash at her waist. Alzaja would not return.

3/Khira

Winter curled icy fingers down the mountain and across the valley. Snow flurries swept lightly upon the leaves, licking at the bare soil of the fields, melting there. The trees of the orchards were stark against the withered grasses of summer. Flowers and fruit had long since fallen.

Khira sat on Borton's Cropping, her auburn hair caught in a loose knot. As she looked across the valley, her face was as pale as winter itself, bloodless. Earlier this morning she had watched a party of lens tenders pass down the mountain, talking among themselves. A little later she had seen a last herder hurry down the slopes with her ewes and lambs. Beyond those, Khira had been alone on the mountain for three hours.

Alone with the first cold presence of winter about her. Alone with the stony ache that had preoccupied her since spring, that had come to painful focus with approaching winter. Soon would be Darkmorning, the time when the people of the stonehalls sealed their doors, scattered sleepdust, and settled into their beds for winter. They slept in families: parents, grandparents, children, aunts and cousins.

But in the palace there were no family quarters, no scatterers, no wintersleep. When the stonehalls were sealed for winter, the barohna left the palace and went to her winter throne in the peaks. Then the

palace daughters were left alone to occupy themselves for long silent
months in the snowbound palace.

Alone. And this year Khira was the only daughter. Her lips tightening, she opened her pack and pulled out a pouch filled with fine grey
dust. Late each summer harvesters went to Terlath's western slopes,
to the woody thickets where sleepleaf grew. They filled large woven
bags with the fallen sleepleaves, then returned to the valley to pound
the leaves to dust. On Darkmorning, when Evefest was done and the
families had swaddled for winter, scatterers came to each door and
sprinkled sleepdust across the floor. And the people of the halls dreamed
until their bodies knew the season for sleep had passed.

Neither barohnas nor palace daughters used sleepdust—not since the
time of Helsa, who had used dust and dreamed of flame. Sighing, Khira
stroked the pouch. She did not have a sunstone to focus flame. Nor did
she have flame to focus. She would not have until she made her challenge. Still the prohibition of generations was strong upon her and she
knew she should not have taken the dust from the store closet.

But to pass the winter alone and awake in the palace, trying to harden
herself against every reminder of Alzaja—

She jumped up, tucking the pouch into her pack, taking up her pike.
If she dreamed of flame, if somehow it burned, it would take only the
herder's cabin where she slept—and her. For the moment, with the
cold upon the mountain and in her heart, neither seemed much loss.

Still she stopped and gazed down over the valley for a moment before
going up the trail. Shading her eyes, she thought she could distinguish
workers trafficking between the palace and the halls, preparing for
Darkmorning Evefest. For a moment her stomach tightened and she
thought of roasted meats, dark breads and rich confections. No one who
went to wintersleep gaunt would survive the sleeping months. At Evefest
everyone ate to capacity—then waited and ate more. And even though
she did not take wintersleep, Khira had always joined the feasting with
full appetite.

This year she would not join the feasting at all. Sharp tears came
to her eyes, tears of anger. She peered down stonily, then turned and
ran up the trail.

She had chosen one of the smaller herder's cabins to take her wintersleep. It sat alone overlooking a frost-killed meadow. She had come
to the mountain five days ago and spent the day preparing the cabin.

First she had harvested vexreed and pressed sheafs of it around the inner walls of the cabin. When the white foam from the reeds had hardened into a dense insulating layer, she had pulled down the overgrown streamers of stalklamp that clung from the ceiling of the cabin. The remaining stubs of stalklamp touched the corners with pale orange light. The lash of the wind did not penetrate the cabin at all and there were ample blankets to swaddle herself in. She had returned to the valley satisfied with her preparations.

But now she re-entered the cabin and shuddered, her hand tightening on her pack. The single room was dim, ready. But to shut herself here alone for the winter, cut off by snow from the valley, to invite the dreams the people of the halls knew... Quickly Khira shed her pack and paced around the cabin. She would wait for night to scatter the dust. And then she would hope that it acted as quickly on a palace daughter as on a child of the stonehalls.

She passed the midday hours restlessly. The cabin already seemed close with dreams. Twice she fled its confining walls and climbed the trail to look down over the valley. The call of the palace was strong, even with its promise of a long and lonely winter. As day passed and the sky greyed, the wind grew harsher, crying down through the rocks and crags. Khira wondered if it read her mood and echoed it.

Then she looked down and saw a white shape below her, in the rocks near the trail, and forgot all bleakness. Instinctively she froze. Snowminx were among the rarer predators of the mountain. They stood no taller than an adult human, but their teeth were savage and their claws cruel. They left their dens each year at this time, just before the snows came, to prey on the smaller creatures of the mountain as they foraged for a last meal before hibernation.

But snowminx preyed on humans as well as on small creatures. Khira stood like stone, willing her pounding heart to silence. The minx paused as it sought among the rocks and gazed toward her, its pink eyes becoming momentarily intent. Then something in the rocks caught its attention, and it sprang, white earlocks bobbing. Some small animal squealed and the minx thrashed after it. When the struggle was finished, the minx did not reappear.

Khira watched until her feet were numb. Then she picked her way down the trail, wary for sign of the minx.

By the time she reached the cabin and bolted the door, snow fell in spiraling gusts and the sky was dark with storm. Khira pulled off jacket and gloves and peered around. She was unprepared for the stark sense of confinement that came to her. Winter in the palace had always been a time for running in the corridors, with no servants to disapprove. And winter had been a time when she and Alzaja had chosen their own mealtimes, ciphered scrolls when it pleased them, sat over the gameboard for as long as they both pleased, a time when there were no set hours to the day.

Here she could only bolt the door, sprinkle dust, and dream. Suddenly her throat closed. She had dreamed before, of course, fleetingly, on summer nights. Winterdreams were different. She knew because she had listened when people of the halls recounted them. Winterdreams were filled with half-apprehended images no one ever saw waking and voices that first muttered, then were siren-shrill. Some of the people of the halls believed the Brakrath powers came into the stonehalls at Darkmorning and stayed the winter, powers as old as Terlath's cragged peaks, powers which revealed themselves to humans only when they lay drugged and helpless.

Khira shuddered. Others said winterdreams were stimulated by sleepleaf. But if the dreams came from the leaf and the leaf came from the soil, and the soil were inhabited by silent powers—

If the Brakrath powers caught her in the long night of winter and would not release her, if she could not cough sleepdust from her lungs and waken—

Or if she spent the entire winter trapped in dreams of Alzaja, if she had to part with her time and again, watch her white shift disappear up the mountainside, if she had to hear that passionless voice—*I care; I do care*— endlessly, through all her winterdreams—

With a flash of fury, Khira snatched up her pack and shook out its contents: bits of bread, dried fruit, personal implements and tools— powdered sleepleaf. The pouch was in her hand, her fingers at the ties. Enough of hesitation, enough of fear. Alzaja was gone. Khira was the eldest now, and she was stone where Alzaja had been flesh. Dreams could not wound her.

She had the pouch open, she smelled the musty tang of the leaf, when she heard the shriek. It startled her into stillness, the pouch clutched tight. The wind?

Did the wind scream like an injured thing, in terror? Without thinking, Khira was at the cabin door, peering down the mountainside.

At the lower end of the meadow were two shapes, locked. She recognized them instantly, with shock. One was the snowminx she had seen earlier near the trail. The other—

"Paki!" she cried, as if the sound of his name could save him. Paki was the foal born on Alzaja's last day—born with white film obscuring his eyes. Worse, he had stepped into a mound of stingbriar near the end of plowing time and his wounds had become infected. Faced with the choice of leaving a single foal behind for the winter or waiting until he was strong enough to make the journey to the redmane plain, Yvala had elected to leave him. If her teams were late for the bonding of the herds in the plain, the mares would have no foals next spring.

Redmanes were known for their ability to travel long distances with no guide but instinct. Apparently instinct had driven Paki to break from his winter pen and set off in search of his herd. Instead, blindly, he had blundered into the snowminx. The minx tore at him with eager claws, trying to rip through his dense winter coat to the flesh beneath.

Every three-year-old knew that to move when a snowminx was near was to invite swift-clawing death. Yet without thinking, Khira ran down the hillside, shrieking angrily at the predator. She stumbled once and sprawled, the pouch of sleepleaf still clutched in one hand. She picked herself up quickly and threw herself at the white-haired minx, bringing one booted foot up sharply against the animal's flank.

The minx spun, its pink eyes blazing. For a moment Khira looked into a face almost human, yet grown with silky white hair that hung down in curling locks. Instinctively Khira froze.

Squealing, Paki squirmed free of the minx' grasp. He backed away, stunned and uncertain of his footing, bleeding from a gash on his nose.

"Paki—" Her cry brought the minx to fury again. With a gliding hop, the animal was upon her, its breath rasping in her ear. Khira took a useless step back, throwing up one arm, the arm that should have held her pike.

Instead it held a pouch of sleepleaf.

Useless. A winter's sleep, thrown against a snowminx in killing rage.

Useless, and still she threw it. The ties were loose and grey dust scattered from the pouch in a dense cloud. The wind caught it, swirling it around the shrieking minx. The animal hesitated in confusion, giving Khira precious moments to whirl away, to race to Paki and wind her fingers into his mane. He trembled against her, his filmed eyes peering up uselessly.

"It's all right," she said in a undertone. "It's all right, Paki."

And it was. The snowminx retreated from the blinding cloud of dust, but too late. Its pink eyes were screwed tight against the sting of the dust and it coughed and choked. It drew its eyes open with effort and peered uncertainly at Khira through the white elflocks that wreathed its face. Slowly, stunned, it brought one clawed hand up and raked at its scalp. Its features twisted spasmodically and its claws caught in its white locks and pulled.

"Paki, this way," Khira said urgently, and drew the shuddering foal past the faltering snowminx toward the cabin. The foal resisted momentarily, then padded beside her, its sides heaving in fear. Khira glanced back once and saw the snowminx rasping at its white-locked skull with both clawed hands. Blood discolored its silken hair. It swung its head from side to side, as if trying to escape some invisible restraint.

By the time she bolted the door behind them, Khira was trembling too. The sleepleaf might have had any effect upon the minx—or none. For a moment she sank to her knees beside Paki, pressing her forehead into his densely furred side. His heartbeat was rapid, tremulous.

Hers must be the same. Taking her feet, she found her pike and went to the door. She opened it carefully, peering out and down the stony meadow. The minx had dropped to its knees and it clutched its head, swaying. Snow flurried around it, momentarily obscuring it. When the flurry swept away, Khira saw that the minx was thrashing in convulsions. Over the sound of the wind, she heard its harsh, cawing cry.

In the end she took her pike and killed the animal to end its agony. By then, the minx had ripped long shreds of flesh from its scalp and lacerated its face. Khira returned to the cabin thoughtfully, wondering if anyone had ever before gone against a snowminx with sleepdust instead of pike, wondering how many young herders might have lived if they had known the effect of sleepdust on the minx.

Broken shells. Terlath's rocky flanks were littered with them. Since the beginning of human time on Brakrath, herders had brought their ewes and lambs to the high pastures and died defending them, just as she had defended Paki.

Broken shells. Khira closed the door and Paki turned and addressed her with blind eyes. "We can't stay here now," she said aloud. Absently she daubed his bleeding nose. The laceration was deep. It would have to be stitched. "We'll have to go back to the valley." Without sleepdust to slow her metabolism, she could not survive the winter without food.

And when she woke the next morning, she knew that one night on the mountain was enough. Her dreams were not bizarre. They did not speak to her with stone voices. There were no strange half-glimpsed images. When Paki nudged her awake, Khira was barely able to recall the content of her dreams. But they were enough. She wanted no more.

She did not want an entire winter of dreams. Better to return to the palace, loneliness and memories.

When they left the cabin, some larger predator had come for the minx' body. And snow had fallen in the night. It lay ankle deep, unbroken except for their footprints.

Paki did not accept their return to the valley with grace. Instinct still urged him to the south, to the redmane plain where his herd had gone. He fought Khira stubbornly down the trail, occasionally stopping to shrill angrily. His cry sounded keenly over the snowbound mountain-side. But no matter how intently he listened, the cry was never answered.

"Come, Paki—you have to be in your pen before dark." Tonight was Evefest, and Khira's reluctance to join the feasting was as great as Paki's reluctance to return to the valley. There were empty chairs at the barohnial table and if she attended the feast, she must sit among them. Somehow she had not felt their emptiness before, when she had Alzaja.

And tonight was the relinquishment of names. The names of all who had died during the year would be released to be used again. There would be bidding for Alzaja's name by the women who expected to deliver children in spring. Khira's hand clenched in Paki's mane. The woman who won the name would be required to change one of its letters, just as Alzaja had altered the name Khirsa giving it to Khira. Perhaps her child would be called Ilzaja or Alzada. Still it would be hard to hear her sister's name again next year and the years after.

Many things would be hard, she reminded herself. She must be hard to bear them. She must be stone.

Yet sometimes she wondered why. Without the barohnial ability to use the sunstone, the people of the halls would go hungry and would dwindle in numbers. Yet once the people of the halls had been without barohnas, before Lensar had polished the first sunstone, before Niabi had discovered its use. And the people had lived.

Why must palace daughters die to provide barohnas for the sunthrone? And why must those who lived let their hearts take stone? As she led Paki down the mountain, Khira thought of these things. Was there an answer somewhere in the scrolls? What was now had not always been. Must it always be?

If I find the answer, Khira vowed, I will name my own first daughter for the person who lettered the scroll that gives me it.

Am I so certain I will have daughters? Pausing by the side of the trail, brushing snow from Paki's forelock, she wondered if Tiahna had been certain of her barohnhood before she attained it. Would she ever know? Tiahna's life scroll was sealed to her for so long as Tiahna lived. And Khira's certainty that she would be next barohna of the valley was a sometimes thing. It came to her at vagrant moments and evaporated just as unpredictably. If her heart had a granular core, why did she feel so much pain and uncertainty? She continued down the trail, carefully guiding the blind redmane, wondering.

Mid-afternoon darkness fell on the valley by the time they reached the pens. Despite Paki's adamant resistance, Khira found a pensman to bed him down with the ewes and lambs. "Try to forget you're a redmane until Yvala comes again," she urged him, combing his auburn mane with her fingers. She knew from the angry lift of his head that he would never forget he was a redmane.

Nor could she forget that she was a palace daughter later, when the bells sounded for Evefest. She lay on her bed, her eyes closed, trying to shut out the sound. She was angry now that she had let herself be driven down from the mountain, that she had not taken another pouch of sleepdust and made her way back, angry that palace walls closed around her for winter. There was no need for her at the barohnial table. The feasting would go on without her. Let her chair be empty—empty beside the others.

Yet when the bells sounded again, she left her bed, pulled on her woolen shift, and descended to the feastroom. As she entered and the gathered people turned to see her, she felt that the chill of winter found expression in her face. She moved toward the barohnial table without sign that she saw anyone in the room and took her chair, the one at the farthest end of the table. Tiahna already sat at the head of the table, her expression as distracted as Khira's was chill.

Khira gazed at her wordlessly and wondered if Tiahna's heart had ever been flesh. Tiahna gazed back and frowned faintly, her fingers restless at her pairing stone. Khira knew her frown from other Evefests.

It had nothing to do with the feast, with the people at the tables. Tiahna's frown came when the days grew short, when storm clouds hid the sun and the lens tenders came down from the mountain. It marked the call of the peaks, where she would find sunlight even in the dead of winter.

All the smells of the feast were in the feastroom: roasting meat, fresh-baked bread, every kind of vegetable and fruit, all served steaming on huge platters. And the people who helped themselves from the platters were sleek with winter reserves, the layer of fat that would permit them to survive a season's sleep. They laughed and sang and ate of everything brought them. Then they laughed and sang again. But beneath the laughter and song was another mood. Some of them would not wake with spring. Each year there were deaths in wintersleep and none knew whose deaths they would be. So some darkness touched the feast too and made the laughter louder and more ragged.

At the barohnial table was silence. Khira stared stonily at her plate. Tiahna frowned at the scarred wood tabletop. Between them were six empty chairs and the words that had never been spoken aloud: *I do care.*

When the feasters reached first satiety, the chanters came, elder women who knew the history of Brakrath as they knew their own lives. They moved among the tables and recreated the first times for the people. As their voices rose, Khira squeezed her eyes shut and the stone walls of the hall dissolved. Instead of a people sitting to feast, she saw a great ship faltering in the sky, then breaking and falling to strand its human passengers upon a harsh mountainous world—Brakrath.

Khira sighed deeply as the chant continued. First the stranded ones looked to the mountains in fear and prayed for rescue. But after a while they felt the protecting power of the mountains and learned to live in their shadow, cultivating the scant valley soil for subsistence. And as passing generations fed themselves from valley soil, they forgot other worlds and became people of Brakrath.

And then, accepting Brakrath, they began to change. At first the alterations were small and scattered. But they spread and grew until they touched every child born, until they shaped every adult who lived within the society of the valleys. The chanting voices fell to a whispered chorus and, under the force of change, a diverse people gradually became a single new race of hardy, fair people who conserved their sparse foodstores by sleeping the winter through.

The chanted history moved quickly from that point, a montage of images. The new people spread through the valleys of Brakrath, driving rock-leopard and snowminx into the mountains. They build their stonehalls, planted their crops, and manipulated the bloodlines of their stock to meet Brakrath's demands. Ewes who had been white gave birth to brindle lambs. Soupfowl became larger and yielded more fat. A people who had gone hungry were fed.

Then in the southern plain, the people discovered the redmanes, a Brakrath species with powerful shoulders and sturdy hindquarters, and would have domesticated them. But at that point the first guardian was born from among the valley people and went to the plain to take up vigil over the redmanes. Soon other guardians were born, silent, dark women who listened to voices that bound them ever more irrevocably to the animals they tended. Centuries passed and one race became two, guardians and valley people.

More centuries passed and Dmira was born, guardian daughter who left the herds and settled among the fair people of the valleys. From her line many generations later came Niabi, who loosed the fire from the sunstone polished by her lover.

There were troubled times, there was conflict, there were periods when the people of the valleys set themselves against each other. But there were far more times when the rising race of barohnas drew the people together and gave them new prosperity. After a while, each inhabited valley held a sunthrone and each sunthrone a barohna.

Khira's fingers tightened on the arms of her chair as the elder women began their recitation of the roll of barohnas who had occupied the sunthrone of this valley. The list was long, and for every barohna there were the lesser names, those palace daughters who had gone to the mountain and not returned.

Alzaja. New courses of meat and bread were served. Puddings steamed on every table. The people ate again and licked their fingers and the chanting continued.

Alzaja. At last the time for relinquishment of names had come and women were bidding for Alzaja's name. They held up greasy fingers, too exuberant with food and drink, too driven by coming darkness, to realize they bid on a living soul.

Alzaja. Her shell was broken. The mountain had loosed her on silver wings and left her sister with heart of stone. That heart could not endure the chanting and cheer and the undercurrent of dread. Darkmorning

Evefest made it feel like flesh, and this flesh was heir to agony. From the far end of the hall a woman with hair that stood around her shoulders in a snowy mass and flashing eyes called out her bid and Khira was on her feet, running through the feasters, running from the wholeness of the others when she was as broken as her sister.

No one called after her, no one followed, although she was aware of startled silence as she fled the hall. Nor did any passionless declaration touch her mind. She pounded down the dim halls—the stalklamp that grew on the stone walls had been trimmed for winter—to her room.

There were precious things there, things left her by Alzaja. She swept past them and threw herself to her bed.

And she cried. The last link was broken. Alzaja's name had been bid out. Next spring a new infant would wear it who had never known Alzaja's grace. She would grow and the name would change with her. It would take her qualities and when she relinquished it at the end of her span, the name would have taken on the connotations of her personality. The next mother who bid for it would not even associate it with the Alzaja who had walked through the orchard on her way to the mountain.

Sometime in the storm of her grief, Khira fell asleep. When she woke, there was no sign of sunlight at her windows. The shutters had been secured for winter. But she knew it was morning and she roused herself reluctantly. She was eldest daughter now and it was Darkmorning. There were small rituals to be met within the larger ritual of a people settling to wintersleep. Some of them were hers.

She did not bother to go to the dining hall. There would be no table set, no food cooked. From now until spring waking, she must make her own meals in the kitchen.

Instead she went to the plaza, where overnight snow had fallen knee deep. She looked up to the mountain and saw that clouds of snow dusted its spired peaks. Darkmorning had come more than by the calendar. It had come to the mountain and to the valley.

Shivering, Khira kept vigil in the plaza until the heavy stone doors of the stonehalls were closed and sealed. Those last people who ran through the snow to their halls had the traces of the night's feasting still on them in their rumpled clothes and sated faces. Now they looked toward the winter's dreams with eyes both expectant and fearful. When the final doors were sealed, Khira withdrew into the palace, towering metal doors closing behind her with a cold sigh. She slipped down silent halls to the throneroom, not knowing which was more to be dreaded, a winter of alien dreams or one of solitude.

Tiahna sat upon the darkly glowing throne, remote today, lonely, ageless. Khira paused to study her. Sometimes she saw in her mother the great cerebhawk of the mountain, splendid in its power and plumage, ever alert, ready to plunge. Yet one of its heads, the lesser, was held mute and powerless by the other. Today as Khira entered the throneroom, Tiahna seemed to gaze at her with the same captive alertness, the same impotent power as the lesser head of the cerebhawk.

Perhaps Tiahna did care.

Or perhaps she cared only for her growing sun-hunger and the delay of ceremony, however brief.

Khira stepped before the throne. Mother and daughter peered at each other in the silent hall. Tiahna's voice was a husky whisper. "Are the stonewarrens sealed now?" The pairing stone hung dark at her throat.

Stonewarrens: the term was archaic, a survival from the time when the people of the halls had been serfs rather than freeworkers. Khira wet her lips, suddenly nervous. Today she must play the part Alzaja had always played on Darkmorning. And although there was no one to hear, no one to see, it seemed important that she bring the same authority to the elder daughter's role that Alzaja had brought. "They are sealed," she said.

"Then the sleepdust is scattered and the people dream." Tiahna stood, her limbs long and bronze, her copper hair bound into a braided crown. The lines of her face were strong: mouth broad, eyes strongly browed, nose thrusting. Power was evident in her every feature. Yet as she paced across the throneroom, her eyes shadowed with pain. "They are dreaming, and so Alzaja lives again, for the winter."

Khira shivered involuntarily at this departure from custom. Closing her eyes, she could imagine her sister beside her now, every feature clear. "Alzaja lives with me always," she declared.

Tiahna turned an unsmiling face upon her. "Does she? And Mara— does she live with you too?"

"Mara too," Khira said with barely a pause. Many times Alzaja had applied a fingertip to a frosted window or a fogged mirror and made Mara's likeness appear. Mara's death on the mountain had become a shared event of their lives, even though Khira had never known Mara.

"Mara lives with you, yet you never saw her?" Tiahna demanded.

"Alzaja remembered her and she told me."

"And Denabar?" Tiahna demanded. "Does Denabar live with you too?"

This time Khira hesitated. Denabar had been the sister before Mara. Alzaja had tried to pass on her features, her ways, her brief legend as Mara had given them to her. But she had not been entirely successful. Khira had never been certain how much was substance, how much shadow. "She—she lives too."

Tiahna peered at Khira bleakly. "No, child. You touched Alzaja, you heard her voice, and she lives with you. But don't imagine that your other sisters live likewise. And don't imagine that when the mountain takes you, you will live with anyone but your next sister, and then only for the time she lives."

Khira stepped back, as if struck. "No," she whispered, not sure what she protested: the coming loneliness, her sisters' loss, the death her mother had so casually pronounced upon her.

Tiahna frowned, wheeling to peer impotently into the darkened mirrors which hung at intervals around the throneroom. She touched her temples, stroking pain. "Snow has banked against the lenses on the mountainside and the mirror tenders have gone to their dreams," she said in a voice hard with pain. "If I stay here longer, I will tear myself apart—and you with me."

It was the inevitable moment, the one against which Khira had steeled herself. She was resolved not to meet it weakly. Yet a plea slipped from her lips, a dry thing, powerless. "No. Please. I'll be alone."

It met the scorn it deserved. "And wasn't Alzaja alone with winter before you were born?" Tiahna demanded with a flash of dark eyes. "Are you less than your sister?"

Was she? Would she cry and beg where Alzaja had silently borne loneliness? Khira drew her slight body erect, appalled by her moment of weakness. Still her voice shook with the question that had troubled her since Alzaja's death. "When—when will you give me a sister for winter company?" It was a presumptuous question, one she had wanted often to ask but had not dared.

Anger stormed across Tiahna's face. "There will be a sister when the tide rises again in my body. And when she is born, she will not be for you or for me but for the throne."

Chastened, Khira stared down at the polished stone of the floor. Stalklamp cast a subdued orange glow across the flaggings. From somewhere she found the final boldness to declare, "I will be for the throne."

Tiahna fixed her ageless gaze upon Khira, mercilessly evaluating. "Perhaps you will."

"I will," Khira said, this time to herself. Denabar, after all, had grasped victory in her challenge, if only in her final moments. Her body had been found on Terlath's northern face two days after she left the valley with the first changes upon it, pale flesh tinged with bronze, delicate profile sharply altered, nose and jaw no longer slight but bold. A mortally wounded crag-charger had been found nearby. If Denabar had thrust her pike deeper between its armored plates, piercing its heart, she would have returned to the valley a barohna.

Instead her pike had broken, the crag-charger had caught her with its rending claws, and the first changes had been the last. Denabar had never claimed the throne she died for.

But who was to say that Denabar was the only one of seven sisters to take stone to her heart? Who was to say that Khira could not do the same?

Suddenly the hall was cold and Khira's certainty wavered. Six sisters had preceded her and six had died. How could she hope to succeed? "If the Arnimi return while you are gone—" she ventured, trying to put away memory of her sisters. The Arnimi had gone in their ship to explore the southern mountains. Khira wished they would remain in the south for the entire winter but knew they would not. At some point they would return to their quarters in the western wing of the palace and she must see them in the halls again and hear their voices on the stairs.

"They will give you no trouble. They know that if they trespass in the stonehalls while the people sleep, I will close their quarters and forbid them the valley." Tiahna strode back to her throne. The black stone glowed darkly at her touch. "Now go while I empty the throne. And don't watch as I leave the valley. I won't carry tears in my memory as I hunt the sun up the mountain."

They had returned to ritual and there were words for this moment. Recognizing the inevitability of separation, Khira said them. "May you find it bright on the peaks."

"May I bring back its light tenfold to make spring for the people of the valley," Tiahna responded, and waited for Khira to withdraw.

Slipping from the throneroom, Khira ran to her chamber. The only light came from glowing stalklamp stems. Khira had refused to let the servants trim them when they groomed the halls and chambers for winter. They groped up the stone wall, clawed suckers holding the succulent stems in place. A single jagged leaf had unfolded from one stem.

Khira knew now why she had refused to have the stems trimmed. Biting her lip, she snapped off the single offending leaf. She must have light this winter, not shadow. She would have light on every wall, light on the ceiling, light growing across the floor. With a strangled sob, she drew water from the melter tap and drenched the stone pots that held the stalklamp roots.

She must have light, if nothing else this winter. And she would not cry. She was elder daughter now and there was stone in her heart, however sparse and fine the grains.

She kept that vow less than five minutes. Winter began with tears and snow.

4/Khira

The first days of winter were the most wrenching. Palace corridors were peopled with ghosts, familiar forms that never quite materialized. Khira slipped between them, wanting to reach out to them, expecting them to speak. But when she turned her head, they dissolved into shadow. Alzaja, Tiahna, the Arnimi commander, servants, monitors, cooks— they all seemed no farther than an arm's span. Yet when she reached, she touched nothing. Each day as she checked the boilers, Khira listened anxiously for the sound of footsteps behind her in the deserted corridors. Sometimes she slipped into the throneroom, hoping to find someone she knew in the sun mirrors. She found only herself.

Occasionally she ventured as far as the sealed door that led to the west wing. But the Arnimi had left no trace of themselves in the stone corridor outside their quarters, not even a musk to prove they were as human as they claimed. Often she climbed the watchtower and looked out over the snow. Terlath was a forbidding white presence in the distance, low-hanging clouds hiding its steep spires. The stonehalls had become white-blanketed mounds and the palace itself was lost in deep drifts. Only towering ventilation chimneys and the tower itself marked the presence of life in the valley.

At no time did she anticipate the sharp terror that was to come. Loneliness was terror enough.

Four hands of days, three five-fingered, one three-fingered, decorated her chamber wall when sound broke the night. By then she had almost accepted her solitary existence, letting it lead her back to a child's state she had thought she left behind. She spent much of her time playing scatter-hop in the deserted corridors, tossing her sharp-edged marker stones with a defiant clatter, then hopping between them on one bare foot, trying neither to scatter the stones nor to step on them. Sometimes at the end of the game, her bare feet bled and she strapped her boots back on with a certain sour satisfaction. Other days she played the board games Alzaja had taught her. Some days she simply patrolled the halls, mentally peopling them with servants and monitors, putting these shades through their usual paces, now making them double-step, now freezing them in awkward postures.

And each day after she had tended the boilers that warmed the few rooms she used, she assiduously watered stalk pots throughout the palace. Alzaja had taught her to leave the pots dry through the winter, but this year Khira flooded the roots, forcing the luminous growth, then trained the tender new stalks into bright patterns. Her bedchamber became luxuriant. It shimmered with light, like the inside of a precious gem. Khira liked to lie in bed and imagine herself a quarri, a mischievous being of infinitesimal size, secreted within a faceted glowstone like Tiahna wore when the Council of Bronze met in the great hall.

She was so hidden, bounded by the wafer-thin walls of the imagined gemstone, when the screaming voice came. One moment she was alone in chill silence. The next she was at the vortex of a terrible storm of sound, a harsh, rending scream. She burst the walls of the glowstone with a sharply indrawn breath and found herself lying taut in her bed, her blankets kicked away reflexively, her eyes wide and staring.

The sound continued, shrieking, grinding, unbearable. She caught another breath, desperately. Her first coherent thought was that one of the great mountain beasts, a crag-charger, a breeterlik, a rock-leopard, had broken into the palace. But she quickly recognized that the shrieking whine was a metallic cry. Arnimi ships, just before they settled to ground, bellowed and screamed like this. Some of their instruments and devices also emitted squallings and bleatings of an inhuman nature.

She expelled her breath with effort and drew another, pulling herself up into a knot, knees to chest. Were the Arnimi returning? So soon? But the continued shriek was much louder than the voice of their ships.

And a moment later an alien energy entered the chamber. Khira sensed rather than saw it. It prickled along her spinal column and raised the hair on her arms, making her teeth clench involuntarily. For long minutes she had the sense of being paralyzed at the center of some unaccountable radiation, some binding but unseen light. She was distantly aware of a curious grunting, her own labored breath.

Then the sensation was gone, and she was alone with the brilliant orange glow of overgrown stalklamp—and her own fear. Her entire body was racked by a shuddering spasm. Her teeth clattered wildly. And still, she realized, the terrible scream continued.

She cowered until shame drove her from the bed and into the hall. What palace daughter could tolerate this intrusion without challenge?

The metal-throated scream was a thing alive throughout the palace. She ran from chamber to chamber, trying to find its source—in vain. Her clattering teeth and her pattering feet were the only other sounds in the empty palace.

Twice again, as she ran through the halls, the unseen shaft of energy briefly caught her, held her, then released her.

She reached the throneroom and flattened herself against the stone wall, peering up into the darkened sun mirrors set around the walls. Briefly the shrieking cry grew deeper, more intense, making the surfaces of the mirrors shimmer. Then, as Khira sidled toward the throne, thinking to find some surcease there, the sound began to retreat. Within minutes it was gone and Khira was alone with a silence deeper than any she had ever known. It seemed to close over her, a deep well of utter stillness. The only sound was the harsh measure of her breath and the continued chattering of her teeth.

Finally, stiffly, feeling infinitely small, she slipped from the throneroom and first walked, then ran down the corridor. If the source of the sound lay within the palace, she would find it and confront it. Otherwise it would hold mastery over her even in its absence.

The sound did not return as she searched palace halls and chambers. Nor did the invisible beam. But she knew as she forced herself to dare each empty room and then to return defeated to her own chambers that those terrible moments had left their permanent mark. If she could confront the source of her terror, if she could assess its dimensions—

but she could not. Nowhere in the palace was there anything that had not been there before.

Nowhere that she thought to search. She did not remember the watchtower. And it was not until late the next morning that she heard the insistent *chink-chink-chink* at its barred door.

She was a ghost in the halls that day, frightened, ashamed of her fright, cold. She neither cast her hopping stones nor sat at the inlaid gameboard. Instead she drifted from place to place, stopping in shadowed corners to listen, to watch.

She had passed several hours in anxious patrol when she heard a distant sound, as if stone struck stone. She froze, her eyes large, her breath caught. The sound was irregular, faint. *Chink. Chink-chink. Chink.* Khira threw off her first paralyzing fear with something close to fierce joy and set off down the hall. Resolution, no matter what its nature, must be better than the haunted, waiting silence that hung over her this morning.

Quickly she traced the sound to the barred stone door that led to the watchtower—the one place she had not searched the night before. She halted short of the door, the hair at the back of her neck rising. Who could summon from the tower in the dead of winter, with the door into the palace barred and the observation dome sealed with heavy glasstone? Khira's eyes sought the stalk-lit hallway to either side of the door and found nothing. She tried to swallow back a sharp rise of panic and choked instead. The sound stimulated a fresh flurry of tapping from the other side of the door.

Khira's first instinct was to run away as quickly as her feet would carry her, to never come near this end of the palace again. Ashamed, she squeezed shut her eyes and bit her lip. Alzaja had gone to Terlath's rugged peaks for her beast carrying only a pike and a day's ration of food, gone in the tradition of palace daughters through the centuries. How could Khira do less than step forward and rap softly at the stone door with a single white knuckle?

The answering clatter was sharp. *Chink-chink! Chink-chink-chink!* Khira fell back, trying to gather fresh courage from the shadows of the corridor. Then, trembling, she fell to her knees and probed the hairline crack at the bottom of the door. She detected a razor-thin edge of cold air. She jumped to her feet, frowning. The glasstone panes of the watchwindows were securely caulked and the double doors at the top of the staircase were as tightly fitted as these. But the chill at her fingertips was unmistakable, as unmistakable as the renewed tapping from the other side of the door.

Alzaja, she told herself, would have unbarred the door immediately. Finally, with trembling hands, she forced herself to lift the bar.

The door swung open of its own weight and Khira's eyes widened. Whatever she had expected, it was not the slight, dark boy dressed in grey who hunched on the lower step. He clutched a fragment of glasstone in one bare hand and peered up at her with eyes as deep as mountain pools—but darker, much darker, and in some way empty. He shivered perceptibly in the cold well of the staircase.

Khira stared at him, at his inappropriate clothing, then peered up the dim stairwell. "You broke the view-window." Her accusing tone surprised her. But she was angry: angry that he trespassed here, angry that he had reduced her to trembling fright, angry that the inexplicability of his presence stirred still deeper fears in her.

Slowly the boy took his feet. His body was sparse, his limbs slender. He met her accusing gaze with a faint, anxious frown and mumbled something that sounded almost like an apology, but with a questioning inflection.

"And the upper doors," she added vengefully. "You broke down the upper doors too, didn't you?"

This time he attempted no hesitant apology, no reply at all. He simply regarded her with bleak eyes, rubbing his chilled fingers together.

Why wasn't he as frightened as she? He seemed only to be cold, and certainly that was no mystery. The suit he wore was pitifully thin. With exaggerated anger, Khira swept past him and ran up the stairs. She found the double doors at the top thrown open, undamaged. She bit her lip. Apparently she had forgotten to bar them the last time she had used the tower.

But she certainly was not responsible for the shattered glasstone that littered the floor, nor for the scorched patch on the stone floor. She peered up at the broken panes, then gazed out over the greylit winterscape. Snow lay deep over the stonehalls and the palace, and Terlath was little more than a looming shape lost in cloud. An oddly dished area marked the frozen white sheet which overlay the main plaza. From the gleaming solidity of the crust, it appeared the snow had melted, then refroze. Narrowing her eyes, Khira distinguished two similar frozen concavities in the distance.

She turned to find the interloper at the top of the stair. He had come silently and his dark-eyed gaze was unreadable, at once steady and empty. Staring at him, chilled, she tried to find some way to bring the encounter into the realm of the familiar, the everyday.

He was only a child. Taking the offensive, she addressed him as one. "All the glasstone is good for now is hopping stones. If you plan to come down with me, you can carry your share." Bending, she gathered the transparent grey shards. When he did not join her, she said sharply, "Well?" This time he complied, copying her action, still watching her without expression.

So his behavior could be manipulated. As she led the way down the stairs, her mind worked furiously. Why had he come? From where? Were his intentions hostile? How hostile could be the intentions of a shivering boy in a thin suit? Her first thought was to bar him from any significant room of the palace: the throneroom, her mother's bedchamber, the pantries and kitchens. Let him see only corridors and lesser chambers. But her second thought, feeling his steady gaze on her back, was to cow him with the scope and importance of the palace. If somehow his intent were hostile, if he had force to back it, there was no one she could call on. But if the spaciousness and grandeur of the palace itself intimidated him—

Accordingly, reaching the bottom of the staircase, she led him directly to the throneroom. Passing through the towering arches, she stepped aside silently to permit him full view of the carved black throne upon its high dais.

If for her the room with its arches, mirrors, polished flagstones and dark throne was invested with power, for him it was not. He stared at the black throne expressionlessly, then turned like an automaton to gaze around the room. He seemed untouched by the stalk-lit walls, by the darkened mirrors. He still held his hands stiffly before him cradling jagged shards of glasstone.

She bit back an angry scowl. She had never seen his like. Children of the halls were sturdy and fair with ruddy cheeks, thick white hair, deep chests and the palest of blue eyes. Palace daughters were like herself, slight, pale, with auburn hair and amber eyes. And the redmane daughters of the southern plain—

This child resembled none of these. He was as slight as she, if a little taller, and there was a haunted gauntness to him. His hair, cut just below the ears, was black and his eyes were so dark she could barely distinguish the iris from the pupil. Frowning, she assayed him feature by feature: neatly formed ears that lay back against his skull, thin lips, narrow, well-defined nose, finely arched eyebrows as dark as his hair, high forehead, hands as slim as her own but much darker. The nails, by contrast, were pink. His skin was slightly rougher than her own and darkly bronzed. He had two visible flaws: a long pink scar on his jaw and one fingernail that looked as if it had recently been torn back.

She felt a superstitious thrill. How had he come to the tower in the dead of winter? And his bronze skin—had he earned it or was it simply his natural pigmentation? Pushing up her sleeve, she stared at her own milk-white skin. Silently the dark child copied her motion, placing his arm against hers. He studied their contrasting complexions impassively.

Despite everything the Arnimi had told her about the people who inhabited other worlds, she could only gaze at his dark arm with perplexed awe. On Brakrath, males never bronzed. The barohnial line ran exclusively from mother to daughter. Indeed a barohna was incapable of bearing sons to full term; Tiahna had aborted five male children. And any children Khira's father may have sired in the stonehalls—she had no way of knowing if she had half-siblings; no palace daughter inquired after her father's identity and no barohnial mother volunteered the information—would never bronze. They were stonehall stock, just as she and her sisters had been barohnial.

Yet this boy stood beside her in flesh of bronze, studying her with eyes as black as the stone of her mother's throne. Threatened by the mystery of him, she pushed her sleeve down. "I know you came in a ship," she said sharply. "I've heard ships before."

His pupils narrowed minutely at the displeasure in her tone. One corner of his mouth twitched.

He had come in a ship, but there was no ship now. And how large must the ship have been to create the metallic scream that had terrorized her? She remembered her cowering fear with mortification. "You can't do this," she challenged abruptly, thrusting out one hand, closing it around jagged shards of glasstone. When she opened the hand, palm and fingers were speckled with blood.

A flicker of his dark brows betrayed emotion. He tongued his lips and deliberately closed the fingers of his right hand. His fingers were still white with cold. And still numb too, she decided scornfully. But quick pain quivered across his thin face and his hand jerked open, spilling the stones. He peered up at Khira, wary of her reaction.

"So you want to play scatter-hop," she mocked him softly. It rankled that he had come secretly in the night, terrorizing her. It rankled that he had tapped insistently at the tower door while she cowered on the other side, afraid to slide the bar. It rankled that he didn't shiver with the cold that was still upon him. Quickly she threw her own shards across the floor and bent to unfasten her boots. "There are two ways to play scatter-hop: the child's way, with boots on your feet, and the midling's way. Are you still a child?"

He hesitated momentarily, then released his second handful of shards. Mimicking her actions, he touched open his boots—how smooth they were; how strangely they fastened—and stripped the thin stockings off his narrow feet. His feet were as dark as his hands and face, but heavily callused. He peered up at her for instruction.

Her eyes sparked with malice. She pulled her hair back into a loose knot. "Watch!" Then she hopped across the field of shards on one bare foot, trying neither to scatter the stones nor to cut her foot on them. The stones had fallen too closely, but when she felt their sharp edges cut her foot, she bit the inside of her cheek and continued until she had crossed the floor. Then she ran a quarter circle around the scatter of shards and hopped through them again on the other foot. When she finished, both feet marked the floor with blood. She counted the dark spots with satisfaction. "Well?"

He gazed at her bleeding feet, then looked up at her.

"Yes, it's your turn!"

He nodded, more in acknowledgement of her anger than in acquiescence. With an almost audible sigh, he raised his right foot and hopped through the scattered stones. His first two jumps were successful. With the third, he miscalculated and landed heavily on a large shard. He gasped and peered at her, warily.

"Go on!" she urged, ashamed of the hot blood that rushed to her cheeks. Alzaja would never have permitted this. It was childish. But Alzaja was not here. "Finish!"

He ducked his head and continued, dark stains marking his course. When he emerged from the scatter, he put his foot down gingerly, his lip quivering. Without looking at her for instruction, he made a quarter circle and changed feet.

He had almost completed his second course when he stumbled. He uttered a wordless cry as he fell across the jagged stones. Khira stepped forward, then stopped herself. He lay for moments as if stunned. When he picked himself up, not looking at her, he bled from half a dozen deep cuts. But he pushed himself to his feet and finished the course, moving with painful deliberation. Then he stepped away from the scattered shards trembling visibly, his face ashen beneath its bronze pigment. He peered at her as if expecting rebuke.

Khira was immediately repentant. She was monitor of her own behavior now, and she had failed in her duty. Quickly she pushed him down on a stone bench to examine his injuries. He quivered at her touch. "Stay here. I'll get ointment from the supply locker."

Returning, she smoothed ointment on his cuts and dabbed his damaged garment with a damp cloth. Then she peered up into his face, feeling the weight of responsibility. However he had come here, whatever his purpose, he was alone in a strange place. And she was the only person he could turn to. "Aren't you hungry?" she wondered.

When he did not answer, she touched her lips and patted her stomach, raising her brows in question.

He bit his lip, as if afraid to respond. Then, hesitantly, he imitated her gestures, watching closely for her reaction.

"Hun-gry," she said again, enunciating clearly. She repeated the word twice, touching lips and stomach again, and watched him intently. It suddenly seemed very important that he respond.

When he finally did, his voice was low, his enunciation alien. "Hungry."

A single word, the first she had heard in sixteen days, and she abandoned all reservation. *"Hungry!"* She jumped to her feet elated. Through some miracle the long days of silence were broken. She no longer needed to reach out to ghosts in shadowed corridors. She had a companion. As she led way down the hall, she prattled inanely, the words spilling from her eagerly. "There's a fire in the kitchen, you know, in the smallest stove. I've kept it fed. And we can take anything we want from the pantry. There's bread, cheese, there's even roasting fowl in the ice locker." She had someone to talk to, someone to talk to her through the long frozen months ahead.

The kitchen was a cavernous place, its great feast-stoves cold now, its dozen pantries silent. Khira lit fuel lamps. When she hung them, the interloper's eyes darted around the shadowy cupboards and his nostrils quivered. For a moment both emptiness and wariness were gone from his eyes. He stepped quickly toward the pantry where fragrant loaves of spring bread were stored for spring waking. He brought himself up short at the pantry door, turning alertly for her reaction, licking his lips nervously.

Did he think she would starve him? "It's all right. I always eat some of the spring bread while the people sleep." She fetched one of the heavy loaves and cut into it. The bread was rich with dried fruits, groundnuts and the eggs of soupfowl. She hacked off a generous slice and offered it to him.

He hesitated momentarily, then snatched the bread and retreated to the shadowy nook beside the warm stove. He hunkered down there, wolfing the bread almost without chewing.

He was starved. Quickly she cut him a second slice. He accepted it without hesitation. As he ate, he peered up from the shadows, his eyes momentarily like live coals. But before he could finish the second slice, he drew a shuddering breath and his eyelids fluttered shut. The last scrap of bread fell from his fingers as his head dropped to his knees.

Alarmed, Khira knelt beside him, monitoring the regular rise and fall of his chest. He seemed simply to have fallen abruptly into the deep sleep of exhaustion. But if this were more than that, if he were somehow, inexplicably, falling into wintersleep...

She frowned. The Arnimi had told her that the Brakrathi were the only human strain that employed wintersleep. And even if the intruder came from some unreported human subgroup, certainly there was no trace of sleepdust in the kitchen.

Still she was troubled. If he fell into true wintersleep, he would never waken. Although sleepdust slowed the metabolism to a crawl, greatly lessening the amount of body fuel required to survive a snowbound winter, even the sturdiest people of the halls woke weak and depleted in the spring. And the intruder had no saving cushion of body fat. None at all.

Khira's fingers clenched as she fought an overpowering urge to seize him and shake him awake. He had already spoken one word of Brakrathi. She would teach him her entire language. She would teach him the games Alzaja had taught her, the songs, the chants. She would teach him to cipher the scrolls stored in the alcove behind the throne. She would teach him everything.

If he woke.

And he would people the winter for her. She would have someone to talk with, someone to share her meals—someone to consider when Adar flared bright in the winter sky and her temper rose red and ragged. She stood, addressing stone walls, and vowed that this year she would forever master Adar's warlike influence—if the intruder woke.

Then, driven by a sudden furious need for activity, she fetched blankets and heaped them over him. She peered down at him a moment before hurrying away again. The bedchamber next to hers stood vacant. Working quickly, still repeating promises under her breath, she made up the bed and assembled all the things he might like to have near: woven hangings, braided chains of rattleweed, tiny carved figurines, an inlaid gameboard, the best from her own collection of stream-polished stones. Some were possessions of her own relegated to storage when she had inherited Alzaja's treasures.

Momentarily her jaw tightened. Perhaps he would not be impressed. There was something troubling about his lack of responsiveness, about the dark vacancy of his eyes. Only food seemed to fully stir his interest. Perhaps if he had been starved, she would have to use his hunger to draw him out. But in any case, he would sleep here and between sleepings, she would teach him to talk to her. Softening, she hurried to rearrange the new growth of stalklamp stems across the stone walls.

Finally, driven by the remnant of anxiety, she returned to the watchtower. The sky was sullen. The dimpled areas she had noticed earlier remained crusted with ice. The wind blew harsh through the shattered pane. Nothing had changed.

She had no doubt he had come from a skyship. The scream that accompanied his arrival had been unmistakably similar to the sound of Arnimi ships landing. But certainly he was no Arnimi.

Did the Arnimi even pass through a child state? She tried to imagine those balding personages as infants, as children—pot-bellied boys and girls with receding hairlines and bulging eyes. She laughed aloud. Yet every Arnimi she had questioned insisted that once he or she had been a child.

Finally, thoughtfully, she went down, barring the double doors at the top of the stairs and the single tall door at the bottom. When she reached the kitchen again, her new companion stood at the counter hacking off chunks of spring bread. He started at the sound of her voice, dropping the knife, his eyes startled.

Her laugh was like a handful of crystals, too-bright, clattering. "If

you keep on eating like that, I'm going to call you breeterlik. Hungry
breeterlik," she declared, drunk with relief. The stones had honored her
vow. He had not fallen into wintersleep.

He relaxed slightly and in an evident effort to please her said indistinctly, "Hungry."

"Breeterlik!" Her voice was shrill. She was not to be alone.

By evening she had renamed him Darkchild. The next day she taught
him her proper name and despite the disturbing emptiness deep in his
eyes and the sometimes slack set of his features, winter was brighter
in the deserted palace for a while. It almost seemed Adar would not
storm from winter skies this one year. Khira had promised.

5/The Boy

The boy came to the palace empty in every way, empty of thought, of preconception, of memory. He came from circumstances he could not remember to circumstances he could not comprehend. He came without weapon or word. He came — somehow — to be sitting on cold stone steps facing a tall door and when he rapped, there was no answer.

Then there was an answer and the boy found himself in the palace, as empty as he had been before the door opened, except that the girl fed him. And with food in his stomach, he realized that although time began abruptly on the cold steps, it did not end either there or in the room where he ate. It stretched ahead into other hours and places. That much hunger and satiation told him, though he could not have said how.

Indeed time did stretch ahead and the boy found it came not only in units of hours but in units of days, a continuity of days. During the first few of those days the boy had little awareness of anything beyond the cold, the girl and the demands of his internal guide, that omniscient presence that instructed him in everything he did. He woke each day in a chill, lofty chamber hung with things that rattled and things that were bright with color. His environment included the bed he lay upon, stone walls and ceiling overgrown with a bright gridwork of glowing stems, two tightly shuttered window-apertures, and an array of articles displayed upon the walls and upon a wooden chest.

Each morning upon waking he lay quietly waiting for his guide to direct him. When his guide was ready, the boy pulled on his boots and made a slow round of the chamber, examining its contents. He touched nubby hangings, polished stones, tiny figurines and dried plant material, and the characteristics of all these were methodically transmitted to that portion of his brain that stored data. After the first few days, the ritual was repetitious. But the boy's brain was empty and it was to be filled in the manner of the guide's choosing. The boy understood this and acquiesced. His guide's will was his will.

One of the first things the guide chose to file in the boy's brain was the girl's language. And she was eager to teach him.

The first night they met, the boy was confused and thought there were many girls in the palace. When the heavy door that confined him opened, the girl who stared at him was a frightened girl. A few moments later, at the top of the stair, he was confronted by an angry girl instead. She was quickly displaced by a girl who was both angry and frightened. He left the tower with that girl and went to a cavernous room with arches, mirrors and polished flagstones. The girl he met there made him hurt himself, but almost immediately another girl appeared to soothe him and feed him.

In appearance the girls were identical: slight and fair with amber eyes and auburn hair. Finally he grasped the symmetry of the situation and was immediately less tense. There was only one girl, just as he was one boy directed by one guide.

When he left the sleeping chamber each morning, the girl met him in the hall and began repeating the words of her language for him. "Tile, Dark-child—tile. This is a floor tile." Usully she caught his arm to be sure she had his attention and pointed to the things she named. Then she held his arm tight and continued pointing—"Say it: floor tile. *Floor tile.*"—until he echoed the sounds she had used. It took him several hours on the first morning to realize that the sounds she made were associated with the objects she indicated. His mind was very empty. But once he understood the relation, he learned quickly.

There were walls, doors, floors and ceilings; beds, tables, cushions and chairs; spring bread, meltwater, roasting fowl and eggs; game-boards, markers, mirrors and throne. And many other things. He learned the sound for them all. He learned the sound for the things he and the girl did together too: running, jumping, walking, clapping. "I'm smiling, Darkchild. See—look: *smiling*." Although he never tested her, he thought the girl would not let him eat if he did not learn, and he was hungry. He felt as if he had been starved.

Perhaps it helped that he had no words of his own for any of the things to be found here. If he did not use the language she taught him, he could not speak at all. And his guide wanted him to speak because there were questions to be asked. The boy felt their pressure at the back of his mind. The tension they created was uncomfortable.

The girl didn't seem to appreciate just how quickly he learned her language. Perhaps she had never taught anyone before.

But there was more than language to be learned. The palace was cavernous and many-chambered. In each room there were things to be examined and classified. The boy moved to that chore automatically during his first days in the palace, touching, smelling, tasting, stroking, weighing, manipulating. At times he paused to puzzle over what he learned, over the relationship of texture and aroma, form and weight. Other times the process of exploration seemed to go on without his conscious attention, as if his senses and his hands knew their work and proceeded unassisted.

There were other facets of himself too, he realized vaguely, that worked unassisted. Sometimes he found his face moving into expressions that mirrored the girl's mood even though he did not share it. Sometimes his head nodded at something she said even though it did not interest him. Often he followed her quietly in activities from which he really wanted to withdraw. She was very fond of board games. They spent hours each day bent over the large inlaid board moving carved pieces according to obscure rules. The boy wanted to explore instead, but his guide instructed him to play. It was important to please the girl.

Later undoubtedly there would be other people who must be pleased. The boy gave it no more than passing thought. It was apparent his body knew its job and would perform appropriately. His guide saw to that. Although his guide had no perceptible external influence, although he could not manipulate the world except through the boy, as far as the boy was concerned, his guide was omniscient and omnipotent. He was a force to be obeyed without question.

There were some things in the palace the boy liked better than others.

At first he liked to be in the kitchen because bread and the warm stove were there. But soon the kitchen offered more than creature comfort. In some unnameable way, it seemed to offer memory. Each day the boy went to the kitchen and explored the long shelves of preserved goods. Then he tapped inside the cold box where roasting fowls were kept in frozen blocks and examined drawers of utensils and containers and implements. From all these things, he drew a sense of life extending into the past as well as the future. The boy liked to caress the wooden handles of the knives and draw upon the presence of the people he imagined had used them. The big boiling pots that hung on the wall hooks were dented and pitted. He liked to place them on the cold stoves and imagine he heard the scrape of carved spoons against their sides and the happy bubbling of things thick and savory. These sensory echoes were his only clue to some personal existence spanning the time before he found himself on the watchtower steps.

The spices and herbs quickly became his special pleasure. They were stored in dozens of small bottles of uniform size and shape. The bottles lined an entire shelf, their contents fragrant, pungent, musty, bitter, sweet. After he had discovered their pleasures, the boy never went to the spice shelf unless he had time to open each container in turn and sample its contents. Most of the spices were stored in ground form but a few of the bottles held loose dried leaves and five held seeds.

He found it satisfying to arrange and rearrange the bottles on their shelf according to their contents. After a few days, he elaborated a set order for the bottles, one that seemed to provide a progression from the mildest spices through the strongest, with those in each range of intensity ordered according to the nature of their taste: sweet, sour, bitter, and so forth. Entering the kitchen, he would carry all the bottles from the shelf to the long cutting table. He liked the table because it showed the scars of many years' use. He could finger its wounds and hear the thump of cleavers, perhaps not here in the palace but elsewhere—in some place he could not even remember. Once the spices were arrayed in a long line, he sampled them at his leisure, one by one, sometimes randomly, sometimes in predetermined order. Then he set them back into place on the shelf jar by jar, arranging them fastidiously.

At first his guide urged him to work in the kitchen. Then his work there was done and the guide grew impatient. There was much to be learned in the palace and the boy was wasting time. When his guide first objected to the extended samplings from the spice shelf, the boy let himself be separated from this most satisfying activity. For a while he came to the spice shelf only once a day to sample and sort the bottles.

But one day he made a startling discovery. He found that if he worked at the spices and herbs very intently, saturating his senses, his guide became too occupied filing the resultant sensory data to direct the boy away from the activity. Apparently the guide could not combine certain activities, and the boy had discovered one activity, sensory filing, that overrode others. The boy experimented over the next few days and found that certain herbs were the most distracting to his guide. There was a complexity to their bouquet that completely overwhelmed the guide. If the boy alternated tasting and smelling from those bottles with sampling from other, less distracting bottles, he could work unhindered.

This realization gave the boy his first intimation of identity and purpose separate from those of his guide. He began to observe the girl closely and soon he wondered why he had a guide when she seemed to have none. She seemed to do as she pleased with no internal direction at all.

At this point, the boy experienced an initial stirring of resistance to his guide. But he was uncomfortably aware of his dependence upon the guide. For soon after coming to the palace, the boy had learned that deep within the wasteland of his mind lay a place of warmth and welcome. That was the trancing room, and within the trancing room lived his brothers.

Had the trancing room been a physical reality somewhere? Had he met there with his brothers before coming to the palace? He didn't know. He could remember nothing. Now the trancing room was a place within his mind. Whenever the boy was tired or confused, he yearned to be there, yet only the guide could open the door. Each evening the boy placed himself at the trancing-room door by resting his forehead on his knees and taking a series of slow, deep breaths. But he knew that if he incurred his guide's displeasure, if his guide chose not to let him trance, he would find himself breathing very quickly instead and the door would not open. He would be left bitter and cold and alone. Completely alone.

It was upon such a bitter occasion—the first—that the boy realized the girl was alone too. He had lingered too long in the kitchen that afternoon, exploring drawers of utensils, resisting his guide's instruction that he play board games with the girl. She had come for him twice, she had pleaded with him, and he had pretended not to see or hear her. The first time she had gone away with an anxious frown, the second time with angry tears. Both times the boy had continued his inventory of the kitchen drawers with no pang of remorse.

But that night when he retired to the corner of the throneroom where he tranced, his guide refused him the trance-room. The boy placed his forehead upon his knees and worked to make his breath slow and steady. Instead he found himself breathing so rapidly he became dizzy. He raised his head and peered around blankly, then dropped his head again. This time he regulated his respiration with painstaking care—and heard his breath huffing rapidly, grunting in his chest. His heart began to hammer and when he jumped up, he swayed dizzily, nauseated.

He gave it up finally and sat shivering and wakeful, staring emptily into the dark mirrors that hung at intervals around the walls. The palace was cold by night and he was hungry for the comfort of his brothers' company, hungry for the sound of their voices, the warmth of their faces. He wondered about them, bleakly. Had he been with them before he came here? Where? Would he return to them someday? Although he entered the trancing room each evening, when he returned he could never remember clearly what he and his brothers did there, what was said among them. Nor could he remember their faces, but he knew they must be much like his.

Sighing, he gazed into the dark mirrors. The only face he saw was his own.

The chill of his loneliness was heavy when the girl approached and knelt before him, her auburn hair falling between them. Her face was shadowed and she touched his shoulder tentatively. "You're going to sleep again, aren't you?" she demanded with the blend of diffidence and hurt anger she sometimes used. "Every night after we eat, you sit here and go to sleep. You never talk to me at night."

The boy peered up at her with some surprise. It had never occurred to him that she noticed his body sitting here while he tranced. There were traces of tears at the corners of her eyes. That, combined with her plaintive anger, touched him. Apparently she felt much the way he felt tonight: lonely, angry, helpless. "I talked to you today," he said finally, not certain it was the right thing to say.

"You talked to me this morning. This afternoon when I came to get you for games, you wouldn't hear me. You pretended I wasn't there." She wiped angrily at her eyes.

"I—I was busy," he said lamely, wondering how he had turned her away twice with no compunction. She had let him explore all morning, and the games were important to her.

"You always talk to me in the morning," she went on. "But at night you sit here with your forehead on your knees and your face cold. It doesn't matter how hard I shake you, I can't wake you. You always leave me alone at night."

"You shake me?" The suggestion startled him. He was never aware of her presence when he tranced. She was always in her own chamber when he returned from the trancing room and walked through the cold halls to his bed. He had never even wondered how she spent the evenings.

"I shake you until your teeth rattle," she said with bleak relish. "And I bring you food, but you never take it. Here—" She produced a rich chunk of fruitbread from a folded square of cloth. "At least you're awake tonight. Eat it."

Touched, he wet his lips with the tip of his tongue.

Something blazed in her eyes when he took the bread: hurt flashing through fresh tears. "You could offer me half," she said with a tearful sting.

And he felt her loneliness. He gazed into her pleading eyes, and before her anger could win through again, he broke the chunk of bread and held half of it for her. She was alone in the palace and she hadn't even brothers to trance with. The sisters she spoke of were dead and mourned. She had only him.

She accepted bread from him, but with lingering wariness. That night they played the board games he had refused to play that afternoon and he enjoyed playing because it helped her forget her loneliness. That in turn helped him forget the trancing-room door that had refused to open. Late in the night they walked the cold corridors together, and before they parted, their hands touched and clung. The boy went to bed with the warmth of her fingers still on him.

This, he realized, was a warmth he could touch any evening. He did not have to wait for the guide to open a mental door for him. And afterward, if he spent the evening with the girl instead of in the trancing room, he could remember what had passed, what had been said.

Was he disloyal to his brothers? He lay in bed wondering. Perhaps if he could remember their faces, if he could recall whether they had ever met outside the trancing room—but no memory came to him and finally he slept.

From that night, he became aware of an increasing tension between himself and his guide. It was necessary for the boy to please the girl. But his guide did not consider it necessary for him to find pleasure in pleasing her. Pleasure was supposed to be granted only by the guide.

It made the guide uneasy when the boy ran through the halls with the girl laughing just because the running and laughing felt good. It made the guide uneasy when the boy and girl bent together ciphering scrolls and the boy enjoyed the warmth of her body near his. It made the guide uneasy when the boy smiled at the girl just because he liked to do it.

Yet the boy continued to steal pleasure from the girl's company, even when he knew his guide would refuse him the trance-room afterward. The trance-room had simply become much less important to him. Sometimes he went for days without thinking of his brothers.

In fact, the boy had entered a period of testing which he would have considered impossible earlier. During the day, he enjoyed the girl's company and ignored his guide's discomfiture. But sometimes he woke in the night and was frightened. Who was he to try to direct his own course of behavior? The girl at least had a name—Khira. As far as he knew, he had none. Or if he did, he could not recall it, no matter how hard he tried. And sometimes he tried very hard.

Ciphering scrolls soon became one of his favorite pastimes. The scrolls were stored in an alcove behind the throne and were made of fine-grained skins laced with inked symbols. The boy especially enjoyed sitting beside Khira on cold evenings tracing the symbols with one fingertip and repeating their meaning after her.

The scrolls related the story of Khira's world, Brakrath. Khira's people had come to Brakrath a hundred centuries or more before—he tried to deal with that span of time in terms of the few days of life he remembered and was dizzied by it—and not by intention. They had been outward bound for another destination when their ship had failed and stranded them here.

They had found Brakrath cold and hostile. For centuries they fought to survive its winter storms and short summers while they waited for rescue. But rescue did not come and after a while they forgot to wait and began to adapt to Brakrath. The scrolls told of the changes they underwent and of the people who underwent them. They told of people who learned to fatten for winter and to sleep through the entire snow-season in sealed halls. They told of people who learned to heed the voices of Brakrath's mountains and of other people who were drawn to the distant plains. They told of the great herds of redmanes that were found in the plains and of the women who became their guardians. They told of other women, daughters of the redmane guardians, who unleashed from blocks of black stone quarried in the mountains capabilities never before dreamed of. Khira was descended from these women, the barohnas of Brakrath.

Khira was never angry or sad when she ciphered from the scrolls. Her fingers flew over the inked symbols and her voice rang. Absorbed, she seemed not to appreciate just how quickly the boy learned to cipher the scrolls with her. Almost certainly she had never taught anyone before.

Often after they finished ciphering, they sat talking for hours. Khira told the boy of the people of the valley, of her sisters, of the mountains she loved and the plains she sometimes visited. She told him of the festivals and feasts that ushered in Darkmorning, the first day of winter, when the halls were sealed and sleepdust scattered. She told him of the lambs that were born when the sheep woke from wintersleep. She told him of spring days when teams of redmanes came to the valley with their guardians to plow the fields. She told him the entire saga of her sisters, and in the telling they seemed to live again.

She seldom spoke of her mother. He had no memory of a mother to make him wonder why.

The boy had nothing to tell Khira in return, in fact. He had no people, no world, no memories. He had nothing but the unremembered faces of his brothers. Sometimes she paused in her tales and flicked a question at him—"Do the children gather summer fruit where you come from? Or do they leave it for the adults to bring in?"—and he couldn't answer. He had never smelled a feast cooking, had never minded animals at pasture, had never watched a field planted to grain. Or if he had, something had happened to his memory of those things.

Instead of memories, he had the guide. He became increasingly restive under the guide's domination. Why should he yield when Khira yielded to no one? And yet at times resistance was useless. If the guide considered the situation merited, he could speak through the boy's mouth without the boy's consent, could use the boy's arms and legs as if the boy himself had no claim upon them.

The boy had been in the palace for five hands of days when he learned that Khira had neglected to mention a very important matter to him. One morning they stood in the watchtower gazing across the gleaming snow that covered the valley. His eyes narrowing, he traced the outlines of the palace in the drifted snow—and realized with surprise that a certain barred door far from the wing of the palace he and Khira used did not lead outside but into another wing.

Somehow, he realized with a sudden sinking, he had missed knowing of the existence of an entire wing of the palace.

He was not prepared for the abruptness or intensity of his guide's anger. Recognizing the oversight, his guide uttered a harsh epithet in a language the boy did not recognize and seized control of his feet, driving him down the stairs. Involuntarily the boy was propelled through the warren of corridors to the closed door that led to the unexplored wing.

"Where does this go?" he had asked Khira when he first encountered the barred door.

"Nowhere," she had said, and led him away.

He had been directed to learn everything, and he had failed. He should have known from the quick drop of her eyes, from the tight line of her lips, that this was not simply another door to the exterior of the palace. It was different from other doors. It was of a different metal, smoother, lighter, newer. Even the hinges that held it were different. Driven by his guide's displeasure, he tested the door with his fingertips, with his knuckles, finally with his entire body. When the door refused to budge, his breath came in a frustrated hiss.

Khira had run down the stairs after him. She watched wide-eyed, frightened, as he fought the door. Finally he stepped back. "This door—" His guide's anger choked him. He could barely speak.

"It leads to the Arnimi wing," Khira said with obvious reluctance. "It's sealed. We can't open it until they return from the southern mountains."

He spun back to the door, his eyes flashing with the guide's anger.

But it was useless to batter at the door. It would not yield. "The Arnimi?" he demanded.

"Yes. This is their wing. The Council of Bronze gave them permission to make permanent quarters here—in our valley."

And who *were* the Arnimi? his guide demanded. His voice was harsh, driven by his guide's anger. "You never told me anyone lived here but your own people. Who are the Arnimi? Where do they come from?" Were they even Brakrathi?

She retreated from his anger, her slight features grim. "They—they come from Arnim. It's on the other side of the galaxy. They've lived there since Earthexodus—since people left Earth to live in the stars. They changed Arnim to make it like Earth. They altered its climate and turned the ground over to Earth-plants. It's still like Earth there."

"They're—the Arnimi are humans? Like us?" Some of his guide's anger ebbed at this revelation.

A tight frown contracted her eyebrows. "They're human—but not human like we are."

Why was she so reluctant to tell him about the Arnimi? As she answered each question, her lips contracted back into a tight line. "How many of them live here? In the palace?"

Her fist clenched and she walked away from him, her voice distant. "There were twenty when they first came. More of them have come since, so now there are fifty-two. They're—they're making a study of Brakrath."

Was that what angered her? That they studied Brakrath? "Why? What do they want here?"

She essayed a resentful shrug. "They're compiling a history of all the human races and what's become of them since Earthexodus. They have—they have three questions they're trying to answer. They want to know if every new world shapes the people who settle it into some unique form. They want to know if humans can adapt to any world that doesn't destroy them in the first few generations. And they want to know if there's some common characteristic that we always retain, something that never changes, no matter where we settle or how."

"And they're trying to answer those questions here?"

"They're trying to answer them everywhere. They're studying worlds all over the galaxy, dozens of worlds. But they're especially interested in Brakrath because no one knew we were here for so long. We haven't traded with other worlds and we haven't fought with them. We haven't been influenced by anything but Brakrath since the stranding."

"And the Arnimi—they've been here how long?"

"The first ones came fourteen years ago and they'll be here another ten or more. The Council of Bronze gave them permission to stay as long as they want so long as none of them leave Brakrath or send information back to Arnim until their study is completed."

The boy felt his forehead pucker in a tight frown. As he listened to Khira's explanation, he was aware of his guide's reactions as if they were his own. His guide was angry that an entire people existed here without his knowledge. Why hadn't he been told about them? He was worried too. Were their purposes the same as his own? Would they be hostile? Would they try to sabotage him? What should he expect of them?

The guide struggled under the concentrated stress of uncertainty. The boy stepped away from the metal door, aware of an unexpected shifting within his mind. It was as if... He shook his head, trying to clear it. He felt as he sometimes felt just before the door to the trancing room opened—remote, detached, drifting.

And then a door did open, but it was not the trancing room door. It was another door, one he hadn't known existed. His mouth opened on a strangled exclamation. For a moment the door stood wide and it was as if a dazzling array of codified information flashed into the boy's awareness, blazing alive too rapidly, too vividly for him to do more than reel back from it, stunned. "What—"

Did he expect an answer? He received none. Swiftly his guide disappeared, blotting out the door behind himself.

His guide had entered the secret room. Without comment or instruction, his guide had slipped into a hidden place where information was stored and closed the access, leaving the boy suddenly alone.

He had never been alone before. At first he did not even recognize the strange, echoing sensation for what it was: emptiness. The boy swayed dizzily, probing his temples with his fingertips. There was another door in his mind. His guide knew how to open it, how to enter. Did *he* have access too? Could he follow?

Did he want to follow? He was aware of Khira staring at him. "You—" he stammered. "Khira—" Was this the freedom Khira knew all the time? This absence of a directing presence? The boy peered down the stalklit corridor, momentarily disoriented. I can do anything I want, he realized with wonder. Anything.

But what did he want to do?

Khira was clutching his sleeve, her face parchment. "Dark-child—"

What *did* he want? It surprised him a little. He wanted to learn. During his days in the palace, he had worked at mastering Khira's language, at cataloguing the contents of every room of the palace because the guide had so directed him. Now, with the guide gone, he found that he simply wanted to learn different things.

He wanted to know everything about the Arnimi, for instance: how they looked, how they talked, what customs they practiced, what crafts they engaged in, how they structured their kinships. If there were artifacts, he wanted to touch them. If there were scrolls, he wanted to cipher them.

"Khira—" Where were the words for everything he wanted to know? "Darkchild—are you sick?"

He shook his head, questions choking him. "*No*. No—I want to know about the Arnimi. I want to know—" Everything.

Khira touched her lips with the tip of her tongue, troubled. "I—I can draw you likenesses of them," she offered.

That was good for a beginning. She had drawn him likenesses of her sisters, each stroke careful and loving. "Yes," he said eagerly.

This time she did not fetch an unmarked scroll and ink. Instead, quickly, she led him down a long-unused corridor to a chamber that hadn't been swept for years. Dust lay thick on the floor. Stalklamp covered ceiling and walls in a dense tangle, creating a garish light. Entering, Khira glanced back at the boy tensely, then knelt. Her forefinger moved through the dense dust and the caricature of a human appeared.

The boy crouched eagerly. The man she drew had narrow hunched shoulders and a pendulous belly. His eyes were prominent, staring, and his lips were bunched in a frown. "They're bad," he said immediately.

Khira shrugged. "No."

"But you—"

"I hate them," she said with a cold hiss. "They want to know everything. They leave nothing private. They go to the stonewarrens when the people are awake and measure them. Not just how tall they are but how large their heads are, how long their legs are, how wide their toes are. They put needles in people and draw out blood and feed it into their machines." She glared at him, scowling with grievance. "They carry meters on their belts and point them at us. They tramp through the fields poking sticks into the ground. Four years ago they tried to butcher a redmane and cut into its brain. Now the redmane guardians don't let them come to the plain anymore. One of them even tried to follow my mother to her winter throne one year. He wanted to meter her when the sun was dim, to study the activity of her brain."

"But I—I want to know things too," he reminded her. "I look at things and ask you questions." There were dozens of questions he wanted to ask her now about the Arnimi.

Frowning, she stubbed out the dust-portrait. "You eat with me," she said shortly. "Techni-Verra is the only Arnimi who has ever eaten with me—and Commander Bullens put her on penalty for it."

That made the difference? He followed her from the chamber, knowing it did not. Perhaps the difference lay in his manner, in the fact that his guide insisted he please her. "Khira—" Then he stiffened, pressing his fingertips to his temples, drawing a rebellious breath. A sense of change—his guide had returned.

And the boy wanted to fight. He wanted to fight for the inviolability of his thoughts, of his mind. Yet how? He pressed his temples, trying to drive the guide away by sheer physical pressure.

The room—did it have a physical site in his brain? Was his perception that information was stored there correct? Could his guide enter it anytime, or only in times of stress? Khira turned with a questioning gaze. He was aware of the rigidity of his muscles, of the perspiration that suddenly stained his suit. Trembling, he drew his hands from his temples.

Who was the guide? The question popped into his mind and he was shocked at its audacity. "Khira—"

But she didn't have the answers to his questions. And his guide restrained him from asking more about the Arnimi. It was obvious Khira did not want to talk about them—and his guide had other sources of information.

The boy frowned. Earlier his guide had uttered an epithet in a language the boy did not know. Now the boy wondered what language it had been—and what language the guide had used to direct him before

Khira had taught him (them?) Brakrathi. Did he and the guide have a language of their own? How many others did they share it with? Or did it exist only to serve the two of them? It angered the boy that he did not know, could not remember.

The room where the guide had gone—were there memories hidden there that once had belonged to the boy? Khira had memories. Surely the boy had them too: places he had seen, people he had known, experiences he had undergone. Perhaps he even remembered a time when his guide had not been with him, when he had been free. If he could find his way alone to the place where the guide had gone, if he could find the key and unlock the knowledge there, if he could find a way to purge the guide from his mind—

Without thinking, the boy snapped off a stem of stalklamp and slit it with his thumbnail. He studied the internal structure of the stem intently, then touched tongue to the bitter sap, screening his thoughts from his guide. The place where his guide had gone, where information was stored . . . But he had no idea how to find that place.

Yet he could not forget one question: *who was the guide?* As the day passed, he moved through the palace distractedly, overwhelming his guide with sensory data as a screen for his own thoughts. The effort yielded nothing but a growing sense of futility. His consciousness seemed to be a single small room, with closed doors at every side. Some must lead to his past, some must hold memories of a time when he had had no guide. But he could not even sit quietly and probe his thoughts. He had to keep moving, touching, smelling, tasting.

Doors . . . His guide was becoming increasingly restive under the barrage of sensory information. The boy moved to the kitchen, to the spice jars, vaguely aware of Khira following him anxiously from place to place.

There was only one door the boy knew how to open, the door to the trancing room. And his guide had final control of that door. Who controlled the other doors, the doors out of this narrow band of awareness? The boy sighed heavily, tired and confused.

That evening he sat in a corner of the throneroom after the evening meal, waiting for Khira to come down from her chamber. He had reached that point of exhaustion where his thoughts had neither substance nor direction. His head hurt and his shoulders ached. He sat on a down cushion, his head resting against the polished stone wall, his eyelids heavy. He had questioned all afternoon and he had found no answers. None at all.

When he first heard his brother's voice, he sighed with relief and let his eyelids fall shut. In the trancing room at least he would not be tired, nor would he be confused. He would be warm in his brothers' company. With another deep sigh, he slowed his respiration, reaching for forgetfulness.

Then his eyes sprang open. *He heard his brothers laughing and he had not summoned them.* He stared around the empty throneroom. Even though his eyes were open, his brothers' voices were still with him. Confounded, he let his eyes slip shut again—and saw the trancing room door. It stood open. He recognized his brothers' faces through the blaze of light that always warmed the trancing room. They were smiling, beckoning him, all those faces so like his own. Some were young, little more than infants. Others were older. Some were men already, smiling men, laughing men—calling him.

He shook his head in confusion. Calling him—*they were calling him by name.* He listened intently, trying to grasp the name they called him. But he couldn't piece its separate syllables into a whole.

They knew his name— it was their name too. And their voices—

He stepped toward the door, reaching out for them.

Before he could enter, Khira bent over him. He hadn't even heard her approach. "Darkchild?"

Darkchild. But that wasn't the name. Moaning, he fought Khira's intrusive voice. The door was so near. His brothers...

Khira's voice was clearer now, anxious. "Darkchild!"

Something of her distress cut through his dazzled consciousness. The door was open; his brothers were calling him; their faces—*Why was the door open now?* He had not put his forehead to his knees. He had not regulated his breathing. Why did his guide offer him the trancing room now?

To reward him? When his guide was angry at being screened?

The boy drew a deep, sighing breath and forced his eyelids open. His head had fallen forward. His chin rested on his chest. He lifted it as if it were a great weight. He could still hear his brothers' voices calling his name.

His elusive name...

Khira's eyes were pleading. "I thought we were going to play magic squares, Darkchild."

Desperately he fought off the trancing room spell. "My name—" He spoke faintly over the retreating murmur of his brothers' voices.

She touched his shoulder, troubled. "I don't know your name—not your real name."

Neither did he. His brothers' voices had faded. They were barely audible. The boy looked up at Khira. "He thought he could distract me," he said slowly, testing the truth of the perception. "He thought he could open one door and make me forget the other." His guide had attempted to play the same game with him that he had played with his guide.

But it had failed. Even as the boy peered up into Khira's uncomprehending eyes, the trancing room door closed, shutting off his brothers' light. The boy sighed deeply. The light was gone and he had become a shadow—excluded by his own will.

Khira had named him correctly. He was a shadow child, a dark child. Exhaustion gripped him, sudden, total. "I'm tired," he said. When had he been this tired before?

Khira took his hand. Her sympathy was direct, tinged with worry. "I'm sorry."

The boy looked up at her. His brothers had been his comfort, his solace. To give them up was unthinkable. But to let his guide use them against him, to maintain dominion over him, was unthinkable too. If Khira hadn't called him back, he would have stepped into the trancing room and his guide's trap. In her loneliness she had pulled him back.

He must be lonely too, he realized. He must give up the comfort of his brothers' company if he was to find the answers to his questions and fill the emptiness someone or something had made of his mind. Sighing, he spoke with great effort. "Do you want to play magic squares?" He could not think while he played. But so long as he was actively occupied, the guide could not lure him into the trancing room.

"Will you?"

"Yes. I will." He rose stiffly and moved to the inlaid board, forcing himself to set the carved pieces into place. He had learned a lot today. Not so long ago he had considered his guide omniscient and omnipotent and had granted him complete dominion over his will. Now he claimed his own will, however painfully.

And in the claiming, he had become the person Khira had already christened him—Darkchild, child of shadow.

6/*Khira*

Two nights after Darkchild discovered the west wing, Khira was wakened by a shrieking metallic cry that jarred through the silent palace. She struggled up from sleep and lay with every muscle clenched, tensely expecting the sound to expand into the terrible metallic scream that had brought Darkchild. Instead the sound was quickly muffled and became the cry of the Arnimi ship as it plunged through drifts of snow to settle on the western plaza.

Khira's racketing pulse had hardly returned to normal when Darkchild materialized in her doorway, his face grey. "That—what was that?"

Khira made no attempt to purge resentment from her tone. "The Arnimi ship. They've returned from the southern mountains." And tomorrow they would walk the palace with their meters, tapping and testing and talking among themselves. Techni-Verra might speak to her, might even take time to ask after her winter's occupation. But the others—if they spoke, it would be to probe, to question. It would be with no care for her, only for whatever information they might elicit from her.

She smiled grimly. Precious little that would be. She had offered Techni-Verra bread and the Arnimi woman had accepted. She would offer none of the others anything.

Darkchild peered at her uncertainly, sensitive to her anger. "They've come back to stay?"

Khira sat, one hand clutching her coverlet. "They won't leave until thawing." And even if you had not come and given me company, she added silently, with sour satisfaction, I would have gone the entire winter without speaking to them. I would have been alone here—except perhaps for Techni-Verra.

"Adar is rising," she said without thinking. Yet the observation was not an irrelevancy. Although she seldom thought about the red star's winter appearance, she kept an internal calendar, and tonight the belligerent surge was in her blood. Quickly she jumped from her bed. "Let's go to the tower."

Darkchild stepped back, surprised at her sudden change of mood. "Now?"

"Yes, and you'll see my host." Watching Darkchild during the first days after he emerged from the watchtower had been like watching a living intelligence emerge from shadow. At first he had been like a person brain-injured: remote, vacant-eyed, slack. Although he moved through the palace touching and evaluating whatever came within range of his senses, he seemed barely conscious of the totality of his surroundings. It was as if he were one of the Arnimi's data-gathering instruments bound up in human flesh. And when Khira worked with him he seemed so little aware of her as a living person that she might have been stone.

Yet he learned, and as she added fingers to the hands on her wall, he changed. His smile became less vacant, his explorations less groping. More and more often, willed intelligence moved behind his eyes. Recently he had given up his evening time of retreat. He played board games with her now instead. And these past days, his eyes often flashed with some covert defiance, some half-hidden rebellion.

Yet through all the changes, one thing persisted: his curiosity. And he had *not* seen Adar.

Nor did she for some minutes when they reached the tower. The wind whipped frosted fingers through the broken window, piling the floor with snow. Khira hugged her down jacket tight and peered into the clouded sky. She knew her star was there. She could hear his drums and the clatter of reeds in her blood, Adar's war-call.

Darkchild was more interested in the shadowed concavity that marked the western plaza of the palace. He held himself stiffly, staring at the dark place where the Arnimi ship had settled, as if at an enemy.

His gaze was black. Adar's was red, and finally heavy clouds shifted and Adar's pinpoint light burned through. Khira clutched Darkchild's hand. "There! There is Adar!" He was a gleaming red light in a misted collar of orange, burning down at them. "Now you see why my feast table is empty."

Darkchild followed her pointing finger, distracted at first. When he found the red star with its misty nimbus, he peered at it with deepening interest. "Because nothing is harvested now," he said slowly. "Your star comes too late. There is nothing to be brought in from the fields now."

"Yes. And no one to bring it. Adar comes only in winter—in the war months."

"But there are no wars. You told me that."

"There are no wars now. In the early days of the barohnas, there were. And this is when raiders came, late enough that the people were sleeping, early enough that most of the winter was still ahead. They never came when there was a barohna in the valley. They took the halls first and they slept for a while. Then they woke and ate and went to lie in ambush for the barohna." Khira should have shuddered as she recounted the brief history of violence that had marked the first centuries of the barohnas. But when the host-markers had been spread for her infant hands, she had reached for the red stone. And in taking it, she had surrendered some of the tenderness of her sisters, moon and blue-star daughters.

War and barrenness. She held Darkchild's hand tighter, until it warmed in hers. Every year on her feast day, there was fasting in the valley. Yet somehow hunger had fed her and the drums of Adar warmed her. She turned to Darkchild, staring at his intent profile. If he were offered the stones, if he took a host, which body might it be?

Darkchild's eyes held the war-star for a moment longer, then returned to the dark concavity on the western plaza. Khira dismissed her moment's speculation. The barohnas had sprung from the women of the halls, and so female infants of the halls took hosts just as did female infants of the palace. But males were never offered choosing stones. They were soil-bound. The sky and its energies touched their realm but did not comprise it.

"Khira—"

She didn't even have to hear his question. "Yes. Tomorrow we will go to the Arnimi wing." Let him see the Arnimi. Let him examine their instruments and appliances. Let him ask them his questions. In the end, he would like them no better than she did.

Still she delayed their visit until the middle of the next morning and approached the western wing with distaste. She had not taken time to train the stalklamp that grew in the remote regions of the palace. As they neared the Arnimi quarters, glowing stems hung in slack streamers. The sealed door to the west wing stood tall and immobile. Normally when the Arnimi were in residence, it opened automatically at Khira's approach. Today, to her surprise, it did not.

She halted and stared up its imposing expanse, puzzled. Then, aware of Darkchild rigid beside her, his gaze flickering tensely from her to the door, she tapped lightly.

A metallic throat cleared somewhere nearby. "Goodwinter, heiress. I see you have acquired a companion."

Startled, she stepped back. Sometime since the Arnimi had returned in the middle of the night, they had recessed a small grill into the door. Beside it was a tiny lens. She peered into the lens, her face tightening into a frown. It was like the Arnimi to suddenly speak to her through the door instead of opening it. "Yes, my friend is with me," she said sharply, waiting for the door to open.

Still it did not move. "How long has this friend been with you, heiress?"

The query, despite its metallic tone, betrayed something sharper than polite interest. "Long enough," she said with asperity. She did not like to be questioned as they might question a child of their own race, condescendingly, through a closed door. "We have come to see the rock samples you brought from the southern mountains."

She heard muttered voices beyond the door. She rapped again, beginning to be angry. Even less than she liked being addressed as a child did she like being barred from a portion of her own palace. "I'm waiting," she prompted.

More muttering, then a whining electronic sound and the door slowly opened.

Khira and Darkchild caught their breath simultaneously. Now instead of a metal door, they faced a shimmering screen of light, beyond which stood two Arnimi. Both Arnimi gazed at Darkchild, their lips bunched severely, their prominent grey eyes cold. One was male—Commander Bullens—and one was female, but to Khira they were almost identical in appearance: potbellied, with greying hair that receded from their high foreheads and hung to their shoulders in thin streamers. Even the characteristic Arnimi expression was identical: remote, chill, disapproving.

"What is this?" Khira demanded, more angry than before. "What have you hung in this doorway?"

"This is a privacy screen, heiress," Commander Bullens informed her. "We saw the shattered watchtower window when we landed and we found your guest's prints on our door. The screen will protect our quarters from unauthorized visitors. If you are eager to see our samples—and you have never been eager before—you may step through the screen. Your companion may not."

"Your companion may wait in the corridor," the female Arnimi said. Although both wore translator buttons at their belts, they had learned to speak Brakrathi without aid. Now, however, Commander Bullens placed his button against his throat. As he subvocalized, the button spoke his words in a tongue Khira did not recognize.

Darkchild clutched Khira's arm spasmodically. He rose to the balls of his feet, his lips parting in shock, his pupils contracting.

The Arnimi spoke again, and this time the alien words held clear warning. Khira stared from the haughty Arnimi to Darkchild, startled by the flush that stained his bronze cheeks. "You have his language in your bank," she realized in surprise, wheeling back to the Arnimi.

"Yes. I told him in his brother-language that while the heiress may enter our quarters and do what she pleases—even though she has never been so interested in entering before—we have guarded the portal against the Rauthimage. He may not enter."

"Rauthimage?" The word was unfamiliar.

"He is the image of Rauth." It was a clarification that clarified nothing. Again the Arnimi placed his button to his throat and subvocalized. This time the alien words were harsh, challenging.

Darkchild dropped Khira's arm. Muscles bunched beneath his thin coverall and his face twisted fiercely. With a quick sideways glance at Khira, he lunged forward, one hand extended.

Whatever invisible force guarded the door became briefly visible, limning Darkchild's slender body in blue light. Serpents of light seemed to snap at his coverall and his bare head. Then Darkchild was propelled backward, to slam against the rough stone wall, his face blanched, his dark eyes staring.

Khira was torn between anger and concern. She ran to Darkchild. "Are you hurt?"

Pain and bitterness mingled in his gaze as he peered at the Arnimi who had blocked his passage. Muttering something in the same language the Arnimi had used, he stood away from the wall and retreated down the corridor, shoulders set. He seemed oblivious to Khira's concern.

She turned back to the Arnimi, her words stinging. "I am heiress here and I invited my friend to enter this wing with me. He was under my protection."

The two regarded her, unintimidated. "Then you would do well to recall your protection. You are a child who has taken a Rauthimage for a friend," Commander Bullens said coldly.

His arrogance made Khira flush with anger. "I am a child who has taken another child for a friend. I am also the palace daughter in my mother's palace."

"Yes, and it is regrettable your mother is not here to deal with the Rauthimage."

Khira felt her gorge rise giddily. "You have already classified him when you have just met him? How do you know he is anything more than a stranded traveler? If you want to use a word in conversation with me, define it or I will consider it nonsense."

She had intended to sting them into anger to match her own. However they consulted silently with an exchanged glance, coldly unconcerned. The female Arnimi said, "We found his prints on our door this morning and we classified them immediately against data in our banks. If you would care to come into our quarters, we will show you tapes containing an exact description of your friend and a number of other verifications of his identity."

Khira touched her lips with a tongue suddenly dry. She could not shake their stony self-possession. And she knew the Arnimi had honed the science of classifying and identifying persons, plants and objects to a degree that confounded even Tiahna. "You—why would you carry identifying data on a stray child in your banks?"

"Because he is not a child; rather he is a child but beyond that, more importantly, he is a Rauthimage. Bring us a sample of his hair; we will show you spectroscopic readouts proving we have already classified samples of his hair. Bring us his fingerprints; we will show you we already have them on file. Bring us a scrap of fingernail, a flake of skin; we will prove that we have already analyzed identical samples and carry the data in our bank to permit exact identification." The Arnimi offered an arrogant grimace. Apparently it was intended as a smile. "We have already satisfied your mother that no two separate persons have identical structures. Even the set of identical twins she brought us were distinguishable in a dozen ways. Isn't that correct?"

Khira refused to concede the point. "You've told me yourself we're a small group of people. There are billions of people on other worlds. Out of all of them—"

"There is no duplication there either, not among people who have not been imaged from a prototype—as your friend has been and as we can prove from our data tapes."

Khira's fists clenched, the nails digging her palms. If they knew where Darkchild had come from, why he had been abandoned half-starved in the tower— But Adar was risen and anger overrode any softer approach. "If you have identification on Darkchild on your tapes, you came to our wing last night and took samples to create it. You came to my personal wing without permission while I slept. You—"

The Arnimi shook their heads. "We have not left our own wing. We carry Rauth tracings in our databanks as a matter of course. Every ship of our flag carries them."

And there was the flaw in their argument. "You're lying!" she flared. "Darkchild is no older than I am. You have been here since before he was born. How could you have tracings in your databanks when he was born several years after you left Arnim?"

She had finally nettled Commander Bullens. He flicked the lank hair off his collar. "We do not lie and we do not argue with children, even imperial children," he said frostily. "We have identifying information on the Rauthimage and if you ask reasonably we will permit you to examine it. If you want our advice, that will be yours too."

Why had Tiahna ever permitted him to quarter his people in the palace? Why had the Council of Bronze allowed the Arnimi to stay on Brakrath at all? "What would that be?"

Commander Bullens laid a proprietary hand on his paunch. "It is very simple, heiress: lead your image-friend to the nearest exterior door, open it, and send him out into the snow. Then seal the door behind him."

She could not believe what he said. Khira stared at him incredulously, for a moment even anger forgotten. "Put him into the snow—to die?"

The Arnimi shrugged, betraying the barest trace of pettishness. "You will only have terminated an image, one of hundreds."

What did he mean? That there were hundreds of Darkchild? Or that there were hundreds of people to whom the ill-defined term Rauthimage could be applied? And what was the meaning of the term? He refused to make it clear. "Hundreds?"

"There are hundreds of Rauthimages scattered through the galaxy. Each one has separate life and awareness—to a degree. But you cannot be said to kill an individual human when you terminate a Rauthimage. It will be simplest for you and for your mother if you disallow whatever individuality you see in this particular Rauthimage and dispose of him."

Khira stared up into his chill face, repelled by his words, by everything about him. At the same time, she felt the first whisper of fear. "And if I don't—don't put him into the snow to die?"

The Arnimi shrugged. "Then he will live."

"You—you won't kill him yourself?" She could guard him of course, but she was one and the Arnimi were fifty-two. She could not stay awake all winter.

This time it was the female who shrugged. Grotesquely, she ran a coquettish hand through her receding locks. "He is no threat to us. We will protect our wing against his entry simply because we do not want him here. It is up to you to protect the rest of the palace."

Protect? "And if I don't?" Were they saying that Darkchild was a threat to her, even in some unspecified way to the palace itself? "He has been here twenty-seven days and he has harmed nothing."

"Physically he will not harm you. But there is a threat, and if you do not care to put him into the snow yourself, we will discuss him with your mother when she returns. She will understand the threat clearly. I think she will take the wise course."

Khira's eyes sparked with rekindling anger. "I will understand the threat well enough myself if you tell me what it is—if there *is* a threat. If it is not simply a lie. And if you ask me, I will tell you which I think is the case."

A glint of malice flashed in Commander Bullens' eyes. "We have discussed enough with you already, heiress. On Arnim we would not have confided any of this to a child. If you want to enter and see the samples we brought back with us, you may do so now."

Khira bit back a dozen intemperate replies before she said, fiercely, "At this moment I never want to enter your quarters again. However your quarters are a part of my mother's palace and I will enter whenever I feel ready."

"Come when you wish then. The portal is not guarded against you." He pressed a button mounted on his control belt, and the shimmering screen of light melted. With a nod, he touched another button and the tall metal door swung shut.

Khira stared up at the expanse of metal, her face set with anger. How could Darkchild be a threat to the palace—or to her? And how could he live by the hundreds all across the galaxy? He was flesh as she was flesh, blood as she was blood. When he was hungry, he ate. When he was tired, he slept. She had seen him cry and she had heard him laugh.

Yet Commander Bullens called him a threat and would not tell her why.

And how did they know so much about him? How could identifying material have been placed in their databanks before Darkchild had ever been born? Commander Bullens had evaded her on that point, retreating into huffiness. Khira paced slowly down the corridor. Had they at any time denied that he was a child, no older than herself?

They had not.

Darkchild crouched in a doorway near the end of the corridor. At her approach, he stood stiffly, his eyes blazing with the same anger that animated Khira. Khira hesitated. She had never seen him angry before. It seemed an alien expression, as if someone or something had taken possession of his features. Yet there was wariness in him too, much like she had seen in his early days in the palace. She caught his arm. "He spoke your language—what did he say to you?"

Mutely Darkchild shook his head, pulling back from her.

"You're not afraid of me!" she said sharply, clinging to his arm. "Whatever he said—"

He answered with a single guttural syllable she did not know. His face twisting, he broke from her grasp and ran down the hall.

For a moment, anger urged her after him. But perplexity held her back. Rauthimage . . . If he would answer her questions . . . But she had long since learned it was useless to ask them. He never gave her more than a dark, unknowing stare or a helpless gesture. And now this single word from his own language. She mouthed it silently.

One word. She knew one word of his language. Probably the first word any child learned to use: no.

She did not pursue him. However she found him a short time later in a corner of the throneroom, his head resting on his drawn-up knees, his eyes closed. She dropped to her knees beside him, frowning. If he retreated now . . . But his respiration was rapid and his face hot. An angry grimace disfigured his features, as if he fought the impulse to retreat.

Impatience overcame her. Khira pressed her fingers into his arm. "Darkchild—what did Commander Bullens say to you? Did he tell you he wants me to put you outside?"

Darkchild shook his head, his eyes squeezed shut, perspiration on his upper lip. His breath came in a harsh grunt.

Khira bristled. If no one would tell her anything, if everyone excluded her, the Arnimi, Darkchild himself . . . Her muscles tightening, she called upon Adar, upon the reservoir of gritty anger he inspired in her. Her grip tightened on Darkchild's arm. "I can't help you if you won't tell me what Bullens said! *What did he tell you?*"

With a strangled sob, Darkchild raised his head from his knees and let it fall back against the stone wall. The motion seemed to require great effort. "The door—" he said in a harsh whisper, his eyes still squeezed shut, his entire face wet with perspiration.

Khira's anger dissolved instantly. "The door—it hurt you! It hurt you when you tried to step through." How could she have forgotten the light-serpents that had snapped at him, then repelled him. Quickly she examined him. But there were no scorch marks on his skin or on his coverall. "Darkchild—"

He caught his breath in a second choking sob and forced his eyes open. They were drowned in tears, half-focused. He spoke rapidly, indistinctly. "He wants me to step through the door. The door—he wants me to go so he can open the other door. He needs to know—" Suddenly he clutched Khira's wrists, his fingers digging into her flesh painfully. *"He wants me to go through the door."*

Dread squeezed her heart. Was he delirious? If the Arnimi privacy screen had burned him—but he had talked about doors the night after he had discovered the west wing too, before he had challenged the privacy screen. "Darkchild—"

He was struggling to his feet, muttering incoherently. She stepped back helplessly as he staggered across the throneroom.

He left the throneroom at an awkward gait, stumbling, lurching, falling against the corridor wall. Khira followed him down stalklit corridors. His thin coverall writhed as if the muscles beneath it were in spasm, as if he fought himself. He made his way to the kitchen and fell against the spice cupboard. His hands shook violently as he opened the cupboard and seized half a dozen small bottles, staggering toward the chopping table with them.

His entire body shuddered as he wrenched open the first jar and inhaled deeply. Khira grimaced. Hathlo was a particularly pungent herb gathered from Terlath's eastern slope just before Darkmorning. The cooks seldom used more than a tiny pinch in a large kettle of broth. Darkchild shook a mound of the dark leaves into his palm and tipped it into his mouth.

"Darkchild—" She had seen him use hathlo before, in small quantities. But to use so much—

His face twisted as he choked down the herb. His arm jerked spasmodically and flung the jar across the stone floor. Resisting his twisting muscles, he squeezed his eyes shut and groped for a second jar. This time his hand shattered the jar on the stone floor before he could wrench off the lid. His eyes flew open. He stared blankly at the broken jar, dark flecks of hathlo on his lips. Struggling against rebellious spasms, he reached for the jar of milo, a sweet yellow powder used in cakes and puddings.

Adar was no host for this occasion. Khira could find no anger to help her. She found only panic. Her hands shaking, she took the milo jar from Darkchild and shook the powder into his palm. He licked it up hungrily, coughing on the dry powder. She ran to the melt-tap and fetched water. He gulped it down, hiccoughing now, tears running down his cheeks. But he continued through the jars, feeding desperately, choking, crying.

And finally he was calm. He stepped back from the table, wiping his eyes with a shaking hand. "The door is closed."

Khira's hands trembled. What door? she wanted to demand. And who wanted him to step through it? But this was not the time to challenge his composure. He turned shakily to the task of rearranging the spice jars on their shelf. She stood frozen, watching him, remembering all the times she had seen him at this task. Had he been confronted with a door each time?

When the last jar was in place, he turned back to her with a faint frown. "Can we eat now?"

Her stomach clenched rebelliously. "Yes," she said faintly.

Nodding, distracted, Darkchild took a loaf from the pantry and cut it. Khira accepted a thick slice but could not choke it down. Darkchild found his mouth too dry for bread too, although he drank three mugs of water.

She stared at him, at his ashen profile. He was a Rauthimage, and when Tiahna returned, Commander Bullens would inform her of the fact. Would Tiahna accept Bullens' warning? Khira's nails dug her palms. Why should Tiahna hesitate over the fate of a castaway child when she had seen each of her own daughters go to die on Terlath? And bade them farewell with nothing more than a nod from her throne?

With a moan of pain, Khira threw down her bread and ran from the kitchen. She slipped down stalklit halls to the throneroom. There she sat cross-legged on the edge of the dais, staring into winter-dead mirrors. She seemed to see images of Darkchild there, starved and empty-eyed as he had been when he first came. She had fed him, given him shelter, taught him her language. And she had defended him against Commander Bullens. How could she consider him a threat?

Her hands fisted in her lap. How could he harm anyone when he was torn against himself? When he muttered about doors and gulped down herbs and spices in some bizarre exorcising ritual? Was that the nature of a Rauthimage, to struggle against himself?

Did she care? For the first time since Alzaja's death, she had a companion—one who was not steeped in barohnial tradition. When Darkchild looked at her, he saw not myth and tradition, not lineage and the potential of transforming power, but simply a child as slight as himself and as lonely, gifted with nothing more than an occasional fit of temper. He did not see a child who would either die on Terlath or accede to the throne. He saw simply—Khira.

Only Alzaja had seen that before, and Alzaja was dead. Slowly tears began to course down Khira's face. She wiped at them furiously, angry with her own weakness, angry with her fear. For the first time in all her years, she dreaded spring and her mother's return. And though she might go to the watchtower night after night, how could Adar arm her against something she could not understand?

Darkchild was a Rauthimage and there was no one to tell her what that meant to either of them.

7/The Guide

Thirty days after the full inception of his mission, the guide found himself stymied, his instructions ignored, his directions rejected, his imperatives contravened. When he spoke, he spoke to the wind. If the boy did not fight him, he ignored him—or worse, screened his thoughts and activities behind sensory data. And when the guide offered the reward that should have insured the boy's obedience, the boy spurned him.

The guide could not fail. Failure was not acceptable. The guide had no alternative but to fulfill the contract by which he had been empowered:

To guide the boy in strange places.

To keep his body safe and fed.

To prompt him to inquire and explore.

To urge him to learn and know.

To divert him from knowledge which was interior.

To direct him to knowledge which was exterior.

To codify those facts and impressions the boy gathered.

To store and preserve them to meet the terms of the contract.

It should have been simple. The boy was naturally curious. He was also intelligent, observant and at first he had been docile.

Now he was docile no more. He had discovered routeways past the guide's vigilance and he used them. He had realized that his brothers were used as a distracting influence and he refused to meet them. He had learned there was information the guide kept from him and he sought it.

The guide was baffled. There were guidelines for the boy's behavior, but the guide had increasing difficulty enforcing them. The boy was strong where he should have been weak, rebellious where he should have been meek, autonomous where he should have been dependent. And uncomfortably the guide knew that for all his troublesome behavior, the boy was still relatively quiescent. He had only begun to test his strength.

The guide's only recourse was to claim the boy's body and use it directly to meet the terms of the contract. Over the past few days, since the Arnimi's return, he had done just that on a number of occasions. He had done it despite the boy's increasingly desperate resistance. Yet he had been given no instructions for implementing that action on other than a temporary basis. It was assumed that the necessity for permanent intervention would never arise, that the boy would remain pliant. Certainly the mastery of the boy's body was an exhausting effort.

The girl now... The guide mused. He could not pace a lonely path upon some stone floor while he thought. He had no physical presence, at least not at this time. His being was expressed within a framework of non-dimensional space. He was bounded by his thoughts, defined by them. And he thought about the girl a lot.

She was the boy's prime source of information. She dedicated hours to him every day, teaching him, coaching him, answering his questions. Despite her occasional impatience, she seemed to take pleasure in the activity and in the boy's company. Yet there were things she had not told the boy.

The Arnimi, for instance. Again the guide mused. The girl had not told the boy about the Arnimi, and his own reference material about them had been difficult to access. He had had to rummage dangerous moments for it and then it had been so incomplete as to be deceiving. He should have known before he encountered the arrogant Bullens, should have known before he challenged the Arnimi force curtain, that the Arnimi would be inimical to him. And the insult the Arnimi had addressed to him in his brother-language—the guide seethed. Apparently he was a threat to the Arnimi, a trespasser on territory they had reserved for their own exploitation.

After his first encounter with the Arnimi, the guide realized it was more vital than ever that the boy please Khira. His very life could depend upon her when the barohna returned. Yet that created a dilemma for the guide. It was Khira who had lured the boy from his brothers' orbit, Khira who drove an ever-widening wedge between the boy and his guide. It was Khira who gave the boy strength, who encouraged him. The guide found himself dependent upon the very person who was wresting the boy's loyalties from him.

The guide was torn. And he felt very much alone. He was silent audience to every conversation the boy had with Khira. Yet none of her warmth touched him. While the boy and Khira laughed and talked, while they ate and played, the guide was cold and solitary in a non-existent space. These past days, out of frustration, he sometimes seized control of the boy's body and tried to take his place with Khira. But Khira recognized the change and drew back from the guide uneasily and he remained as isolated as before.

Sometimes the guide fought the boy for control of his body anyway and used it to propel himself around the palace. He always ended the experience in anger. Things that were fresh and bright to the boy turned cold and dull when the guide motivated the boy's body. Tastes and scents grew insipid, colors dull, textures bland. Somehow only the boy could bring alive the magic of the palace and the guide did not understand why that should be.

He also did not understand how he could experience anger and loneliness when his functions were limited to fulfilling the contract. But he did, more and more.

Certainly he experienced anger on the fifth day after the Arnimi's return. Various of the Arnimi had emerged from their quarters on each of the previous days and performed a ritual metering of the palace's public chambers. The guide had watched them silently from room to room, grimly determined not to be cowed by them. They were an unattractive people. The guide found their thin, greying locks offensive, their wobbling potbellies distasteful. The arrogance in their chill grey eyes was most grating of all. They seemed to be mocking him for his humiliation on that first day, every one of them. And although they pretended to ignore the boy, when they spoke among themselves it was

in their own tongue rather than in Brakrathi. Afterward Khira told the
boy they had never committed such discourtesy in her presence before.
Certainly her own stony silence when addressed by Commander Bullens
was a discourtesy as deliberate—and as grave.

On the fifth day after their return, a female Arnimi appeared in the
throneroom as the boy and Khira sat on the dais ciphering scrolls. She
was the youngest Arnimi the guide had seen and with her dark hair and
deep-set eyes, she was less unattractive than the older Arnimi. Even
the characteristic abdominal fat deposit was only in its incipient stage.

The boy glanced up warily when she entered the room. He had
conceived a dislike of the Arnimi entirely separate from the guide's
dislike. But the Arnimi did not address him. She smiled at Khira instead
and indicated the instrument she carried. "I'm sure you remember how
this instrument works, Khira," she said.

The guide recognized Khira's resistance to the Arnimi's overture in
the stiffening of her shoulders. She had not spoken directly to an Arnimi
since the day after their return. But she had told the boy once that she
considered one Arnimi—Techni-Verra—her friend, and apparently this
was that Arnimi. Because now Khira said grudgingly, "I remember."

The Arnimi nodded, ignoring Khira's reluctance. "Well, it slipped
out of my hand this morning. The case didn't shatter, but I'd like to
test my instrument to be certain it is working properly. Will you help
me?"

Khira eyed the instrument, her lips tightening in suspicion. "You can
test it on your own people."

"Yes, of course I could do that," Verra responded without offense.
"But I want to test the instrument's entire range, and for that I need
someone who is not an Arnimi." Turning, she finally acknowledged the
boy's presence with a direct glance. "It's too bad I left my translator
in my quarters. Your friend could help me test the meter too."

The guide was stung. The Arnimi claimed to know who he was. Did
this one think then that he required more than thirty days to learn a
language as simple as Brakrathi? Impulsively the guide seized the boy's
tongue. "You don't need a translator to talk to me. I speak Brakrathi
as well as you."

The Arnimi's brows rose in exaggerated surprise. "You do? Then
you have worked hard this winter."

She dared condescend to him. "Khira has worked hard to teach me," he said with a rush of scorn. "She has answered every question I have asked her." His challenge was clear. Would Khira have done as much for an Arnimi? For any Arnimi?

Never.

"And you have understood all her answers?" The Arnimi touched her hair in a coquettish gesture. A second flick of her brows made her expression sceptical.

Stung, the guide fought the resistance in the boy's jaws. "I understand everything that is presented to me!"

The Arnimi woman nodded, becoming thoughtful. "Yes, that is characteristic of Rauthimages, their ability to assimilate information quickly and completely. You understand what you are, of course; that you are a Rauthimage."

Without glancing down at the meter in her hand, Techni-Verra had activated it, setting its tiny needle aflicker across its printed dial. Drawn, the guide moved the boy's body nearer. "I know my name," he said sharply, peering at the printed dial. When he spoke, the tiny needle danced nervously between ranges of printed numbers.

The Arnimi noted its movement before saying, "Then I would like to know it too." The needle flickered lightly in response to her words.

The guide caught the slight movement with narrowing pupils. Curiosity was the boy's province, but the guide found it moved in him too. And there was challenge in the Arnimi's query. Did she think his name had been kept from him? "I am Iahnerre Trigonne Rauth-Seven," he said, drawing himself erect. Again the needle swung wildly. The guide felt the boy struggling to assert himself. He squelched the effort with impatience. "What is this instrument?"

"You're probably not interested in its technical name," Verra said. "I call it simply a response evaluator. It's very sensitive to the electrical responses within the human nervous system. The needle's movement tells me if a person is speaking the truth as he knows it—or lying."

The guide narrowed his eyes. Again the needle had flickered lightly in response to her words, while it had swung wildly both times he spoke. "Then who is lying—you or me?"

The Arnimi laughed at his challenge. "Neither of us, actually. There are certain differences within our nervous systems that cause us to give different readings even though we are both telling the truth. If I were to ask Khira a question, the needle would stand completely still when she responded—if she answered truthfully. And I've found that I can't use my instrument in the presence of Khira's mother at all. Her field makes the readings meaningless. Isn't that correct, Khira?"

Khira frowned at the boy, obviously troubled by the change in him. She responded to Verra's question distractedly. "Yes, you've shown us that."

The needle stood completely still at her words. Techni-Verra shrugged lightly. "I believe my instrument is working quite properly." She directed a smile at the guide. "So you are an IT-7. Can you tell me how many IT-7 brothers you have?"

The very casualness of her tone made him stiffen. Belatedly the guide recognized his error and flushed with emotion: fear, anger, confusion. He should never have spoken to the Arnimi. Hadn't his encounter with Bullens shown him clearly that they were inimical to him? And certainly he should never have spoken out in the presence of Khira— *and the boy.* Oh yes—*the boy.* He had been listening. And now the guide had been tricked into giving the boy his name—the one bit of information that might have had the most potency in keeping the boy under control.

Iahnerre Trigonne Rauth-Seven. He had uttered the precious syllables arrogantly, forgetting the boy's hunger for possession of those same syllables. He had almost drawn the boy into the trancing room several times by offering him his name. Now he would never have that potent enticement to offer again. He had let the Arnimi make a fool of him.

Techni-Verra misinterpreted his silence. "So you miss your brothers," she said. "Well you might. But I'm sure you've been taught to connect back into the consciousness of Rauth when you need support." When he still did not respond—*how had she tricked him so easily? why hadn't he been alert?*—she turned to Khira. "Isn't that true? Doesn't he leave you sometimes to trance with his brothers?"

Khira glanced from the boy's taut face—taut with the guide's consternation—to the instrument in the Arnimi's hand, obviously torn between loyalty and her own need to know. "I don't watch him every moment," she said noncommittally.

The needle remained completely still.

"And you don't betray him either," Verra concluded. "Well, it's a lonely life being a daughter of the palace. Your sisters are spread from you in time and you have no way of linking back to them. Of course for that matter, your friend doesn't actually link to his brothers, but the illusion is there and that's some comfort. Wouldn't you welcome a link, even an illusory one, now that Alzaja is gone?"

"A link?" The question erased the troubled frown from Khira's face, replaced it with stark emotion. *Alzaja, Mara, Denabar, Hedia, Kristyan, Sukiin*— she recited the names like a litany sometimes, when she was troubled, trying to conjure up something of her sisters' presence. He could see the names on her lips now.

"But then of course you might find yourself burdened with a guide, as your friend is," Verra continued.

Khira purged the litany of names from her lips. She darted a glance at the boy, then back to Verra. "Darkchild has no one but me."

The Arnimi shook her head. "You're his only flesh and blood companion, yes. But he has inner direction—an internal force termed a guide. Whatever he says, whatever he does, however he responds—even down to the fact that he is standing here listening to me tell you this—all his activities are in direct obedience to his guide. Never mind that there is no one you or I can see. Your friend is very much aware of his guide. His guide's instructions are buried so deeply in his mind, embedded so completely, in fact, that your friend doesn't even realize that the voice that instructs him is not a living entity at all but a programmed response of his own mind, just as the link with his brothers is a programmed response."

Fear, anger, confusion—if the guide had suffered them before, now they choked him. He drew the boy's body up tight, fighting down an angry flush of blood to his cheeks. That she could speak of him as a programmed response, that she could call him *no more than a part of the boy himself*—

That she could call him that *in the boy's presence*—

And the boy was listening. There was no mistaking that. The guide had commanded control of the boy's motor muscles, but there was no provision for cutting off the boy's sensory awareness without luring him into the trancing room.

At least the guide knew of no such provision. The guide raged. Why had the contract been implemented so clumsily? He had been told that the assignment would be simple, that the boy would be totally subordinate. He had been told he had only to follow rudimentary guidelines. Instead the assignment was turning into a nightmare of complexity.

There was another betrayal too. He had been told that he would be the rational, directing force, that he would go about his duties without suffering emotion or attachment. What were fear, anger and confusion if not emotion?

Both the Arnimi woman and Khira were staring at him. The boy wanted to speak to them. The guide fought him, making his lips stiff. And at the same time the boy blocked the guide from speech. The guide clutched at their throat, choking. He had to take the boy away from the Arnimi before she gave him more destructive information. With a dry croak, he forced the boy around and brought him to a staggering half-run.

He ran painfully, awkwardly, muscles knotting and cramping in resistance. The guide could feel the boy fighting to hold him back, grappling for control of the body. Once the boy turned and looked back at Khira and the Arnimi, pleading.

The guide would not yield. He dragged the boy unwilling from the throneroom and down the corridor to the watchtower stairs. Perilously he staggered up the stairs, groping at the wall for support. When he reached the tower, he threw the boy's body down against the wall and forced his head to his drawn-up knees, oblivious of the cold. The desperate heaving of the boy's chest was his own, pained, spastic.

Grimly the guide worked to slow the boy's respiration and draw the pounding blood from his head. Gradually the boy's struggles weakened and he sat with face cold and still, breath slow and regular.

If the boy's brothers were illusion, then the guide was master of illusion. He released the brothers' voices into the boy's consciousness, from the cry of the youngest infant brother to the reassuring murmur of the elder brothers. When the boy's attention was fixed, the guide slowly brought the trancing room door into visibility. Light spilled from it, and within hung the faces of the boy's brothers, brilliantly lit. Yet there was a swirling, misty quality to the air of the trancing room that diffused detail. The boy's brothers smiled out at him, beckoning, their features bright but indistinct.

At some level, the boy still fought. A moan escaped him. The guide disregarded it, spinning out his illusion, playing it against the boy's trapped awareness.

Then without warning his own awareness quaked. He felt the boy's head snapped sharply back against the wall, felt pain in his shoulder, quailed under the angry lash of Khira's voice. His eyes flew open. She bent over him, shaking him angrily. Her lips were a taut slash, her cheeks hotly flushed. Her eyes blazed.

Anger. He was dependent upon Khira and she was angry. Hurriedly the guide abandoned the trancing room illusion, letting the brothers' voices die. He worked the boy's lips stiffly. "Khira—" Her name did not come hard. The boy was struggling to call it too.

She was not appeased. Adar burned from her eyes, bright for war. "Do you know how many times I've asked you questions and you've pretended you could tell me nothing? And then an Arnimi comes to the throneroom with an instrument in her hand and you talk to her. Now you're going to talk to me too."

"No!" The guide and the boy fought to utter the same word. It emerged a dry husk. "No! I—I can't. I can't—"

"But you can," Khira retorted immediately. Her fingers dug deeper into his shoulder. "You talked to Techni-Verra. You told her your name. Now you're going to tell me the things I want to know. You're going to tell me where you came from. You're going to tell me why you were left in the tower. You're going to tell me what you want here. You're—"

"No!" The guide spoke alone this time, in furious indignation. "The Arnimi tricked me!"

Khira matched his anger. "Yes—she tricked you because she knows all about you. She knows where you came from, who your people are. She knows how you got here, why you came. She knows all about you—and she's never done anything for you."

He had to please her. "And you have done everything," the guide said with forced humility.

"Yes! I've done everything! I've fed you and given you blankets and taught you to speak and cipher. But you ignore my questions and answer hers. And you've changed since the Arnimi came. I talk to you and your face changes, your voice changes, everything about you changes. You're—I don't like you when you change. I don't like you when you're stiff. I don't like you when you're like an Arnimi!"

"I—"

"You're like an Arnimi! You're like one now! You're looking at me like an Arnimi, like you want something from me and when you have it, you won't even see my anymore."

The boy responded to the pain behind her anger and his hand came up in a pleading gesture. The guide snatched it down in panic and tried to make his voice appeasing. "Khira—"

She refused to be appeased. "You—how many times have you done this? How many times have you gone to someone and used them like an Arnimi?"

That she could compare him to the arrogant Bullens, to the deceitful Techni-Verra— But the boy broke through the guide's guard. "Khira— I can't tell you—I can't—even if I knew, I—"

Khira's pupils narrowed, recognizing the change in him. But her anger remained caustic. "Why? Because your guide won't let you talk to me? And tell me this—if your guide guides you, who guides him?"

The guide felt the boy grasping desperately for an answer. "I—don't know. I—"

Fiercely the guide snatched for control. The boy was eager to please Khira. But he could not be trusted to do so without betraying vital information. The guide crushed the boy's windpipe with tightening cords of muscle and the boy's voice became a strangled sob. "He's angry! He won't let me talk! Khira—"

Khira seized his arm, hardened to his distress. "Well, I can talk, and this is what I have to tell you, Iahnerre Rauth-Seven. If you won't answer my questions, I'm going to go downstairs and bar the door on you. If you won't talk to me, I'll leave you here to freeze."

"No!"

"I will." Her eyes were fire and stone at once. They brimmed with her anger. "If you won't talk to me like you talked to Verra, I'll send servants for your corpse next spring."

Frantically the boy leapt free of the guide's control. "You wouldn't!" His hands were clenched, white. "You wouldn't! You've done everything for me, Khira. You've taught me Brakrathi. You've shown me everything in the palace. You've taught me about the plants and animals that grow outside. You've told me about the mountains. When the snow thaws, I have to go there. I have to climb the mountains. And your people—"

Khira drew back from him, her face set. "And after all my lessons, you haven't learned what I am? I'm the imperial daughter of this palace and I have stone in my heart. Yes—my heart is rock. It's hard and cold. If you're still here when my mother returns, the Arnimi will tell her about you. They'll tell her what they've told me and everything else too; they won't tell me more because they consider it demeaning to talk to a child. But when they tell my mother, she will have you taken to the mountain to die. She'll do that and never care. What makes you think I'm softer than she is?"

"Be—because you are."

"I'm not. I'm hard where other people are soft, and if you won't answer my questions, I'll lock you here and never look back."

Her words carried a gritty conviction. The boy's mouth opened in appeal, but the guide was caught in a frenzy of sheer panic. *She meant it; she would lock him here to freeze and never care. He was no more than an Arnimi to her.* A sharp spasm of fear cut off the boy's words. The boy pressed himself against the rough stone wall, his eyes glazing as repeated muscle spasms closed off his breath. The guide drew up the boy's knees and pressed his forehead against them in instinctive retreat.

Khira uttered a fierce cry and shook the boy until his head snapped back against the stone wall. "If you leave me now—if you leave me, I won't come back! I won't come back until the snow thaws!"

The threat hardly touched the guide. He did not even notice the tears in her eyes. His panic seized the boy's throat and choked consciousness from them both. As if from a great distance, an unfamiliar voice spoke to him. It spoke in a droning voice. *Tell her nothing.* The message was repeated, and a hypnotic force uncoiled in his mind, dulling it. *Tell her nothing. Tell her nothing.*

Yes, he must tell her nothing. Because nothing he told her would be right. She could not be appeased and she must not be informed. She had succored the boy but she despised the guide. There was no way to please her now without betraying himself to her.

And the questions she had asked him—if he was the trainer, who had trained him? Who had placed him in authority over the boy? Who had sent them both here? He had answers. But behind those answers, was there meaning—or deception?

Why did he wonder? Why did he doubt—if there were no cause for doubt?

Tell her nothing, tell her nothing, tell her nothing. Desperately the guide threw aside doubt and clung to the voice. It was his lifeline. It would save him when nothing would. He had only to tell her nothing. *Nothing.* And that was easy, so easy, with his head sagging back to his knees, with awareness slipping away on the tide of repeated command.

Tell her nothing. The boy's head lolled loosely against his knees as he lost consciousness.

8/Khira

Khira's anger still rang in the chill tower as she ran down the stone steps and bolted the lower door behind her. But what rang in her heart was hurt and bewilderment. How had Darkchild slipped away from her? She had taught and tutored him from his first day in the palace, she had fed him and given him a warm place to sleep, she had coaxed him free of whatever it was that shadowed him—she had made him her own.

Yet these past days he had undone her making. He had become a stranger to her. All too often he spoke in a changed voice, he looked at her with hard eyes, he pressed her with questions she did not want to answer. Before the Arnimi had come, he would have recognized that she did not want to answer them. Now he was frequently insensitive to her reluctance.

Yet each time she reached a peak of irritation, he slipped back into his old manner and she could not lash out. She could only put aside her anger and wonder at the change in him.

Was this what it meant to be a Rauthimage? Was he some soulless being? Like the mythical benar that lived high in the mountains and rolled down the slopes each spring in invisible avalanche, moaning and crying for lost memories? Certainly Darkchild's memories seemed lost.

They had seemed lost—until today, when he had arrogantly pronounced his name for the Arnimi.

And Khira—she had told him she was stone, hard where other people were soft. But was she? If so, why did his behavior wound her? How could he touch her feelings if they were guarded by a rocky core? If she was stone, why were there tears on her face?

She wiped at them angrily and ran through palace halls, deaf to the echo of her feet. If he would not answer her questions, if he would not show her the courtesy he showed an Arnimi, why should she care if he froze? What was he to her?

She was just stone enough to run to the throneroom and hide herself behind the throne until her heart stopped racing. Then she began to sob. What did it matter that Darkchild didn't answer her questions? Was that the price of her friendship, words he didn't want to give? The Arnimi knew where he came from, who his people were. Techni-Verra had tricked him into telling her his name. But Khira knew the sound of his laughter, the touch of his hand. And where did friendship lie but there, in warmth?

She was weakening. Smothering her tears, she pulled a scroll from the alcove and tried to concentrate on it. If she had not intended her threat, she should never have uttered it. To release him now would be to admit defeat. She ran her fingers down the scroll, trying to distract herself. Darkchild was nothing to her, a boy from nowhere, torn against himself. He was not even whole.

But her eyes would not focus on the scroll. The symbols swam before her, meaningless. She was not stone where Darkchild was concerned. She was butter. Melting, she threw down the scroll and ran back to the watchtower, ran up the stalklit stairs, burst through the upper door.

Darkchild lay on his side on the stone floor, his face grey, one hand outflung. His eyes were open and staring, but he made no sign when she threw herself across him and pressed her ear to his chest. She listened, breathless. His heart beat to a faltering rhythm.

Her own heart quivered with panic. Why was he like this? He had retreated often enough, sitting with his forehead on his knees and his face cold. But she had never found him unconscious on the floor. She rolled him to his back, seized his shoulders and shook him. "Darkchild! *Darkchild!*" When he did not respond, she slapped first his cold cheeks, then his wrists. "Iahnerre!" The name was alien, but if it would call him back . . . "Iahnerre!"

He shuddered and squeezed his staring eyes shut. Khira released him, thinking he was about to waken. But his facial muscles relaxed and he lay completely still again. Sobbing, she pressed her ear to his chest. His heartbeat had become barely perceptible.

She couldn't have destroyed him by shutting him in the cold tower for less than an hour! He had stayed here overnight when he first came. But if she left him here much longer, even the faint throb of his heart might cease. She jumped up, her heart clenching in panic. There was no one she could go to, no one to help her—

Except the Arnimi. She bit her lip, hesitating, then ran to the stairs. If she could carry him down, get him to his bed—

It was hopeless. She was no larger than he and the stairs were steep.

There was no one but the Arnimi. She pounded down the stairs and ran through the halls to their door. It opened and she plunged through the protective screen and peered around urgently.

Three Arnimi approached, one of them Techni-Verra. Choking back panic, Khira summoned as much authority as she could master. "My friend is sick in the tower. I want two people to carry him to his bedchamber." Her voice sounded reedy, thin.

The senior Arnimi's response was aggravatingly deliberate. "The Rauthimage is ill?"

Throttling her anger, Khira turned to Verra. "He's unconscious and there's snow on the floor. We can carry him down, the two of us. He isn't heavy." Wasn't it Verra's fault she had locked him in the tower in the first place?

Verra hesitated, glancing at her superiors. "He isn't in trance with his brothers, heiress?"

Desperately Khira seized her arm. "He's unconscious. I can barely hear his heart." Why had she played for even a moment at ruthlessness? Why hadn't she simply accepted him as he was, with all his inconsistencies?

Verra's superiors eyed her coldly, but her hesitation was brief. "I can see that you are concerned. Tomer, I will return to the conference as soon as possible. If necessary, I'll call back for Medi-Torrens." Quickly she followed Khira.

"Will your medical officer treat Darkchild?" Khira demanded as the metal door closed behind them.

"It probably won't be necessary, heiress. Rauthimages are bred hardy."

Bred. Khira's lips tightened. "Here we breed animals," she snapped. "We have other terms for human generation."

Verra frowned faintly. "I am aware that you do, Khira. But in some places, under some circumstances, these things are different."

And why should Khira be angry with Verra over the fact? When Darkchild was dying in the tower? Fighting to tame her indignation, Khira led way.

Darkchild lay as she had left him, on his back, eyes closed, arms reaching for nothing. Verra bent over him quickly. She tapped his eyelids and pressed his scalp, then stood. "I think we must get him downstairs to his bed and warm him," she decided. "I'll carry his shoulders. You take his feet."

"He—he isn't—"

"I think he will recover when he is warm."

Khira bobbed her head in relief. They inched down the steep stairs tread by tread. When they reached the bottom, Verra assumed Darkchild's full weight while Khira bolted the lower door and led way to his quarters.

Verra catalogued the furnishings Khira had provided Darkchild with a slight elevation of her brows. "You have made him comfortable here." Carefully she laid Darkchild on the bed and examined him again, listening at his chest, lifting each eyelid in turn, lightly slapping his pallid cheeks. She frowned, unconsciously coquetting at her hair. "From what I've read of Rauthimages, I would guess he has been overstressed."

Khira stared at her in puzzled dismay. Did Verra mean he would not recover at all? "I locked him in the tower," she said hesitantly, "but for just a few minutes."

"You did? Why?"

Khira's face colored. "He answered your questions and then wouldn't answer mine."

"Ah." Verra's brows rose. "You questioned him then, after you left me. Harshly?"

Khira was instantly defensive. "He's asked me hundreds of questions since he came here and I've answered them all, no matter how he asked them." And since the Arnimi had come, the manner of his asking had often rankled.

"I know you have taken pains with him. That much is apparent in how quickly he has learned here. But a Rauthimage is not trained to give information—only to gather it. And a Rauthimage is provided with protective programming to prevent him from violating his training.

Can you imagine any better protection against a loose tongue than falling unconscious?"

Khira peered up at Verra with dawning incredulousness. "You mean he can't answer even simple questions? If I ask him where he was born, how he was raised—" But she had asked him those questions. She had tossed them at him at unexpected moments, trying to catch him off guard. He had not answered, but neither had he fallen unconscious.

Verra shook her head. "The harm isn't entirely in the asking, heiress. There are times when it's easy to turn a question aside. Imagine that one of my fellow officers and I decided to have information from you which you knew we should not have. If we approached you separately, whom would you find it harder to resist—my fellow or me?"

"You," Khira said promptly.

"Yes, because you and I have something together that you have with none of the others. We haven't spent a lot of time together, but we have shared bread and kindness."

"And the others are as cold as the glacier," Khira said with venom.

"Exactly. Or so it seems to you. To them—because my science is a softer one, because I was trained differently, because I come from a rural province and was reared within a family while they were raised in nurseries—I seem to be the deviant one. I suffer a dangerous lack of objectivity. I let myself read things into charts and graphs that cannot be proven mathematically or in any other way. If your mother had not insisted that every Arnimi who comes here remain until our evaluation is completed, Commander Bullens would have sent me back to Arnim long ago.

"But your friend has never exchanged kindness with me. He refused my questions easily once he realized I had tricked him—because he had no bond with me. But he does have a bond with you, a deep one. If you questioned him, if you questioned him ruthlessly—"

Khira winced. "Yes. I did."

"Then you placed him in an extremely stressful position. On one hand, I'm sure he wanted to answer you because you are his friend; on the other, his guide could not permit him to answer. It is against his programming. Ultimately his programming took the choice out of his hands and he fell unconscious."

"So I'll never know anything about him," Khira said bitterly.

"You'll know enough when the barohna returns," Verra pointed out.

"Commander Bullens will tell her far more than he told you. And I have observed that she regards you as less of a child than my people do."

Khira's clenched muscles relaxed. That much was true; Tiahna would not keep information from her. But if this were information she would regret having...

Verra bent over the bed again and laid the back of her hand against Darkchild's ashen face. "He is warmer. Let him sleep for a few hours. If he doesn't waken normally then, come for me again. But I think he will recover with no problem."

"And if he needs care from your medical officer—"

Verra sighed. "Then I will try to prevail upon Torrens to come. But I hope that won't be necessary. And if I don't return to quarters for conference now, I will be on penalty for the next three clock-days."

Anxiously Khira watched her out the door. Then she ran after her. "Wait!"

"Yes?"

"At least tell me—how long will be be here? Will he leave before—before very long?"

"I have no way of knowing, heiress. That apparently depends upon the contract."

"The—contract?"

"Heiress, I can't tell you more. The information must come through your mother."

And perhaps it would be information she would forever regret having. Khira let Verra go and returned to Darkchild's chamber, her mind teeming with questions. Where had Darkchild come from? Why had he been subjected to training, to programming? Could he be freed of his guide, of his illusory brothers? Her shoulders sagging, Khira sat on the side of his bed, occasionally touching his hand. No matter what the provocation, she vowed, she would never question him again. Never.

Darkchild recovered slowly from his somnambulent state and for hours that day lay staring at the wall, bleak-eyed and unresponding. Khira watched over his recovery anxiously. It was two days before he began to eat again, three before he left his room. For a full hand of days, he spoke to Khira in cautious monosyllables when he spoke at all. And she was aware that he studied her with silent wariness when she was not looking.

But at last he did recover, although he no longer asked questions.

He leashed his curiosity just as Khira leashed hers. The effort created an atmosphere of constraint between them. They bent over the game-board day after day in silence, tense with the effort not to trespass upon each other. Sometimes Darkchild went exploring the palace alone, trying to answer his own questions, and Khira did not see him for most of a day. Occasionally they experienced a brief revival of mindless conviviality, running through the corridors shouting and laughing until they were exhausted. But even then, as they caught their breath, Khira would look up to find Darkchild gazing at her intently, anxiously.

She watched him too, at odd moments. Since their encounter in the tower, he seemed to have settled into a condition of internal truce. He always spoke in his own voice, never in the harsh demanding voice he had employed sometimes after the Arnimi returned. He seldom moved with the stiff, awkward gait she had seen during the same period. But the effort of maintaining inner truce apparently cost him vitality. He moved at everything more slowly, as if he deliberately held himself back.

When Khira had drawn eighty days on her chamber wall, it was time to open the shutters high in the vault of the throneroom. Khira did so reluctantly. Despite the strain between herself and Darkchild, she cherished their winter isolation. She couldn't guess what spring would bring for either of them.

For three days after opening the shutters, she watched the throneroom mirrors and saw no sign. On the fourth day they flashed once and on the fifth they flashed three times. On the sixth day the light came in a steady beam that bathed the dark throne for minutes. When the light died, the throne briefly continued to glow and Khira retreated to her chamber, evading Darkchild's silent question. He had read the scrolls. He knew that the flashing of the mirrors meant the end of winter. There was nothing she could tell him.

That night they stood side by side in the watchtower, looking out over the frozen valley, neither of them speaking. Snow was mounded on the stone floor beneath the shattered window and chill wind reached into the tower. Yet Khira thought she felt the first balm of spring in the air and the clear night sky revealed a universe of stars.

"You came from one of them," Khira said finally. "You came from one of the stars, didn't you?"

Darkchild stiffened. Silently he turned and left the tower.

Khira's hands clenched into fists. It was the first question she had asked him since he had recovered and he had walked away from it. If Adar had still been in the winter sky, she would have felt anger.

But Adar was gone and she felt only emptiness.

Five days later they sat together over the gameboard when there was an insistent rapping at the heavy metal doors that led to the central plaza. Darkchild's head snapped erect, his eyes dark with quick fear.

"It's the servants," Khira reassured him, and ran to unbolt the door.

Five of the palace caretakers had wakened and tunneled through the snow from their stonehall. Normally sturdy people, they were gaunt now from wintersleep, their eyes hollow, their hands gnarled. They nodded to her gravely. "We will begin to clear the plaza now, heiress," Palus, eldest of the group, governor of his hall, told her formally. "We feel the energy. The barohna comes down the mountain."

"She comes," Khira acknowledged. She felt the energy too, crackling through her nervous system. It had moved her through the palace with increasing restlessness the past three days. "Dig."

Darkchild materialized beside her when she closed the door. His gaze was intent. "Your mother will be here soon."

"In a few days." She was surprised at the bleakness of the words. She and Alzaja had always celebrated when the flashing of the mirrors signalled that Tiahna had melted the snow from the relay lenses stationed upon Terlath's snowbound slopes.

Sensitive to her mood, Darkchild kept silence as Khira retreated to the throneroom. She stood at the center of its great emptiness, peering up at the vaulted ceiling, at the dark mirrors and dull throne. Winter had delivered the silent palace into her custody for seventeen hands of days. Now spring was about to snatch it away.

She turned. Darkchild peered at her with an intensity she had not seen for many days. She sighed. What did it matter if she relented, if she answered the questions she saw struggling just beneath the surface of his self-control? There were many things the scrolls did not explicate. If they had only a few days left together, why thwart each other?

"We can watch them dig from the tower," she said, suddenly eager to escape mirrors that had begun to beam sunlight again and throne that answered with its own dark glow. Surrendering to the spiking energy that signalled her mother's return, she ran from the throneroom and through echoing corridors. Catching her mood, Darkchild ran after her.

They went to the tower to watch each morning for three days. Each day Terlath's rugged silhouette grew more distinct through the dissipating mists of winter. And each day more gaunt people appeared with shovels and barrows to excavate the deep-drifted plaza. They worked with monotonous strokes, moving to the imperative of the approaching barohna.

At first, when Darkchild realized that Khira was receptive to his questions again, he voiced them hesitantly, rationing himself, testing her reaction. But on the second day after the appearance of the servants, he already monitored the activity in the plaza when Khira reached the tower. He turned slowly. "Khira—why do they dig back the snow if your mother can melt it when she comes?"

Khira approached the window reluctantly. Tiahna was nearer today and the energy played restlessly through Khira's nervous system, making her fingers twitch and her toes tingle. Her voice seemed flat, overcontrolled. "It's custom for the people to gather in the plaza to greet her when she comes."

He seemed not to notice her tension. "She looks for them there? She will be angry if they don't come to watch her return?"

Khira shrugged. "They're always there when she comes."

"But if the servants rebelled," he probed, watching intently for her response, "if they didn't want to dig snow when she could easily melt it herself, if they—"

She frowned, unable to fathom the direction and intent of his question. "They *do* want to dig the snow. They want to see her," she said sharply. "When the barohna is near, everyone gathers on the plaza and the families stand in pyramids. They pile the lighter members of the family, the children, the smaller women, on the shoulders of the men and the sturdier women. Every family wants to be the first to see her."

"Because they worship her?"

Was he baiting her? "Do you think my mother is a stone image to be carried from valley to valley? They are eager to see her—that's all. Everyone is eager to see her. She takes the snow from the fields and soon there will be fruit and crops." She hugged herself, trying to control her rising irritability.

He studied her intently. "Khira—there are so many things I haven't asked you. In the first scrolls after the barohnas discovered the sunstone, the people did worship them. And the barohnas ruled the valleys. But in the later scrolls—"

"The people became serfs when the barohnas found the sunstone—

yes. But that changed centuries ago. Now the people are freeworkers. And my mother is simply barohna of this valley."

"But she sits on a throne."

Khira frowned. He seemed to be trying to fit information into some preconceived framework. Perhaps where he came from there were still rulers and serfs.

"She links to the sunstone of the throne—and of the bathing slab in the plaza. She draws the sun's energy and invests it in the stone. Then she discharges it to melt the snow. If she didn't concentrate the sun's energy at this time of year, it would be wasted on the mountainsides and spring would come late to the valley. There wouldn't be time to grow enough crops to feed all the people."

"But she directs the people in their work—like a ruler," Darkchild persisted.

Far on the mountain, a single mirror flashed. A tremor passed through Khira's body. "She—my mother is the brain and the people are the arms and legs. Together they are the body. The body can't live unless the brain directs and the limbs work. The people choose the governors and jurises to govern them in their halls, but my mother selects the people who will oversee the work teams in the fields. She picks those who understand her directions best."

"But even in the halls—"

"She makes no decision concerning the halls unless the juris sends people to her. Then she sits to hear them."

"She settles disputes, you mean."

A second mirror winked brightly in the distance and prickling energy surged through Khira. She turned from the view window, her voice crackling. "Disputes are for stock animals, not for Brakrathi."

Darkchild's pupils narrowed minutely. "You disputed the Arnimi."

Khira colored. "I've watched here long enough," she snapped, pushing past him to the stairs. Sharp spikes of energy danced through her nervous system. Later in the season she would harden to them. She would hardly notice them. But today they made her nerves quiver. And she had no tolerance for questions. She wanted only to run down the stairs—to run through the palace until she was too tired to think. Then she wanted to cry until she could cry no more. At all cost, she wanted to quench thought.

Darkchild ran down the stairs after her and caught her arm. "Khira—"

She twisted away from him with a flash of anger, throwing herself against the corridor wall, her body unconsciously arching into a posture of defense.

Darkchild stepped back, his eyes widening. A long moment passed before he said, "Khira, you're—you're afraid today."

Angry blood flowed to Khira's cheeks. She was afraid—and he didn't know why? "I wouldn't be afraid if it weren't for you!" she snapped. "Soon my mother will be here and the Arnimi will tell her what they told me—to put you into the snow to die. How do you expect me to feel?"

His finely arched brows drew into a tight frown. He wet his lips with the tip of his tongue, thoughtfully. "Why do you care? Why do you care what happens to me?" The query was more curious than probing.

Why indeed? Because he had made a lonely winter short? Because she had taught him to speak much as she might have taught an infant? Because she had knelt hours beside his bed while he lay unconscious? Why did one human care for another? "Wouldn't you care? If I were the one to be put into the snow?" she demanded bitterly.

His lips parted. He said slowly, as if discovering something he had not known before, "I would. Yes, I would care."

"Well, I care too!" Before he could see her tears, she broke free again. She ran down empty corridors, blinded by tears, dimly aware that this time he did not follow.

She cared because he had won his way past the stone in her heart to the flesh. She cared because even the scars of Alzaja's death had not hardened her where she lived. Pain had not come once and put an end to her vulnerability. Instead it had heightened her to new vulnerability.

She pounded through echoing halls until her legs ached, until her mind was numbed. Then she ran to her room and threw herself against the pillows of her bed, sobbing. Winter ended as it had begun, with snow and tears.

9/Darkchild

It was early morning, and the upper halls of the palace held a spectral emptiness, as if the stones waited in hollow silence for the barohna. Darkchild moved along the corridor at a deliberate pace. This sedate gait was one of the tricks he had mastered since Khira had locked the guide in the watchtower. The experience had stirred the guide to a state of chronic anxiety—and frightened, he was amenable to compromise. Darkchild had learned that so long as he did not agitate the guide by darting through the palace impulsively, moving too quickly for the guide to anticipate his direction or intent, so long as he did not screen his thoughts from the guide, so long as he refrained from worrying at questions that made the guide anxious, he could go where he pleased, studying what interested him, ignoring what did not.

On the whole, the equilibrium they had struck served Darkchild well. But sometimes compromise was unsatisfactory, and today was one of those times. Darkchild paused in the corridor outside the printing room. He had been here often these past days, slipping between the tables where during the warmseasons printers inscribed scrolls. It was as if hidden memory drew him here. Whenever he thought of the printing room, of parchment, pens and ink, his fingers contracted involuntarily, as if tightening on the shaft of a pen. And his breath quickened, creating an impatient flutter in his throat. He thought he knew what this meant: that he had taken pen in hand somewhere before...and his hand was impatient to scribe again, to form inked figures that would tell stories only his fingers remembered.

Those stories were exactly what the guide did not want to think about. Frowning, ignoring the guide's discomfiture, Darkchild pushed open the door and stepped into the printing room. The room was cold and smelled of soured ink. Darkchild paused, sampling the distinctive odor. Then, deliberately, he moved across the room. On each long table was a selection of scrolls to be copied. Some of the older scrolls were so brittle Darkchild hardly dared touch them. Others were soft and pliant. Carefully he unrolled a scroll he had not examined before.

It was a tale from early times, a story of sheep that strayed and a herder who searched for them and found a beast like no one had seen before bathing in a mountain pool. Darkchild caressed the parchment, as if he could touch the herder's time with probing fingertips. The early scrolls made him hungry for the world beyond the palace. Mountains, meadows, plains—he had never tasted water fresh-drawn from a valley spring. He had never climbed a slope and looked back over diked fields. And he had a strong sensory curiosity. He wanted to record the texture of every kind of stone with his fingertips. He wanted to see Terlath through all its seasonal moods. The quality of daylight was important to him. And the rush of storm clouds across the valley, the pattern of rain and snow—he had a hunger for them all. Hundreds of experiences awaited him beyond the palace, and each would tell him something about the people who lived here, who they had been, how they had become as they were.

But he had a more immediate hunger: to snatch up a pen, dip it in ink, and let his hand have free rein across clean parchment. However when he reached for a pen, his hands clenched into claws and he jumped back involuntarily, a sharp rise of panic in his throat—the guide's panic.

Darkchild frowned, reluctantly averting his eyes from the pens. It was the same each time he came here. And each time he found that much as he wanted to scribe, he wanted more to preserve the balance he had struck with the guide.

Still he lingered for a while, skirting the tables, occasionally examining a scroll, hoping the guide would be soothed by his desultory activity. There were other things in the palace that seemed to promise memory too: certain utensils in the kitchen, the silk mourning sash Khira had shown him once, a crudely carved pebble he had found on the floor behind the wardrobe in his room. And twice recently thunder had sounded from the mountains and he had found himself crouching and peering behind himself—for something he could not name.

But none of these things promised so much as the pens and ink, and those he could not even touch without disturbing the guide. Finally, dissatisfied, he left the printing room.

A short while later he sat at the gameboard with Khira when a group of workers appeared under the great arch at the entrance to the throne-room. Darkchild glanced up with quick interest. The scrolls told of a sturdy people who had survived on Brakrath against great odds. But the people he had watched clearing the plaza had appeared uniformly gaunt, their shoulders bent, their white hair ragged. And now, seen more closely, they looked no hardier.

One of them, a woman, stepped forward, inclining her head stiffly. "Heiress, Palus sent us to trim the stalk. It has overgrown."

Khira looked up with an irritable frown. "Yes, I watered the pots. I wanted light."

"Now the barohna brings light," the woman said without rebuke and withdrew. The others followed.

Darkchild stood, drawn. He had barely had time to catalogue their appearance: the coarseness of their clothing, the crumpled quality of their flesh, the arthritic stiffness of their limbs. And none had so much as glanced at him. "Didn't they see me?"

Khira slumped back against her cushions, glancing up irritably. "Of course they saw you."

"But none of them said anything."

"What would they say?" Khira's hands tightened on the edge of the playing board. "They have the manners of Brakrathi, not Arnimi."

And it was mannerly not to see a stranger? Darkchild frowned. Khira was tense today, distracted. She moved her gamepieces clumsily, as if she were a learner. And she spoke to him either absently or sharply. He knew he should stay with her, but he was drawn to the people he had glimpsed so briefly. "They won't mind if I watch?"

Khira shrugged, and he jumped from his cushions and ran after the workers.

They had fetched ladders, trimmers and a cart from the store room. They began their work in the corridor nearest the throneroom. At first they seemed constrained by Darkchild's presence, carefully avoiding his curious eyes, never glancing directly at him. But after a time they forgot him and moved to their work without self-consciousness. There was a musty smell about them, clinging to their clothing, to their hair, and their voices were hoarse, as if from a winter's disuse. They worked stiffly, slowly, and talked little. Yet Darkchild observed that there was no confusion among them. Each moved to his or her chore readily, without stepping in the way of anyone else. When one had cut down the overgrown stalks, another stood ready to sweep the stems into the dump-cart and another to wheel the filled cart away.

After watching the cutting and sweeping for a while, Darkchild followed the carter and found that the glowing stalks were emptied in a barren, windowless room beyond the kitchen. When the carter turned from dumping his load and found Darkchild standing in the doorway, he rolled his cart to a halt and gazed fixedly past Darkchild's left shoulder.

Darkchild glanced behind himself uneasily, then stared up at the carter. "Will the stalks rot here?"

The carter inclined his head quizzically, as if harking to some faint sound, but said nothing.

Darkchild bit his lip, puzzled. The carter waited—but for what? Some ordinary courtesy that Darkchild didn't know how to render? Guessing, he said, "My name is Darkchild. Did you—did you bring the stalks here to rot?"

At that the man honored Darkchild's presence with a direct glance. His eyes were grey and sharply alert in his crumpled face, as if winter had tried to quench them and failed. "I'm Rabbus from the seventh hall of Tiahna's valley." He nodded with careful formality. "I bring the stalks here to make root so we will have more for the pots."

Darkchild's eyebrows rose in surprise. He glanced past the carter to where the stalks lay on the bare floor. "But there's nothing here for them to grow in—Rabbus."

Rabbus inclined his head. "Then perhaps they require nothing. Do you intend to stand aside and let me pass, Darkchild from nowhere, when you've told me your hall?"

Darkchild flushed, stepping aside quickly. "I'm—my hall is here. In the palace."

"A warm hall with sound beams." The comment was ceremonial. Briskly Rabbus wheeled his cart into the corridor.

Darkchild ran after him, encouraged. "Rabbus—why didn't you speak to me at first? Before I told you my name?"

Rabbus' matted brows rose in feigned surprise. "Would you speak to a shadow on the wall, Darkchild?"

"No," Darkchild said quickly. "But I'd roll my cart past it without stopping—if I really thought it was a shadow."

Rabbus inclined his head, his eyes glinting in appreciation. "Ah, but there are shadows and shadows. If you suspect the shadow might eventually give you name and hall, it is inconsiderate to injure it. It is as well to be considerate—don't you think, Darkchild?"

"It—yes."

"And if you are considerate and there are people working, it is good not to tax them with questions," Rabbus went on with a sideward glance. "Because if you are considerate, you know there are times when people like to answer questions and times when they do not."

Darkchild nodded, rebuked—not so much for the few questions he had asked as for all the others he had intended to ask. "But you won't mind if I watch—without talking?"

"I'll tell my mates you're not a shadow and none will mind."

They did not, but neither did Rabbus' mates talk among themselves as they worked. As the day went on and they trimmed corridor after corridor, Darkchild was increasingly tantalized by the unstudied efficiency of their work. He watched silently, doggedly testing unspoken questions against their silence.

At midafternoon the workers left the palace without explanation, silently putting down their tools in the middle of a half-trimmed corridor and going without word. Puzzled, Darkchild followed them to the plaza door. Rabbus turned and lifted a single finger in parting salute.

Disappointed, Darkchild went to find Khira. But her chamber door was closed, and when he called she did not answer.

Nor did she join him in the kitchen for the evening meal. He ate uneasily, puzzled at the behavior of the workers, wondering if he had hurt Khira by leaving her alone to watch them. There were things, he began to realize, that he had not gathered from the scrolls—a host of cues and nuances that he would have to gather in person instead.

It was dusk when he discovered Khira's chamber door open and found her at the window of a nearby chamber. She had removed the shutters and night air chilled the very stones of the room. She stood unmoving, her hands clenched at her sides, and from her expression Darkchild thought she was angry because he had left her—until he reached the window and saw the people gathered on the plaza below. They stood silently, men, women and children, peering toward the mountain, shadowed now by dusk. It took him a moment to understand, and then his heart leaped. "Your mother's coming!"

Khira stood like stone, pale and graven. "She's coming. We'll see her light in the night."

Quickly Darkchild's eyes flicked toward the cloud-veiled mountain, toward the gathering darkness there. Khira had sketched her mother for him, tall, bronzed, sunlight her captive. She would come wearing a sunstone circlet at either wrist, and each wristlet would glow with winter sunlight gathered at her mountain retreat. "Will we have to wait long?"

He was surprised to see a tear slip down Khira's cheek. "Yes," she said, making the word bitter. "As long as we wait for dawn."

Darkchild frowned. "Khira—" But something in her face told him it wasn't the time to talk.

And even the sight of her distress did not quench his eagerness. He leaned out the window, his arms resting on the cold stone casement.

Dusk passed into darkness and for a time the sky cleared and stars were visible. Then clouds came again and hours passed. Through them all, the people on the plaza were silent, Khira motionless. Darkchild watched with barely flagging eagerness, occasionally stamping life into his feet or chafing his hands, refusing to let the cold dull him.

It was near dawn when he distinguished a cloudy glow far in the distance, barely perceptible through the last mists of night. As he watched, the light grew more distinct and moved toward him, gliding slowly through the dark. He caught a ragged breath. "Khira—look!"

The light drifted down the lowermost flank of the mountain, a ghostly nimbus, yesterday's sunlight cast against today's pre-dawn darkness. No limb of the barohna showed from within the drifting cloud of light. There was only a gash of brilliance at its center, featureless, floating. But as Darkchild watched, he could imagine Tiahna striding over tumbled rock, striding toward the palace she had deserted months before.

When Darkchild turned from the window, he was surprised to find his lips stiff, his tongue dry. "Khira, can we—can we watch from here? When she comes to the palace?" Did Tiahna expect Khira to wait in the plaza with the others?

Khira lidded her eyes, her face silver-pale. "We always watch from here." A whisper.

Darkchild felt a momentary pang. "Khira—you don't have to be afraid. Not for me." Because that was why she had been angry earlier, why tears shone on her cheeks. She was afraid her mother would listen to the Arnimi and put him into the snow.

She turned, the cold light of dawn silvering her tears. "How can you say that? When Commander Bullens talks to her, when he tells her about you—"

"Khira—"

She shook her head, refusing to let him speak. "When Commander Bullens talks to her and she calls you and questions you—what can you tell her?"

For a moment he was caught by the plea in her eyes. For a moment he wanted to tell her he would find answers for Tiahna if she questioned him. But he bit the lie from his tongue. "I—can't tell her anything, Khira."

Her eyes narrowed in pain. "Darkchild—" She caught his hands, clutching them. "Darkchild, if you could just tell her—if you could just tell her the things you couldn't tell me—I locked you in the tower, but you knew I would come back. My mother won't. If she sends you to the snow, she won't call you back. She—she's never exiled anyone. And she's never turned anyone to ash. But she could do it. If you could just tell her—"

What? Briefly Khira's fear infected Darkchild. Tell Tiahna that sometimes when he heard thunder he was afraid? That he thought there were stories in him that he didn't know how to tell? That there were doors in his mind he could find no way to open? "Khira, I—I don't know anything to tell." Desperately he groped for words to explain his helplessness. *"He* does. *He* knows things—or where to find them. But I don't."

Her hands tightened on his, bruising. *"He?"*

Darkchild caught his breath, surprised he had told her so much. "The guide."

"The guide?" She frowned. "Your guide? The one who tells you what to do?"

But he couldn't explain. "I can't tell you. Khira—I can't tell you about him. And I can't tell her either."

She pleaded silently a moment longer, then dropped his hands in quick hopelessness. She turned back to the window, her lips trembling. "You can't tell her anything. And she's in the orchards now."

He glanced out the window and saw that all across the plaza families had grouped themselves in pyramids, lighter members standing on the shoulders of the sturdier. Momentarily his throat closed. But he had waited a cold night to see Tiahna. With will he drove Khira's fears from mind.

The gliding light passed through the skeletal orchards, across the diked fields. At last Terlath's jagged peaks were limned with dawn and Tiahna herself was visible, tall, bronze, striding toward the palace. A child cried out below and dozens joined her.

"Tiahna comes!"

"The barohna!"

"Warm days! Warm days!"

Darkchild leaned out the window, caught. Even from here, he felt the heat and power of Tiahna's presence. Her features were stern, strong, and her hair fell rough to her shoulders, torn ragged by the winds of the mountain. She wore a woolen shift that might once have been white. Now it was stained and torn and there were streaks of blood at its hem.

Tiahna did not acknowledge the people as she moved across the plaza. She clutched the pairing stone at her throat, and occasionally it surged with light. The glow of the sunstone circlets at her wrists was constant, as if winter sun fought the dawn-darkness of spring.

Tiahna's bathing stone was located at the center of the plaza, oblong, black, dull. Tiahna approached and touched it amost absently with the fingertips of one hand while the pairing stone glowed in the other. The sunstone circlets at her wrists blazed, then dulled, and the bathing stone glowed briefly with diffuse light. Bowing her head, Tiahna closed her eyes and stretched herself full-length upon the stone.

She lay motionless for a long period, eyes shut, face stern. People tumbled from their pyramids and total silence fell across the plaza. Then the sun peered over the shoulder of the mountain, pale, morning-hazed. Tiahna's eyes slid shut and she tipped her head forward sharply to direct her gaze to the rising sun.

Darkchild felt an involuntary tremor, as if he were about to see something that should be secret. "Should—should we watch?"

Khira's answer was barely audible. "We always watch."

He watched. The sun hovered upon the horizon, diffusing energy across mountain and valley alike, across sterile rocky slopes and fields waiting for cultivation, across pasture land and waste land. Then Tiahna caught its orb in her suddenly blazing eyes and drew the energy it diffused to her, concentrating it into a single intense beam.

The beam quivered from sun to glowing eyes, quickly becoming so finely concentrated that it exactly matched the aperture of Tiahna's distended pupils. Mountainside and palace fell into darkness. Even the plaza became jet with blackness.

Darkchild thrust one hand before him and could not see it. All he could see was the concentrated energy that linked sun and barohna. Silently she drew it through her distended pupils and invested it in the black stone slab upon which she lay. The slab began to glow, until it became an ill-defined white radiance at the center of the plaza, Tiahna's form a shadow upon it.

Although he could not see the people, Darkchild knew they had drawn back from the bathing stone. He turned and tried to penetrate the darkness of the chamber. He could feel Khira's arm against his, could hear her irregular breath, but he could not see her. "Khira—"

She clutched his arm, her fingers cold. "Darkchild, if your eyes burn, don't look at the stone."

"But I can't see anything else." There was only the blazing sun-stone—and darkness.

Her fingers tightened. "Darkchild—the stone can blind you. Look toward the edge of the plaza."

Reluctantly he obeyed, but only when the blaze of the bathing stone seemed to fill his consciousness, blocking out every other image. For a long time after he turned away, he saw the glare of the stone as clearly as if he still gazed at it.

As the sun slid up the sky, Tiahna's head moved to maintain direct visual contact. The cold in the room where Darkchild and Khira watched became profound, even when the sun hung at the crest of the heavens, a pale yellow disk. Solitary, immobile, it continued its path down the darkened sky. Tiahna arched back upon the stone slab, her eyes tracking its motion.

At last the sun slipped behind the western mountains. Tiahna lidded her eyes and dusk came diffusely to the valley. The sunset sky was briefly rosy, then fell into hues of violet and indigo.

Slowly the people stirred from the plaza, stiff, silent. Khira continued to stare down, her shoulders rigid. Below Tiahna lay motionless, her woolen shift falling from her in ashes, the flesh beneath dully gleaming. Staring at her, Darkchild felt that she was stone upon stone, that she had never been flesh, that she had never walked, had never done the things other women did. But as he watched, the stone at her throat glowed and her hand moved to clasp it.

He turned to Khira and for a moment was frightened by her pallor. Her face hung like an ashen moon in the dim chamber. "She—will she sleep there tonight? On the stone?"

She spoke bleakly. "She'll lie on the bathing stone until day after tomorrow. Then she'll carry the energy to the fields to melt the snow. That will take three days more."

"And we'll watch here every day?"

"And burn?" She turned and stalklamp cast shadowless light into the hollows of her eyes, haunting them. "No one watches while she finishes drawing the sun and spreading the heat."

He drew back. "Not even from the tower?"

"No—*no*. If you look before she comes to the throneroom a hand from now and strikes the gong, if you go to the tower to watch—"

"What?" His voice was husky.

"You'll burn as fine as the ash of her shift."

His heart bumped once, softly jarring his ribcage. "Khira—there's nothing in the scrolls about that."

"Not in the scrolls you've seen. But there are hidden scrolls. Alzaja ciphered them with me the winter before she left, some of them. That's how the sentence of death was carried out in the troubled times. The people who were condemned came to the plaza on the second day of spring and stood to watch the concentration. And they were turned to ash. If you look, you can see where they stood. When the troubled times were past, black flaggings were put down there."

Darkchild shuddered involuntarily. He had seen the black flaggings from the tower window when the workers shoveled away the snow. "I won't watch," he assured her. "And Khira—I won't leave you."

Instead of being reassured, she drew away from him, her eyes suddenly glinting. "You say that. But you'll leave me if she sends you."

"No—"

"*You will.* You'll leave me just like Alzaja did. You'll promise to be with me—and you'll go." Choking, suddenly sobbing, she pushed past him.

Surprised, he ran after her. But when she reached her chamber, she slammed shut her door, leaving him helpless outside. Twice he knocked. Once he took the knob in hand. But he did not turn it. Instead, after a while, he withdrew, the sound of her sobbing still with him.

Alzaja had left her and now she thought he would too. Slowly, troubled, he went to his own room. It seemed as he had left it the morning before, bright with overgrown streamers of stalklamp. There were cushions scattered on his bed, small artifacts waiting on the bureau for him to touch them. Yet today Tiahna lay on the stone in the plaza.

And in a hand of days, when she came to the throneroom and sounded the gong? Frowning, Darkchild paced his chamber. He had no fear at the prospect of meeting Tiahna. Instead he felt anticipation. To stand near enough to study the texture of her dark skin, to feel the heat of the sun radiating from her sunstone wristlets, to listen for the sun's power in her voice . . . He was eager for Tiahna to come to the throneroom, eager to see the throne catch her light and burn with it.

But Khira knew Tiahna and Khira was afraid. Pensive, Darkchild walked the stone floor. It was long before he slipped into his bed, longer still before he slept. Twin images came to him as he dreamed: Tiahna dark against the glowing stone and Khira graven pale at the window. For the first time, dreaming, he felt something that might be fear—fear that he would leave Khira despite his every promise—and he moaned in his sleep.

10/Khira

The next day the palace seemed caught in vacuum. Its stalklit halls were silent, the very stones like living creatures, their tongues muted in anticipation. Stems of stalklamp took life, dipping down into the chill silence. Khira woke with the memory of harsh words and slipped from her bed to find Darkchild.

She found him in the corridor that led to the plaza, peering up at the tall stone doors at the end of the corridor, at the glare of concentrated sunlight that poured through the narrow scissure between door panels and casement. Khira stopped in the shadows, breath held, and gazed at his intent profile. She was hardly aware that her hands tightened and her lips drew hard.

He felt her gaze and turned, his glance briefly wary. "It's much hotter today." He seemed to test the words against her mood.

She nodded, unconsciously loosening clenched muscles. "We can't come to this side of the palace at all tomorrow. We'll have to stay in one of the other wings until she goes to the fields."

Darkchild's brows arched. "And the day after—when she goes to the fields?"

"Then it will be cold again. Almost like winter—for three days." But without the sense of unstructured time stretching ahead. Instead there would be—*should have been*—sharp anticipation of the freedom of the warmseasons. Biting her lip, Khira turned away. If they had only five days and she ruined them with her anger, the memory would be forever gall. "And after that it will be spring and I'll show you the valley," she said quickly, as if she could convince herself with the words. But she was aware that he studied her, weighing the strained tone of her voice against the promise of her words. And the effort of keeping back tears was painful.

The next five days passed slowly, as if they were caught up in some ceremonial ordeal, able neither to escape it nor to hasten its conclusion. Whenever Khira felt the rise of anger, of fear, of the tearful sense of impending desertion, she quickly damped it. But she knew Darkchild heard more than she said, saw more than she let her face tell, and sometimes his silence was more than she could bear.

By night she slept uneasily. Once she dreamed vividly of Tiahna. In her dream, she saw Tiahna slip from the glowing bathing stone and cross the plaza. As she approached the fields, banks of snow and ice melted before her and frost-hard soil turned to mud. Although Khira had never witnessed the spring melting, she visualized it in minute detail. And she woke with a cry of pain when Tiahna's radiant cloud touched a small animal and turned it to ash—a small animal with eyes she knew, intent eyes, questioning eyes.

The next day Khira was silent, knowing that beyond palace walls Tiahna moved as in her dream.

Finally on the sixth day she and Darkchild waited in her chamber for the sound of the gong. When it rang, Khira took the shutters from her window with trembling hands. Instead of snow, mud and water stood in the valley. The air was clouded with moisture and Terlath was lost in steamy clouds. Darkchild drew a disbelieving breath.

"It's time for the sharing," Khira said, turning from the window. And an emptiness far more disturbing than fear took hold of her, a protective numbness so profound her own words seemed distant. "Come."

By the time they reached the throneroom, it was crowded with people from the halls, pale, cold, crumpled. Tiahna sat upon the softly glowing throne, her eyes hooded, her flesh burned black. She had not taken time to trim the singed strands from her hair or to wash mud from her feet. Her hands lay motionless on the arms of the throne and the pairing stone hung dark at her throat.

Darkchild halted, and Khira's heart hurt when she saw how he looked at Tiahna—breathlessly, as if she were a myth taken flesh. "We sit to the left of the throne," she said, drawing him through the crowd to the dais. The sunstone throne radiated warmth, but Darkchild seemed not to notice. He perched on the edge of the dais, peering up at Tiahna with parted lips.

At a gesture from Tiahna, Palus struck the gong again. Without instruction, the people formed a line that wound through the throneroom and into the corridor. When Tiahna raised her hand again, the line began to move, each person coming before the throne and pausing, hands folded, to stand briefly in the warmth of the sunstone. Through the ceremonial sharing, the untended mirrors flashed intermittently, making the throne pulse with light. Tiahna sat unmoving except for the occasional flicker of an eyelid. Darkchild stared up at her in breathless silence, every pore open to her presence.

It was mid-afternoon when the sharing was done and Tiahna closed her eyes again. Darkchild shot a wordless question at Khira. She shook her head, her stomach suddenly leaden, her shoulders and arms weak. It was time to stand, to speak...

Before she could do either, the abrupt clatter of boots announced the arrival of four Arnimi. Darting a glance at her mother, Khira caught the slight tightening of Tiahna's lips before she opened her eyes.

"Goodsummer, Barohna," Commander Bullens said, stepping forward with stiff ceremony. He had groomed carefully for his audience with Tiahna. His lank grey hair was combed back smoothly from the crown of his head and he had plucked his brows and underscored his prominent eyes with a thick-pencilled black line.

"Goodsummer, Commander." Tiahna's voice was husky with disuse. "I trust you found our mountains of interest again this winter."

A sharp pang brought Khira to her feet. "Mother—" But Tiahna silenced her with a raised hand.

And Commander Bullens spoke as if she had said nothing. "We find everything on Brakrath worthy of study, Barohna: your mountains, your palace, the persons of your people." He permitted a small, chill smile to touch his lips. "We hope the Council of Bronze will kindly grant us another year's extension to continue our studies."

Absently Tiahna's fingers rose to the stone at her throat. "The Council has granted you an extension every year since your arrival, Commander."

His smile grew and became smug. "Yes, and this year we are in a position to return some favor for your continued hospitality." He glanced covertly at Darkchild. "While we studied in the mountains this winter, while your palace was deep beneath the snow—"

"*Mother*—"

Tiahna stirred restively. "Speak plainly, Commander. My intelligence is as sound as it was last fall."

Bullens tossed lank hair off his collar, glancing irritably at Khira. "Very well. While you were gone, a ship of the Rauthfleet came and deposited an image here—the image your daughter has brought with her today."

Khira saw a ripple of tension tighten Darkchild's face. Her eyes flashed. "He is not an image," she said angrily. "He is my companion and he has a name: Darkchild. And nothing the Arnimi tell you about him is true!"

For the first time Tiahna looked directly upon Darkchild. Her impassive gaze brought him to his feet, stiffly, his lips parted. Tiahna frowned, clasping the stone at her throat. "So he is not one of yours, Commander Bullens?"

Bullens colored. "You know we brought no personnel for creche and training facilities. This is a Rauthimage."

Tiahna continued to gaze at Darkchild. "You will have to define the term, Commander. I see a male child, of the same age as my daughter. He is not one of my people nor apparently one of yours. Whose child is he then?"

Bullens stroked back his smoothly brushed hair, recomposing himself. "Properly no one's, Barohna. His predecessors had their origin in a cell specimen taken illegally from a man named Birnam Rauth one hundred and thirty years ago. His creators are the Benderzic, a ship race—a human strain that has never taken a world of its own. They inhabit a constellation of mother ships orbiting a small yellow sun in the vicinity of Betelgeuse. At the time they proclaimed autonomy, their gene pool was too limited to assure normal offspring over a period of generations. They chose a specialized form of reproduction to overcome that limitation: imaging.

"A cell scraping is taken from the parent, male or female, put through a series of procedures, and an offspring is grown from each separate cell. Some are implanted into human uteri. Others are grown entirely in the laboratory, as in the case of the Rauthimage—although it is not properly an offspring of the Benderzic but a tool."

Displeasure passed briefly over Tiahna's features. "You have told me a number of incredible things in the years of our acquaintance, Commander."

Bullens smiled, a chill baring of teeth. "I'm telling you nothing incredible now, Barohna. Consider. Each human body cell contains the genetic information required to reproduce the characteristics of the original. It is only a matter of stimulating a single selected cell to reproduce and then of stimulating the multiplying mass of cells to differentiate and take on the various specialized functions of the human body. The image you see here is one of hundreds identically grown, programmed, then dropped throughout this galaxy and others by the Rauthfleet."

Tiahna inclined her head, her singed hair falling over her sun-blackened shoulders. "I assume then that the Rauthfleet is an entire fleet operated by this child's—siblings?"

"No, Barohna. The Rauthimages have no hand in Rauthfleet operations. The fleet is simply a group of ships given over to producing, programming and distributing Rauthimages—a lucrative operation. It contributes considerably to the Benderzic's ability to maintain autonomy." His thin lips quirked in an arrogant smile. "Of course I advised your daughter immediately upon finding a Rauthimage here."

Khira surged forward angrily. "Mother—"

Tiahna raised one hand. "You advised her—how, Commander?"

"I told her to escort the Rauthimage to the door and lock him outside to freeze. She chose to ignore my advice—as you can see—and so now it is up to you to dispose of the image."

Tiahna's gaze returned to Darkchild, lingering until the blood ran from his face. "Is there some particular reason I should dispose of him, Commander Bullens?"

Khira knew Tiahna's moods, knew that her disinterested tone hid anger. And her anger, Khira realized with quick elation, was not directed at Darkchild. It was directed at Commander Bullens as he postured in his dress uniform, stroking at his lank hair. *She despises you as much as I do,* Khira mocked him silently, pleased.

But Bullens was insensitive to Tiahna's mood. "In the first place he exists without the consent of Birnam Rauth, the man from whom he was imaged. The cells from which he derives were taken illegally and by force. He has no right to independent existence under the circumstances."

"Birnam Rauth himself has demanded that the images be destroyed?"

"Birnam Rauth is a hundred and twenty years dead, Barohna." Momentarily Bullens lidded his eyes. "He was a resourceful man but careless of his safety. The Benderzic have had to program considerably more caution into his images."

"But before he died, he requested the termination of these images?" Tiahna persisted.

Bullens was scornful. "Apparently he never recognized the gravity of the offense. But my people recognize it and are repelled by it—as I am sure you are. And there is a more immediate reason for disposing of him: the threat he poses to your people."

"Ah—and what is the nature of that threat, Commander?"

He flicked at his hair. "Your isolation from the mainstream of human civilization has given you false confidence, Barohna. You are not invulnerable."

"No one is invulnerable. I am far less vulnerable than most."

"And your people are far more vulnerable than many," he said smoothly, as if the evaluation pleased him. "This image has one purpose here—one only. That is to learn everything possible about Brakrath, its resources, its people and culture—and to relay what he has learned to the Benderzic."

Tiahna's fingers curled around her pairing stone. For a moment its light glowed from between her fingers. When she spoke, her voice was husky, intimate. "In other words, his purposes here are the same as yours—to learn about us and to communicate to others what you have learned."

Bullens frowned faintly. "His goals and purposes are entirely different from ours, as different as his origins. We have come to analyze your world and your way of life for scholarly purposes."

"And he?"

The single female Arnimi stepped forward, her uniform stiff, her bearing stiffer. "Baronha, you think you see a child here, an ordinary human child. But no, this is a data-gathering instrument, nothing more—a tool. Birnam Rauth was an explorer, a man who flirted at the very edges of human civilization. He had very special qualities of mind:

resourcefulness, a probing curiosity, and a particular ability to form data into patterns. This image possesses those qualities and in addition he has been programmed in various ways to increase his utility to the Benderzic.

"He appears harmless to you. Many hosts even find him appealing. But if you permit him to live, he will study your resources, your customs, your weaknesses and limitations. He will learn about your land, your mountains. He will learn what grows here, what minerals are available to be extracted. He will learn how you can be overthrown and how your people can be welded into a slave labor force. He will learn everything you permit him to learn.

"Then the Benderzic will send a ship for him and draw what information he has gathered from him and place it in databanks very similar to our own. They will sell that information to the highest bidder."

Khira drew a shivering breath. She recognized Tiahna's mood now, her scorn for Bullens and his arrogance. But if she believed the female Arnimi—*if what the woman said were true*—

Fiercely Khira turned on the Arnimi. "Let them come for him! We won't let them have him!"

Bullens reacted with a cold flash of irritation. "Then they will take him by force."

"If they can find him! He doesn't have to stay here. There are mountains—and hundreds of valleys. He can hide anywhere. We—"

The female Arnimi tossed her head emphatically. "Heiress, you could bleach his hair white, put blue lenses in his eyes, make his skin as fair as your own, and the Benderzic would find him. There is a small unit embedded deep in his heart muscle. They can pick out its signal from the stratosphere of your planet and home on it with great precision."

"Then we'll remove it!"

"And kill him in the process. The device contains a minute amount of extremely potent poison—which it will release into his bloodstream at the slightest trauma to the heart muscle. No, they will find him easily."

"And thereafter," Bullens said, "he will disgorge every bit of data he has accumulated for sale to whomever will pay most to exploit Brakrath. No matter if he swears he will say nothing. He has no control over the process by which the Benderzic program their databanks directly from his brain tissue."

Distractedly Khira noted Darkchild's rigidity, his pallor. She glared at Bullens, groping for some definitive argument. "That's not true! No one would send a child to spy! No one—"

Tiahna silenced her. "Yes, Commander. Why would anyone send a child to gather information he can hardly be expected to understand?"

"But who learns more readily than a child?" the female Arnimi countered. "The younger the child, the greater the ability to assimilate language and cultural nuances. And the less ready his hosts to dispose of him. Virtually all human cultures conserve human young. The surprising thing is that they've sent a Rauthimage as old as this one. He has obviously had previous assignments. But he will have no memory of those. And he needn't understand the information he gathers. He need merely record the raw data to be transferred to the Benderzic databanks and interpreted there."

Tiahna nodded, dismissing the Arnimi's argument. "In any case, there is little here to be exploited."

"There is a great deal to be exploited," Bullens said immediately. "I can show you reams of data about the mineral content of the mountains to the south. Your own Terlath has deposits valuable enough to make export mining extremely profitable. And we have documented dozens of unique plant specimens. I can project commercially feasible uses for many of them.

"On the other hand, you have no military strength and you have a potential slave labor force numbering into the hundreds of thousands. A winter strike, when the barohnas are in their mountain retreats and the people are in wintersleep, would meet virtually no resistance."

Khira chilled. But Tiahna remained aloof from Commander Bullens' arguments.

"And in addition to the conventional resources, Barohna, there is the sunstone. Perhaps you don't appreciate the value of a block of stone no larger than your throne which can absorb sufficient energy to melt the snow from a valley this size—or to raze entire mountain ranges. Because I appreciate very well that you use only a tenth of the capacity of your stones."

Tiahna considered him with remote impassivity. "I use only a hundredth of the capacity of my stones, if that. Only what is necessary to maintain a valley this size. And I have capabilities you haven't guessed at, Commander. But I stress the personal pronoun: *I* use the stones.

There are just four hundred living barohnas on Brakrath. Without us the stones are useless."

"To your people, yes. To mine perhaps. But there are commercial combines that would gamble on finding ways to use the sunstone. The Benderzic may not have sent the image here on speculation, you know. They may have a sponsor for his services, some group that already suspects Brakrath is worth its attention."

For the first time Tiahna brought the full force of her attention to bear on the Arnimi, studying him from deep-set eyes, her voice falling to a husky whisper. "It seems you know enough to endanger Brakrath yourself, Commander."

Bullens flushed. "We do not deal in information."

"Yet you plan to disseminate the information you gather."

"To responsible scientists and scholars, yes. But never for gain. We will not sell a scrap of information."

Tiahna's long fingers tapped a measured beat upon the arms of the throne. "And none of your responsible scientists or scholars will sell a scrap of information either? Despite the value you ascribe to data about Brakrath?"

Bullens' prominent eyes bulged with quick anger. He tossed the hair off his collar with a flick of his head. "People of the caliber of those who will be privy to our study do not deal commercially in information."

Khira smiled with savage pleasure at his discomfiture. *Yes, she despises you.*

"I see." Tiahna's fingers drummed. She leaned forward, her hair falling across her scorched shoulders. "Of course you are my only source of information about the behavior of all those peoples beyond Brakrath. I have no one else to consult."

Bullens' voice crackled with impatience. "Then you must take my word, Barohna, that if you permit the Rauthimage to live, you place your sovereignty at peril."

"And if I permit you and your colleagues to live?"

For a moment Bullens seemed not to understand. Then his florid face drained. "We have enjoyed your hospitality for fourteen years."

"Yes." Tiahna leaned back, pleasure playing lightly at her lips. Khira could see it there. "Yet you understand me so poorly that you don't know if I'm threatening you or toying with you. You don't know if the Council is permitting you to amass a fund of information which only we will see, or if we intend to let you return to Arnim one day."

Bullens' lips seemed stiff. "The Council has permitted us to augment our research staff from Arnim three times in the past ten years."

"We have permitted you to bring in fresh personnel, yes. Under the terms of agreement, however, you have not been permitted to send personnel or data back to Arnim. You don't know, do you, if you are our guests or our prisoners? You have always asked if you could stay, never if you could leave." She smiled faintly. "This winter a breeterlik wandered into my mountain quarters looking for prey. You know the breeterlik, Commander. You have hand weapons that could destroy it despite its size—if you kept your wits. I didn't need a weapon. I drew energy from my wrist-stones and the breeterlik fell in ashes.

"I can render this boy ash in a fraction of a second. Within the same quarter moment I can do the same to you and your companions. Why shouldn't my daughter have a companion until I can give her another sibling?"

Commander Bullens gathered at visibly dissolving stores of nerve. "Barohna, this is no companion. This is not even a human. He is the image of a man who died over a century ago. And his training has made him a creature of conditioned reflexes, nothing more. He appears to respond to the stimulus of the moment, but actually he responds only to the instruction of his guide."

"As you respond to the instruction of your superior on Arnim? Even though you have not seen him for fourteen years?"

Bullens' features tightened into grimness. "There are two ways to prevent this image from betraying you. You can wipe his deep brain centers and leave him a vegetable, if you have that ability—or you can dispose of him entirely."

Again a shadowed smile lingered on Tiahna's lips. "I hope you will remember that you prescribed the suitable measures for dealing with a guest who has become unwelcome." She raised one hand in a dismissing gesture. "We'll talk again, Commander."

The four Arnimi seemed not to comprehend. They stood frozen at the center of the polished floor.

Tiahna repeated her dismissal. Lips seaming, Bullens wheeled and stamped from the throneroom. His companions followed, stricken. The clatter of boots turned their recessional into flight.

Their discomposure was fuel to Khira's flame. Her eyes flashed with triumph. "Darkchild can stay then!"

Sighing, Tiahna leaned back against the polished throne, closing her eyes. Absently she caressed her pairing stone. "Did I say that, daughter?"

"You said—" Khira surrendered her elation reluctantly. "You said—"

"I asked the Arnimi why my daughter should not have a companion until she has a sibling to occupy her."

"Then—Darkchild will be my companion," Khira declared. "The things the Arnimi said about him—"

"They are to be considered."

"No! They're lies! They told you lies!" The words emerged shrilly, unconvincingly—because Khira had observed Darkchild's curiosity herself, his determination to master the Brakrathi language, the searching questions he asked.

"Perhaps they did," Tiahna said. "Even so, I will have to know much more about your friend before I decide whether he can stay." Slowly her deep-set eyes opened and rested upon Darkchild. He gazed into them as if held in spell.

"I'll tell you everything you need to know about him!"

"And how do you know what questions I intend to ask him, child?"

"I—I know everything important. He's—he's told me everything."

"I doubt that he's told you what I need to know." Tiahna sighed, deeply, and clasped her pairing stone. When it dulled, she said, "Rahela needs me now. Bring your friend to me tomorrow at first gong, after I have slept. I will talk with him then." She lidded her eyes, dismissing them.

Khira caught Darkchild's hand and drew him away, hardly noticing his stunned gaze. Tiahna would question him at first gong. Twelve hours until she found he could not answer her questions—would never answer them.

And then? Khira had never seen her mother ash so much as a stingmadder. But Tiahna had bid Alzaja a tearless farewell—and five daughters before her. And Darkchild was nothing to her.

A spy instrument. If she were to believe the Arnimi, Darkchild was nothing more than a data-gathering instrument, dropped by a soulless people to determine if Brakrath was a ready victim for exploitation. Khira halted in the corridor beyond the throneroom, trying to order her thoughts. But they eluded her, lashing out chaotically in every direction.

"Khira—" Darkchild's voice was thick.

She drew breath in a half-sob. "I have to think. I have to...Go to your room and I'll—I'll come there later. When I've had time to think." She could not imagine the depravity of a people who lived by exploiting others. How did they structure their private lives? Did sister fight sister for food and trinkets? Were Benderzic young trained to subordinate each other to the greed of the strongest? Or did the women who governed them see that their venality was directed entirely outward?

"Khira—"

She gazed at him distractedly. At least he was not one of them. He was their victim instead. His very flesh had been taken by force from Birnam Rauth. And his mind, deliberately programmed—

"*Please*—I'll come to your room later."

He honored her distress with a silent nod and slipped away. She turned back down the corridor, her mind racing. If only he could lie when Tiahna questioned him—

If only he could lie...

Khira frowned, her thoughts turning in a new direction. Why hadn't the Benderzic simply programmed him to lie? Then he could have told her any tale he pleased about his people and his origins. And tomorrow he could tell Tiahna the same tale: that he was a stranded traveler, separated from his people by accident; that someone who wished his family ill had abducted him and abandoned him here; that he was a student sent to study Brakrath ways; that—

But he could tell Tiahna none of those things. He had not been taught to lie. Caught in her thoughts, Khira paced the corridor. She looked up in surprise when Techni-Verra spoke; she had not heard the Arnimi woman's approach. "Khira—were you in the throneroom when Commander Bullens spoke with your mother?"

"I was there. Verra—"

"He says your mother threatened to hold us here indefinitely—to terminate us if we try to leave. He's going to message Arnim command immediately."

Terminate. It was like Bullens to use a word that had neither flesh nor blood. "She was toying with him," Khira said impatiently. It surprised her that Verra didn't understand that. "He tried to tell her the Council of Bronze couldn't protect Brakrath. And he tried to tell her Darkchild was nothing but an image—something you see in a mirror." Insubstantial, without independent life.

Was he only that, a shadow cast on a reflective surface? She could not believe it. No more than she could long believe he was only a data-gathering instrument.

"It's—it's only a term, heiress," Verra said, distracted. "A translation. There are any number of words we could use if you spoke Arnimi. But Commander Bullens is very upset. He wants us to leave immediately. He's going to call for fire-support ships from the nearest CoSignators."

Khira shook her head, rejecting Verra's digression. "Verra—why can't Darkchild lie to my mother when she questions him tomorrow? If he could tell her he's never heard of the Benderzic, if he could tell her—"

Verra ran a splayed hand through her hair, disarranging it. "Child, we're talking at cross-purposes. The threat your mother made Commander Bullens—"

Khira flung out her arms in frustration. "Verra, she was toying. She was angry. If you had spoken to her instead of Commander Bullens, she would have said nothing. And he won't be able to reach his command anyway. That was part of the agreement with the Council, that no messages be sent off-planet unless they're monitored by a member of the Council. That's why all your message-casters had to be turned over to the Council when your group was given permission to quarter here."

"Yes, yes, of course. But Khira, Commander Bullens didn't turn over all the casters. He kept one, a small unit."

Again Khira was surprised by Verra's ignorance. "I know. Alzaja showed it to me three winters ago."

Verra became very still. "She—she couldn't have. We told no one about it. It looks—like another kind of instrument entirely."

"Yes, a weather instrument. Don't you remember Commander Bullens let Alzaja use your databank keyboard and screen the winter she was learning to read your language?" Alzaja's interest in Arnimi was an enthusiasm Khira had never shared. "She was screening inventory lists and she learned that one of your weather instruments was really a message-caster."

Verra's face was suddenly ashen. "She—"

"She told my mother of course."

"The barohna knows we have a message-caster in our quarters?"

"She knows it's there. But it hasn't been useful for three years." Khira suppressed a momentary pang at Verra's distress. "Some of its components were very delicate."

"Yes," Verra said softly. "They were. Very delicate."

Impulsively Khira seized her arm. "Verra, my mother won't hurt you. She was toying with Commander Bullens—because he's arrogant. But she's going to talk with Darkchild tomorrow, and if he can't lie to her, if he can't tell her he's a lost traveler, that he's never heard of the Benderzic—Verra, why can't he tell her that? Why didn't the Benderzic teach him to lie?"

Verra finally seemed to focus upon Khira's concern. She clasped Khira's hand, shaking her head. "Khira, sometimes I think we take the information in our databanks too literally. We've told you what the Benderzic intend when they produce a Rauthimage. They intend to send out a child who presents the semblance of a human but performs with the precision and predictability of a machine. Certainly that child should be able to lie to your mother, to you and to me—effortlessly. A lie should have no meaning to him.

"But the Benderzic are working with human flesh. And from what I've learned of Birnam Rauth, he was a man who trusted his life to his own senses and resources and little else. Certainly not an easy man to subdue, even at the level of a single cell. Your friend probably shouldn't have slipped into stress-state under less than physical torture. He shouldn't have cared enough for you to reach that level of distress—if his programming were fully effective."

Yet he had. Khira groped to clarify her thoughts. "Then—a Rauthimage shouldn't care for anyone?"

"I doubt a properly programmed Rauthimage cares for anything but his guide and his brothers. But there is something else we haven't considered, heiress. A Rauthimage is first sent out at a very young age—before his fourth birthday. He is most valuable when he is very young—when his mental capacities are fully plastic. The major part of his programming is completed before that age. Your friend has had at least seven years then to outgrow his programming. And the programming—even the refresher programming the Benderzic impose between missions—is suited to a much younger child than your friend. If the Rauthfleet retrieved Darkchild from his last assignment and dropped him again without realizing that his programming had partially failed, that he was outgrowing it—"

"Then he wouldn't be as Commander Bullens says! He would be—"

"We don't know how he would be," Verra cautioned her. "All we know is that he wouldn't be as the Benderzic intended him."

Khira's pulse sang with momentary elation. It died almost immediately. "But tomorrow then, when my mother calls us—" What Verra said accounted for the difference between Darkchild as Khira knew him and the person Commander Bullens insisted he should be. But what help would that be when Tiahna questioned him?

Little.

None.

Verra felt her distress and responded to it. "Khira, perhaps you're letting yourself be frightened unnecessarily too."

"I—" Dumbly Khira shook her head. "I don't know." Perhaps after Tiahna had rested, she would accept Khira's word that Darkchild offered no threat. Or perhaps when he could not answer her questions, Tiahna would simply dismiss him until another time.

Perhaps. It seemed unlikely.

But if they left the palace before Tiahna could question Darkchild—

The snow was melted from the valley now. The fields were ponds of mud. But she and Darkchild could run along the tops of the levees until they reached solid ground.

And then run where? To the mountain, where snow still lay deep and predators were waking hungry from wintersleep? Khira was surprised to find she clutched Verra's arm. She squeezed it urgently. "Verra, she won't harm you. I promise it." Then she turned and ran.

Her feet clattered down the corridor, up the tower stairs. Cloud hung dense over the valley, shrouding the mountains. Even Terlath's lower slopes were lost. The air would be unstable for days, cold air masses from the mountainside rushing down into the valley, warm air from the valley rising to form towering clouds. There would be storms; thunder would bring avalanches grumbling down the mountainside.

But they would not have to climb far to reach the tunnel that led to Mingele's valley, deserted for almost three centuries now, since Mingele's last daughter had died without bronzing and Mingele's powers had waned. The snow would be as deep in Mingele's valley as on the mountain. There was no barohna to bring early spring. But they would have Mingele's palace for shelter and game for food. They would be safe there for a time.

Perhaps a time was all they needed. If Khira could tutor Darkchild to claim to be something other than a Rauthimage—

For the first time since she had locked Darkchild into the tower so many hands ago, Khira found hope. She had taught him to speak, to cipher, to play board games. Now she must take him to Mingele's valley and teach him to lie. Quickly she slammed down the tower stairs and ran to the kitchen to pack supplies. Her heart hammered with elation, counterpoint to her running footsteps.

11/The Guide

The guide fought his way from dreams of ice and fire, perspiring, and pushed himself erect in bed. Beyond the palace thunder rolled, the voice of the mountain. Stiffly, troubled, the guide left his bed and unshuttered his window. Below, the plaza was deserted under the occasional trembling brilliance of lightening. Cloudy mists closed around the darkened bathing stone and the smell of night was the smell of wet soil. Somewhere a solitary cock celebrated some remembered dawn.

Remembered. The guide turned from the window and stared bleakly across the room. For Darkchild thunder carried the promise of memory. It brought alien images into his dreams and made him toss and strain for them. But the guide knew he must not be permitted to touch them. There was not just memory in Darkchild's dreams—there was loss and aching pain. More pain than Darkchild could bear if he came upon it at the wrong moment.

The guide retreated from the window, bleakly whispering the terms of the contract by which he was empowered:

To guide the boy in strange places.

To keep his body safe and fed.

To prompt him to inquire and explore.

To urge him to learn and know.

To divert him from knowledge which was interior.

To—

The guide started as his door swung open and Khira hurried into the room. For a heart-stopping moment he thought Darkchild's dreams had summoned her.

But she was urgent with some other concern. "Darkchild?"

The wardrobe and bureau cast shadows along the far walls of the chamber. Instinctively the guide edged toward them, speaking with Darkchild's voice. "I couldn't sleep."

Khira frowned, momentarily distracted by the tension in his voice. But her own concern was uppermost. "I packed supplies for us and took heavy clothes from the storeroom," she said hurriedly. "They're downstairs in the kitchen."

The guide understood at once. She intended to take Darkchild from the valley rather than permit Tiahna to question him. "We're leaving."

"Yes. And we have to be out of the valley by dawn." She turned toward the door, then turned back when he did not immediately follow. "Darkchild, we have to go now, before anyone wakes."

Yes. Before they could be stopped and brought back to the palace. Still he hesitated. *To guide the boy in strange places; to keep his body safe and fed...* He was charged with these duties. And beyond the palace were beasts and perils.

But within the palace was Tiahna. Softly the guide shuddered, remembering her deep eyes and the power she held. She slept tonight, but tomorrow she would send for Darkchild and question him.

Unconsciously the guide's hand rose to his throat. Darkchild could not lie, and the guide knew that if he faced Tiahna in Darkchild's place, he would not be able to speak at all. His windpipe would close and he would fall unconscious. Panic squeezed a premature beat from his heart. Why *had* the Benderzic sent him out without the protection of a lying tongue? It seemed such a simple defense, to glibly tell Tiahna some tale of a fallen ship and lost people.

Tensely he stepped from the shadows. "I have to put on my boots. I'll meet you in the kitchen."

Khira studied him for a moment, frowning, then hurried away.

The guide didn't notice until he tried to close his boots that his hands shook. He clenched his fists and stared at them with a rising sense of helplessness. All the things he had been promised: that he would not be troubled by fear, by uncertainty—not only were they untrue; when he tried to remember the person who had promised him, shadow fell across his memory and he could not see. If he was to believe the Arnimi, his masters were the Benderzic—but he could not remember their faces.

And he *was* troubled by fear and uncertainty. Since the day Khira had locked him in the tower, they had been his constant companions. It was hard to believe his former arrogance. Now he saw danger in every corner, heard threat in every sound. Even Khira frightened him when she frowned, when she spoke sharply—frightened him so much he was afraid to answer her. That he left to Darkchild, because Darkchild at least knew how to please her.

But now the guide realized, sitting on the edge of his bed, that he had left too much to Darkchild. For hands of days—out of fright, out of anxiety—he had permitted Darkchild to go where he pleased, to touch and sample and question at will. He had interfered only in moments of sharpest panic. He had abdicated all responsibility, conscious not of the contract and his obligation to enforce it, but of his own fear.

With will, the guide stood. If he could think of fear as a tool, a warning, surely he could master it. And by that measure, uncertainty was a tool too, a sign that he must give more thought to his activities, that he must not let events sweep him along. That he must meet his responsibilities.

Now, tonight—there was thunder, and thunder moved Darkchild to reach for images that hovered just beyond the brink of consciousness. The guide must forestall that seeking, even if it meant mastering Darkchild and going with Khira himself. Even if it meant facing her anger and scorn. Because she had made it clear in the days after the Arnimi came that she despised him.

Quickly, before his resolve could slip away, the guide left his chamber and hurried down the corridor toward the kitchen. All he had to do, he told himself over the anxious thump of his heart, was go with her as Darkchild would go, answer her as Darkchild would answer her. If he were careful, perhaps she would not even notice, in the dark.

But for a moment, when he stepped into the kitchen and she turned and glanced sharply in his direction, he wavered. She would know him immediately from his stiff gait, from the timbre of his voice, from a dozen other clues.

Even so, better Khira's anger than Tiahna's fire. "I had trouble fastening my boots," he excused himself, trying to keep the harsh note from his voice.

She nodded distractedly. "Here—try on these leggings. If they don't fit, I'll have to go back to the store room." She frowned at the bulging packs. "Everything else is packed."

The leggings fit and within a short time they slipped from the palace, each carrying a pack and a bundle. The guide stayed well behind Khira, hoping she would not notice how awkwardly he moved.

On the plaza, the night air was at once steamy and chill, as if the heat Tiahna had brought to the valley struggled to repel the intruding cold of the mountains. They ran across the plaza and Khira seemed not to notice that the guide moved stiffly. But when they climbed the broad steps that led to the tops of the leveed fields, he forgot himself. He peered into the turbid water that stood in the fields. And stopped. Slowly his tongue circled his lips, wetting them. "It's—deep."

She turned, surprised. "It's over our heads," she said with a shrug. "You're not afraid?"

Wasn't he? His fists clenched at his sides and he struggled to subordinate his fear. The levee tops were broad and smoothly paved. Even though he didn't have Darkchild's easy coordination, why think he would fall into the water?

That reassurance didn't wipe the perspiration from his lip, didn't make his feet any less reluctant to move.

Khira gazed back at him with rising irritation. "It'll be just as deep an hour from now," she reminded him sharply.

Yes. He could not stand here until the water sank. Reluctantly he forced himself to follow Khira. But he ran painfully, conscious of each footfall.

When they left the last levee, his knees weakened with momentary relief. But now they were in the orchards, running through skeletal trees, their feet sinking in mud. And what might live in the mud he was afraid to think. Once as he ran after Khira he tripped, stifling a frightened cry. Khira turned back and helped him up without reproach.

The air grew colder, and near dawn they reached Terlath's lower slopes. There they stopped to pull on quilted jackets and leggings. Khira stuffed her hair into a fur-lined cap and the guide chafed trembling hands before pulling on thick mittens. Harsh winter winds swept down the mountainside, pushing beneath the warm, steamy air of the valley and raising it in dense clouds. The sound of thunder was closer, sharper, and lightning flashed in sheets across the clouded sky.

Memories. The guide put them back and climbed the snowy slopes after Khira, plunging through snowdrifts and over fresh rockfalls. She moved as if she were made for the mountain. He moved gracelessly, constantly stumbling, frightened. After a while they reached a great glasstone lens set in a supporting frame that swiveled to beam sunlight down the mountain and concentrate it upon the throneroom mirrors. They rested there for a while, thunder grumbling on all sides. The guide hugged his bruised knees until he realized that Khira studied him, faintly frowning. Anxiously he forced his body into a more relaxed posture, but he suspected she had already seen what he had wanted to conceal. When she got to her feet and continued up the slopes, she went without speaking.

At last she raised one hand, calling a halt. "There, ahead—" She pushed at a straggling strand of hair and gazed narrowly back at him. "There beyond the cleft in the rocks—there's a tunnel leading to Mingele's valley. We can shelter in the palace there." Her lips hardened and she studied him more closely. "But there may be rock-leopard in the tunnel. They sleep there sometimes in the winter."

Rock-leopard. The words scoured his nerves. He knew about rock-leopards from the scrolls. They dragged prey to their dens live and devoured it by bits over many hands of days. Sometimes they kept partially eaten prey captive for an entire season, kicking up barricades of rock to contain it while they hunted the mountainside for fresh tidbits. The guide couldn't contain the blood that drained from his face, couldn't keep the shrill panic from his voice. "We can't go in there!"

Khira's lips twisted in a scornful grimace. "If there is a leopard, he'll be sleeping. All we have to do is slip past without waking him—if you can do that. You've kicked enough rock down the mountain to wake a hundred leopards this morning."

And Darkchild wouldn't have stumbled once. Unconsciously the guide wiped at his eyes. "Is there stalklamp? In the tunnel?" The demand was brittle with fear. But if he could at least see whatever beast they met—

Khira's smile was small, satisfied. "A few strands at either end. The main part of the tunnel is completely dark at this time of year."

He shrank. But this was no time to hesitate, wounded by her scorn.

She turned and moved up the trail, challenging him by the careless set of her shoulders. Tensely he followed, fear singing in his nervous system. Perspiration broke out on his upper lip. As she entered the tunnel, he tried to gauge how much time he would have for flight if a leopard rose from the dark and attacked them.

In the end there was no leopard in the tunnel. They burrowed through drifted snow into a chill darkness that smelled of damp stone and stagnant water. The tunnel was broad enough for two to walk abreast, tall enough that neither had to bend. The floor was worn smooth from the traffic of centuries. Near the inception of the tunnel, occasional tendrils of stalklamp clung to the tunnel roof, offering anemic illumination.

The guide crept along the wall of the tunnel after Khira, his nerves quivering. Loose rock littered the floor and in places there were animal droppings. He felt them underfoot. Disoriented, the guide clutched at the rough walls for reassurance.

The tunnel twisted twice. At each bend, the guide paused and listened. Each time he heard nothing but his own breath and Khira's. Each time, following Khira, he found nothing but a further stretch of empty tunnel.

The guide's nerves ebbed abruptly when they reached the far end of the tunnel. He collapsed against the rock wall, breathing hard against the whine in his ears.

Khira had already begun digging at the drifted snow that blocked the end of the tunnel. She turned on him with a scornful flash. "Well? Do you expect me to do all the work?"

Stung, ashamed, he joined her, working awkwardly, and after a while the last of the drifted snow fell away and they looked down over Mingele's valley. It lay deep in snow, the empty palace girdled in white, its watchtower blind. Tall breathing chimneys marked the sites of the deserted stonehalls. Occasionally a brief stretch of levee was visible, breaking the layer of frozen white that covered the dead valley. The air was clear and biting.

And there was no thunder.

For a moment, looking down over the snowbound valley, tasting the crisp silence of the mountainside, the guide felt a sharp sense of elation. He could walk here and leave footprints where no one had left footprints before. He could shout and there would be no ear to hear. He—

He stiffened as sunlight caught the strangely carved stone mounted at the peak of the watchtower below. The stone was large, darkly translucent, and for some reason sight of it made his mouth go dry. "Khira—there at the top of the watchtower—"

She shrugged off his agitation irritably. "An eyestone. The barohnas used them during the troubled times to watch the valleys. No one uses them now."

Then why did he have the feeling that the stone watched him?

Khira returned to the tunnel, warming her nose and mouth in her mittened hands. The guide remained outside, trying to recapture the first sharp ecstasy of freedom. Instead he found only a sense of threat.

When he turned back to the tunnel, Khira crouched on the floor, her pack open. His pack lay kicked against the wall beyond her. She looked up, and it seemed to him that she deliberately challenged him to step past her to retrieve it.

"I'm hungry," he said, aggrieved.

Her pupils narrowed at the harsh tone of his voice. "Then eat." But she made no move to let him pass. Glancing down, he saw that her pike lay on the tunnel floor at his feet. Angrily he snatched it up. "I'll hunt for my dinner."

Khira jumped to her feet, her face flushing. "With my pike? For what?"

"Brownfowl. They nest under the snow. I'll have those." If she would not feed him, he would feed himself.

Her eyes glinted, challenging. "You don't know anything about hunting brownfowl."

But he did. "I know to look for a place where three hollow reeds stick up through a deep drift. The nest will be there. I know to kick the snow back and strike for the largest fowl—the drake. I know to leave the hen with the eggs so there will be young at hatching time."

Khira's voice crackled with scorn. "You know what you've read from the scrolls! You've never used a pike in your life. And predators hunt this valley. There are no people to drive them away. You don't even know how to tell if they're nearby."

He was stung. "Do you think I won't notice prints in the snow?"

"You won't—if it snowed last night and a minx has been waiting behind a boulder for three days. They wait that long at this time of year, you know. And if you move when there is a minx nearby—"

She didn't have to tell him. He knew from the scrolls of the snowminx' killing fury. His gaze dropped. *Make fear a tool,* he reminded himself.

A tool this time to keep him from doing something foolish out of wounded pride. He was charged with keeping the boy safe—even at sacrifice to his own pride. Silently he dropped Khira's pike. "I want my pack," he said in a harsh undertone. "I'll eat from my pack."

She glared at him disbelievingly, then hurled the pack at him, her teeth clenching in an angry grimace. "Take it! And eat at the other end of the tunnel!"

He turned without defending himself. But he didn't retreat to the other end of the tunnel. He ate a dozen meters from her, choking dry bread down a dry throat. Then, although it was only midday, he slumped against the cavern wall and fell into exhausted sleep.

It was dark beyond the cavern mouth when Khira shook him awake, her fingers digging into his shoulders, her voice pounding shrilly at him. With a frightened gasp, he pulled himself to a sitting position, trying to escape her gripping fingers. Instead they tightened. By the stalklamp that clung sparsely to the cavern ceiling, he saw wild anger in her eyes and tears on her cheeks.

"You're not Darkchild! *You're not Darkchild!*"

The guide's heart shuddered and the blood left his face. The way she loomed over him, the way she held him . . . "Khira—"

"I thought you were Darkchild, and I didn't understand why—why you were acting that way. The way you acted all day. And then I dreamed. I dreamed about you, about the way you acted after the Arnimi came back to the palace. I dreamed about your voice and the way you walk—the way you kept falling down today. I dreamed you fell down and when you got up, you got up twice. You were two!" Fiercely she pushed him back against the wall, releasing him with a violent shove.

The guide raised one hand, imploring. If only she would listen; if only she would understand. "Khira—I'm—*I keep Darkchild safe.* I guard him. I—"

Her lips twisted. "You keep him safe—by falling down? By stumbling every time you put one boot in front of the other?"

"I—" How to explain his clumsiness when he didn't understand it himself? Darkchild moved easily, surely, and without fear. But something seemed to bind the guide's muscles, making his entire body rigid and ungainly. It bound even his throat, so that his voice came harshly. "Khira—"

"You're the guide!" She leaned near him, her eyes blazing. "You're the one he tried to tell me about. The one who knows things! *You're not even Darkchild!"*

So she hadn't known. She hadn't guessed until now. He slumped back against the wall, his muscles feeling as if they had been pounded. "I'm not."

His admission quieted her for a moment. She drew back and slapped angrily at her tears. "I don't understand," she said finally, like a child lost.

He sighed. He didn't understand either. Why should they be two in one body, one anxious and frightened, the other unafraid? One holding back, the other pushing ahead? Because the Benderzic had made them thus? Because the Benderzic had given him fear to guard Darkchild with? Because there was no other way to control and protect?

"I don't understand," she said again, with new force, her eyes suddenly dry and angry. "But I know one thing. Darkchild promised not to leave me." Her lips tightened. "That's what he told me—that he wouldn't leave me."

How could he answer her? He couldn't tell her about thunder and dreams, about his contract, about responsibilities too long neglected.

What would Darkchild tell her? The guide peered up at her hopelessly. Khira, when he leaves you, he wanted to say, whenever Darkchild has to leave you, I won't. I won't leave you alone. The words and the emotion he found in them moved him strangely and he wondered at his feelings. Why should he care that she was angry and hurt? There was nothing in the contract about her.

Still it mattered. "Khira—"

"He promised not to leave me," she said with finality. Quickly she took her feet and strode away into the darkness of the tunnel.

Her hurt touched him, ached in him. He wanted to go after her, to reassure her. But he knew the only reassurance she wanted was Darkchild.

And he could not give her Darkchild. Because when he finally slept again, curled uncomfortably against the stone wall, his dreams were of thunder: the thunder of storm in some damp jungle, the thunder of a ship in the sky, the thunder of Darkchild's heart. And all through his dreams, he felt Darkchild groping for images he must never grasp: violet eyes and midnight hair, a silk that sang in the sun, golden skies.

Darkchild was searching for things he must not find. And when the guide woke, he knew that he too had reached for something he must not have. He had reached for Khira; he had cared for her. And he must not. He could not fulfill the contract by caring.

He must not care for anyone or anything.

Still it mattered that the next morning Khira would not meet his eyes, would not speak. She ate silently, as if she were alone. And when the guide followed her from the tunnel, she did not look back. She walked as if she were the only person on the mountain.

Her rejection was a physical pain. It ached the same way his bruised knees ached, the same way his strained thighs hurt. But he followed silently, making no effort to reconcile her. He knew he must not.

Morning sunlight glinted off the snow crust that covered mountain and valley. Everywhere were signs of game. Hollow reeds poking above the snow created breathing chimneys for nests of brownfowl. A series of icy potholes marked the spot where dens of heapers slept. Coveys of early-hatching groundrunners squawked and scattered at his approach. Twice Khira froze and the guide saw signs of snowminx in the snow. He stood utterly still, not breathing, listening with bristling hair for the slithering approach of Terlath's eeriest predator.

Both times they passed without seeing the minx that had left its sign.

It was midday when they reached Mingele's valley. The guide peered uneasily up at the eyestone on the peak of the watchtower. But today it did not seem to look back.

He followed Khira across the valley with a hollow sadness. If he were Darkchild, he would absorb every new sight and sound eagerly. He would run with Khira across the snow and they would laugh together.

Instead they walked separately, silently, until they reached the deep-drifted plaza of Mingele's palace. Breathing chimneys stood like giant straws, ringing the palace. The watchtower cast its shadow across the snow.

They shed their packs and Khira threw herself down in the snow to catch her breath. Dully the guide explored the perimeters of the plaza. Mingele's palace was centuries older than Tiahna's, built in an era when the climate had been briefly milder and crops had grown lush. Assured of a rich harvest, the people had lavished time and skill upon the palace. Windowed turrets grew from its four corners, rivaling the watchtower. Carved forms were set into stone recesses at intervals around the exterior walls, native forms alternating with forms that had accompanied the stranded humans. A snowminx stood half-crouched, razor claws raised. A stone ewe grazed at non-existent grass. A bellowing breeterlik reared on its hind legs, stomach sphincter gaping. Its neighbor was the legendary horse, driven from the valleys during an early famine period. Then came the cerebhawk, poised ready to fly, its opposing heads glaring at each other in frozen anger.

Poised...

The guide experienced a momentary twinge of apprehension, transitory, unexplained. Frowning, he returned to where Khira rested and stretched out in the snow. When he closed his eyes, he was for a moment keenly aware of the ache of his muscles. Then weariness anesthetized him and he drowsed.

He woke at Khira's sharp exclamation and sat instantly. Khira was on her knees, peering tensely around the plaza. She turned on him wildly and for the first time that day spoke to him. "Darkchild—there's something—*something*—don't you feel it? In the air?"

At the sharp panic in her voice, the guide jumped up and without thinking scooped up her pike. Was there a crackling sense of electricity in the air? And did the eyestone watch again, from its high tower?

"Darkchild—" Turning, Khira had found the focus of her fear and stared up at it, her lips parting in disbelief. "The cerebhawk—"

The guide gazed up, his pulse pounding. Slowly the stone bird moved, its dominant head turning on its extended neck. The bird peered around, then flexed its wings. Every motion was deliberate, as if the bird were testing the responses of an unfamiliar body. The dominant head drew back and swept the plaza with an angry stare, while the secondary head remained locked in position, helpless, its eyes glittering bleakly. Then, abruptly, the dominant head shot forward and the stone bird uttered a strident cry.

Khira struggled to her feet, one hand flying to her throat. "I thought it was a legend. I thought it was just a story people told—"

Dreadfully the stone bird glared at them, shrieking again. The sound tore at the air.

The *warm* air, warm and crackling, as if an unseen web of energy had fallen across the plaza. Khira and the guide were caught in it, trapped. All around them ice and snow began to melt. The guide stared, open-mouthed, fear chattering through his nervous system, his fingers and toes tingling with it.

With a third tearing cry, the bird launched itself from its perch. The guide knew that if it were a bird of flesh, it should have mahogany and white markings. It did not. Instead it was grey—even its claws, which should have been black. The stone bird swooped across the plaza, one head still locked helplessly into position, the other extended, stone eyes staring, beak parted.

Finally Khira found words. They came weakly, dry husks of sound. "It's my mother. The legend—she can make stone live."

The pike fell from the guide's clenched fingers and color ran from his face. *Tiahna.* There was a legend in the scrolls—he had not read it, but he had seen reference to it—that a barohna had the power to invest herself in stone, to make it move like a living creature, to make it leap, run, scream, cry.

Kill.

"I never believed it," Khira whispered.

Nor had he taken it for more than a legend. But now the legend flew at them, death in its eyes. And they faced it helplessly. The guide wanted to run, to hide. But his muscles were locked in shock.

Struggling against paralysis, Khira bent and retrieved the pike the guide had dropped. The terrible energy of Tiahna's presence snarled and crackled around them, rendering everything unreal: the empty plaza, the melting ice crust, the carved figures, immobile in their niches.

"Mother, no! I made him come with me! I made him run away!" Her voice came in shrill bursts. "The Arnimi told you lies! *Mother—*"

The guide felt his intestines coil with fear. Him—*she had come for him.* She was going to tear him with stone claws. As he stared up, the hawk snapped its stone beak. Its cry was deafening, harsh.

Khira dropped to her knees, the pike falling from her fingers again. As the guide watched helplessly, Khira tried to shape her babbling plea into coherent words, words to save Darkchild by. But her throat closed as the great hawk swooped near and she did not even scream.

A moment later she shrieked with pain. For the hawk flew not at Darkchild but at Khira, dragging its stone claws across her cheek, then swooping up again and soaring away. Khira clasped her bare hand to the bloody wound, unbelieving. The guide stared at her with the same mute disbelief.

Tiahna had not come for him. She had come for Khira.

Why? There was no time to wonder. The hawk passed again, this time snatching at Khira's hair, tugging tufts of it bloody from her scalp. For a moment the hawk hung before them on beating wings, glaring at Khira with eyes the guide knew, Tiahna's eyes. Then the hawk soared away.

"Khira—"

She turned numbly, staring at him with fixed pupils. "She—she's—"

The guide's heart hardly seemed to beat. He stood like a carved figure, rigid, cold, helpless, as the hawk returned, wings spread, head thrust, beak ready to tear. Returned—*for Khira*.

In his fear the guide had forgotten Darkchild. And if the guide could not move, Darkchild could. Bending, he snatched up the pike Khira had dropped and raised it. Startled, the guide struggled silently with Darkchild's renegade muscles, making them writhe and cramp.

Run! The guide broadcast the shrill warning to every muscle. *Run!* Tiahna would have Khira. How could he stop her? But she could not have them both at once, and that meant he had bare moments to race across the plaza and hide himself.

Darkchild fought the guide, rejecting his directive. The screaming hawk burst upon them savagely. With knotting muscles Darkchild threw himself between Khira and the bird, raised the pike and loosed it.

Incredibly the pike placed home in the ghostly grey beast. The bird hung in midair, a shriek frozen in its throat. Then, with a choked cry, it plummeted to the plaza, wings drawn tight in agony, and sank through the melting crust. Steam boiled up furiously, shrouding the place where it had fallen.

Instantly the air of the plaza was cold again. The momentum of his thrust had slammed Darkchild to his knees. His arm sank to his side. When he stood again, when he turned, he looked at Khira with pain in his eyes.

Numbly Khira stepped forward and peered down through the icy crust. The stone hawk had melted its way to the surface of the plaza. It lay there unbroken, the pike buried in its chest. Khira's face twisted. "Mother—" She turned back to Darkchild. "The legend—no one ever killed a barohna when she was stone."

The guide seized at Darkchild's feet, trying to spur them to flight. He succeeded only in taking a single stumbling step back.

Grief, anger, pain—they passed across Khira's face in swift succession. Then both she and the guide realized the air had warmed again. They spun.

High above them the carved snowminx stirred to life. It tossed its stone head, stiff ringlets sweeping across its shoulders. From its throat, Tiahna spoke. "I told you I must know more about your companion, Khira, before I could decide whether he could stay."

Khira faced the stone figure, trembling. "Yes," she whispered. "You told me. Mother—"

"Now I know more. You may stay, Rauth-Seven."

It took the guide a moment to realize he had been reprieved. Then he set aside Darkchild's quick surge of elation for the trembling weakness of relief.

"Go to your redmane cousins for the warmseasons, daughter. Take your companion and teach him whatever he wants to know. We have no need for secrets. Leave when your grandmother tells you and come back to the palace for winter."

Khira nodded. Her words seemed dry, as if her mouth were packed with wool. "Yes. We'll—go."

"Goodsummer then, daughter. Travel well." The snowminx became immobile again.

With Tiahna's going, a cold wind swept down into the valley. The guide looked down and saw that his boots had sunk into the melting crust of the snow. As he watched, the crust froze again, imprisoning his feet.

Laughing giddily with relief, Khira freed her feet from the crust. The stone hawk lay at the bottom of a deep well in the snow. Khira slipped down the frozen well to retrieve her pike. But when she touched its haft, she drew away quickly and scrambled back to where the guide waited. "It's—it's stone! My pike has turned to stone."

The guide peered down the ice well and shuddered. He had felt the pike's smooth wooden haft in Darkchild's hand just minutes before. Tiahna had made stone live and now she had made wood stone.

He could not escape another thought. If Darkchild had accepted his command, if he had run, would they both be ash now? Was that what had decided Tiahna—that Darkchild had defended Khira?

Stricken, the guide drew to the back of Darkchild's mind. He had been charged with keeping Darkchild safe. But if Darkchild had yielded to his instruction, if he had run—

The contract—its terms seemed so clear. To guide Darkchild, to keep him safe, to urge him to explore and learn. But how could the guide know what course of action would protect and what endanger when he could not see beyond the moment and his own fears?

He had been told he would be coolly rational, a safeguard against Darkchild's recklessness. Then where was his own safeguard?

He had none. This time, only Darkchild's recklessness had saved them.

Preoccupied, the guide did not notice that Khira peered at Darkchild narrowly in recognition and held her hand to him. He did not notice that Darkchild and Khira clambered away together across the freezing crust. They pushed at heavy palace doors and stepped into an entryway harsh with the light of long-untrimmed stalklamp. The smell of winter was heavy in the deserted palace. Long corridors were deep in dust. Somewhere a small animal squealed and fled.

That might have been him—squealing, running, crying. Tiahna had told Khira to take Darkchild to the redmane guardians for the warmseasons, but the guide wanted only to retreat to some dark place and hide.

Yet where Darkchild went, he must go. What dangers Darkchild faced, he must face. And without the rewards that were Darkchild's: Khira's hand in his, the warmth of her smile. They were together. He was alone.

12/Khira

From Mingele's valley they traveled ten days through snow-frosted mountains and steaming valleys. Sometimes they heard rockslides in the distance, sometimes the sharp crack of thunder. Shy mountain creatures ran across their trail and they saw frequent signs of predators. During those ten days came many hours Khira cherished—hours when she showed Darkchild her world and saw it freshly through his eyes. His was an eager curiosity. He wanted to know every sign in the snow, wanted to touch every exposed rock and twig. Khira indulged him. There was no hurry to reach the plain.

But interspersed with the good hours were the others, when Darkchild hardly seemed to see the trail before his feet. Times when his eyes gazed inward, times when what he saw hurt. He was especially withdrawn in the mornings when he woke—from what dreams?

She wondered about his dreams sometimes, crouched over a quickly kindled cookfire, turning foraged foodstuffs and staples from her pack into a morning meal. Too often Darkchild joined her silently, eyes averted, hardly aware of her presence.

And sometimes, when he had been particularly troubled, she found she served food to the guide instead of Darkchild. There was no mistaking the guide once he raised eyes to hers. His gaze was flinching, frightened, yet in some way pleading. She might have been touched by it—if his very presence hadn't turned her first brittle-cold, then hotly angry. She could never see him without remembering her dream: Darkchild clumsy on the steep trail, crying out, falling; then, before she could reach him, some shadow of him pushing itself up from the ground—and as the shadow walked away, a second shadow rising to follow the first.

How could he be two and still, at any time, be wholly one? And the other—the guide—who was he but a creature of the Benderzic? Darkchild shared his body with an entity who was stuff of his exploiters. And that must diminish him in a dozen small ways—ways that might someday take him away from her.

He was two, and she must not let the one win her with pleading eyes. She must shrink him with silence and scorn.

Silence and scorn. She honed them to perfection as they traveled through the mountains. She learned when silence would drive the guide away and she learned when scorn would do it. She even learned which of his fears were the greatest and played on them. Shamelessly, since one of his fears was that she would be injured. Another was that she would abandon him. And was that so different from her own fear that Darkchild would leave her?

She examined that thought only once, and it made her so uncomfortable she put it from her mind.

At the end of ten days, with the sun scarlet in a dusk-violet sky, they finally reached a rocky cropping overlooking the plain. Red rock and winter-bitten grasses stretched below them, broken by stunted trees and bare-limb bushes. The sun seemed enormous, as if it might consume the plain. Yet the air was bitter-chill.

Khira looked silently over the plain, stirred. The redmane guardians who had been her remotest ancestresses had patrolled these dark rocks and desolate trees for tens of centuries, watching for breeders come to steal redmanes. They patrolled still, silent in their umber capes—not because breeders often came these days but because the guardians had become a plains people. And now for a summer Khira would be a daughter of the plains too, wading streams with guardian daughters and clinging to the backs of redmane foals.

Darkchild crawled to the edge of the rocky ledge and peered across the plain intently. "We'll have to walk another day before we see the herds," Khira told him, her fist clenching on the strangely carved pike they had brought from Mingele's palace.

He turned, his eyes bright with anticipation. "And the redmane guardians—"

"They'll be with the herds. The plowing teams won't leave for the valleys for at least another hand of days." She gazed across the plain. The wind was sharp on the mountain by night. On the plain, it would be just as bitter and there would be little shelter. "We'll have to shelter here tonight and cross the plain tomorrow. My grandmother and Upala make their kefri in a guardian campment near the northern rim of the plain. We can reach their kefri in a day and a half." She was not surprised to find herself suddenly eager to see her grandmother again, and Upala, Kadura's stone mate.

She turned and peered back up the mountainside. Dusk already cast shadows behind the rocks and made the air grey. She climbed back the way they had come and found a cove of boulders. "We can sleep here."

Darkchild scrambled after her to inspect the rocky cove. "I saw nesting signs back the way we came. I'll bring something for the cookfire."

"Yes." He had made himself a hunter these ten days. Giving him the pike, she crept into the rocky cove and sat down, resting her head against the rocks. Without intending, she fell asleep.

When she woke, the sky was dark. She sat, momentarily disoriented, groping for her pike. But Darkchild had taken it. And he hadn't returned. Alarmed, she crawled from shelter and peered around. Nindra rode low on the horizon, amber in a starred sky. Gazing into the darkness, Khira distinguished only the shadows of the mountainside and, below, the darkness of the plain.

But somewhere something moved. She heard it and caught her breath. "Darkchild?"

He spoke from nearby, whispering. "Khira—someone's coming."

She turned quickly, peering around until she found him in the shadow of a boulder, tensely alert, his eyes gleaming. A string of fresh-killed brownfowl hung from one shoulder. "Where?"

"Up the trail from the plain—there." He inclined his head.

"A guardian," she guessed, but it could be a renegade breeder scouting the way for a stealing party. She slipped forward, peering down the dark mountainside.

After a moment she distinguished a single figure moving in the rocks below, head bowed, limbs lost in the folds of a dark cape. As if summoned by Khira's gaze, the figure paused, raising its head. "Kadura!" Khira cried and ran down the trail.

She threw herself into her grandmother's arms and was enveloped in the black cape Kadura wore. Then she stepped back and peered up into her grandmother's face. "Mother's mother—" But the words died in her throat. She drew back involuntarily.

She had never found age in Kadura's face before, only strength and the promise of compassion. But tonight there was pain in her eyes and her face was visibly thinner, lined. And there was something in her eyes ... Without thinking, Khira glanced down. Beneath Kadura's cape, a white scarf bound her waist, its ends hanging to her knees.

"Upala—" Khira said with sinking heart.

Kadura's shadowed face contracted and she touched the mourning sash. "Yes. We lost good friends among the guardians last warmseason, and her heart suffered. I found her dead beside me at the end of wintersleep."

Upala ... gone. For a moment Khira was stricken, then sharply alarmed. "But you—you're not ill?" Quickly she took Kadura's hands. They were as strong as ever, but the veins stood more prominently, and the skin felt dry and loose.

"I'm well, daughter's daughter," Kadura assured her. "But I'm too much alone. Ice is forming where it should not. I'm pleased you've come."

"And I've brought a friend," Khira said quickly.

"Yes, Nezra's stone brought us that message. That you were bringing a child from elsewhere who wants to know how we live." Kadura peered up the mountain, her brows drawn in a faint frown. "Do you suppose he intends his pike for my heart, child?"

Startled, Khira turned and peered up the trail. It was no longer Darkchild who stood on the rocky cropping. Instead the guide hunched there, pike raised. Indignation seized Khira. Angrily she launched herself up the trail. Catching the guide's arm, she spun him around, blind to the quick fear in his eyes. "Would you pike my grandmother?"

He shrank, licking dry lips. "How—how could I tell who it was? In the dark? She came without calling—she pulled you under her cloak. She—she could be anyone!"

"Well, she isn't! She's my mother's mother and she's come to take us to the herds. But she can go back and leave us here if she wants. Or we can both go and leave *you*."

The guide's face twisted in panic. *"You wouldn't! Khira—"*

"Wouldn't I?" Khira seized the pike and tapped the string of fowl he carried forgotten in one hand. Her anger was not calculated; it was genuine. "I could leave you and you'd starve in a day. You don't know how to pike these—you don't even know how to pluck them for roasting. Do you?" She refused to be touched by the trembling fear in his face. "Do you?"

Kadura had followed Khira up the trail, tall and silent in her dark cape. Now she spoke. "Do you always abuse your friend, Khira?"

Khira spun, bristling at the rebuke. "This isn't my friend!" She snatched at the string of fowl, and the guide jumped back, letting them fall. "I'll pluck these myself," she said, directing a fiery glance at him. "Maybe by the time they're ready for roasting, someone will build a fire. If anyone here knows how." She stalked away, leaving the guide gazing up empty-handed at Kadura.

Khira set to the plucking with a fury, hardly aware that the guide had slipped away to gather moss and twigs for the fire. After a moment Kadura joined Khira and Khira found herself uncomfortable in her silent presence. Was it judging? Stern? Khira's anger turned sour in her mouth. She glanced up at Kadura, expecting some further rebuke for her temper. But Kadura looked at her from shadowed eyes and said only, "You've had a loss too since I saw you last, Khira."

For a moment Khira did not know what she meant. Then her eyes fell to Kadura's mourning sash and she said in surprise, "Alzaja is gone." It was long since she had thought of her sister. The summer they had spent with Kadura and Upala seemed a lifetime ago, although it had been just three years before. Her eyes narrowed, trying to penetrate the shadows that fell upon Kadura's face. "Did you know—"

"Did I know she wouldn't succeed in her challenge?" Darkchild had returned to the rocky cove—Khira knew instantly it was him and not the guide—and had begun building a fire. Kadura watched as he worked, her face shadowed, her voice remote. "I guessed it, of course. Alzaja was tender—in ways I'm sure she explained to you before she went."

"She told me about—about the ice and the stone," Khira said with frowning reluctance. She had put those things behind her when she left the valley and she was not eager to take them up again now. She had enough to concern her with Darkchild.

Kadura nodded, her eyes lingering on Darkchild's intent face as he worked over the fire, striking the spark, kindling it to life, blowing carefully on the fledgling flame. "The boy who was here a few minutes ago was not your friend. This boy is, I think."

Unexpectedly Khira flushed. "He—is."

"And the other?" Kadura probed. She threw back her hood and shook down her hair. It was dark, sparsely streaked with white. It fell heavily across her shoulders, making her seem like some dark-maned plains legend, wise in her age. Her face, shorn of shadow, had the barohnial strength Khira remembered.

"The other—the other was his guide." Stubbornly Khira gazed at the ground. If Kadura wanted to know more than that—

But Kadura only nodded and continued to watch Darkchild as he spitted the birds and roasted them. He did not glance up at her until the birds were browned, and then it was her sash that drew his attention.

They ate, Kadura silent, Darkchild flirting glances at the white sash that gleamed beneath her cape, Khira tensely poised. When the cookfire flickered into nervous embers and they had thrown the bones of the roasted fowl aside, Kadura turned her attention fully to Darkchild. "No one has told me your name, Khira's friend."

He wrenched his gaze from her sash and met her eyes with a moment's flinching wariness. His voice was husky. "I'm named for the shadows: Darkchild."

"Ah. Then the shadows have eyes—do they not, Darkchild? Bright eyes?" Kadura stroked her scarf.

Darkchild dropped his gaze, flushing.

"No, no, I'm not rebuking you. I like to think about names, about how they define the people who carry them. Tonight you are a child looking out of the dark—but you see everything around you, no matter how shadowed. So you make your own light, and perhaps one day you will have to change your name. Is that permitted among your people?"

He raised his head warily, trying to read her gaze. "I—I don't know. It isn't among yours."

"No, but then our names seldom have any particular meaning. I've wondered sometimes—" For a moment she seemed to recede into her thoughts. "I've wondered if having a name with meaning molds the person who carries it. Upala, my stone mate, was one of the few whose name described something other than herself. And in my mind, she came to resemble the stone her name described. But did she become as the stone because she carried its name—or because that was her nature, no matter how she was named?"

"She was named for a stone?" Khira said, surprised.

Kadura nodded, fingering her mourning sash. "The upala was a milky white stone the first timers carried when they were stranded. You'll read of them in the very earliest scrolls. When you gazed into the upala, deep inside you saw fire of every color. The gem masters never faceted it. They simply polished it to bring out the fire."

Khira frowned. "I've never seen a stone like that."

"Because they no longer exist. They were fragile and they crumbled. Upala was like that to me—a still surface that hid fire. I had to look deeply, but when I did, I saw the fire. Not to be touched—only to be glimpsed, and then only if I looked closely."

"And now she has crumbled," Darkchild said, and Khira glanced at him sharply.

Kadura nodded, gathering her hair, pulling the hood over it. Her face retreated into shadow again. Her voice fell to a husky thread. "She has crumbled, but she's left me memories, Darkchild. I remember the day I took my pairing stone from the gem master and put it on my neck. I felt Upala's fingers in my mind for the first time that day, but it seemed to me I had waited all my years for her cool touch in my mind." Her eyes studied Khira, but they seemed distant, as if they saw herself instead, younger. "You'll know that touch one day, Khira. And when it comes, you'll realize how alone you have been."

Khira recoiled, glancing quickly at Darkchild. "I'm not alone."

Sighing, Kadura returned from a distance. "You have your friend, of course. And I'm an old woman who needs to sleep before we walk tomorrow."

An old woman. Khira watched her grandmother as they crossed the plain the next day. Her stride was still firm, her shoulders steady. Khira knew she would never be old in the withered, helpless way of valley women. But there were long times when she walked blindly, absorbed in some reverie, hardly aware of Khira and Darkchild. And by daylight the strength in her face seemed eroded by loss.

Yet whenever one of them spoke to her, she made the long journey back and answered with attention. Sometimes it seemed to Khira that she regarded Darkchild with special thought as the morning wore on, as if she were heeding him with some sense Khira did not possess. And he seemed aware of her attention and walked silently beside her, his eyes lingering on her sash.

When they stopped for their midday meal, Kadura said, "We may see stray 'manes from the herds this afternoon. Stay near me, Darkchild, until they accept you. The plow teams have seen people from the valleys, but most of the herd 'manes have never seen a human male."

Darkchild had been studying the ground, absently drawing one forefinger through the dirt. He glanced up in quick surprise. "There are no men in the plain at all?"

For a moment Kadura studied the lines he had made in the dirt. "No. None."

"But the guardians bear children. Khira's told me that."

Kadura smiled faintly. "There are men in the valleys, Darkchild. When a guardian wants to bear a child, she must go there for a time."

"Then—if her child is male?"

For a moment Kadura's eyes lingered on him regretfully. "No guardian ever bears a male infant to term, any more than a barohna ever does so. We have no sons here, Darkchild—only daughters." Deliberately Kadura slid back her hood and shook her hair over her shoulders. "The Arnimi outworlders tell us there are human cultures where no woman considers herself complete until she has a son. Have you heard of places like that, Darkchild?"

"I—I don't know," Darkchild said in confusion. When she said nothing more, he touched his lips with his tongue and finally, in hurried confidence, said, "I have brothers."

"Ah." Kadura drew her fingers through her hair, holding the dark strands to the breeze, calculating the effect of her words. "But no sisters, Darkchild?"

"No." Softly. Tentatively.

"Still perhaps you know of people where some women have only daughters and think of sons."

Khira squirmed resentfully. There were things in this conversation she did not understand: the patterns Darkchild's finger made in the dirt, the calculation in Kadura's words. Somehow they excluded her much as Tiahna excluded her when she paused in conversation to touch her pairing stone. "He has no people," she said sharply. "He's a Rauth-image."

Darkchild glanced at her uncomfortably. When Kadura did not respond to Khira's comment, he wet his lips with the tip of his tongue again. "The silk you wear—may I touch it?"

Khira jumped up, clutching his arm. But Kadura gestured her aside. "Of course you may. There are tens of these in the memory house near our kefri. I chose white because Upala was named for a white stone."

He nodded, touching the scarf carefully. His fingers tensed, and Khira thought he would bunch the scarf. But he did not. He only permitted himself to stroke it lightly, once, then drew back. When he sat again, his finger did not return to its absent marking. Instead his fists lay clenched on his legs.

Kadura spoke softly. "You may touch the others when we reach the campment if you want."

Darkchild nodded, but Khira noticed that he had averted his eyes from the scarf and stared intently at the ground, his jaw muscles clenching.

Khira's fists knotted too, but with a different tension. She wanted to protest—but protest what? That Kadura said things to Darkchild that she could not understand? That Kadura seemed instinctively to know Darkchild at some level where Khira did not? "I want to see the 'manes," Khira said abruptly. She flung her pack over her shoulder and hurried away, fleeing some vagrant thought that hurt.

When Kadura and Darkchild followed, it was at a distance. Khira turned several times as she ran ahead of them, but she could not tell whether they talked or whether they walked together silently.

It was an hour before Khira joined them again. The three of them walked together without speaking, Darkchild's manner silent, distracted—as if Kadura's presence directed his attention inward. Khira frowned uncomfortably, feeling that some communication had passed between them that excluded her.

Kadura touched her arm lightly. "Tomorrow we will reach the campment, daughter's daughter. Then you and Darkchild can ride the 'manes and wade in the streams and do summer things with the guardian daughters."

Khira bristled. Was she a child, to be appeased with a child's pleasures when her intimacy with Darkchild had been compromised in some way she did not understand? "I have other plans," she said stiffly.

Kadura regarded her with a thoughtful frown. "Does it disturb you so much that I study your friend?"

Khira scowled. "Study him all you want!" she snapped, wondering at her spite. It was like some harsh new jealousy, disturbing in its intensity. "Study his guide too, and tell me what you learn." Without waiting for a reply, she ran ahead again.

They ate from their packs that night, building a fire to brew drinks. Again Darkchild drew sparks from the tinder and breathed the fire alive. Then he slipped back into the reverie that had gripped him earlier in the day. Though neither he nor Kadura spoke, Khira scowled into the fire, her hands tight on her mug, and felt alone.

Alone...Absently she remembered what Kadura had said of Upala's first coming, of cool fingers of thought joining hers. Her own stone mate would find Khira's thoughts an angry chaos—so angry perhaps she would withdraw and never return.

She looked up to find Kadura studying her. "You'll have your companion back, granddaughter."

As if she had traced the line of Khira's thoughts simply by studying her face! "How do you know I want him?" Khira demanded bitterly. "I was alone for months after Alzaja and I did well enough."

"Ah. Then why have those months left a mark on your face, Khira?"

Involuntarily Khira touched her face. "You—you see nothing there."

"I see a great deal," Kadura rebuked her. "You're how old? Twelve? You had your day just a few days ago, didn't you?"

"I—I didn't observe it." In fact she had forgotten her day until now.

"Even unobserved, it made you twelve. But do you know how many years I've lived? Over two hundred. In that time I've given birth to a dozen daughters, raised them and saw two bronze and ten die. I brought early spring to my valley more years than I care to remember. I worked the stones—the sunstone, the eyestone and the pairing stone.

"I took a stone mate and we lived almost a century in each other's thoughts. Then when your mother bronzed and my heart turned flesh again, Upala and I knew a period of hardship that neither of us ever forgot. Upala's only surviving daughter was a child of six, years from bronzing, and suddenly because I had lost the power of the stones, Upala was alone in her thoughts—and she lost the power too. It went right out of her heart.

"She left her valley—she had no choice—and came to the plain with me. And for years we lived here while the valley she had nurtured grew cold and barren. Each year the crops were smaller, the people fewer. Some left, some died—everything she had spent her life for slipped away. We were together, but the pain was between us every day.

"Her daughter made her challenge at her first majority, when she was thirteen, and died—and there was more pain between us. It was eleven years before Melora, Tandara's second daughter to bronze, came to take the throne and restore the people. Eleven years before our own good years could begin.

"Do you wonder that after all I've known I can read things in your face that you think are hidden? I see the loss you had when Alzaja died, the joy you had when your friend came. And I see all the fears and angers you've had with him in the interval—including those you have now."

Khira's muscles pulled tight. How could Kadura see so much when she hardly seemed to look? "Then what do you see in Darkchild's face? Or can you read that?"

"I can, granddaughter." Kadura glanced at Darkchild. He had removed himself from them and peered into the fire, lost in thought. "You consider him two people and so does he. But he is one with a divided awareness—one person divided from himself. As your friend Darkchild, he is shut into one room of his life, unable to find doors into the others—rooms he knows must exist because he hears sounds from beyond the walls. There are certain things that make him feel he is about to find those doors. My scarf is one. He thinks he might open doors with my scarf.

"But the guide is afraid that if Darkchild opens doors, he will find things behind them that will hurt more than being divided and alone. And so when Darkchild reaches for those doors, the guide holds them ever more firmly shut. The guide is even trying to keep his own feelings shut against you—but the harder he tries, the less he succeeds." Kadura smiled, the lines of her face falling into repose. "That's what I see in your friend, Khira."

"He talked to you!" Khira exclaimed, nettled.

"Very little."

"Then how do you know any of that?" If he hadn't said things to Kadura he had denied her, if he hadn't openly shared his thoughts . . .

"Perhaps you're too angry to understand me, Khira. I need very few words from other people to know them. Very few indeed. Often I need no words at all."

Khira stared at Kadura, suddenly frightened by the serenity that had come to her lined face. Great coldness gripped her. "You've learned to move among minds," she said, stricken. There were whispers among the people that certain barohnas who had left their stones could exercise that power. Khira had never given the rumor credence.

Kadura pulled up the hood of her cape, shadowing her face from Khira. "You could call it that, granddaughter. I think of it as bridging— reaching from the loneliness of my mind to the loneliness of another's. When Upala and I could no longer enter each other's minds through the pairing stones, we found we must communicate in other ways. Because we knew each other so well, we found it easy to read small signs in each other: an inclination of the head, a passing frown, any small gesture. We learned to read both the thought and the feeling behind these. Soon it was hardly necessary for us to speak to each other.

"Later we learned that others shared the same unspoken language. We learned to read what they said to us with their bodies and we learned to read what time and experience had recorded in their faces. Perhaps we read far beyond that—it's hard for me to set boundaries between myself and another and then to calculate how far within those boundaries I've penetrated.

"If you want to call this moving among minds, then I do it. I can't help doing it, anymore than you can help seeing the prints of a breeterlik in the snow or storm clouds in the sky. It's become so customary I hardly realize now that I do it."

Khira stood, tense, angry at Kadura's revelation. When Darkchild looked up, she demanded, "How do you like that? How do you like being read like a scroll? How do you like my grandmother knowing what's in your mind from what she sees on your face?"

Darkchild frowned faintly, troubled. "Does it disturb you?"

"Don't quiz me! I want to know how *you* feel!"

He glanced covertly at Kadura and sighed. "I—I don't mind it."

Not only did he not mind, she saw. He was comforted—comforted to have Kadura see into him and speak to what was there. Slowly Khira sank back down beside the fire. If he was comforted, why should she be angry? Because she could not share the intimacy of his mind as

Kadura could? Because what the two of them shared excluded her? Or because she did not want to admit that Kadura could read her as clearly as she could read Darkchild?

No, she did not want her thoughts bare to anyone—because of their very pettiness. There was no order to her thoughts and no serenity. They were colored with angers and jealousies that she would hide even from herself if she could.

She bit her lip, peering up into Kadura's shadowed eyes. Not only were her thoughts filled with pettiness. She had spoken to Kadura with the greatest rudeness, doubting her, challenging her, all but accusing her. And Kadura had answered with nothing but patience. "My grandmother—" she pleaded. There was much to forgive. If Kadura could forgive at least some of it—

"I always forgive the young, Khira," Kadura said from the shadows of her hood. "At your age, I was much the same—full of energies and needs and what I considered pettinesses. Over the years other things gradually took their place. That is the natural order of life. Age never comes before youth."

But did youth have to be thoughtless? Rude?

"No," Kadura said. "Youth is the time to learn not to be thoughtless. To grow in spirit as you grow in body. And if you wish to grow, you can begin with your friend."

"Darkchild?"

Slowly Kadura shook her head. "The other—the one you despise. Or think you despise. You have some tenderness for him too. You can begin growing by examining that tenderness, by fostering it. Your friend has trouble within himself. If you support him, even that aspect of him you like least, you will strengthen him to deal with his inner difficulty."

"And if I—if I do that—then Darkchild won't leave me again?"

Kadura sighed. "Granddaughter, I can't promise you that. But if you can bring yourself to support both aspects of your friend, to tolerate him when he speaks to you as the guide just as you do when he speaks to you as Darkchild—if you can bring yourself to care for him whichever face he presents—certainly the support will make him stronger."

Khira drew back from the fire, shrinking from Kadura's suggestion. Care for the guide? When his very presence meant Darkchild had left her? Her fists tightened and the muscles of her arms cramped. "I'll never care for him! I can't!"

"You feel that way now," Kadura said. "You may always feel that way if you permit it. But I think you are old enough to begin to manage your feelings, to begin to master them."

"No. No, mother's mother—" How could she care for the guide when she felt angry at the very sight of him?

"It is really very simple," Kadura answered her. "Now when you see him you feel confused and angry and you lash out. You address your anger to him. The first thing you must do is refuse to behave in an angry way. You must learn to put on the face you want him to see—the accepting face.

"That seems hard. But after a time it will no longer be just a face. You will no longer be making a pretense. Eventually the act becomes the reality, Khira. If you behave in an accepting manner toward the guide, soon you will accept him."

"No—"

"Yes, even the guide, Khira."

Khira recognized the finality in Kadura's words and argued no more. But as she settled for the night, she had to stifle a rebellious desire to disavow everything Kadura had said. Darkchild and the guide were two—and she could never learn to care for the guide. If she had her wish, she would never see him again.

Never.

Khira lay awake long after Kadura wrapped herself in her cape and closed her eyes. The fire died to embers and Darkchild curled near it. Dimly Khira realized that he was wakeful too.

If only he could answer her questions. If only he could tell her where he went when the guide appeared, what he did; if only he could describe the state of his awareness then—

At last she stirred and sat. "Darkchild—" But it was the guide who gazed at her across the embers.

Her anger came so quickly it took her breath. *The guide!* He made anger flare in her like fire in dry leaves. And Kadura wanted her to control the fire? Biting her tongue, Khira jumped up and backed from the embers, backed into darkness. She stumbled from the fire in anger and confusion, finally throwing herself down beside a boulder a distance away. The night was bitter cold but she hardly noticed.

Manage her feelings? Master them? Put on a face that was a lie in the hope that even her feelings would become a lie? Khira wanted to run back to where Kadura lay, to throw herself into her grandmother's arms and tell her that she could do none of these things.

But she did not. She huddled against the boulder until her anger ebbed, leaving only a gritty residue of shame. Then she returned to the fire and lay down again, wide-eyed, sleepless, making herself promises she could never hope to meet.

13/Kadura

Kadura felt the dream as if it were her own, as if she had become transparent and it passed through her.

It was daylight and the boy walked a white-pebbled path beneath trees that wept silver leaves. He was younger than she knew him, slighter, and he moved along the path with stomach-knotting tension. Far ahead he heard voices. Singing? Calling? No—laughing. Hearing them, he felt the familiar leap of joy—and then turned rigid. The dream seldom went past this point: the path, the voices, the reaching. Beyond these lay only anger and loss as the dream was snatched away.

But tonight—Kadura frowned: was it because of something she had said? was it because she had let the boy touch her sash?—he continued down the path. The images continued to form before him: the branching of ways, one fork leading to the dancing glade, the other to the hamlet. He chose the second fork, and when the dream still was not snatched from him, his heart began to pound against his ribs, making his breath short. If he could move quickly enough, if he could run, perhaps he could reach the edge of the hamlet before the dream vanished. Perhaps—

Afraid to hope, he forced the dream to flow ahead. It carried him quickly through the nesting bushes where bluerunners chuckled, past the first and second kneeling posts—he paused, but only momentarily, to press his forehead against the polished stone pillars—past the public ponds where the untempled must sow their seed. By then the voices were clearer and he stood at the edge of the hamlet. It was a place of rambling, airy structures, roofless houses sheltered by the bending trees that stood around them. When it rained, the people felt a light, cooling mist through the leaves. When the sun shone, its light fell dappled everywhere.

He paused, hardly daring to breathe. It was so fragile, this dream, and so full of longing. He had reached for it so many times. If it vanished now—

But it did not. It remained. With an eager rush, he ran down the path. When he reached the house where the family lived, when he passed through its open door, an entire montage of faces and scenes came to him so quickly he could scarcely sort them.

His dream was a reunion, a return to people he had almost forgotten he had lost. He rejoined them with tearful eagerness: the violet-eyed woman who knelt beside him as he took pen in hand and made his first marks upon a thick block of yellow bond, the girls who sang in the next room, the men who talked outside while silver leaves whispered.

He had been nowhere, hungry and frightened and alone, his mind an emptiness. Then the woman had found him and suddenly he had a home and sisters, three of them. They wore robes of sunset colors and they chattered happily, each word clear and singing, while he struggled simply to make himself understood. But he was the one the woman bent to each day after he had bathed. He was the one she taught to use pen and paper.

Because he was the one whose presence gave the family license to kneel in the sky-roofed temple with the other families. No family could kneel there until there was a son to sign the family names in the yellowing pages of the register. And until he had come—how? from where? and why had his mind been so empty?—there had been no son for this family.

Now he was the son.

Came the day—in the way of dreams it came swiftly, before its time—when he could form the characters of each name properly. Then the entire family walked beneath the arched span of the temple with proud shoulders and knelt to hear the wind singing through the strings of the godsvoice.

While they listened to the voice of the templed god, the women and the girls combed out their midnight hair with their fingers and let the god speak through those strands too. No man was permitted long hair, so no man could ever hear the godsvoice in that intimate way. But once the godsvoice had spoken through the hair of the woman and her daughters, the seeds they cast on the family pond would sprout in plenty and in the brown mud the sweetest bulbs would multiply more rapidly than they could feast on them. They would never have to cast seed in the public ponds again and they would never again be hungry.

Godsvoice—the woman had told him how it was created, by finely drawn strands of metal stretched tight and raised to the wind. She had told him how the godsvoice worked too, how it touched the people in a secret way that made their prayers powerful and their wishes accessible. Their first wish, of course, was that their pond feed them well. Their second—

The boy moaned, suddenly hearing something else in his dream—not the woman's voice, not the godsvoice, but another metal voice. It came first as a deep, droning sound in the distance. Then it was nearer, a tearing metallic scream.

Abruptly the fabric of the dream tore. The boy sat with a sharp cry, clutching his bedding, struggling for breath. *The droning, the scream—and something in the sky, a shape he could not distinguish*...For a few moments, the remnant of the dream clung in his mind, making him tremble with terror. Beyond the terror was something worse, something he could not bear. He shuddered and abruptly, as if a door had been closed, the dream vanished. No shred of it remained, visual or aural. There was only fear.

Fear so intense Kadura had to will herself shut against it, before the undisciplined rush of blood damaged her heart.

The boy's cry had wakened Khira. She sat in confusion. "Darkchild?"

He stared at her numbly, as if he looked beyond her into emptiness. "I—I had a dream."

Khira dismissed her waking confusion quickly. "A nightmare? Darkchild—what did you dream?"

As yesterday, Kadura was touched by the depth of Khira's concern. Time had passed since the summer Khira had run the plain with the guardian daughters and Alzaja had watched and secretly wondered if she would ever settle from her wildness.

"What did you dream?" Khira pressed when Darkchild did not answer.

He shook his head. "I don't remember. I thought—I thought it was good. But—"

Yes, a joyous dream that had ended in terror. And now he remembered nothing. He had only the dregs: fear. He turned to Kadura, and for a moment she saw herself with his eyes: the spent power of her presence, the face set so long in its folds and creases that it told nothing of her present thoughts, and her eyes—eyes that saw, relieving him of the necessity of words. "Kadura—"

"Yes, Darkchild. You need to get away for a while. It will be light soon. Walk until then. Khira—"

"I'll go with him."

"Yes." Kadura watched them into the greyness and then continued to sit, her hood sheltering her face against morning chill. So strange to deal with fears and passions after the silence of winter. So strange to feel the rush of youth in her thoughts, keen and clear and aching. She wondered, for a moment, if her heart still had the elasticity to meet what she found in these two. The first ice had touched her heart when Upala died and it gave her pain now, as she waited for Darkchild and Khira to return.

Troubled, Kadura rose and began gathering sticks and moss for the morning fire.

Khira and the boy returned as she had instructed them, Darkchild calmer but distracted, still reaching for lost images. They traveled soon after dawn. The plain was desolate in the cold shadows of morning. Only an occasional gnarled tree broke its brown monotony. Within an hour they met a solitary redmane, an elderly buck with faded mane and fat haunches. He accepted the boy readily and carried both Khira and the boy without protest. Later, when they met a small herd, Khira and the boy selected younger mounts. Soon they rode as heedlessly as if there had been no dream of metal voices.

Kadura's mood lightened as the sun warmed the plain. They reached the campment at midday: caped guardians silent at the doors of their mud-walled kefris, bright-haired guardian daughters running through the sparse, early spring grass, redmanes grazing, and for Kadura the welcome shelter of her own kefri. She pushed aside the stretched skin that served as her door, pleased to return to her own fireside.

But Khira was restless and soon took the boy with her to visit favored spots. It was near night when they returned, wind-bitten and hungry, smelling of dust and redmanes. "Mother's mother, there's a teaching tonight. Can we go with you?" Khira demanded when she pushed through the door.

The boy paused behind her, touching the coarse netting that covered the sloping interior walls of the kefri, studying the lamps in their brackets and the soft mats arranged around the firepit. Then he turned to Kadura and raised his brows experimentally. *Will the guardians let me come to the teaching?* In his mind was the image of the tall silent women he had seen that afternoon, their faces shadowed and forbidding.

Kadura nodded to his silent question. "We will go to the teaching together, Khira, if you can keep your eyes open."

Khira laughed sharply, throwing herself down by the firepit. The wind and the company of the guardian daughters had burnished her spirits. "I won't sleep. Mother's mother—"

"Yes?" In the boy's mind, carefully framed, was another silent question. *If I can talk to you this way, why does Khira ask you aloud, Kadura?* Kadura smiled, declining the question although she was pleased he had realized he could address her directly without speaking.

Khira frowned impatiently. "Mother's mother—if Darkchild sits for the teaching—"

Kadura finished the groping thought for her. "If he were to listen as the guardian daughters listen for as many years as they listen, I think he would learn the same things they learn."

"Just as I would learn, if I stayed here?"

"Just as you would learn if you stayed and listened in the proper way. Not with your ears, but with the soles of your feet, with the palms of your hands, with the marrow of your bones." She was aware of the dampening effect her words had on Khira, who was a creature of sight and sound. At the same time she felt the boy's heightened excitement. He had left his morning fear behind. The afternoon had left him eager for everything the plain had to offer. "But first you must eat and then you must put on the nightcloaks I took from the storehouse for you. Otherwise you will take chill."

They left the kefri when Nindra rose and walked through the campment with the others, the guardians silent in their heavy nightcloaks, their daughters laughing and running, auburn hair like silk on the night breeze. The teaching place was an area of hard-pounded soil beyond the campment. It was grassless in every direction and sloped gently to a shallow basin filled with spring water.

"We sit here, at the top of the slope," Kadura instructed Darkchild. "The guardians and their daughters sit nearer the pond."

And they learn about the redmanes by listening with their bodies? They learn—?

"I can't tell you what they learn, Darkchild. The ways of the redmanes aren't the ways of people. Each person who learns here learns something different."

And that's why the guardians are so silent, he rushed ahead eagerly. *Because they listen to the redmanes. They don't have to talk with each other when they're lonely. They hear the animals.*

"You've learned a lot today. A guardian can train herself to pick out the footfall of an individual animal within its herd—and from a great distance. She can monitor the rhythm of its heart, the surge of its blood. If that animal becomes alarmed or angry, the guardian will know. A guardian can even tell which mares are carrying live foals and which dead—and when they will deliver."

His eyes darkened in excitement. *They bridge to the redmanes like you bridge to me.*

Kadura nodded, aware that Khira was struggling to hold back possessive anger. "A little like that—yes."

But they don't bridge to each other?

"No—and I'm surprised you haven't noticed that Khira is uncomfortable when you speak to me without talking."

A quick narrowing of his pupils marked his discomfiture. "Khira—" But Khira averted her eyes, frowning, and refused to respond to his apology.

Then it was time for the teaching. The time was marked, as always, by the arrival of the first redmane at the spring. The elderly buck who earlier had carried Darkchild and Khira appeared from the dark and approached the water. His mane hung ragged and the coarse hair of his tail was tangled. But by Nindra's light, his haunches seemed more powerful than fat and he ignored the wind that tore at his dense coat.

He stood for a while beside the spring, gazing up at the assembled guardians and daughters. When the last restless daughter settled quietly in her mother's shadow, the buck lowered his head to drink.

"We place our palms to the ground now," Kadura instructed Darkchild. "And our feet."

"But my boots—" Darkchild gazed at the buck in fascination.

"He's different tonight, isn't he? And your boots won't hinder you if you make yourself still—very still everywhere, in your mind, in your body."

If I reach out to him—

"No, don't reach out. Make yourself empty—totally empty—and wait. And don't expect anything tonight. This is your first teaching. You don't yet know how to listen with your body." But she realized, as he placed his hands lightly on the packed earth, that to some extent he did know. Listening with more than ears was inbred in him.

The buck raised his head from drinking and peered at the girls and women who sat so still, so empty. Kadura sighed, letting the world slip away, letting the buck's heartbeat enter her. There was pain in one of his legs, an irritation of the joint, and deep in his abdomen a blood vessel had become twisted and the blood did not pass as readily as it should. But he felt the rising of spring throughout his body and he raised his head and shrilled.

Kadura withdrew her consciousness from him, making herself empty again as the mare padded to the spring to join him. She was even older than he, but her body held memory of a younger time, of bondings and matings and foals, and she moved with pondersome grace. She grunted in answer to the buck, then bent her head to drink. She was the oldest mare of her herd and she carried the knowledge of their kind in the very tissues of her body, carried it like a compendium of redmane wisdom. She knew where to look for the tenderest grass whatever the season, knew how to find water even in the driest days of summer, knew how a foal should look and smell in the first moments after birth, knew everything a redmane must know to live.

Behind her gathered others, younger, stronger, restless. They waited as she drank, their heads lowered, their ears soft flaps lost in coarse fur, their eyes empty as they opened themselves to her. Teachings had happened on the plain long before the first guardian had come. At the springs and at the streams, redmanes had always gathered on moonlit nights and stood in the presence of age to learn.

Kadura let her breath sigh away. Sometimes the cares and responsibilities she had put down so many years ago still burdened her: decisions made, mates chosen, daughters sent to die. When she emptied herself of all those things and let the secrets of the redmanes enter, she became ageless. She joined the dust of the plain, and in dust there was no weariness and no pain, no loss, ever.

Dust.

Take care, my herd. Pondwater smells different when stingmadders nest in the rocks. It smells this way...this way...and when it smells so you must not drink or you will surely be stung.

Beware, my herd. There are places on the plain where you must not walk. Corrosives have been dissolved from the underlayers and have come to the surface and your pads will burn. When you near such a place, you will know it immediately by the dusty shimmer in the air, a shimmer that will look to you...this way.

Mind me, mares. There are years when you must not foal. In those years, the egg has formed improperly and to conceive would be to misconceive. You will know that is the case by the tightness in your abdomen when your mate approaches you. It will feel to you...this way...

Listen, foals. Near the end of summer, you must eat certain barks and leaves to balance the nutrients you have taken from the fresh grasses. At those times, there will be a sensation at the back of your throat that will feel to you...this way...

So the teaching went. The buck had wisdom too and the younger animals received it from him, as did the guardians and their daughters. As the teaching went on and the second moon rose, Kadura saw that Khira had curled down in to her nightcloak and fallen asleep. The boy sat with hands and feet flat to the ground, the day's excitement still vividly in his mind despite his effort to empty himself.

"Child, this way," Kadura instructed him. "Close your eyes as I do and with each breath, let one thought leave you. Let it slip away on your breath, until all are gone."

Everything?

"Yes, everything. You must let your mind become completely empty."

He sighed, lidding his eyes, letting his head fall forward. He attuned his breathing to Kadura's, inhaling deeply, extending his exhalations. Slowly Kadura felt the level of his thoughts sinking. His body relaxed until his forehead rested against his knees.

Doors. They formed dimly in his mind. His body tensed again and his hands clenched.

"Let the doors go," Kadura instructed. "If you want to learn, you must empty yourself of everything, even those."

He wanted to learn. He attuned his breathing to hers again, and with each sighing exhalation, the doors became fainter. Unconsciously he opened his hands and pressed them to the soil. His face had become pale, his mind barren.

He was empty.

Empty—and then his consciousness filled with light, faces, fear. Kadura recoiled, feeling the panic-surge of blood to her heart. Swift-riding images filled the boy's carefully emptied mind. He was in a place of metal walls. He lay on a metal table, restrained by straps. Cold-eyed people stood over him. They wore black and their eyes were the grey of the metal walls. They spoke incomprehensibly among themselves, their voices muffled. Helpless on the table, the boy had fresh memory of the sting of a needle. It numbed him, removing him from the people who surrounded him. Even if his arms were free, he could not reach those people.

But they could reach him, effortlessly. He struggled to keep his eyes open, fought to plead with them in the only language he knew, even though it was not a language they would understand.

They would understand it soon enough, because now the metal helmet hung over his head, its needles ready to pierce his scalp and steal his thoughts. Desperately he fought the straps. Relentlessly the helmet drifted toward him. With terrible effort, as its needles touched his scalp, he drew a deep breath and released it in a scream.

Kadura shuddered, clutching her chest, and the boy jumped to his feet, startled from his trance by his own scream. He stared down at her wildly, his lips working. Then, his body stiff, every movement forced, he turned and ran from the teaching place.

Kadura tried to fend away the clenching pain in her chest. Had he screamed aloud or had it been a remembered cry that had stiffened them both? Khira had not stirred, nor did the guardians or their daughters turn to peer. The teaching continued.

No matter which the nature of the cry. The boy should not be alone and she had no strength to follow him. His cry had driven fresh swords of ice into her heart. "Khira—" She hardly had breath for words. "Khira—your friend needs you."

Khira blinked owlishly, struggling to wakefulness. "Darkchild?"

"Your friend—be with him. He went back toward the campment."

It took Khira moments longer to waken. Then she said, "I'll take him to the kefri," and was gone.

Kadura remained at the teaching place until the pain in her chest eased. Then she stood and slowly made her way back to the campment, even less certain than before that her heart had the strength to meet what she found in the boy. There was a great coldness in her chest.

Khira and the boy huddled on opposite sides of the firepit, silent, still buried in their nightcloaks. Kadura paused at the door, armoring herself against their tension—the boy's pain, Khira's anger. When she stepped into the kefri, she went first to the boy. "You must take off your cloak when you sit by the fire. If you perspire too heavily, you'll take chill."

Instead of obeying, he stared up at her with trapped eyes and hunched tighter into the garment. She read his dilemma clearly in his face. She was the one who had tricked him into letting the doors dissolve. She was the one who had prompted the emptiness into which the Benderzic had come. She was the one he must guard against.

Yet she was also the one who understood. She understood the darkness that lay behind him—in its fullest extent.

Sighing, Kadura sat beside him. "Yes—too well. I understand too well what you're trying to protect yourself against." Because she had caught not just the horror of the helmet but the deeper nuances of what had happened to him, of how he had been used against the people who had fed him and given him comfort.

He gazed up at her tensely and she read conflict in his eyes. He should say nothing to her. But the terror was heavy upon him, and if he could not dissolve it in words—

"Not me—*him*," he said, clutching her hand. "I have to protect *him*."

Darkchild. Kadura touched his cloaked shoulder, trying to reach past the fear that sundered him. "Child, you are him. You are Darkchild." Was he ready to hear it?

"No," he said. "I am his guide. I'm the one who keeps him safe. I'm the one who keeps the doors closed."

"But do you want to live behind closed doors? I think you've lived behind those doors long enough. You aren't responsible for the use the Benderzic made of you. If you can accept what has happened—"

"*No!*"

Kadura drew back involuntarily, willing her heart not to contract at the despair behind the single word. It was easy for her to see what he must do; hard for him to do it. Even as she studiously dismissed tension from her shoulders and upper arms, she watched him set himself at a distance from his own emotion. Memory became grey, feeling diffuse.

She clasped his shoulder again, trying to draw him back. "Child, what do you achieve by erecting these barriers? What do you accomplish by putting your fear so far from you? You—"

"I have no fear," he said in a harsh voice, forcing the words through clenched teeth. Perspiration glittered on his forehead. *"He's* afraid— Darkchild's afraid. I'm not."

Khira had listened impatiently. Now she threw off her nightcloak and leaned toward the fire, her eyes glinting. "Darkchild isn't afraid of anything. You're the one who's afraid!"

The boy stared across the fire at her, wounded by her scorn, and Kadura felt fresh conflict in him. He wanted to reach out to Khira, to make her care for him as she cared for Darkchild. But he was afraid of the emotion she evoked in him, afraid of all the other emotions it could call to life.

"You're afraid of your own shadow," Khira hissed with fresh scorn.

The boy cringed; and for Kadura it was enough. "Khira, go to the shelf and take down the powdered terris root. Then bring me mugs and water. You both need sleep more than you need argument."

Khira turned on Kadura, forgetting all her promises in a flash of temper. "He *is* afraid!" she snapped. "Just look at him! He was shaking when I found him—and mumbling to himself. He—"

"Child." Kadura spoke with such chilling authority that Khira drew back, paling. "Child, this is your friend and he needs you. Won't you accept him?"

Briefly Khira's eyes flashed, and angry rejection reeled through her mind. Accept the guide? What was he but the Benderzic's creature? Certainly he was Darkchild's enemy—and hers. He—

"No, he is simply one aspect of your friend," Kadura said. "He is the aspect that guards the past—but he wants to touch the present too. He wants to reach out to you. And the other aspect of your friend— Darkchild—is searching for the past the guide guards. If your friend can't touch what he reaches for in both his aspects, he may always be as he is now—divided."

Khira sank back to her heels, bowing her head as if Kadura's words were physical blows. "If I can't accept him—if I can't accept the guide—"

"But you can. You are strong."

She had chosen the right words. Khira's temper and uncertainty deserted her. She sighed, peering across the fire. The guide sat stiffly hunched, guarded. But he could not hide the pleading in his eyes. "I'll try," Khira said finally.

"You will succeed," Kadura assured her. "And now the terris root, Khira." Her heart was stabbed with ice again. The pain would not ease until she saw them both sleeping.

Over the next hands of days, some sense of serenity returned to her kefri. The boy continued to reach, the guide tentatively seeking Khira's company by day, Darkchild dreaming by night, waking to find his dreams gone. Sometimes he followed Kadura as she went to her morning chores and addressed her silently. *Kadura, you know what I dream. If you would tell me—*

She refused him every time. "You hide the dreams from yourself, Darkchild. When you're ready, you will find them."

No, the guide hides them. If you will help me find them—

"Child, we each choose our own path. When you are ready to remember, you will put your feet to that path and you will remember." When he might be ready for that new path, she could not guess. Khira worked at accepting the guide, but she was often tight-lipped and strained in his presence. And no matter how carefully Kadura guarded herself, Darkchild's dreams frequently brought her awake, perspiration clinging to her body and wetting her hair. Some nights she silently left the kefri and went to the memory house to sleep.

It was there Nezra found her one morning three hands after Khira and the boy had arrived in the plain. Kadura woke and found the failed barohna standing over her, her mottled stone clutched in one withered hand.

Kadura sat, chilling. Three centuries before Nezra had taken her bronzing prey prematurely. She had gone to the mountains a willful child of ten and returned not a barohna but something other, something never before known on Brakrath. She had the stature of a child, the face of a barohna, and just one gift. Although the gem masters had polished sunstones for her, she had never learned to invest them with light. Instead she had gone to the mountains again and found a stone of her own, dark, discolored, untouched by any hands but her own. With it she found messages in the air and, when the mood moved her, delivered them to the appropriate parties.

Kadura looked into Nezra's withered face and read nothing. Nor had she ever been able to read anything there beyond the fleeting expression of the moment. "Is there something?" she said.

Nezra's hair was fair and silken, shining incongruously against her withered cheek. Unconsciously she touched it with one clawed hand. "There is something," she said, looking down at Kadura with indifference.

"Then what is it, Nezra?" A message from Tiahna? Some notice from the Council of Bronze? It was many hands before the Council was due to convene, but if there were some unforeseen eventuality—

Deliberately Nezra turned away. "Someone comes," she said, and left the memory house.

Kadura's hands slackened on her bedding. Go after her and demand to know who was coming? But Nezra would not tell her. She knew that from the indifference of her gaze. Time and circumstance had created a unique perversity within Nezra. Sometimes she carried her messages in good fellowship, sometimes indifferently, sometimes with malice. Whatever her mood, she delivered them as it pleased her.

Today it pleased her to say simply, "Someone comes."

Stiffly Kadura stood and unfolded her bedding. She was troubled as she went to her morning chores and she felt warning jabs in her heart and a coldness that ran to her very fingertips.

Khira and the boy rode to the pinnacles that day with a group of guardian daughters. They returned late in the afternoon and Kadura saw immediately that the boy was bleeding. She stood from the firepit to tend him, but Khira went to the medicine jars herself and found bandages for his injured leg.

See what happens when I try to make friends of myself? Darkchild chided Kadura as Khira cleaned his scrapes and cuts and applied an herb dressing. *I let the guide climb the pinnacles and he fell and left me with the pain. I had to ride all the way back with it.*

"Was it a bad fall?"

Khira frowned over the herb jar. "He wouldn't have hurt himself at all if he had relaxed when he felt himself falling. But he stiffened."

"And you were kind afterward, just as you were patient before," Kadura said. "You *are* strong."

"The guide just doesn't know how to fall."

Kadura nodded, as pleased with Khira's off-handed acceptance as with Darkchild's good-humored rebuke.

It was dusk by the time they finished their evening meal. "Will you come to tonight's teaching?" Kadura asked.

As usual, the boy exchanged a glance with Khira and Khira said, "We'll come." She would sleep, Kadura knew, and the boy would sit stiffly, watching but afraid to participate.

So it might have been. They reached the teaching grounds as Nindra rose and the first redmanes gathered. Although summer had come and grasses grew deep on the plain, the night breeze was still chill. And as soon as she sat, Kadura felt a ripple of apprehension. The redmanes were restless, passing the same news among themselves, silently, that Nezra had brought to the memory house: *Someone comes.*

Kadura touched the soil and emptied herself. It was a woman who came, she found, and the woman was not a guardian. She came from the direction of the mountains, her face lost in the folds of a cape. She came slowly, heart-sore.

That was all Kadura found in the redmanes. The woman's face, her identity, were not significant to them.

The eldest redmanes approached the water to drink and then looked up at the gathered women. The younger redmanes moved restlessly behind them, ready for the teaching. It did not begin.

My herd, a woman comes.

My foals, she comes now.

Kadura gazed into the darkness, distinguishing motion from the small grove of trees west of the teaching place. The woman, whoever she might be, was there, hesitating in the shadow of the trees. Then she stepped into the moonlight and Kadura knew her immediately.

She was a barohna, her white shift stained, her dark hair wind-torn. She moved to the edge of the pond with eyes downcast, one hand clasping the pairing stone at her throat. The redmanes moved aside, and the barohna's reflection fell on the water. She was a woman shorn of the sun. Nor did her pairing stone glow between her fingers.

Kadura's hand clenched over her heart, trying to press away pain. She read everything that had happened from the woman's face even as the woman snapped the chain that held her pairing stone and threw the stone into the pond.

The water rippled and the gathered guardians sighed collectively. The barohna raised her head. Her voice trembled against the wind. "The sun has gone from my stones and the stone from my heart. I have come to live my quiet years among you."

Kadura turned to see the blood drain from Khira's face. She stood slowly. Her features seemed carved from ice, they were so pale, so immobile. The boy jumped to his feet, shocked by Khira's reaction. "She—Khira, who is she?"

Khira's eyes were huge with shadow. "Rahela—my mother's stone mate. She's turned flesh and left my mother alone."

The boy licked dry lips, trying to understand. "She—"

"I have to train." Khira's voice was flat.

"But—*why?*" This was Rahela, who made Tiahna's stone glow? She'd left her throne? The boy did not understand.

"I have to train," Khira repeated, this time with a note of hysteria. Turning blindly, she fled the teaching ground, fled the women who turned to look after her, testing her with their eyes.

The boy hesitated, not even able to formulate a silent question for Kadura. Then he turned and ran after Khira. When their footsteps faded, Kadura let her head fall to her breast, the icy pain in her heart greater than any she had known. She drew a fluttering breath and as she expelled it, she let her resistance to the swiftly proliferating ice crystals ebb away. There was pain in the ice, pain as the jagged crystals gouged the tender flesh of her heart, but eventually the cold would bring her numbness and peace. Then she would not have to think of Khira called so young to meet her beast.

14/Khira

"The sun has gone from my stones and the stone from my heart."

Khira stumbled from the teaching ground, blind to everything but the afterimage of Rahela at the pond. Shock had driven her blood to some deep place and left her entire body cold. Numbly she pushed back the nightcloak and extended her arms. They were grey. Like stone.

Every part of her was stone. She wanted only to stand, a graven monument to this moment. But she had to have her pike. And her pack, with clothes and supplies. She had to have those things to train. She stared down at her empty hands, the fingers pale, stiffly clenched. Would they always be this way, cold and useless? How could she strike if she could not close fingers around the haft of her pike?

How could she find her beast if her legs would not carry her?

She was dimly aware of Darkchild calling behind her. She did not turn. He belonged to another time, a time before Rahela had committed her pairing stone to the water. A time when the sunthrone had waited in the distant future.

Now it shadowed her life, darkening her eyes so she could hardly see.

"Khira—*please!*"

The plea in his voice touched through her shock. She stopped and turned, stiffly. Darkchild had thrown aside his nightcloak and wore only the grey suit Timar had tailored for him when they first came to the plain. Moonlight glinted upon his face and glanced from his eyes. Perplexity sat upon him like pain. "Khira—I don't understand. That woman—"

"Rahela."

"Your mother's stone mate—why is she here?"

Khira shook her head dumbly, trying to dismiss the dull pounding that filled her head—the rush of slow-pulsing blood through petrified veins. "She's lost the power of the stones. Her daughter—Lihwa must have bronzed." Impatient Lihwa—but no one had expected her to go this year. She still had a sister to raise, a child of four.

"She—Rahela's not a barohna anymore?"

"She's a barohna without stone. Like my grandmother. Like Upala. And she's left my mother alone. My mother has no one now."

Darkchild's pupils narrowed in quick comprehension. "She threw her pairing stone into the water because she can't use it anymore. And now that your mother is alone—"

Briefly an image of Tiahna flashed to mind. How would she look without the sun in her eyes? With the sunthrone dull behind her? "Her heart will turn flesh too. She will have to leave the valley."

"When?"

"Whenever her heart turns. Now—or hands from now. If it turns before I bronze—" Then the valley would taste the slow death of prolonged winter: scant crops, dying stock, debilitating cold.

"But you can't go now. You're too young. What you told me—about Nezra—"

Khira shuddered. "I'll go on the day of my first majority."

"On your birthday? Next spring?"

"Yes." Her whisper stood between them, thready, and she quivered with sudden cold, realizing that all of her had turned to stone but one vital organ: her heart. That had begun to ache with what she saw ahead: the hardship, the loneliness, and finally the challenge. "I have to go, Darkchild. I have to go to the mountain in the spring. And I have to go there now to train." She peered up at him, begging him to understand.

He studied her from a great stillness. She could see that he wanted to protest. But at last he took her hand and held it between his, warming it. "Yes. I'll help you."

And suddenly she wasn't stone at all. Suddenly she was weak, her blood rushing a dizzy course through her head. With the blood came tears and panic—and shame. Alzaja had gone in serenity—would she go in fear? She caught at Darkchild's arm, pleading. "Darkchild, if the guardians come from the pond now—if they come—"

He held her, hiding her face against his shoulder. "I won't let them see you cry," he promised.

Her relief that he understood made her tears come that much faster.

They left the campment at dawn the next day with packs on their backs and pikes in their hands. Kadura watched from the door of her kefri, her cloak tucked around her as if to hide a mortal frailty. When they reached the edge of the campment, Khira turned to look back, knowing it was not the campment she left behind but childhood. She would never again run through the coarse grass with guardian daughters. If she one day rode a redmane again, it would not be for sport. And if she ever returned to the plain, she would not sleep through the teaching. She would listen and begin to learn.

They reached the mountains two days later, tired and dusty, and sheltered the night in the same rocky cove where they had slept before. Khira lay awake as the moons progressed across the sky, listening to the wind in the rocks, to Darkchild's sleeping breath, to the anxious throbbing of her heart. Tomorrow they would weave targets and fashion other training devices. They would cut staffs for sparring. And they would run, but not as they had run together before, in play. This time they would run to harden her legs and strengthen her wind.

Khira tried to distance herself from fear by listing all the things she must do in training: all the things Alzaja had not done because she knew they would never be enough; all the things Mara had not done because she hadn't thought them necessary; all the things Denabar had done— and had almost won the throne by doing.

Still her fear was not quieted. *Heart, be stone. Flesh, be fearless.* Sliding deep into her bedding, she whispered long verses from the earliest scrolls. Her voice rasped in her throat. But that was not the way past fear either. The verses only emphasized how little had changed since the first palace daughter had gone to make her challenge. These many centuries later breeterlik still slept in deep caverns, fouling the air with the stench of meat that rotted between their teeth. Crag-chargers still tumbled down mountainside in horny armor and stingmadders still slipped along the surfaces of quiet ponds. Snowminx still crept like white shadows.

Palace daughters still trained.

Hand, be sure. Eye, be vigilant.

Finally she slept, restlessly. When she woke the next morning, it was not to train. She fought from sleep as if from a smothering blanket, perspiring. Darkchild bent over her anxiously. "You were crying, Khira. In your sleep. And your face—" He tested her flushed cheeks with measuring fingertips.

Fever. She had tried to be strong, but this morning the fear that burned in her spirit burned in her body too. She pushed aside her cloak and sat. Dizziness forced her down again. "I have a fever." She would not train today.

Nor did she train for many days. Later Darkchild found a small cavern higher on the mountain and helped her to it. Then he searched for the herbs she directed him to find and brew. Those did not help. The fever persisted, a physical manifestation of her weakness. Alzaja had been wrong. Her heart was not stone. It was flesh and the flesh was failing.

She dreamed in her fever, dreamed for most of many nights and days. She often woke to find Darkchild sitting beside her, trying to hide his worry. Or she woke to find the guide bending over her, pressing her hand, silently pleading for her to be well.

One? In her dreams Darkchild and the guide melded and become one person manifested in two personalities. In her dreams she even recognized why the guide was awkward, why his voice was harsh. He was afraid too and fear drew his muscles tight, binding his joints. Fear stiffened his throat and made his voice grate.

He was afraid. She was afraid. Beasts came to her in her dreams and she struggled against them until her bedding was soaked with perspiration. When the beasts did not come, Tiahna did, her pairing stone dull, the sunstone circlets dead at her wrists. Then Khira fought to throw off sleep, driven by a growing sense of urgency. She must go to the valley. She must go to the people. If she did not, they would die.

But each time she tried to go, the beasts were upon her again.

The beasts...Tiahna...the valley...

Finally on the seventh night of her illness, the fever receded and she lay weakly in her bedding. Darkchild sat against the cavern wall, sleeping with his forehead resting against his knees. She studied his profile, the clean line of forehead, nose and chin, seeing him with a new clarity. He was the one who had taken the stone from her heart. He was the one who had made her flesh. She had let herself care for him as she had not cared for anyone else—even Alzaja—and in her caring, she had lost her gritty substance.

Weakly she stood and groped to the mouth of the cavern. The night was clear, the stars white. If she could see Adar instead of these serene points of light, if she could fill her eyes with his war-fires—

But she would not hear the rattle of Adar's drums tonight. She would not feel his anger rise in her, expunging fear and shame. This was not Adar's season.

I'll never go to my beast, she realized, except to die. I've given Darkchild the stone from my heart. Now nothing can make me strong.

She turned back to the cavern. She was relieved that Darkchild did not stir as she slipped back into her bedding.

They left the cavern the next day, traveling slowly through the mountains. As they went, they fashioned staffs for sparring and wove targets for striking. But when Khira trained, she did so reluctantly, with no heart. Darkchild pressed her gently, he watched anxiously when she withdrew from activity, he hunted and cooked for her. At night, she knew, he often watched while she slept. He thought her reticence, her reluctance, were remnants of illness. She did not know how to tell him otherwise.

They traveled through the mountains for five days. On the morning of the sixth, Khira woke at a sound from beyond the cave where they slept. As she reached for her pike, her heart hammering, a shadow fell across the mouth of the cave. Carefully Khira slipped from her bedding and touched Darkchild's shoulder. His eyes slid open, the pupils glistening in the dim light. She held a finger to her lips and indicated the cave's entrance.

Before he could slip from his bedding, Nezra stepped into the cave.

Slowly Khira lowered her pike, the hair prickling at the back of her neck. Nezra's child's body was lost in a black cloak, but her silken hair hung free on her shoulders. She carried a walking stick in one withered hand, clutching it like a sparring staff.

"My mother—" Khira said without thinking. Had Tiahna already lost command of the stones?

Nezra's pale eyes glinted child-bright and malicious in her withered barohna's face. "Tiahna requests that you come to the palace immediately to celebrate midsummer. The people ask to see you."

"She—" Was that all? Had Nezra come just for that? And was it midsummer already? So soon?

"You will meet the Arnimi at midday in the northernmost meadow of Ladana's valley, below. They will take you to the palace in their aircar."

"The—the Arnimi are still in my mother's valley?" Khira was surprised to find she had not thought of Verra and Commander Bullens since she had left the palace.

Nezra lowered her stick and thumped the ground with it. "Is there some reason they would not be?"

"No." She had never taken Tiahna's threats against the Arnimi for more than a moment's temper. "Nezra—"

"I have no time," Nezra said with a second impatient thump of her stick. "Midsummer comes to the plain too and my redmane waits for me. Join the Arnimi below."

"And if I don't go?" Khira demanded, stung by Nezra's arbitrary manner.

Nezra peered at her from unwinking eyes. "Is there some reason you should not?"

Khira shuddered. Something dark looked from Nezra's pupils, something not at all human. It made her think of a stingmadder resting on the surface of a pond, waiting. "I'll be in the meadow."

Nezra nodded, drawing lids over the threat in her eyes. Swirling her cape, she vanished. For a giddy moment, Khira wondered if her feet had even left prints in the dirt.

Prints there were, and when Khira went to the cave mouth, she saw a black shape tramping down the mountainside, golden hair gleaming. Seen from behind, Nezra might have been a palace daughter in her mother's cloak—a child born three centuries before to an unkind destiny.

"You don't want to go to the midsummer festival?" Darkchild asked softly.

Khira turned back to the cave, refusing to meet his gaze. "I'll go." The words were hollow. She would go and the people would know when they saw her that their valley was lost. Lost for the lack in her heart. Lost because there was fear where there should have been courage.

They descended silently. When they reached Ladana's valley, it was midday and the Arnimi aircar waited. Khira approached silently, too preoccupied to notice that Darkchild hung back momentarily before following her.

The aircar rose across the mountains. Khira stared down on rocky spires and jutting formations, letting the grumble of the car's rotors relieve her of thought. Had she been less preoccupied, she would have seen that Darkchild sat stiffly erect, his jaws clenched, his hands gripping the arms of his seat.

Soon they passed over Terlath's dark spires and the valley lay below, green fields and bright orchards. Sunlight shone in broad beams from the lenses on the mountainside and converged on the throneroom mirrors. Khira saw with relief that there was no sign of dereliction in the valley.

But when the aircar landed, the people who had gathered on the plaza were silent in their bright festival robes. Khira shrank in her seat, not wanting to face them.

Silence and watching eyes—no one could miss the shadow that lay across the people as Khira disembarked from the aircar. She felt unreal under the gaze of so many eyes. Shrinking, she picked out Letra, the weaving mistress, in a gown that shimmered with centuries of embroidery. "Letra, are you well?"

The weaving mistress inclined her head, her pale eyes studying Khira, evaluating her in every detail. "As well as ever, daughter."

"And my mother is well?" Again Khira managed to keep her voice from trembling.

Again the weaving mistress inclined her head without lowering her gaze. "Well but lonely. She waits in the throneroom to see you. We all wait, daughter."

And now you see. You see that I am not the daughter you thought I was. You see that I am lacking in the very thing you require: heart. "I will go to her," Khira's lips said, completing the exchange of their own volition.

With Darkchild, she descended from the ship and crossed the plaza, conscious of each person who watched. Did Tiahna feel this shrinking loneliness when she returned from her winter throne each spring? The

weight of so many eyes—Khira wanted to hide. These were her people
and they were strong. But if the throne stood vacant, not one of them
could command the stones and bring warmth to the valley.

Nor could she. If she had guessed that in the mountains, she knew
it now. As she crossed the plaza, there was nothing but flesh beneath
her ribs, aching flesh. She clutched Darkchild's hand.

The great iron doors of the palace cried open for her. The stones of
the entry hall were oppressive. She had never noticed how dark they
were, how crusted with centuries. Even the clinging glow of stalklamp
could not brighten them.

She hardly saw the people who stepped aside to let her enter the
throneroom. Light, color, motion—the throneroom was hung with ban-
ners, thronged with dancers. But she saw only the blazing throne and
the swords of light that stabbed down from the throneroom mirrors to
inflame it. She halted, letting her breath seep away. To sit there, to
grasp the sun's bright blade and turn it to her people's use—

But she could not. Could not.

Tiahna stood. Her summerfest gown was black, embroidered with
sun-emblems that struck light as she stepped forward. Her strength
remained visible in the blaze of the throne and in the fire of her sunstone
wristlets. But the pairing stone hung dull at her throat and her eyes were
like Kadura's now, looking back rather than ahead.

Had she already begun to enter minds? If so, in Khira's mind she
would find the lost wraiths of anger, drowned in fear. In Khira's mind
she would find the same darkness that soon would consume the valley.

Tiahna's voice was husky. "Goodsummer, daughter. We are gathered
for the midsummer dancing of the tides. Bring your friend; join me."

The flagged floor seemed to stretch for spans beneath Khira's feet
as gowned dancers parted to let her pass. Walking among them, Khira
could feel their tension. Where the people on the plaza had been silently
vigilant, the dancers were eager and perspiring. It was time to call up
the tides, and nothing mattered more today.

Without word, Khira took her place beside the throne, drawing Darkchild down beside her. Tiahna seated herself and raised her hand to the
dancers. They were paired, woman and man, their dance gowns rich
with centuries of embroidery. Many were pairs who had produced a
child together that spring. Others were pairs chosen to produce a child
the next spring. As they began to dance to the soft thump of drums,
the year's infants were carried into the throneroom in the arms of their

paternal grandfathers. Each child was wrapped in an investiture robe woven centuries before and embellished with the embroidered devices of every generation since.

The dance was as old as the gowns of the dancers, older. It began with a stamping of sandaled feet, with a clapping of hands, with a solemn turning and bowing and nodding. Each gesture was a stylized promise to the infants in arms and to the community, a vow of guidance and care.

As the dance continued, the stamping grew heavier, the clapping faster, the turning and bowing and nodding more emphatic. Gradually the dance became a promise of the dancers not to the infants but to each other, man to woman, woman to man. Tonight when woodsmoke fires burned on the plaza and all who had been selected gathered there, the tides would rise, those sweet inner tides, and man and woman would yield to them in the fullness of joy.

The tides would rise, and their response would be of more than the body. It would be a response of the spirit, calling up the unjoined elements of the child who was to be conceived that night, urging them to union. Flesh would yield, fluids would flow, and the child would feel the call of the parents, the call to life. Sperm and egg would make their separate magic and two halves would become one whole.

We call you, spirit, the dancers whispered, clapping. *We call you, child. You bring us together. We bring you to union. Come, use us as your tools. Come, make yourself of us.*

We call you child, the dancers chanted, clapping: *We have a name for you. We have a name with grace and strength and intelligence. Come—make yourself of us.*

We call you, child. We have a robe for you. It is embroidered with the thread of centuries. You will be one strand of that thread. Beyond you will be others. Come!

The dance continued, and the valley itself called. The mountains called. There were paths to be walked, ground to be tilled. There were garments to be woven, songs to be sung. Later there would be other children to be summoned to conception.

The drums gave the call its heartbeat. The dancers spun and clapped and chanted, perspiration staining their embroided gowns. Without thinking, Khira turned to Tiahna. She had turned each year, looking for some sign that the tide rose in Tiahna too.

Foolish to study Tiahna's impassive profile this year. She was

Tiahna's last daughter. Perhaps next year there would not even be a dance. Perhaps next year—

Khira felt Darkchild's hand on her arm. At the back of the throne-room, the elder women had come with torches. Tiahna stood. At a gesture, the men who held the ropes to the throneroom mirrors turned the mirrors. Swords of sunlight were immediately sheathed in darkness. Only the throne gave light—and the torches.

The torchwomen strode through the dancers, the light of fire shining from their sweated faces. "We call you, we call you!" The dancers chanted louder and louder, until they were shouting, until the throne-room echoed with their cry to the tides.

"We call you!"

Khira closed her hand over Darkchild's as the dancers reached the peak of frenzy. Abruptly the dancing pairs shouted once and stopped mid-stride. The drums fell to silence, as if the heartbeat of the palace had ceased. The torch bearers pounded their feet on the floor, making their own ululating cry as they ran to the perimeter of the throneroom where vessels of water waited. They plunged their torches into the vessels. Flame died in the roar of steam.

As the steam dissipated into the throneroom, shrouding the throne, Juris Fenilis stepped before the dais. "Torch and vessel—join tonight as your parents joined before you, as others have always joined. Go!"

The mirrors remained dark as the people left the throneroom. Tiahna sat in silence, dark against the captive sunlight of the throne, until everyone had gone. Then she turned to Khira and studied her impassively. "This is your last year to take midsummer feast with the children, daughter."

Khira shrank against Darkchild. "There will be no other," she whispered. She had not expected Tiahna to be so direct.

"Next year," Tiahna continued, as if she had not heard, "you will feast with the women. You will drink the ovulants and if the tides are right, the year after there will be a new daughter in the palace."

Disbelief brought Khira to her feet. Could Tiahna look at her with clear eyes and not see the truth? "Next year I'll be dead—or in exile in the mountains!"

Tiahna accepted her outburst with faint surprise. Unconsciously she clasped the dulled stone at her throat. "I don't believe you will be either dead or living in the mountains next midsummer, daughter. I believe you will sit here on my throne while I celebrate midsummer in the plain with Rahela." For a moment her gaze touched Darkchild. "Your friend, I expect, will be here beside you."

Couldn't she see? *Wouldn't* she see? "I'll never take the throne!" Khira cried, pain and rising anger mingling in her voice. "If I were fit to command the stones, my heart would be ready. I would be ready to train!"

Again Tiahna expressed faint surprise. "Most certainly you are ready to train, daughter."

"For what? To die?" The vehemence of her response surprised her. Faced with Tiahna's bland insistence, Khira felt muscles draw tight that had grown slack. Had Adar come into the heavens out of season? "If I go to my challenge like this—afraid—I'll never come back."

Tiahna's brows rose. "So you are afraid, Khira." It was more statement than question.

Khira stared up at her, wanting to deny it. But surely the truth was apparent. "Yes!" Angrily.

Tiahna stood and paced across the dais, her gown rustling. When she turned back, her customary impassivity had fallen away. For the first time she spoke to Khira as to an equal—as to a younger friend who was also sister and daughter. "You're the only daughter ever to tell me that, Khira. You're the only one strong enough to voice your fear."

"I'm—" Khira's mind turned blank. Strong enough to voice fear? If only she were strong enough to hide it!

"Khira, you think the stone is gone from you. No—I'm not moving in your mind. I'm simply reading your face. You've studied your heart so closely you no longer see its nature. You see confusion. You see fear. Pain. Caring that gives you as much pain as joy. You see such a conflicting range of emotions in yourself that you can no longer distinguish one important element—courage. And so you think you are weak."

"I am!" Khira admitted, a whisper. Tears stung her eyes.

"Yes. You are as weak as I was when I began my training. That weak, Khira."

"No."

"Yes. You are as weak as your father. I've watched for him in you for twelve years now and today I see him. Today I see your father as

he was before he went to the mountains that last time. No, I won't tell
you his name and I won't tell you the name of the valley where he was
born. He made this valley his home for a short time before he went to
find new veins in the mountains."

Khira caught her breath, unbelieving. Surely no barohna ever told
her daughter even this much of her father. "He was a gem master," she
realized.

"Yes, and I trust he found some stone that pleased him when he left
here. I've always hoped that for him, that he held it in his hand when
the avalanche caught him." She turned to address Darkchild, who peered
up at her with darkly questioning eyes. "A barohna does not choose her
mate in the way the women of the halls do, Rauth-Seven. In the halls,
the families confer and study genealogies and when they make a selection of mates, it is the culmination of a long thoughtful process. At
midsummer the proper tides rise and the contractants conceive. If the
selection has been a good one, there are healthy offspring and the
contractants enjoy the mating through many years.

"A barohna pursues no such course. She moves through the months
of the year watching for a man who will make her tides rise. Sometimes
she finds him at midsummer fest, and then she goes to him and dances
with him. Other times she finds him when she least expects—as she
walks the fields, as she talks with her people. A man who has never
been of interest to her before suddenly becomes so and she arranges to
meet with him.

"And sometimes she is alone on the mountain when she meets a lone
lens tender or a herder—or a gem master."

Darkchild spoke hesitantly. "Gem masters—are the only men sensitive to stones."

"Yes. They are the only men who have feeling for the stones that
a barohna can use. Lensar was the first gem master—though since he
was the first, he did not call himself that. And he did not live to see
how the sunstones he found and polished were ultimately used."

Darkchild nodded. "Because when Niabi learned how to release the
sun from the stones, she turned him to ash."

"Yes—you've studied the scrolls. Niabi had no way of knowing
what she could do with the stones until she had done it—and then it
was too late. Lensar was dead." Tiahna turned back to Khira. "Your
father came to the valley to bring me a pairing stone to replace one that

had chipped. When he placed it on my neck, when his hands touched me, I wished it could take me into his mind instead of Rahela's. He had many of the strengths and sensitivities of a woman, and when the avalanche caught him, I knew it. I felt it through the pairing stone he had polished for me. If he had lived, he intended to polish an eyestone and wear it at his neck as I wore the pairing stone. He intended to wear it wherever he went."

"So you could see what he saw," Khira said softly.

"Yes. I would have accompanied him on all his travels that way. I would have gone everywhere with him, seen everything he saw. And if he had come back to the valley midsummer next, I would have danced with him and you would have had younger sisters."

But he had not returned, and the tide had never risen for Tiahna again. "But I'm still afraid," Khira said.

"I've been afraid for most of my life, Khira."

"You?"

"Yes, afraid of every event of my life. Afraid I would fail in my training and then in my challenge. Afraid I would fail on the throne. Then afraid I would never bear daughters, afraid the daughters I did bear would never bronze—afraid Nezra would not find you and bring you to midsummer.

"The test is not in the absence of fear, Khira. The test is in acknowledging fear and living beyond it."

"Yes." The sighing word was Darkchild's. Tiahna acknowledged it with a nod, then turned back to Khira—waiting.

There were centuries behind her waiting—and all the stones of Brakrath. To Khira's surprise, she felt fear and inadequacy ebb away to be replaced by quiet certainty. Her father had lived by the stones and died by them. Tiahna had lived by the stones too.

Now it was her time. Without thinking, she raised one hand to her breast. It clenched there, clutching at the stone that was suddenly in her heart again. Not the stone of harshness, of uncaringness. Tiahna was not harsh and uncaring, although she had often seemed so in her loneliness. Nor need Khira be harsh and uncaring to take the throne. "I'm ready to begin training," she said.

Tiahna returned to her throne, silhouetting herself against its captive fire. "Yes, you are ready. But not tonight. Tonight there is a feast to be eaten. And then I would like you to return to the plain for the bonding

of the herds. Your grandmother is not well—I have that message. If
this is her last bonding, I would like you to be with her.

"Then you may train."

Yes, she would use pike and targets. She would spar with staffs.
She would run and do all the things necessary to build her body. But
her heart required nothing. It was whole again. She caught Darkchild's
hand and felt the strength of the stones between them.

She was whole.

15/Darkchild

Kadura was not well. Darkchild saw that immediately when they reached her kefri. She waited near the door, wrapped in her nightcloak despite the afternoon heat. There were new lines in her face, as if the flesh had fallen, and there was a shadow upon her eyes. But what it might hide—

Khira seemed not to notice. She ran to Kadura eagerly. "We haven't missed the bonding, have we?"

The old woman embraced Khira, then studied her closely, looking deep. Khira wore her auburn hair knotted loosely over one ear, and her skin had taken a healthy sun patina. There was no mistaking her buoyancy or her new confidence. "The herds haven't gathered yet. You've had a good journey, daughter's daughter."

"Yes—I've begun training. I've trained for ten days now in the mountains."

"You've begun well. I see that in your face." Kadura turned to Darkchild, the shadow upon her eyes deepening. "And your friend— Darkchild, have you helped her?"

"When I could," he said, passing off the question hurriedly. "Kadura—" *Kadura, why do you look this way: ill?*

But she nodded away his unspoken question and led Khira into the kefri. This was not the time to talk about the change he saw in her.

This was the time to undertake a new phase of Khira's training: night stalks. They made the first that night, leaving the campment at sunset, taking only their pikes and a few bars of dried fruit. "I want to go to the grove beyond the pinnacles," Khira explained as they passed the deserted teaching ground. "Whispreys come there sometimes in the summer—and nightcallers. And sometimes a whitemane comes from the forest beyond the plain."

"A whitemane?" Darkchild responded distractedly, still wondering about the change in Kadura. If she would not tell him what made her ill—and if what he had heard about the bonding were true—

"They're—" Khira halted, listening. Then she shook her head. "Nothing. Some people think they're a form of redmane. Other people think they're descended from animals that came with the first timers— horses. Guardians go to the forest sometimes to try to learn their ways, but no one has ever found their teaching grounds. So no one knows how they live. If we could stalk one and find their teaching ground—"

"We wouldn't learn anything," he reminded her. Certainly neither of them had learned the ways of the redmanes that summer. He always sat stiff, cold and guarded through the teachings, while Khira slept.

She sighed, surrendering her moment's enthusiasm. "Someday I'll learn to listen."

Except for the browsing redmanes, the plains were sparsely populated. There were occasional groundfowl, chortling sleepily from nests deep in dense clumps of grass. Khira paused at every sign, listening intently. Then she studied the ground for droppings and for the scratching tracks the fowl left in the soil.

But there was not much cunning to be gained in tracking groundfowl. Soon the moons rose and found Khira and Darkchild making a steady pace toward the pinnacles. Occasionally they passed a solitary redmane or a buck and mares.

Several times they skirted guardian campments and passed places where groups of redmanes and guardians gathered around pools or streams. Darkchild guarded himself against the urge to stop, to try to fathom the animals' silent communication.

Sometimes riding, sometimes walking, they reached the pinnacles in the middle hours of evening. The sterile rock peaks cast bizarre shadows upon the plain, and by moonlight Darkchild could believe their legend: that once a party of breeders had come to abduct the most ancient mare of all the redmanes as she stood teaching at the pond, and that upon lashing their ropes to her neck, the seven breeders and their five helpers were turned to stone. There was frozen agony in the craggy rocks, as if they were caught in a timeless scream. By moonlight there were eyes too, staring from deep-shadowed crevices.

And tonight an ancient redmane stood teaching at the pond, younger redmanes gathered near. Darkchild followed Khira with stiff reluctance, feeling the cold of the summer night for the first time. Nindra and Zan rode upon the surface of the pond in silver silence. No redmane moved.

Listen, my herd—

Darkchild could not listen. With choking panic, he ran, not even looking back.

He stopped, breathless, when the pinnacles were faceless crags in the distance. *Doors*—when he emptied himself to the redmanes, he saw doors. He wanted to move past them, into the dreams that still troubled his nights. But the doors were guarded by dragons. Shaking, he wiped cold sweat from his face. If he could capture a fragment of his dreams, a scrap—a color, a face—

Khira had caught up with him and studied him anxiously. "I couldn't stay there," he said shakily. "I saw their faces in the crags—the breeders—"

She accepted that explanation and they rested for a few minutes, then continued their stalk.

As they neared the grove, Khira walked with silent stealth, watching and listening. A crushed leaf, a fallen feather—she must be alert for every sign now. She had come to pit her cunning against the most elusive creatures of the plain—not to take them for meat, but to sharpen her instincts and her senses in stalking them.

Darkchild let her walk ahead, let her search for the faint signs marking the passage of prey. Even so, he was first to see the wisp of grey fur caught in the coarse grass near the edge of the trees. "Khira—"

Khira turned and quickly saw the direction of his gaze. "Whisprey." Her lips formed the syllables silently.

There was no second wisp of fur, but as they slipped through the trees, they found other signs: the faint track of small feet, a shredded seed pod, raw dirt where the animal had scratched for insects. The trees of the grove were tall but widely spaced. Darkchild and Khira passed through an intricate gridwork of moonlight and shadow, searching.

Then Khira halted, raising her hand for silence. Darkchild peered around. A small shape crouched at the base of a nearby tree. Its pear-shaped body was lightly furred and soft with fat. Its feet were tiny and man-like, with pink-nailed toes. There were two small arms with man-like hands. But there was no neck and no distinct head. Instead there was a cluster of tiny oval eyes near the rounded peak of the body. As Darkchild studied the creature, it peered back at him, lidding and un-lidding its many eyes with confusing rapidity.

Carefully Khira eased herself to the ground. She moved her head from side to side, closing first one eye, then the other. In response the whisprey rocked too, its eyes flickering even more rapidly than before. When the animal quieted again, Khira reached into her pack for a fruit bar.

The whisprey considered the offering with much blinking of eyes. Then it edged forward, and from the palms of its pink-nailed hands came a buzzing whisper. The creature accepted the fruit bar and the whispering rose to a whining peak. Quickly the whisprey tore the bar into two pieces and closed one hand around each section.

After a moment its hands opened and it began to rock from foot to foot, whispering again, this time with a note of demand. Darkchild edged forward. There was a stickiness in the palms of the creature's hands—nothing more. And still the whispering petition continued, ris-ing to an angry buzz when Khira did not offer a second fruit bar. "No more," she said, closing her pack.

Film appeared immediately upon the whisprey's clustered eyes. It stood utterly still, clenching its small hands until even the residual stickiness was absorbed. Then, abruptly, it stood and ran, fat and wad-dling, comical.

However comical the creature, it was much harder to track this time. It left scant trace on the dry-thatched ground: an occasional fallen hair, a drop of spittle, a barely perceptible disturbance of the fallen leaves that matted the ground. It took all Khira's concentration and skill to follow its trail.

Then they spotted the plump creature crouched beneath another tree, waiting. Again it peered up with rapidly blinking eyes, again it begged a fruit bar and absorbed it. Again it retreated in indignation when refused further offering.

The third time the whisprey was still more difficult to track. Darkchild and Khira wandered through the trees with little clue until the animal showed itself and buzzed for its reward.

The fourth time they found the animal, the clues that led through the grove were so tenuous Darkchild was not certain the animal they found was the same animal they had been tracking. But the animal agitated to be fed almost immediately and this time vanished without being verbally refused a second offering.

"I don't think we'll find him again," Khira said.

They searched anyway, studying the ground minutely for traces. Several times they crossed their own trail and followed it a distance before branching away again.

They had passed under the same hollow-trunked tree three times, its feathery leaves brushing their hair, when Darkchild glanced up and saw a faintly glistening shadow in the distance. He froze as the shadow slipped from sight, knowing that in the grove were black shadows and grey shadows, but none the color of moonlight. "Khira—there—"

She looked in time to see the shadow reappear. It stood poised among the trees, a dewy white form with graceful neck and slender legs. It seemed to watch them from the center of a great stillness. "A white-mane," Khira whispered, moving forward slowly. "If we don't move too quickly—"

The animal watched with quivering alertness as they crept toward it. With each deliberate step, Darkchild distinguished more detail: long narrow head with pricked ears and flared nostrils; eyes that glinted pink by moonlight; a silken white mane; powerful shoulders and hindquarters supported by delicately formed legs. The whitemane peered at them across the shadowed grove, a creature of grace and strength.

It was also a creature of easy frights. It tossed its glistening mane nervously as they approached and danced backward through the trees. They halted until the animal forgot its fright, then inched forward again. This time the animal rose to its hind legs, pawing the air with anxious hooves. Darkchild caught his breath, afraid the animal would overbalance and fall. But it sank to fours again and danced away into the trees, uttering a shrill cry, its hooves striking the densely thatched soil with barely a sound.

The whitemane's trail was not difficult to follow. It led to the far edge of the grove—and beyond, to the north. Darkchild and Khira stood at the edge of the trees and Darkchild was torn between feelings of privilege that he had glimpsed the elusive white creature at all and sharp feelings of loss.

"It's gone back to the forest," Khira said finally. "We frightened it away."

"How far is the forest?" If they could reach there before daylight, if he could see the whitemane by moonlight again, enchanted . . .

"We wouldn't reach the trees until afternoon, unless we found redmanes to ride. And if we stayed more than a day or two, we might miss the bonding."

The bonding: the gathering of the herds of the plain to select mates for the coming year and to cull their numbers. Darkchild felt a moment's uneasiness, the return of a question he had silently nursed as they made their way back to the plain after the midsummer feasting. *Kadura* . . . But this was not the time for that question, and he put it aside. "We'll have to go back to the campment," he agreed reluctantly.

They encountered the whisprey again as they made their way back through the grove. It hissed and buzzed and finally shrilled angrily when they did not stop. By silent agreement, they stalked no more that night but walked back across the plain. The ancient mare still taught beneath the pinnacles and the moons still made the plain silver-bright. But a white shadow stood between Darkchild and his surroundings. He could not forget the whitemane's alert grace.

Each time they passed a guardian campment, Darkchild noticed that there were more redmanes than he had seen earlier. Many were dusty with travel and they moved restlessly among the other, quieter animals, stallions nudging mares, mares rubbing against stallions in silent inquiry.

"The herds are gathering," Khira explained, frowning distractedly.

Kadura—he must talk to Kadura tomorrow.

But Kadura left the kefri before he woke next morning. And when he dressed and ate and went asking for her, no one could give him word. He searched with rising anxiety. The herds were gathering. Everywhere were dusty, tired animals. He studied them covertly. They walked heavily on padded feet, their coats dense, dull, grey. Their manes hung tangled and rust-red across stocky shoulders. They scarcely raised their heads as he passed.

He had caught only isolated glimpses of the whitemane in the trees, but he could imagine how it would look moving aloof and pale among these heavyset animals, how it would bend its long neck to graze, how it would pause, raising its head, gazing around with quivering alertness, ears pricked. How anyone could think the whitemane related to the redmanes . . .

Kadura still had not returned to the kefri late that afternoon. There was only Khira, stirring a pot of soup, ladling some for him. "Tonight is the night of veils at the teaching ground. Will you come?"

"Veils?" There were so many customs he had not heard about.

"The oldest guardians, the ones who think they may not come back from the bonding, wear veils tonight and join in the teaching."

Darkchild shuddered. That would answer his question, if he went to the teaching and Kadura sat veiled beside the pond. But to have his answer that way, to see Kadura's face shadowed as if death already fell across it—

"I'll stay here," he said shortly.

He kept vigil in the kefri while Khira went alone to the teaching. Despite his rising anxiety, the warmth of the kefri and fatigue made him drowsy. He lay down and without intending it went to sleep.

It was much later when he woke. The fire had died to embers and Khira and Kadura had returned and gone to bed. Darkchild sat, looking at Kadura's shadowed face and aching with hollow uncertainty.

Tomorrow. Tomorrow he would ask her: *Kadura, I know that guardians die in the bonding. The old, the unfit, the tired—they fall then. Khira has told me that. But no one has told me—do barohnas fall in the bonding too?*

You look old now and tired—so much older, so much more tired than when we first came to the plain. Will you die when the herds gather?

Kadura stirred, the light of the single hanging lantern falling across her face, making a death-mask of it. Darkchild squeezed his eyes shut and burrowed into his bedding.

The next morning there was the sound of many padding feet in the campment. Redmanes passed in weary numbers, heads bowed, flanks dusty. Darkchild stood at the door of Kadura's kefri watching. There were dark-cloaked shapes among the animals, guardians walking silently with the migrating herds. And there were bright-haired figures—guardian daughters, laughing and making a game of the pilgrimage.

Again Kadura had slipped from the kefri before Darkchild woke, but this time she returned at mid-morning. She was wrapped loosely in her heavy nightcloak, and the shadow upon her eyes had darkened. "We go with the herds this afternoon, Darkchild," she said without preface. "The bonding will begin at tomorrow moonrise. You will be the first male to see the bonding in many centuries—very many."

He peered up at her, stricken dumb by the darkness in her eyes. *Kadura—*

At the last moment, afraid, he tried to call back his silent question. But he had rehearsed it too often. It came of itself.

Her response surprised him. She smiled, her eyes clearing. "No, child, barohnas never die in the bonding. There is something in us so enduring we must will it dead before it can die. But we lose our guardian friends in the bonding and sometimes we realize then it is time to take the ice and follow."

Again he could not hold back his question. *Kadura—this year will you take the ice?* Without her stone mate, without the oldest of her friends, without health, how long would she choose to live?

Kadura sighed, her eyes sinking into shadow again. "Do I look so old to you—and so ill?"

You look older than you did just hands ago, when we first came here. You look like something hurts you. That was the shadow in her eyes—pain.

She nodded, completely shadowed now. "There are many things to hurt a person like myself, Darkchild. The loss of my mate, the loss of friends—but so many other things too. Imagine yourself moving among minds as I do. Imagine all the things you might see and feel—and wish you had not."

The burden of everyone's pain. The ache of everyone's loss, and all of it as immediate as if it were her own. Without thinking, he reached for her hand. It was unexpectedly fragile, as if the bones had turned dry and brittle beneath the weathered skin. *That's why barohnas finally take the ice,* he guessed. *Because they learn to read more and more in other people until someday they read too much.*

"Someday . . ." she agreed, a dry whisper, and stepped past him into the kefri.

They left that afternoon, walking eastward. Padding redmanes surrounded them in every direction, walking with weary purpose, heads lowered. No one rode. They walked together, women, children and animals. As they walked, Darkchild held himself stiffly aloof, clutching his pike. Something in the migration made him feel that a great teaching was taking place on the plain, that every animal was silently speaking to the consciousness of every other.

Although he tried, he could not entirely close himself to the teaching. It was too pervasive. The very soil of the plain pounded with it, like an earthen heart. It reached him through every sense.

He dreamed that night, a confusion of dark images. Terror moved scarlet in his dreams; despair stalked them, black. He saw everything through the screen of those dark colors: faces, structures, trees, paths. He woke half a dozen times, trembling. Each time Kadura watched him from her blankets, her face grey. He didn't try to speak.

The last time he woke, Kadura had gone. Khira bent over him, concerned. "You—you shouted."

"A dream," he muttered hoarsely and turned away to darker dreams still.

Late the next afternoon they stood on a promontory overlooking the bonding ground. Below them redmanes stretched as far as the eye could see, a massed assemblage of thousands. Upon reaching their destination, the animals had thrown off their plodding weariness. From below came calls and shrills, piercing, excited. Although the massed animals gave the appearance of a solid field of grey, individual animals moved constantly, shrilling at each other, rubbing necks, chewing manes in greeting and courtship.

Darkchild looked down upon them as if upon a nightmare. He had not brought a single concrete image from his night's dreams into consciousness, no more than ever. But he remembered the colors of his dreams and he remembered terror. And somehow the redmanes were responsible for his recalling that much.

"They've already begun pairing," Khira said, and he watched reluctantly. Pairs of redmanes rose on their hind legs, jabbing the air with padded feet, tossing their tangled manes. Foals darted among the courting pairs in noisy excitement, stirring the red dust of the bonding ground into obscuring clouds.

Uneasily Darkchild gazed around. Caped and hooded, guardians lined the promontories that commanded the plain. He had never before been so aware of their silence. Tonight it was a watching silence, a waiting silence. He caught his lower lip in his teeth. There were perhaps sixty barohnas among the guardians, and they waited too, in silence as deep.

Darkchild and Khira sat atop a boulder until sunset. With dusk an acrid odor rose from the plain, a musk that drove the redmanes to shrilling excitement. Darkchild sucked at the cold evening air, his hands gnarled into fists. More than once Khira glanced at him in concern but said nothing.

Finally, with darkness, the plain became still. Courting bucks and mares fell to fours and stood motionless. Even the foals ceased their running and shrilling. Darkchild stirred uneasily as thousands of animals became as stone. After a while the silence was complete—and terrible from so many animals. Darkchild turned to Khira. She had grown rigid, hardly seeming to breathe.

Then Nindra appeared over the crest of the horizon, her silver face looming silently in the dark sky. She had never been so luminous, so large. She cast a glimmering radiance over the redmanes, a blessing of silver light. The animals raised their heads, suddenly shrilling and tossing their heads again, loping and cantering around the plain, necks arched, padded feet kicking.

As Darkchild watched in growing astonishment they played teasing games, charging each other, darting away. Some danced on their hind legs, flailing the air with their manes.

And with the silver shadow of the moon upon them—

"The whitemane!" Darkchild whispered. "You can see the whitemane in them." Before, they had been stocky and grey, without spirit. Now there was beauty in them: grace, swiftness, joy. As he watched, the plodding bodies, the tangled manes, the heavy feet became guises quickly tossed aside. Whitemanes courted and danced in the spell of Nindra's light.

"Khira—they're like whitemanes!"

Khira seemed not to hear. And Kadura stood like stone, her eyes hard, black, lusterless. Her face had become a petrified mass, deeply fissured, only the harshest edges weathered smooth.

Darkchild turned back to the dance of redmanes. Then Zan's silver rim appeared above the horizon and the redmanes were suddenly still again. They stood in frozen silence until the second silver circlet completely cleared the horizon. Darkchild waited in poised tension. *Dance!* he wanted to cry. *Dance, whitemane!*

But when both moons glided up the black sky, the animals did not dance again. Instead they uttered a long quivering sigh and began slowly to stamp their padded feet.

They stamped in unison, heads lowered, as if they listened to the sound of their own feet. At first the beat was slow, a gentle pounding that reverberated across the plain like the beat of an earthen heart. Shivering, Darkchild drew up his feet from contact with the soil. If he could make the boulder an island, a place where nothing could touch him, if he could look out upon the thousands of animals, yet isolate himself...

The stamping grew stronger, more emphatic, gradually accelerating. Gazing around, Darkchild could see that the guardians had spread their feet, bracing themselves against the softly vibrating earth. He shuddered, trying to shut out the reverberation that reached him even as he sat on the boulder, feet pulled up.

Khira clasped his arm for a moment, then released it, sliding down from the boulder. When her feet touched ground, she spread them as the guardians did. Darkchild stared down at her in frightened fascination. Khira was invulnerable to the teaching. She always slept when the elder mare taught at the pond. But now the slow heavy rise of her chest told him her heart had slowed to meet the beat of the plain.

The redmanes pounded the ground harder, faster. Darkchild held his breath, refusing to empty himself, refusing to make room within himself for the spell the redmanes cast.

But were they redmanes? As the mesmeric pounding continued, it seemed to him he saw the whitemane dancing among them again, throwing its silken mane as it raised delicate hooves to strike the earth. Its neck arched, it pounded the earth in the same rhythm as the redmanes—heavier, faster, ever more emphatic. Its hooves clipped at the ground, striking a sharp repetitious note.

Later he could not remember when he slipped down from the boulder to stand beside Khira. Could not remember when he spread his feet. Could not remember when he let the pounding of feet and hooves become the pounding of his own heart. But Zan had not risen far above the horizon when Darkchild's will seeped away and his heart's rhythm altered to meet the rhythm of the bonding.

The pounding of thousands of feet went on and soon all were one: redmanes and guardians, soil, mountains and moons. They bonded.

One. The feet pounded and barriers fell. The feet pounded and doors were splintered. The feet pounded and all the memories the guide had hidden were revealed.

Memories: the violet-eyed people who had found the boy in the forest, hungry and alone, and fed him. The woman who had bent to him, teaching him to scribe symbols that would admit the family to the temple where the godsvoice sang. Then the long, good years, the godsvoice strumming for them and the family pond yielding all the good things that were to be desired: tender bulbs, delicately flavored stems, rich seeds and pods.

Memories: his sisters' hair combed out between their fingers to catch the godsvoice. Only women and girls could hear the godsvoice in that special, intimate way. But sometimes—yes, sometimes he imagined he heard a thin, high singing too. And then he wondered if his prayers too might be made more powerful, if his desires might become manifest.

Because beyond the silver forest and the people who were his family there lay still earlier memories: plain people in plain clothes. People with dirt under their nails and the smell of the soil on them. They were scattered thin across their rich world and peace was their wish. The plenty in the soil and in the mountains, the rich, fine things that could be made of the elemental stuff of their world—not for them. They had no desire to mine their world and make themselves wealthy. They were few and their simplicity was special to them. In physical austerity, they believed, lay the source of spiritual riches.

The plain people: they found him—so small a child to be crying and alone—and fed him on plain foods and love. They filled his emptiness and helped him grow, until one day—

Darkchild gasped, trying to force his way out of the trap of memory. But there was no escaping. He could not build back the doors. They were shattered. How could he refashion barriers of a handful of splinters?

Two peoples had cared for him. Two peoples had taken him in and fed him. Two peoples had fostered his growth, had formed him in the ways of love. Without them he could never have learned to care for Khira. They had taken an empty, hungry child and made him human.

And both times had come the droning in the sky. Both times had come the screaming ship. Both time grapplers had reached down for him and taken him to where the Benderzic helmet waited.

Then the helmet had stripped his mind of all the detail stored there and used that detail to strip the peoples who had cared for him of their very way of life.

Yes. He knew that now—now that the doors were gone. That was what the guide had been hiding from him. He had been used against the people who fed him like a tool of destruction. He had been sent among them to record in infinite detail their resources, their defenses, their weaknesses, their ways. Then what he had learned had been codified and analyzed and exploiters had taken the processed information and used it for their own ends.

He didn't have to be told what they had done then. He could guess. They had come to the silver forest in ugly ships and stripped the very tongue from the temple—from every temple. They had muted the godsvoice, for the metal that sang in its taut strands was exceedingly precious in trade. Then they had brought in blasters and loaders and haulers and taken away all the ore from which the metal of the godsvoice was refined.

The exploiters had taken every smallest part of that essential metal— he didn't have to be told; he knew—and left the gentle people to starve. What else could they do, with their temples silent and the women stripped of the mystical power that lived in the presence of the godsvoice? If by some chance the people took straggling crops from the public ponds after that, surely the poisons excreted by their own festering spirits soon made their souls bloated and gangrenous.

And the plain people—he could guess the terrible things that happened to them when factories and refineries rose in their farmlands and trade ships came and gaudy people of every race bought and sold in hurriedly constructed marketplaces. They had retreated to the stone-deserts, surely, and there their simple austerity had become hard-bitten poverty. And while a chosen austerity had made them strong, exile and poverty could only weaken the fibers that held them together in love.

Darkchild shuddered. Dead, the two peoples who had befriended him. Dead at his hand as surely as if he had been a Benderzic or an exploiter. Dead because they had not murdered the strange child they found hungry on their lands but had succored him.

And the people of Brakrath? Khira? Tiahna? Kadura? Darkchild trembled, cold sweat standing on his face. The redmanes' feet pounded faster, ever faster, making his thoughts whine by dizzily.

The Benderzic ship would come again, droning, screaming. The

grappler would come again. The helmet would slide over his head again
and the Benderzic would learn of the sunstone and the barohnas and
of a people who slept for many hands while the snow lay deep in their
valleys. And then—

Then the exploiters. He could not guess who they might be or how
they would turn the sunstone to their ends. But they would come and
they would destroy.

Blindly he turned his head, trying to grasp reality through the ever-
accelerating fury of thoughts and images. Below, padded feet pounded
faster and faster, until the beat of every heart was swift and violent.
Darkchild's blood raced dizzily, singing in his ears. Guardians stood
braced against the frenzy and guardians lay fallen in the dirt. Below,
redmanes had begun to fall too, those whose hearts were too weak to
sustain the pounding fury of the bonding.

And Kadura—Darkchild stared and hardly knew her. Her face was
the grey of stone. Her eyes hardly seemed flesh. They stared at him in
stark agony as her body swayed. Her hands, he saw, were clenched on
the folds of her cloak, bloodless.

But she had told him barohnas never fell in the bonding. She had
told him she must will her death. She had told him—

She had told him of the pain she took from the minds around her.
Now, he realized, it was his pain that made stone of her. It was his
pain that made her rock on her feet, as if she would fall and shatter.

And before—so much suddenly became clear—before *he* was the
one who had made her old and ill. He had come to the plain with Khira
and brought the poison of hidden memories with him. The guide had
protected him against memory—but Kadura saw everything. She had
read his memories, she had read his dreams, and they had hurt her so
much she faltered in her will to live.

What had he ever loved that he had not destroyed? The people of
the silver forest, the plain people—and now he would destroy Kadura
and Khira too, one with pain, the other with unwilling treachery. With
terrible effort—feet pounded and his blood whined—he pressed his
hands to his ears, ground his fists against his eyes. He could not quench
the gouting rush of memory.

Colored stones, singing scarves, a strangely familiar voice pleading
with him in a jungle clearing—he had destroyed another people too.
He—flesh of Birnam Rauth, creature of the Benderzic. The Arnimi
commander was right. He was not human. He was a killing-tool.

A tool—but a unique tool, one that could at least choose its own obliteration. On the plain more redmanes had been culled by the heart-stopping frenzy. On the promontory another guardian fell, her body slowly sinking until she lay lifeless, her face hidden from the watching moons by the hood of her umber cape.

He could fall too. Already the singing of his blood had become a buzzing, the buzzing a whine. His heart beat a useless frenzy against his ribs, robbing him of breath. He choked on rising bile.

He could fall if he gave himself totally to the bonding. He could fall and never hurt anyone again.

He could fall and at last he did, his knees bending, his body slumping against the throbbing soil. He felt its roughness against his cheek and made a pledge upon the soil of Brakrath: he would not rise again; he would not kill again.

The last thing he saw as his senses faded was Khira's face, moon-misted, staring. He did not know if she really bent over him or if he just wished it. But as she drew nearer he repeated his pledge and released himself into the oblivion of her eyes.

16/The Guide

The guide left the kefri on the tenth night after the bonding, slipping away silently while Khira and Kadura slept. He didn't take pack or supplies. He took only Darkchild's pike—and that only because his hand felt naked without it. He had never learned to use the pike properly, only to carry it.

Nor had he learned to ride properly, but when he reached the edge of the campment, he summoned a redmane, a staid mare well past breeding age, and climbed to its back. The animal's gait was wandering and uneven. But if he fell, there was no one to see. The plain was empty tonight, its barren sweep mirroring his own emptiness.

Gone—Darkchild was gone. In the ten days since the bonding, the guide had sent mental feelers in every direction. Everything Darkchild had experienced on Brakrath was meticulously recorded in the brain they had shared: the smell of spices in the palace kitchen, the texture of stone beneath his fingertips, the sound of the whitemane's hooves on the floor of the grove. Even now, ten days after Darkchild's death, every detail was fresh. But Darkchild himself was gone.

The guide sighed. Even the body they had shared felt different now: stiffer, thicker. Now that he was alone, his hands were perpetually cold, his lips and tongue dry and thick. Food had lost its taste and when he spoke, his voice grated.

And Khira—bleakly the guide clung to the redmane's neck. Better if Khira had openly rejected him. Instead she treated him with elaborate kindness—and she watched. He felt her eyes on his face a hundred times a day, watching for Darkchild there. She listened for Darkchild in his voice.

Gone. Darkchild was gone. And now, if he had the courage to let himself go too, if he had the courage to let ice form in the living cells of his heart, as an aging barohna might...

When he neared the pinnacles, the guide slid off the redmane's back. There was no teaching tonight. There were no redmanes at the pond. This was the season when redmanes roamed and mated. The guide walked stiffly until he stood at pond's edge. Zan lay upon the water's surface, white, crater-marked, shining.

A single step and another face lay on the pond too: dark, with thin lips, a narrow, well-defined nose, finely arched brows—and empty eyes. The guide stood for a time gazing at his own reflection before he realized that his lips were moving, that he was whispering a teaching of his own:

I am empowered to guide the boy in strange places.

To keep his body safe and fed.

To prompt him to inquire and explore.

To urge him to learn and know.

To divert him from knowledge which is interior.

To direct him to knowledge which is exterior.

To codify those facts and impressions which the boy gathers.

To store and preserve them to meet the terms of the contract.

It had seemed so simple in the beginning. The terms of the contract were clear. And if he had been properly prepared, if he had been as devoid of feeling as the Benderzic had intended, his duties would have been simple. He would have guided the boy without compunction. He would have used Khira and cast her easily aside. When the ship came, he would have returned the boy to the helmet without hesitation.

Now?

Now, he realized numbly, he could still return the boy to the helmet. The required data was there, carefully stored, waiting for analysis and classification.

But so were doubt, indecision, regret—and thwarted caring. What would the helmet make of those?

Sighing, he summoned up courage to do what he must: invite the cold into his heart. He left the pondside and walked to the place where the spires rose so abruptly from the floor of the plain. He stared emptily at the cragged rocks. Then he lowered himself to the ground and sat with his knees drawn up, arms encircling them. He stared into the empty plain for a time before he lowered his head to his knees, letting the cold of night, the cold of the plain, penetrate him. He thought of cold things: mountain snow, winter wind, fear—helpless fear.

He thought of those things and after a while he became so cold his thoughts froze and awareness slipped away. With distant relief, he let it go.

It was daylight when he thawed to life, unwillingly, pain in every muscle. He opened his eyes reluctantly, not sure what had wakened him, and stared blankly at the ground, at the tall shadow that lay at his feet. It was a long, painful time before he raised his head. "Kadura."

She looked down from the folds of her cape, the strength of stone in her face. "Did you think it would be so easy, child?"

Easy? Tears stung the guide's eyes and filled his throat. "I'm taking the ice," he choked. "Like you, Kadura." And it had not been easy.

"But I'm not taking the ice," she said, kneeling before him. "I've put the ice out of my heart. You said something the day we left for the bonding. You told me you thought barohnas took the ice when they had taken too much loneliness, too much pain, from others. Do you remember?"

He shook his head stiffly. "I didn't say that. Darkchild—"

"You said it and I thought about it when we carried you back from the bonding. No one has ever brought as much fear and pain among us as you have. I can't believe you came to us without purpose. I think you came to test us and to teach us. You came to show us—to show me—that we must learn to erect barriers against what we find in others.

"We think ourselves strong, but I see now that we must be stronger. Those of us who have mastered the stones remember times that are only tales to the people of the halls. Their legends are our memories. What they read from the scrolls we know in the cells of our bodies. The past lives in us—we carry it into the future.

"And Brakrath's future is in the crucible now. The Arnimi are among us. One day there will be other humans here—and non-humans as well. The time is past when those of us who can bring past and future together can permit ourselves to take the ice and die. The time is past when we can let ourselves grow tired and then take the easy way from our weariness.

"You tested me ten nights ago, child, and I thought I would fall. I thought I would be the first barohna ever to fall in the bonding.

"But I did not fall. I walked away from the bonding and from all the pain of your memories. You provided me a tempering fire and now my blade is more resilient than ever it was before. I won't let it be broken when my people may soon need it.

"Child, you must be resilient too."

He stared up at her. He had hardly noticed, in his self-absorption, that the shadow was gone from her eyes. Her face still fell in creases, but there was no longer weakness there. Kadura no longer looked like a woman old and ill. She looked like a woman seasoned and strong again, a source of stability for her people, a foundation.

"Darkchild—" He caught his lip between his teeth, fighting back tears. Where had the blessed, numbing cold gone? She held his hands in hers and drove it away. "It was Darkchild!"

"You are Darkchild."

"No." He peered up into her eyes, pleading. "No!" *If I were Darkchild, I would be with Khira now, helping her train. But I can't spar with her—I'm too clumsy. I can't ride with her—if I try to keep up with her, I fall. She's tried to teach me to strike at targets but my pike flies wide.*

Now she wants me to go to the mountains with her. If I go, I'll only hinder her. I was weak, I let the doors fall, and Darkchild is dead. If I go with Khira, I'll fail her too.

"But you aren't weak, child," Kadura said, his hands still captive in hers. "You're afraid—so afraid you have set one part of yourself completely aside. Of course you feel diminished.

"But you can reach for that part of yourself. You can take back all the things that are yours."

"No." He didn't want to hear. He was responsible for what had happened to Darkchild. He would not be responsible for whatever might happen to Khira too. He pulled his hands from Kadura's, struggling to his feet.

He had been sitting too long. His feet cramped, his legs were barely able to hold him. Fighting weak muscles, he turned and stumbled away, fleeing the old woman and the weight she would place on him.

None of it—he would have none of it. He would have the ice and he would have peace.

His heart fluttered as he fled the pinnacles. He looked back only once. Kadura remained where he had left her, black-caped, immobile. She might have been stone—a thirteenth pinnacle. He cried with relief that she did not follow. How many times could he wrench himself away from her strength and stability?

He did not want to go to the grove. Darkchild had left behind carefully stored memories of the grove, of the whisprey and of the white-shadowed whitemane. But where else could he lose himself in cold shadow at mid-morning?

Painfully he made way toward the tall trees. The grove was an alien place by daylight, the trees broadly spaced, sunlight striping the ground with shadow. The soil was soft and moist underfoot. Occasionally he saw phalanxes of insects marching from hive to hive bearing unidentifiable objects. He saw no sign of whisprey, heard nothing that might have been a nightcaller.

But then it was not night. It was day, and when he sat at the base of a towering tree, in the deepest shadow he could find, and closed his eyes, he could summon no night-chill. He thought of cold things and his body remained warm. He imagined a network of crystals forming jagged and white in his heart—but his pulse continued its steady throb.

At last, thinking of the things Kadura had said to him, thinking of what she wanted of him, he put his head on his knees and cried.

He dozed fitfully through much of the day, his arms wrapped around his drawn-up knees. It was not until night that he woke and began to draw the cold into himself again. Moonlight was like silver crystals spilled out across the sky, then pounded into smooth metallic sheets. He had only to stare up long enough and the sheets broke into crystalline form again.

He let the dancing crystals dazzle him, let them carry him away from the grove, back into some deep place where brother-voices spoke. And the brother-faces—if he gazed steadily into the crystalline light, it turned warm and golden and deep inside it he could see the brother-faces. How many times Darkchild had reached for those and come away with no clear concept of their beckoning features.

Now the guide reached for them. He wanted to lose himself in them, to become another diffuse image among the many, smiling and empty, without awareness. An image had no responsibility, no care. An image could never fail anyone. Certainly an image had no life to dash away on shores of ice.

An image did not hear his name spoken in a voice he had not wanted to hear again. "Iahnn! Iahnn!"

It was Khira's voice, using the name she had given him since the bonding. He pushed out a trembling breath and tried to lose himself among the brother-faces.

No use. "Iahnn! I saw the whitemane. It was standing beside you. Iahnn—don't you want to track it?"

The whitemane? He raised his head, bewildered.

"Iahnn! Look—you can see its prints."

No. But he looked anyway, peering down at the soft soil. There was the unmistakable mark of a hoof—and another beside it.

Chill moved along his spine. The whitemane had stood beside him, so close he might have touched it. The elusive creature that had en-thralled Darkchild had come to him as he sat unseeing.

Now it was gone. But it had left its prints. Slowly, reluctantly, the guide raised eyes to Khira's. She was watching him intently, as if she expected something profound of him.

As if, he realized with a sharp rise of bitterness, she expected Dark-child to resurrect himself to follow the whitemane. As if she thought this was the stimulus that would finally call him up.

The guide caught his breath in an angry sob. She had called *his* name—the name she had given *him*—but she wanted Darkchild to answer. That was all she wanted from him. Never mind that she treated him tenderly, as she would treat someone she tried to cherish from the grip of illness. It was only Darkchild she wanted to raise from this particular sickbed.

Stiffly the guide stood, setting his jaw against angry tears. "Leave me alone," he said. His voice was at its harshest.

Khira flinched. "Iahnn—"

"I didn't ask you to follow me. I don't want you to follow me. I don't want to see you again." Because she did not want to see him. Never mind her tolerance, her patience—they were for Darkchild, not for him. *"I don't want to see you again!"*

He stumbled crazily as he fled, his legs cramping. She called after him, she ran after him, but she didn't know the right things to say. When finally she caught her foot on a protruding root and fell with a cry, he didn't turn back. He ran through the grove and across the plain blindly. It was true—he never wanted to see her again. It hurt too much that she did not want him, and it hurt too much that if he went back to her, he would fail her.

He ran until his lungs burned and a cramping pain in his side brought him to his knees. As he gulped raggedly for breath, he stared blindly at the crescent-shaped indentations in the soil before him.

Hoof prints—running blindly, he had followed the whitemane's trail. When he could walk again, he pushed himself up and stumbled on, blindly again, wondering.

Again he followed the whitemane's trail without intending it. Sweat poured from his face, his heart labored, his eyes refused to sort images. But whenever he stopped and his eyes cleared, the whitemane's trail lay before him in the dirt. Finally he threw himself down, trembling with fatigue. Why follow the whitemane? The animal meant nothing to him.

Only to Darkchild.

Still he kept to the animal's trail. Finally he accepted the fact that he was tracking the whitemane—just as Darkchild would have done.

And Khira was tracking him. He glimpsed her a dozen times as he stumbled across the plain. She made no attempt to overtake him. Nor did she call out. She simply limped a distance behind him, a lonely figure.

As lonely as he.

By late afternoon he was exhausted and hungry. He stopped several times to gather berries and once he used the tip of his pike to dig edible roots. They were crisp with moisture.

Dusk came and soon he tracked the whitemane by moonlight, glancing up frequently, as if he expected to see the animal before him. As early evening wore on, the vegetation on the plain grew denser. Thorny thickets appeared and sometimes small stands of trees smudged the landscape. Peering intently ahead, the guide saw a larger smudge on the horizon—the forest. His heart thumped against his ribs, a beat of anticipation. He hurried ahead, walking less stiffly.

As in the grove, the trees of the forest were widely spaced, the ground shadow-laced underfoot. There had been rain recently, and the soil was soft and damp. A woodsy musk hung in the trees, a forest perfume that seemed to promise mystery. The guide walked among the tall trees with his pike clutched tight, walked alertly, on the balls of his feet. He hardly noticed that Khira followed just paces behind him now, as watchful as he. There was something here, something in the trees... He peered down at the hoofprints in the damp humus, wondering where they led—wondering why he followed.

He followed until he reached a small clearing where grass grew, moon-silvered, and the ground curved in a shallow bowl. Sighing, he sat down to rest and soon curled in the grass, dozing. He heard Khira step through the trees, felt the warmth of her body as she curled next to him, but he was too tired to confront her.

He woke to her warning touch. He opened his eyes, drawing a cautious breath.

The whitemane stood on the other side of the small clearing, and for the first time he saw it distinctly. The silky texture of its mane, the glistening white hairs of its coat, the pink transparency of its eyes—he stared in awe. The whitemane held its head alertly poised, ears pricked. Its lips were pulled back to reveal strong white teeth.

A distillation of moonlight? An hallucination? Or a living animal, studying him with a curiosity as keen as his own?

Khira's hand tightened on his arm. "Iahnn—do you hear? That sound—I think the whitemanes are bonding. Somewhere in the trees."

He listened. The sound grumbled almost subliminally through the soil. He felt it in his teeth more than he heard it. But as he listened, it became louder—sharper.

Droning. It was not the sound of bonding, not the sound of thunder. The guide's throat was suddenly dry. He took his feet.

No, not a bonding—except of himself with the Benderzic helmet, the metal helmet come to take Darkchild's carefully stored memories and convert them to objective information.

Information about Brakrath. About the stones that stored the sun's energy and the women who controlled the stones. Information about the barohnas' weaknesses and strengths, about the customs and habits of their people. Information about the resources of the mountains and valleys.

Information to be bid away to whoever would pay most richly for it.

Information to destroy a culture by, to make dead a people who had struggled for centuries to live.

The Benderzic had come. The droning of their ship was unmistakable now, sharp, high, ominous. And the guide couldn't move. He stood as frozen as the whitemane.

"What is it?" Khira's nails drove hard into the guide's arm. "Iahnn—what is it?"

He couldn't answer. He was caught helpless in the web of destiny. This was the moment preordained from the time Darkchild had found himself on the tower steps. It had always waited for him. And he knew too well what came next: the flash of a metal hull by moonlight, dark markings upon it; an opening port; a capsule reaching down, metal grapplers engaged; a suited figure stepping from the capsule; the glint of a needle—

He had forgotten the paralyzing beam that came before anything else. It moved across the clearing before the shrieking ship appeared. At the last moment the whitemane panicked and reared to its hind legs, slashing the air with delicate hooves. The beam caught it that way, its powerfully muscled body helpless, its dancing hooves frozen in midair.

Then the beam caught Khira. The expression of shock on her face became a mask, staring. The guide hardly noticed when the beam froze him. Shock and anticipation had already made him helpless.

The contract—this was the moment the contract had directed him toward. This was the culmination of its terms. This was its ultimate end: to see him loaded aboard the Benderzic ship without struggle, data ready for extraction and use.

A tool—He was even more a tool than Darkchild had been. He was the tool the Benderzic had used against Darkchild, to hide the truth from him, to keep him ignorant and docile.

He was—

"Darkchild!" Khira raised her pike as the beam released her and the port opened.

"No!" the guide cried, frightened by the protective anger that glinted in her eyes. "They have weapons. Khira—they have blazers." He remembered now. He had seen the Benderzic turn fire against the damp vegetation of the last world they had taken him from, just for sport. He remembered how wet leaves had curled and blackened, how moss-grown trees had blossomed with clouds of damp smoke.

It was familiar now: the capsule reaching down on its hinged metal arm, grapplers working. He was supposed to aid the retrieval process by stepping forward and letting metal fingers catch in his clothing. Inside the capsule was one suited figure, at the port another—expecting him to cooperate, without question or hesitation. The guide stared hopelessly at Khira. If she slipped away into the trees, if she did not anger the Benderzic—

Because he remembered more about the Benderzic now. He remembered so much he had forgotten. There was fury in them—laughing fury. They spent too much time in ships' holds, biting back all the things they could not direct against each other. How could they survive in close quarters if they set darts of jealousy and anger flying there?

So they set them flying other places—and laughed.

Now the figure in the capsule threw back its head and the guide cringed. He had forgotten how wet Benderzic lips were, how moist Benderzic eyes. He had forgotten the way their brows grew low over their eyes. That much was clearly visible by moonlight.

He turned. "Khira—" His voice caught. He had run from her today. He had told her he never wanted to see her again. But he had not thought of saying goodbye to her this way, with a Benderzic mocking them both and grapplers reaching. "Khira—run! They don't want you. Run!"

She stared at him, momentarily uncomprehending. Then her mouth tightened. "No."

"Khira—" He glanced up urgently. The second Benderzic crouched in the shadowed port.

"Darkchild—how many are there? Just two?"

It was his turn to stare. Her first anger had turned to calculation. Her eyes narrowed with it, and that frightened him more than her anger. "Two—in this ship. But this is only the retriever, Khira. There are others on the carrier ship. Khira—" There were so many things he wanted to tell her, things he had never dared: how bright sunlight looked on her hair in the mornings; how well she walked, boldly yet lightly at once; how kindly she had treated him even when she looked for Darkchild in his face.

How he wanted to cry at leaving her—and at being used against her.

Yes—he would be used against her and against Kadura, against Tiahna, against all the people who had been kind. *Again.*

Used. Without warning, a change came in his throat, as if the muscle tone changed, as if the tension on his vocal chords altered. *"Two,"* he said. The word shocked him because he said it in Darkchild's voice.

Her eyes glinted up at him with triumph. "Then if we can get them out of the ship—"

And take them with pikes, two hand-flung weapons against blazer-armed Benderzic? The guide waited for the thought to shrivel him.

It did not. Because the alternative was not just his death in the helmet, a spiritual surrender, but Khira's death and the death of Brakrath. Without thinking he caught her hand and pulled her with him from the clearing, evading the grapplers. Get the Benderzic out of the ship? "They want to come out," he said, remembering more about them. The Benderzic liked to crush soil under their boots. They were a ship-people, with laughing scorn for the web of life that constituted the environments cherished by others. A thought struck the guide and he glanced back toward the clearing, alarmed. The whitemane—

But the animal had fled without harm.

And the capsule was opening. The first Benderzic was stepping out, putting his boots down heavily, as if he relished the death of land-borne microorganisms beneath them. His voice was heavy with scorn. "Rauth-Seven, you are called."

With a shock, the guide recognized the brother-language. For a moment he experienced a sense of giddiness, as if some part of him prepared to step forward—called. He conquered the impulse easily, almost without thought. If he could answer in the brother-tongue, lashing out with withering words—

But the tongue had deserted him. And his bravado was fading. How could he think of going against the Benderzic? Although Darkchild was a skilled hunter, the guide had never so much as brought down a groundfowl with his pike. "Khira, you have to run," he said in a low voice, hurried. "They have blazers—there are two of them—and I can't help you." He held out his pike uselessly, pleading.

She stared at his stiff arm, at the extended weapon. She stared so hard that he stared too, then caught a sharp breath. He didn't hold the pike in a gesture of surrender. He held it in strike position, raised, ready to fly.

And he held it in Darkchild's hand. There was no mistaking that. His own hand had never closed so lightly, so cleanly around the haft of a pike. Nor had his arm ever risen so smoothly, the muscles like bands of elastic. Slowly, stunned, he looked up and watched the second

Benderzic slide down a cable and drop to the moonlit clearing.

"You can help me!" Khira said and laughed sharply, a challenge.

The guide stared in frozen horror as she darted to the clearing and faced the Benderzic. They grinned, pleased by the game she offered, their wet lips curled with pleasure. She turned back once to the guide, moonlight glinting on her hair, challenge bright in her eyes.

The Benderzic unsheathed their blazers, ready to sting her, ready to torment her with a dozen little burnings before they dispatched her and took their prey. The guide had no choice. He joined her at the edge of the clearing—not stiffly, not jerkily, but boldly, with a smooth stretching and contracting of muscles.

Darkchild's muscles.

"What is this, Rauth-Seven?" the first Benderzic mocked, snapping off a beam of fire at the ground, making the damp grass sizzle. "Deserted your brothers for a dirt-witch?" He made a second patch of grass steam at Khira's toes. "Your brothers call you, Rauth-Seven. They wait for you in a place where your boots will make a decent sound when you walk." The Benderzic stamped the ground. "What kind of sound is that for a walking man? There's no ring to dirt, Rauth-Seven. And this dirt-witch—" He raised his blazer, tiny muscles contracting beneath his eyes as his finger closed on the fire pin.

For a moment the guide thought he would watch, helpless, unable to move. But Darkchild's muscles tautened as the Benderzic darted flame at Khira. And Darkchild's hatred moved in his blood. With a scalding cry, the guide raised the pike and sent it slamming across the clearing. Sent it slamming not just at the Benderzic who touched Khira's shift with fire, who burned the pale flesh of her leg, but at every Benderzic who had ever come to laugh and destroy.

Khira cried with pain. The Benderzic staggered, his blazer dropping as he clutched at the pike buried in his chest. His mouth sagged in surprise and then filled with blood, a dying tide. His eyes glazed. He fell slowly, in stages, and the ground did not ring at his impact.

"Darkchild!"

The second Benderzic crouched, laughter dying in his throat, and flashed fire across the clearing. The guide dodged aside at Khira's shrieked warning, feeling heat on his face. He caught Khira's hand, pulling her into the trees. He threw her to the ground to smother the fire that ate a bright hole in her shift. "Your leg—"

"He shot at you!"

That surprised her? His mind worked rapidly, sorting possibilities. Few of them promised hope. "Can you run?"

"He shot at you—Darkchild, he doesn't want to kill you! He—"

He caught her hand again, pulling her to her feet. Behind them the second Benderzic had gone mad with his blazer. Fire ate at the trees and bit at the damp soil, raising clouds of smoke and steam. "All he needs is my brain," the guide said through gritted teeth.

"But alive," Khira insisted, staring up at him in disbelief. "He—"

"He needs me alive long enough to use the helmet. No longer." The helmet would extract the data Darkchild had stored in a matter of moments. And in extremis, the data would be available for minutes after his heart stopped beating. Brain activity would continue at the necessary level for that long.

Oh yes, he remembered a lot now. The Benderzic had no ultimate need for him alive. His conditioning had failed and he was past the age of greatest usefulness. The guide choked on a bitter laugh. He was too old to be the Benderzic's tool now. He was a child no longer; there was a dead man in the clearing to prove it.

They ran. The Benderzic shouted hoarsely, and when Darkchild turned he saw that the trees blazed reluctantly behind them. Thick smoke stung his throat, making him cough. Nearby he heard rustling sounds of alarm. A dark animal shape flashed through the trees, fleeing the smoke.

The whitemane? But the shape was too slight, too dark. Distracted, the guide stumbled over a fallen limb. He caught himself, his lungs burning, the Benderzic's angry shouts in his ears.

The Benderzic continued to direct his blazer at the trees, raising clouds of damp smoke. The guide and Khira ran, coughing, stumbling, gagging. Numbly the guide was aware of forest creatures running with them, silently, invisible in the dense smoke. The woods were damp. If he could fell the Benderzic, the fire would smother itself.

"Khira—your pike—" The guide fell against a heavily mossed tree, fighting for breath. "Your pike—"

She looked at him dumbly, her face streaked, then peered back into the dense smoke. Although her face was set, a carved mask, her eyes seemed to take fire from the burning trees. She turned back to the guide and he saw a stoniness in her he had never seen before, a hard strength that would not be denied. Adar burned in her eyes. Deliberately she raised her pike, the muscles of her calves stretching, pulling her to tiptoe.

The Benderzic plunged through the trees and halted, glaring. He didn't laugh now and he didn't cough, despite the smoke. His eyes rolled with anger and his wet lips were dry and cracked. Perspiration stood like melted wax on his face. "You—image!" He made the word obscene. Then he saw Khira, saw the same thing in her eyes that the guide had seen. Momentarily he faltered, letting the blazer waver in his hand.

Adar flared in Khira's eyes and it seemed to the guide that she raised her pike with taunting deliberation, to the sound of drums. It seemed to him that her every muscle and tendon did its job with mocking slowness. It seemed to the guide that she made the Benderzic wait an eternity for his death.

Then the pike rode the air with blinding swiftness, just as the Benderzic's flame reached out. Without thinking, the guide leapt aside, pulling Khira with him. The matted leaves where they had stood blazed damply.

The Benderzic fell as the first Benderzic had fallen, slowly, the pike quivering in his chest. Again the soil did not ring with his impact.

Two Benderzic—dead with their faces pressed to living soil rather than to ship's metal. Both damned, in their way.

Khira stared at the dead Benderzic, Adar's brightness dying from her eyes. Unconsciously she raised one hand to her face. Smoke swirled around her, wreathing her as it would a figure of stone.

The guide was first to recover from shock. He seized Khira's hand and pulled her away from the dead Benderzic, leaving flames to lick unenthusiastically at the body. They stumbled through the thinning smoke, the guide trying to understand what had happened to him. When first the Benderzic had come, he had been stiff and afraid—and then, inexplicably, he had been neither. First he had stood helpless, ready to throw down his pike—and instead he had killed with it.

And now—he shook his head, trying to clear it. Something had happened to him and something continued to happen. Because so many things were coming alive as he ran. Memories: the savory taste of roast fowl, the smell of rain in the mountains, the bright color in Khira's cheeks when she walked against the wind. None of these were his memories. They were Darkchild's—yet they were suddenly vivid and alive.

He frowned, coughing. Darkchild's courage, Darkchild's memories—Darkchild's awareness. Confused, the guide felt it stir and waken in him, as if the Benderzic's death had terminated some long estrangement. He had called upon Darkchild's courage. He had called upon Darkchild's physical prowess. And now he felt himself caught up in Darkchild's rousing consciousness.

As if it were his own. Dizzily, he fought a sharp rise of panic. If he was afraid and daring, if he was curious and frightened, if he was strong and weak—all at once, all within himself—if there were no partitions, no barriers—if there were no doors—if he could touch the past and reach for the future, all at once—

That should have been release. That should have been freedom. But if his consciousness and Darkchild's co-mingled, if he could use freely all the gifts that had been Darkchild's exclusively, if he could not extricate himself from the resurrecting network of Darkchild's memory—and he could not. He tried to shut back the flow of images and failed. They continued to pound at him, color, sound, event, emotion. If he could not retreat from them—*who was he?*

Who was he if he halted in the moonlit forest, fire dying damply behind him, and found he could not say his own name? Who was he if he could not look down at his hands and name them either as Darkchild's or the guide's? Who was he if he touched his face and knew that it was his—*his*—but could not identify by name the person who bore its features?

He drew a shuddering breath and his heart raced with panic. What was happening to him? He was no longer the guide, but neither was he Darkchild. Before he had been afraid—either of the past or of the future—but at least he had known his own name. Now he did not. Incredibly—*he did not.* Neither of the names he had used fit him.

Nameless, he bit his lip, squeezing his eyes shut. He tried desperately to partition himself—tried to separate guide from Darkchild. But something had happened since the second Benderzic had died. He could not extricate the awareness of the guide from the consciousness of Darkchild.

Kadura had told him he was one. He had insisted he was two. Now, suddenly, he was—neither. And his confusion was overwhelming.

Behind, the dampness of the forest slowly stifled the Benderzic's flames. The boy threw himself down in damp leaves, trembling, lost. Unconsciously he drew up his knees and dropped his forehead to rest upon them. He was hardly aware of Khira beside him.

"Darkchild—"

The boy raised his head, shaking his head dumbly, unable to speak. Whose voice would he hear if he did?

"Darkchild—" Deliberately, reluctantly, Khira moved from the shadows where she stood and knelt before him, moonlight full on her face. "Darkchild—I think it was too soon."

Too soon? Uncomprehending the boy stared at her. It was moments before he realized what he saw, and then he did not believe it. The pigmentation of her skin could not have changed so quickly. The bone structure of her face could not have altered in minutes. And her eyes—

They were deep now, dark by moonlight. They held the same ageless power he had seen in Tiahna's eyes—and the same helplessness, as if Khira found herself shaped by forces she could not control—forces she must live by nevertheless.

"Khira—your face—" Forgetting his own dilemma, he reached out, cupping her chin in both his hands. Slowly, disbelieving, he explored the contours of her features. Her chin, the line of her jaw, the pressure of her cheekbones against the visibly darkening flesh—

"Darkchild, if I took my prey too soon—" She held out her hands— her changing hands—to him in appeal. "Darkchild, if it was too soon, I'll be like Nezra."

Nezra, the failed barohna, trapped in a half-changed body, her powers perverse and unaccountable. The boy felt his hands tremble. Khira had taken the Benderzic with her pike months before her first majority. She had taken him with all the stony deliberation she should have directed against her bronzing prey. She had taken him as if he *were* her prey— and now the first marks of a barohna were upon her.

The boy set aside his own pain and confusion and cradled her face in his hands. Tears gleamed in her shadowed eyes and spilled down her face. They were like acid on his fingers. *Too soon?*

17/Khira

Neither of them had intended to sleep. But at some point Khira curled against Darkchild and they slept, heavily, exhausted.

It was morning when Khira woke, alone. The sun reached through the trees and stung hazily at her eyelids. The faint smell of smoke clung to her shift and to her hair. She roused herself slowly and lay for a moment in the warm hollow of leaves, unwilling to confront the thoughts that came with waking.

She had taken a human for bronzing prey. No barohna had done that before. Indeed no Brakrathi within her knowledge had deliberately taken human life, and she should have felt diminished. She should have begun preparing to offer herself on the plaza on the second day of the next spring concentration.

But she had only to close her eyes to hear the Benderzic's mocking laughter, to see the glint of his eyes by moonlight, and she felt no regret. He had shown less respect for Darkchild than a hunter for an animal caught in his snare. And that had made the Benderzic himself less than human. That had made him a predator to be exterminated.

Khira sat, putting the Benderzic's death behind her. The pike was thrown. Now she had the present to consider. Frowning, she stretched her hands before her. They had changed. The flesh was darker, the fingers longer, the tips blunt instead of tapered. But they were not the hands of a barohna. They were too delicate, the texture of the skin too fine. And when she stood, she was little taller than the day before, although her legs were darker, their muscular structure more clearly defined.

Perhaps her delayed physical transformation was significant; perhaps not. It was her inward sense of herself that troubled her, the feeling that the stone had come fully into her heart for a few instants—and had immediately deserted her when the Benderzic lay dead. Certainly she did not feel it now. She felt only the ache of stiff muscles and a yawning sense of uncertainty.

She turned at a sound from the trees. Darkchild stood in the shadow. When he stepped forward, her chest tightened. There was something in his gaze—a tentativeness, a moment's apprehensive wariness—she had seen before, but in the guide's eyes. And this was Darkchild. She knew him from the easy way he moved, from the way his brows arched in question. "Did you see the whitemane?"

Darkchild's voice—but with a hint of the guide in the inflection. And something more too, something she didn't recognize at all. Khira frowned, puzzled. "No. I just woke."

He nodded and stepped from the trees, his pack thrown over one arm. "He was watching from the trees when I woke. I followed him as far as the retriever ship." He glanced at her, the guide's tentative eyes momentarily looking from beneath Darkchild's arched brows. "It set down and burned. There wasn't much left except the hull. I salvaged two blazers and a stunner, but the stunner has no pack." Squatting, he tumbled the three weapons to the ground. "Have you thought about where we want to meet them?"

"Them?" Blankly.

"The Benderzic—from the carrier ship."

Her lips turned cold. The three Benderzic weapons seemed to absorb light, creating a small darkness at her feet. "They'll come down?" Somehow in her self-occupation, she had set aside thoughts of the carrier and its contingent.

He frowned at her preoccupation. "They'll come, Khira. I don't know if they'll send another retriever first or if the carrier itself will come. But they'll be here." His eyes held hers, searching, troubled. "Khira, if we separate now—if we go different ways—"

She chilled. If they separated, she could go to the campment, to the mountains, wherever she pleased, and the Benderzic would not interfere.

They had no interest in her separate from him. "No," she said.

Still he held her gaze. "I thought of leaving you," he said. "This morning I thought of following the whitemane and not coming back."

"But you came."

He nodded, looking down at the ground, saying nothing. After a while he stood, sighing, and slipped the three Benderzic weapons back into his pack. "Will you come with me if I track the whitemane now?"

Again the deep-biting chill. "Yes." Did it matter where they met the Benderzic? If the strength she had felt when she raised her pike against the Benderzic was to return, it would come whenever she went.

And if it was not to return?

Then she would be like Nezra for however long she lived, caught in a half-matured body, her command of the stones perverse and unpredictable. The valley would grow cold and even Darkchild would eventually turn away from her bitterness.

No—and this time the chill was bone-gripping. If the strength did not return, they would be two children against the Benderzic carrier ship and the blazers he had brought from the shuttle would do nothing to even the odds.

If the strength did not return, the Benderzic would take Darkchild and she would not live to become like Nezra. She would not live to repel anyone with her bitterness.

She bit back those thoughts, helpless against them. Darkchild studied her with a detachment she had never felt in him before, gauging her anguish with more pity than concern, as if he had withdrawn from her even though he had invited her to join him in tracking the whitemane.

Troubled, she followed him into the trees. As they walked, almost peripherally, around the obscuring mass of her other concerns, she wondered about the change she saw in him today. He was clearly Darkchild, returned from whatever limbo he had occupied since the bonding. The easy way he slipped among the trees told her that. But there was a remnant of the guide in him, an occasional brief awkwardness, a moment's uncertainty. And there was something entirely new in him too, something she could not fathom. She could only see its outward manifestation in the detachment of his gaze, in the repressive set of his lips. He held some secret from her and it created a distance between them.

The whitemane's trail was clear in the deep leaves. It led them far into the forest, through the area where the Benderzic had set his fires and beyond. There were places in the forest where the trees grew close, towering up like living spires, their trunks darkly mossed, their sparse leaves breaking sunlight into dancing tatters. There were other places where the ground sloped gently and there were no trees at all but only lush vines.

There were still other places where springs bubbled up from rocky outcroppings and tall grasses grew. It seemed to Khira that there was a special stillness near the springs, as if only the voice of the water would be heard there and sometimes the answering call of the wind in the trees.

It was beside one such spring that they sat down to fashion pikes of stout limbs cut from hardwood trees. It was beside another that they sat to eat their midday meal from their packs. And it was beside another, late in the afternoon, with the sun reaching horizontally through the trees to cast its halo around them, that they found the whitemane.

He stood beside the spring, his head raised, one leg flexed, the hoof resting on a mossed boulder. Nearby, in the grass, his mate lay curled protectively around their foal.

Darkchild's fingers closed on Khira's arm. The whitemanes regarded them steadily from eyes that were pink transparencies, the pupils scarlet pinpoints. The setting sun cast a rosy light upon the three animals, making their smooth coats gleam.

The very directness of the animals' gaze was disconcerting. So was Darkchild's utter stillness, his concentrated awareness. Khira caught his hand. "Darkchild?" Somehow he was slipping from her. He met the animals' gaze and she felt as if he were caught up in a teaching that could never include her, as if he were losing himself in it. *"Darkchild!"*

He shook his head, freeing himself from her claim. Wordlessly he slipped his hand from hers and stepped forward. The whitemanes did not tense or shy at his approach. They continued to gaze at him, the rosy dazzle of the setting sun in their eyes. Silently Darkchild approached them, knelt and placed his hand on the foal's brow, touching the silken hairs gently. He knelt there for minutes and only the voice of the water broke the silence. Then he stood and stepped back.

When finally he took Khira's hand again, she felt the foal's warmth still on his fingers. Darkchild's voice was husky. "He has my mark now."

Khira looked back to the whitemanes, uncomprehending. Then she caught her breath in surprise and incomprehension. The mark of Darkchild's fingers lay like a shadow on the foal's brow. As she watched the mark darkened, until the foal carried a flame-shaped black blaze where Darkchild had touched it.

"How—how did you—"

Darkchild shook his head. "I don't know. I don't know why I put my mark on him. I don't know how. But I think—I think he'll wait for me. Even if I don't come back." His eyes narrowed and he gazed past the whitemanes into the forest. "There are others—other whitemanes. I don't want to bring the Benderzic here."

Khira followed his gaze into the trees, trying to see what he saw. If there were other whitemanes nearby, they had hidden themselves well. Perhaps instead they were scattered over many spans of forest, gathered in small groups around dozens of small springs.

If I had touched the foal instead—But she bit back the thought. She would never have thought to place her hand on its brow. It was not her the whitemane had stood over in the clearing. She had never felt the compulsion Darkchild felt to follow the whitemane. Certainly she had not seen whitemanes at the bonding. Her presence here was incidental.

She understood that if she understood nothing else. She turned back to Darkchild and found he had slipped back to some inner place where she could not follow.

Where? Why? As they turned back through the trees, she thought more about the distance he had set between them than about the whitemanes, the Benderzic, or the lack in herself.

They returned the way they had come, walking until the moons rose. Then they made their bed in the leaves, each wrapped separately against the night chill. Khira lay awake for a long while, wanting Darkchild's warmth against her. But when she turned to him, he stared at her blankly from moon-silvered eyes. There was no invitation there for her.

Was he repelled by the change in her? Was that why he made himself a stranger? Or was it the change in him that created the distance? Khira fell asleep reluctantly, alone.

They emerged from the forest early the next morning, speaking little. The emptiness of the plain was absolute. No breeze stirred the occasional tree. No redmane offered companionship. Even the swarming insects had taken to their burrows. Khira walked with head bowed, trying to feel something new in the touch of sunlight on her shoulders. If only she could find heart-wholeness, if only she could find certainty...

But how to recapture the wholeness she had felt at Tiahna's throne? How to find certainty when Darkchild hardly spoke to her all morning, when he gazed past her at nothing and walked toward that nothing as to the distant mountains—steadily, silently, with a frown of concentration.

They reached the pinnacles late that afternoon and by silent agreement made camp there for the night. Darkchild fell asleep early, curled in the protective shadow of the craggy spires. Khira lay beside him, feeling curiously suspended, as if the world had fallen into unreality around her and only moonlight were real.

Finally, when she could not sleep, she threw off her cloak and stood. She had avoided the pond earlier, afraid to glimpse her reflection. Now she was drawn there. She knelt beside the quiet water, eyes closed, and let her breath ebb away, let her will seep after it.

Slowly she opened her eyes and gazed upon herself in the moon-silvered water. One hand rose, touching her face. She was dark now where she had been fair and her hair hung copper upon her shoulders. From the vestigal features of childhood a new face had emerged, the eyes deeper, shadowed, the nose longer, broader, the mouth wide and unsmiling. There was new strength in her jaw, new prominence in her cheekbones. Even her eyebrows had darkened and become bolder.

It was a stranger's face—but not yet a barohna's.

No. These were only the first changes. She looked now as Denabar must have looked when they carried her down from the mountain. But Denabar had lived only seconds after taking her bronzing prey. For Khira it had been two days. Her head dropped and reality flowed back, weighting her like a stone.

The next morning, Darkchild sat watching her when she woke. She felt his scrutiny for moments before she opened her eyes, but she was not prepared for the sadness she saw in his face. She sat, her heart closing in painful spasm. "Darkchild—"

"I'm going to stay here," he said, as remotely as if he were reading from a scroll. "The Benderzic will find me here. I want you to go back to the campment."

"Without you?"

He sighed and placed a hand over his eyes. "Khira, you can't do anything for me here. If you go back—"

"*No!*"

"Khira—"

She could never be as remote as he. "*I won't,*" she hissed, making an icy thread of her voice. "I won't go back to the campment unless you go."

He shook his head. "I won't go to the campment. I won't bring the Benderzic there."

"Then I won't go either."

She had the pleasure of seeing a moment's helplessness in his eyes then. She had the pleasure of seeing quick tears. He quenched them with a shaking hand, stood, and walked away, his shoulders stiff.

She saw little of him that day. He climbed among the pinnacles, making his way up the steepest of the craggy spires. He didn't climb as they had climbed with the guardian daughters, for sport. He climbed with silent concentration, deliberately picking his way up the jagged and treacherous faces of the three tallest spires, Upquir, Falsett, and Principe. There were places in the pinnacles where a fall would do little physical injury beyond scrapes and bruises. There were other spires from which a fall would inevitably be fatal: Upquir, Falsett and Principe.

Khira watched, her nerves leaping with tension. He knew how to fall, she reminded herself—loosely, unresisting. But even that would not save him if he fell from the tallest spires.

In any case, he did not fall. He returned to the pond at dusk, his face streaked, his hands bleeding. Jagged rocks had ripped his suit and scarred his boots. He ate without a word. Khira could find no emotion in his face: sadness, regret, anger.

Nor did she find any change in her own face when she knelt beside the pond again at moonrise. Darkchild made his bed at a distance from hers that night, curling up with his back to her, his face lost in shadow. Khira lay wrapped tight in her cloak, her heart empty.

They were waiting for the Benderzic and the night was a trap, set to spring. A snare waiting to close—not on the Benderzic but upon them. She stared up into the stars, watching for some light moving among them that should not be there. She studied the moons, expecting the shadow of the Benderzic to fall across their bright faces. She and Darkchild were prey to the Benderzic—not formidable prey but totally vulnerable prey. They had no defense beyond their pikes and the two blazers Darkchild carried in his pack. When the carrier came, the Benderzic it brought would be wary—as the first two Benderzic had not been. And they would be many.

Khira sat, fighting against a sudden sense that the breath was being squeezed from her chest. The emptiness of the plain called her. Her feet knew the path to the campment, to Kadura's kefri, and her senses knew the comfort of settling beside the embers of Kadura's fire with all the friendly smells and sounds of the campment around her. And Kadura, silent but understanding.

Yes, understanding that she had run away and left Darkchild to face the Benderzic alone. Fighting tears, Khira got up and walked silently to the pond. She knelt and peered at her reflection, trying to make a friend of her altered face, trying to establish some familiarity with it.

She sat until she was stiff, until her hands were numb with cold. Then she rose to return to her bedding. Self-absorbed, she did not notice at first that Darkchild no longer lay asleep. She glanced at his empty bedding without registering his absence.

Then chill moved into her heart. He was gone, leaving not even a print on the hard soil or a hint of warmth in his blankets. Wildly she peered around. She wanted to call his name but the irrational fear that the sound of her voice would betray them to the Benderzic stopped her. Unspoken, his name formed an obstruction in her throat.

She searched the rocks at the base of the pinnacles, probing shadows for some clue to his presence. At last she looked up and saw him far above, silhouetted against the stars. He clung precariously from the tallest spire—Upquir, the master breeder. The craggy peak reared against the stars, and Khira felt the malevolence of the petrified breeder, caught so many centuries before in his quest for the eldest of the red-manes and turned to stone. Tonight, glinting from his dark face, she saw eyes—vengeful eyes. Upquir had only to shrug, to bend, to stoop his steep, stony shoulders, and Darkchild would fall to his death.

Darkchild. But she could not call his name around the obstruction in her throat. And she could not see his face. It was too distant, shadowed.

But now, beyond the spires of the pinnacles, she saw the alien light she had watched for earlier in the sky. It was winking and red and it passed among familiar constellations like the blinking eye of death. It moved, steadily, inexorably, growing nearer, until the body of the ship it announced slowly blotted out the surrounding stars. As she watched, the Benderzic ship created a larger and larger darkness in the sky, a strangely empty darkness, a growing shadow.

The snare was closing, its jaws moving slowly shut, and she stood paralyzed. She could not call out, she could not run. She could only watch as the Benderzic carrier ate the familiar stars. At last the ship was a visible presence over the plain, a dully glinting metal form that hung so silently above the ground that she could not believe she saw it there in all its massive presence. It moved, pondersomely, until its shadow made dark the ground at her feet. Nindra and Zan cast down their silver light futilely, creating no more than a pale halo around the perimeter of its obscuring metal body.

Then the ship moved silently away and settled to the ground beyond the pond. With the return of moonlight, Khira felt suddenly exposed. She watched, still caught in silent paralysis, as multi-colored lights appeared from recessed wells and illuminated the area around the ship, dimming the moon's light.

She expected the metal hatch to open with some groan of sound, some metal protest. Instead it slid aside silently, creating a rectangular darkness in the flank of the ship. A metal ramp appeared and slid smoothly into place.

Darkchild. She tried again to call his name and could not. She could scarcely breathe around the mass in her throat.

Three Benderzic appeared upon the metal ramp, black-uniformed, with gleaming metal at their wrists, at their necks, at their waists. They were much like the Benderzic of the forest landing, short-limbed, compactly built, with thick dark hair, wet lips and rolling eyes. But they were not laughing. They were not mocking. They were stiff with vigilance.

She stepped back involuntarily as the multi-colored lights winked out and the Benderzic and their ship sank into the relative darkness of moonlight. It took Khira's eyes a moment to adapt. Then she saw that the Benderzic still stood stiffly upon the ramp, gazing up at the pinnacles.

Up . . . *Darkchild!* He clung from Upquir's precipitous peak, his face white by moonlight. Khira stared up at him and could almost feel the shuddering breath in his throat, the soft jarring of his heartbeat, the cramping tension of his muscles. He was so far from her—not just because of the physical distance that separated them but because he had moved away from her in spirit.

The three Benderzic who stood upon the ramp did not speak. But the ship did, in a carefully modulated tone. "Rauth-Seven, you are called," it announced.

And gazing up, Khira suddenly knew what was in Darkchild's mind. She knew why he had insisted upon meeting the Benderzic here. She knew why he hung so high upon Upquir's face. She knew why he had drawn away from her.

The Benderzic had come to return him to the helmet, but they didn't care if they returned him as living flesh or simply as brain tissue, briefly electric with residual life, then darkening into death. All they wanted of him was the information he had stored in the cells of his brain.

And he would not let them have that information. He would not permit them to take either him or his dying brain.

He had climbed Upquir and he knew how to fall. He knew how to release himself to the jagged rocks below in such a way that his skull would be crushed and his brain turned to a useless bloody smear.

He had calculated his victory over the Benderzic. The prime element in that victory was his own death.

"Rauth-Seven, your brothers call you to join them," the ship's amplified voice reminded him. "The door stands open and your brothers are gathered. Your brothers wait, Rauth-Seven."

As Khira watched, the ship's interior took a warm golden light. The light had a misty quality, as if a golden haze circulated within the ship, spilling lightly from the open hatch, enveloping the three black-clad Benderzic.

Then came the voices, not in chorus, but speaking out randomly, calling. Voices of men, voices of boys, voices of small children. They spoke a coaxing language, a summoning tongue. Their message, she knew, must be the same as the Benderzic's: Darkchild was called.

Called to the warm light, called to the beckoning voices. Hardly breathing, she peered up to where he clung to the rock of Upquir. Did the golden light tempt him? The voices? She could not read his expression. The distance between them was too great. But she could see that his face was white and strained.

Then, as if her vision had become telescopic, reaching out to bring in detail she could not normally distinguish, she saw Darkchild's fingers loosen, surrendering their grip on the rock. And suddenly the obstruction in her throat filled her chest instead, crowding aside her lungs, squeezing the breath from her in a loud pant. Her ribs cracked loudly.

No, not her ribs. It was the stone of the pinnacles—of Upquir, of Falsett, of all the others—that cracked loudly and began to heave and grind and tumble and fall. Khira stood with open mouth as the pinnacles shook apart in sudden fury, stone from stone, and boiled in the air. For a moment it looked as if the stones might simply hang in midair, suspended. Then it looked as if they were fashioning themselves into a giant hand that reached to cradle Darkchild as he fell.

Numbly Khira turned to stare at the Benderzic. How had they done this—sundered the pinnacles and robbed Darkchild of his victory? But the Benderzic were as startled as she. They retreated toward the hatch of their ship, their faces twisting with panic, their rolling eyes for once frozen and still—bulging with shock.

As they watched, a stone hand did form from the sundered rocks of the pinnacles. It formed beneath Darkchild's falling body and lowered him gently toward the ground even as the rubble that boiled all around him whipped through the air and pounded toward the Benderzic ship. Driven by invisible force, the stones caught the retreating Benderzic and knocked them from their feet. The Benderzic screamed and the stones pounded, raising a haze of blood from their quickly battered bodies.

With the blood came further fury. Khira felt it as if it were her own. Felt it as if she were sister to the stones that hammered against the metal hull of the Benderzic ship, sister to the stones that hurled themselves through the open hatch and raised cries of fear and sounds of pounding destruction from the interior of the ship.

Khira felt as if she were the stones, as if they had become an extension of her will—as if she flew with them into the carrier and sought out the black-uniformed Benderzic wherever they tried to hide and pounded them to limp, bleeding masses. She felt as if she were the stones that rattled and thumped at all the shining equipment of the ship, smashing and shattering. She felt as if she were the stones that destroyed everything in their path.

Everything except the four empty children who sat silent in one compartment of the ship and watched the destruction with vacant eyes. Them the stones did not touch.

Strange how she smelled the perfume of the orchards as the stones rattled and pounded. Strange how she glimpsed Alzaja through the hail of rocks, walking serene and pale up the mountain. Strange how she heard Alzaja's voice.

Strange how she heard herself sob with concentrated fury. Darkchild had tried to leave her as Alzaja had left her. He had tried to leave her and the stones of the pinnacles had borne him safely to earth and flung themselves at his enemies.

Now Khira stood in the rubble of the Benderzic ship staring at the destruction and tears ran down her cheeks. The obstruction in her throat, the mass in her chest, had shrunk and become nothing more than her heart. Shattered glass lay at her feet. Nearby, beneath a mound of rock, lay a dead Benderzic. His blood spattered the ravaged metal wall.

"Khira?" It was a voice from somewhere far away, from a place she could never visit again—a place of innocence. "Khira?"

She shook her head, the tears burning her face. There was blood on the stones and there was stone in her heart. She felt it there now. It lay heavily in her chest even as she felt all the changes come to her body that had not come before. She gazed down numbly and watched her fingers grow. She felt her hair fall ever more heavily upon her shoulders. She touched her face and knew that it was a barohna's face now.

It was the face of a barohna who, under the threat of loss, had made stone live and used the living stone to kill. It was the face of a barohna who had done these things almost without knowing she did them.

"Khira—these are my brothers."

The empty children. She turned to Darkchild and saw that he had led them to where she stood. They looked up at her emptily. They were slight, their eyes so dark she could barely distinguish iris from pupil. Their black hair was cut just below the ears and their thin lips were encased in grey garments. As they gazed at her, she expected to see their brows arch in question.

But they were too empty to question her, even silently. They simply stared.

She sighed heavily, putting aside the burden of guilt. These were Darkchild's brothers, but they were not even children, not now. The Benderzic had made tools of them, just as they had once made a tool of Darkchild. And in the making the Benderzic had surrendered their own humanity.

She was a barohna who had made stone live and used the living stone to destroy evil. "These are your brothers," she acknowledged huskily. Then she stepped past him to the hatch of the ruined ship.

Where once the pinnacles had stood there was only rubble now. But the pond was undisturbed, its surface clear. Khira walked to it and gazed down at her reflection: at the strength of her limbs, at the power of her features. While the stones flew, she had become as tall as Tiahna and as strong. There was the same mystery in her eyes, the same impassivity upon her face—the same stone in her heart. Not the stone of harshness, but the stone of strength and caring.

Slowly she raised her head. Darkchild stood behind her, still ashen with residual shock, his empty brothers gazing vacantly after him. From the starred sky Nindra looked down with silver serenity.

We'll always walk together. Khira frowned. Those were the words Alzaja had said before she walked to meet her beast. And those were the words Khira had heard her say again as the stones flew against the Benderzic. Khira raised her head and for a moment saw the blue of sunlight falling through orchard blossoms.

Then she turned back to Darkchild. If she had changed suddenly, in the flight of stones, he had changed slowly over the past days. He had breached the barriers that divided him and become one, and that one was more than the sum of the two.

Even so, he looked at her with reticence and white-lipped awe. "You're a barohna now," he said, holding himself back from her, as if he were afraid of violating some new boundary her barohnhood set between them.

"Yes," she said. She was taller than he and she was a woman. But he was no longer a child either. He had seen things no child saw and done things no child did. He was a man and he knew the nature of her heart. And now that they were both changed, they must learn to know themselves again—and each other. Silently she held her hand to him, dissolving whatever boundary change had created between them. They left the ruined pinnacles together and led the four empty boys back in the direction of the campment.

We'll always walk together. Alzaja's words, but Khira used them herself now, and with some measure of Alzaja's certainty.